Sharon & Bill

May your days be filled
with Joy and serenity as
you Remember to Remember who
you Really are!

J.W. Rich [signature]

Mystic Travelers:
Awakening

F. W. RICK MEYERS

Edited by
Tarah Michaels

iUniverse, Inc.
Bloomington

Mystic Travelers:
Awakening

iUniverse books may be ordered through booksellers or by contacting:

iUniverse
1663 Liberty Drive
Bloomington, IN 47403
www.iuniverse.com
1-800-Authors (1-800-288-4677)

ISBN: 978-1-4759-0070-5 (sc)
ISBN: 978-1-4759-0071-2 (hc)
ISBN: 978-1-4759-0072-9 (ebk)

Library of Congress Control Number: 2012904494

Printed in the United States of America

iUniverse rev. date: 04/04/2012

Dedication

To all those who have struggled to find their way in the wonderful environment we call Mother Earth, Gaia, including all the ancestors of all beings throughout the ages. I'm awed at what we've become in the past six hundred thousand years since we discovered fire. A little closer to home, I dedicate this work to my dad and my mom, who overcame amazing obstacles to provide a better life for my sister and me. I dedicate this to my wife, son, and daughter, who have received much to be able to give much. I also dedicate this work to my family and friends, known and unknown, who have helped me grow and wake up to the possibilities and potentialities available in this life, and finally to all our children, their children's children, and beyond. Because I have been able to stand upon the shoulders of others, I am challenged to be stronger and more aware every day so those present and yet to come will have strong enlightened shoulders they can stand on. For all our relations, I dedicate this sacred work for ongoing awakening and transformation.

Preface

In the Beginning
How *Mystic Travelers* Came to Be

I found myself in a liminal state in a lucid dream in the middle of the night, not knowing how I could be both asleep and awake at the same time.

"It's time to write the book," a voice said to me.

"What book?" I responded.

"The one you've been preparing for from before you were born."

Curious at this strange conversation with an unknown voice, I decided to play along. After all, it was just a dream. "What am I supposed to write?"

"A novel called *Mystic Travelers*."

"What's it about?"

"You'll have to write it to find out."

"I've never written a novel and haven't even read many. Why do you want me to write a novel?"

"Everybody loves a good story. This story needs to be told, and you're the one to tell it."

I was now beginning to wonder if this was really a dream or some projection of my egoic mind playing with me again. "How is this supposed to happen?"

"We want you to get up at three o'clock every morning for the next two weeks, go to your desk, turn on the computer, and write. We'll be with you to help if you're willing and open."

"This is crazy. What if I don't do what you're requesting?"

"Then you'll never know if this is real or imaginary."

"And, if I get up at three o'clock in the morning every day for the next two weeks and go to my computer, what then?"

"You'll have to do it to find out."

"Who, may I ask, are you?"

"We're messengers from another altitude that have been with you for a very long time. You've been asking for help in dealing with the many planetary problems and crisis of consciousness within yourself and the species, so here we are, ready and willing to help."

"Thanks," I responded, and rolled over to look at the clock. It was three in the morning. I pulled on my housecoat, skeptically went to my study, turned on the computer, and nine months later, *Mystic Travelers* was born. Dare to receive!

At this stage in my evolving existence, I have to acknowledge everything life has given me during the extraordinary second half of the twentieth century and first tenth of the twenty-first century. I am a product of this environment of amazing change, and I hope to bring my compassion, appreciation, and transitions to the next phase of life for the highest good. I want to acknowledge the dancing universe, which has been and will be expressed in the ceaseless flow of energy, diversity, and rhythms of creativity and destruction, death and new life that are everywhere present. As we come to know the subatomic world as rhythm, synchronized motion, and continual change, we will come to understand our own dance in new, more awakened ways. In the meantime, I will continue to realize that the more I know, the more I don't know, and the more I don't know, the more I can know. From this place, I will continually live in thanksgiving, for all of it!

Please take your time reading this novel. It's a different kind of story. It seeks to touch parts of you that long to be touched and rarely are. Herein are many layers of meaning for you to discover, not only in this story, but also in your own story. Use this work as a mirror. Find yourself in each character and movement so that a new picture of the *who* that is you can appear to inform and even transform you and our global community. Notice the polarities and prejudices, the fears and fragmentations, the meanings and motivations. Awaken to the possibilities and potentialities, the common unity, the radical empathy that seeks to end all wars and bind all wounds.

We live in a troubled time that offers dangers and opportunities. This crisis of consciousness is an invitation and challenge to grow beyond where we are, to learn from all that's happening, and to become the ones we've been waiting for. Do you want to bring a radical new peace and prosperity into being for all? Could it be that you are here for some higher purpose beyond what you presently know? Is it possible that you are much more than you appear to be? If so, are you willing to spend your courage, caring, and compassion for the greater good? Can you find the optimism, hope, and intention to forge ahead with others of the same mind? Let us dare to embrace a radical grace and face each day with a renewed spirit of reverence and joy. Let us build upon the best and leave the rest. Let us recognize that we are the Mystic Travelers, invited and challenged to continue the awakening!

Prologue

"I don't know how long we can hold her!" Will shouted above the raging wind and water to his first mate, Miguel. "The storm is just too strong!"

The sailing vessel *Mystic Travelers* slid safely down the wall of a massive wave despite the razor's edge trajectory. Any miscalculation would topple the schooner and drop the five-crew members into the raging waters of Lake Superior.

"Get below and prepare the transporter! We may have to abandon ship at any moment. Put Sonja between us to relay the order on my command. We must prepare to transport immediately!"

Miguel responded with haste. Will's voice grew hoarse from the continuous shouting necessary to communicate over the roar of this rogue storm. The mainsail was reefed, the jib and genoa furled. The line of sail necessary to descend the massive waves was almost impossible to follow. The storm relentlessly tested Will's masterful sailing abilities. He used every ounce of his energy to hold the wheel, direct his first mate, and make the necessary adjustments to keep the vessel from capsizing.

Once more, Will executed the slide of the vessel down the wave with perfection, giving his four colleagues time to prepare for the transport. A Coast Guard helicopter appeared overhead but couldn't help due to the enormity of the gale. The lake swelled again. Will, still at the helm, worked diligently guiding *Mystic Travelers* down another steep and narrow trajectory along the wave. A third of the way down, the wind abruptly changed direction, gusted, and then blew hard and steady. Will was unable to correct for the aberration. The ship began to fall off the wall of water.

"Energize!" Will yelled.

He heard the command echoed by Sonja.

The ship toppled off the wave, rolled, and dropped four fathoms through the air into the turbulent water. The wave crashed down upon them cloaking the schooner. Everything went dark. The ship and crew disappeared and never surfaced. The storm raged on.

Chapter 1

Time is not at all what it seems. It does not flow in only one direction. The future exists simultaneously with the past in this present moment. The distinction between past, present, and future is only a stubbornly persistent illusion.
-Albert Einstein-

I don't know how I found that place when I did. I was lost in the north woods at three o'clock in the morning. I'd been driving all night. The lights were illuminated in the café and I saw the OPEN sign. I noticed that mine was the only car on the street. I crossed the threshold into Sunnyview Café. A tiny bell above the door jingled and an adventure began I never could have imagined.

I picked up a menu from the host's stand, noticed a wooden model of a sailing vessel, and sat down in a booth. I opened the menu and saw nothing but blank pages. On the back of the last page in the lower right-hand corner was a question in small print that simply asked, "What do you want?"

What do I want? I thought to myself. *How about a glass of water, a cup of coffee, and a new life? What kind of joke is this? The night cook's way of saying, "Get lost," or did a disgruntled employee decide to be a smart-ass?*

What do you want? The question began to sink farther into my tired mind when I heard a rustling in the kitchen and looked up to see the most beautiful woman I'd ever seen walk out. She approached me carrying a glass of water and a cup of coffee. She wore a dark blue flowing gown over a white robe that showed at the wrists and neck. An attached hood hung down from the neck of her gown onto her back underneath her well-coiffed auburn hair. The attire reminded me of a religious habit I'd seen somewhere in my travels.

She placed the water and coffee in front of me and sat down. Her eyes were brown, strong, and compassionate. They looked right into my soul. I could feel my pulse race as my metabolism shifted.

"What do you want from this new life?" she asked without introduction or hesitation.

I don't know why, but I felt as if I was going to pass out. Was her question rhetorical? What did it matter to her? How could she know what I was thinking?

The fragrance of her presence was like wild roses with a hint of mint. Her eyes spoke of a vastness that reminded me of a clear night in the Canadian Rockies, a billion stars shining and touching the depths of one's being. Her presence was that of a Greek goddess, although I'd never met one, and the sound of her voice was as beautiful as a rainbow, as bright as the sun, and as deep as the ocean. She seemed ageless. I couldn't tell if she was thirty or sixty, which added to my confusion. The silence that ensued after her question seemed to linger into eternity. I was speechless and stunned. Who was this person? Where had she come from? The silence persisted, as did the steady gaze of the look in her curious eyes. *What do you want from this new life?* echoed in my ears.

Remembering Alice in Wonderland, I pinched myself to see if I was dreaming. A sharp pain traveled from leg to brain and verified I was not dreaming. I was sitting in the presence of a very eccentric and stunning woman. I couldn't speak, so I picked up the glass of water, took a drink, and tried to get a grip. In my many years of life, never before had a question or a person had such a profound effect on me. I returned the water glass to the table and willed myself to relax. Not sure where to look, I closed my eyes and bathed in the moment. *Relax . . . remember . . . surrender . . . renew.* The mantra I'd been working with for some time emerged as I became aware of my breathing. The short shallow breaths elongated and calm washed over me. *Relax . . . remember . . . surrender . . . renew.* I could feel my body releasing its tension from the night driving and this new dark night experience. The energy of life seemed to be awakening in me and as it did, I was caught up in a vision.

I sat by a small campfire in the Black Hills. A woman laid beside me wrapped in a buffalo robe. The night sky was shimmering with stars. The howls of wolves sang the end and the beginning of an era. It was the end of the world, as we had known it. The Wasechu, the crazy white people, had come to the land and were overtaking her. The ways of the reds were over, the ways of the whites beginning. The two of us were medicine people for a tribe who had lived and loved in the plains and mountains of what was to become the state of Colorado. We represented the last of our band and were making our way north to make a new life for as long as it was given. The spirits of the deep, who accompanied us along the paths of the ancestors, were our guides and protectors. We saw the end of our place in the grand design and were now traveling to the beginning of another. The night was cool and opened to the infinite possibilities of life. We were at peace.

The café sign flickered on and off and finally went out. The smell of freshly brewed coffee drifted into my nostrils and brought me back to the question, the present moment, and the woman. I shook my head slightly, trying to shake loose from this strange vision.

"What do you want from this new life?" she asked again.

"What new life?" I blurted out. "What the hell do I know? How about peace on earth, good will for all creation? How about the enlightenment of humanity? How about a whole new way of being together in the world that honors and respects the dignity of everyone and everything? How about the end of exploitation, greed, hunger, and war? An end to anxiety, regret, despair, blame, and humiliation? No more condemnation, hopelessness, fear, craving, enslavement, antagonism, scorn, righteous indignation, pain, suffering, and . . ."

Tears began to seep from my eyes. The sadness from all the journeys, all the difficulties, and all the despair I'd witnessed and experienced began to pour forth. I tried to control myself, but the dam broke and I began to cry. My grief sparked a flashback.

"I can't stop the bleeding!" I yelled, as I grabbed more gauze. "The whole side of his head is gone!"

The other medic came to my side to assess the situation. "Move on, he's gone. The casualties are coming in like a wave. We can only do so much. Save the ones you can and let the rest go. That's the choice we've been given. Move it!"

The blood, the sounds, the pain, the suffering, the futility of war . . . and for what? Another foothold in another part of the world so we can drink more oil and eat off the backs of the peasants? Patch 'em up, sent 'em home or back into the fray, so we can eat another Big Mac and clear-cut another forest?

The scene changed and I was wiping my teary eyes with a napkin. *Where am I?* I looked down at the table. There sat the steaming cup of coffee and glass of water that reminded me I was still in the strange café somewhere in the middle of the night. I looked up; the mystery woman was still there with an angelic glow around her. Embarrassed, I ran my hands over my face and tried to rid my mind of the war scene I hadn't remembered in decades. I had no explanation for my behavior or my surroundings. In defeat, I put my elbows on the table, rested my chin on the heels of my hands, and looked up curiously at the woman. I was growing more tired by the moment.

"It's been a long dark night," she said, "and it's a brand new day. It's time for some rest. There's a cottage and a bed with clean sheets out back. I'll lead you there."

She got up. I followed. The darkness enfolded me. We walked for some time. All I remember was hearing a door close as my skin embraced the cool cotton sheets. Was I home?

Chapter 2

*You have now found the conditions in which the desire of your
heart can become the reality of your being. Stay here until you
acquire a force in you that nothing can destroy.*
-George Gurdjieff-

I woke up not knowing where I was, who I was, or why I was. It
was a strange experience. It seemed like I'd been traveling forever
to unknown and familiar places. The experience lasted only a few
seconds, and yet there was a lingering sense that way more was
going on in the universe than I was conscious of when I opened
my eyes. I reflected on the paradox of my reality: the smallness
and spaciousness, the constriction and expansiveness. *Is it possible
to hold two apparent opposites together at the same time?*

I lay with my eyes open in the bed I'd been so graciously led
to the night before, trying to recall my thoughts and impressions.
It ranked in the top ten of the strangest experiences of my life:
the mystery woman, the vision and flashback, the outpouring of
grief, my not knowing, and now my own place to stay. Something
was very strange about these happenings.

I scanned my surroundings and realized I was in a clean and
efficient one-room cottage constructed out of what I assumed
were native logs and timber, and it looked to be a perfect square
with a window in every wall. I saw a small woodstove, a desk with
a chair, a wingback chair with a floor lamp beside it, and a small
closet that was simply a wooden bar with hangers. A nightstand

stood next to the bed that held a small lamp. I was lying on a very comfortable double bed covered with a handmade quilt and down comforter. I sat up and saw above the bed a framed aerial photograph of a tropical island covered in palm trees. The cottage was heavenly. I laid back, stared at the ceiling, and attempted to make sense of the night before. Strangely, I didn't feel afraid. On the contrary, I felt safe and renewed.

As I pulled back the covers, I noticed the crispness of the north woods air. I looked at my watch: five o'clock in the afternoon. I'd slept through the day. Eager to get moving, I made my way to the restroom, splashed some water on my face, and walked out into a world I didn't know. To my great surprise, I was standing on a porch looking out over a lake in the midst of a forest. The sun was dropping in the sky directly in front of me casting a reflection on the lake. I looked west, felt the sun on my skin, wondered where I was, how I had arrived here, and gave thanks all at the same time.

I sat in one of the two chairs on the porch that faced the lake to enjoy the warmth of the sun. I scanned the shoreline to my left and right and noticed other cottages like mine interspersed among the trees. Curious, I got up and walked to the shoreline twenty yards from the cottage. The trees, trimmed to create a park-like atmosphere, felt friendly, inviting, and even embracing. Each cottage seemed deliberately placed to create both a private and a public feel. Each had its own space and yet, there was a sense of community among them. I counted a dozen cottages scattered through the forest, all enjoying a serene view of the lake and western sky. When I reached the shore, I noticed a series of docks that extended a couple sections out into the water in front of each cottage. Attached to my dock was an aluminum rowboat, and upside down on the shore, a one-person kayak waited to be flipped over, slid into the water, and paddled across the stillness. The water was clear and the bottom displayed light brown sand that gradually dropped off into the depths. I removed my shoes and socks, rolled up my pant legs, and walked a couple feet into the water. The approaching winter cooled the autumn air as well as the lake, both clearing my head a little more.

Be still and know, I heard from within, presumably prompted by the serenity of the moment. *You're on sabbatical with no agenda, and you're exactly where you need to be.* I closed my eyes and rested in what I'd been working on for decades—inner peace.

Stop, look, listen, breathe, don't try to hang on to anything. Let come. Let go. Pure awareness. My inner voice was speaking freely, and I was attending to it in awesome silence.

The birds sang their salute to the sun as mother earth rotated through her movement around the great fireball in the sky. As the sun dropped toward the horizon here, it was beginning to bring light and warmth to the other side of the globe. I backed out of the water and sat on the dock. What was happening to me? What was it about this place that prompted all this introspection? I was beginning to see the ordinary as extraordinary. It felt strange and at the same time perfectly normal.

I put my socks and shoes back on, rolled down my pant legs, and backed off the dock caught up in the stillness and beauty of the moment. A massive blow to my body broke my trance, and I was knocked off my feet and landed in the sand. I looked up to see a young man half my age stumbling to catch his balance before he too hit the ground. While I was slowly getting to my hands and knees and assessing any possible damage, I noticed that he avoided the fall and was quickly coming back to help me.

"I'm so sorry, sir. I was in the zone and didn't see you until it was too late. Are you all right?"

"I'm checking on that at this very moment. Help me up and we'll see," I replied.

A little embarrassed, I quickly checked my body as he helped steady me. "Looks like the only thing hurt is my pride," I said, extending my hand to the runner. "My name's Michael Wyman from Denver."

"My name is Anthony Amir from San Francisco. I really am sorry for running into you like that. I was in my third mile coming down the stretch, and well, I'm glad you're not hurt."

"Not a problem, Anthony. Are you a resident here?"

"No, I'm on a vacation retreat. A friend from college days works here. He does research, design, and development in alternative energy. We haven't seen each other in years, so I decided to visit him in this remote outpost that he raves about. It's an amazing place with awesome people. How about you?"

"I just got here." Not wanting to elaborate, I asked a deflective question. "You mentioned college, what did you study?"

"I wanted to study political science and economics, but my dad wanted me to study physics and chemistry, so I majored in physics and chemistry and minored in econ and poly sci."

"Was your dad a scientist?"

"He was an astrophysicist in Iran doing research and development for the Shah's government in collaboration with the Americans before the Shah got ousted. When the government fell and was eventually taken over by the Ayatollah, Dad moved to the United States with my mom and sister. That was in the early eighties. I was born here. He worked for Lockheed Martin until a few months after nine-eleven when he lost his security clearance for no reason. That was when I . . . whoa, I've opened Pandora's box here. I'm talking way too much. What's the deal, are you a psychologist or something? I don't usually spill my guts to strangers." Anthony paused. "I'm sorry again. I don't know what got into me. Maybe it's the silence. I'm not used to being so quiet. Maybe that's it, or maybe it's everything about this place that's making me loony."

"No apologies necessary, and if it makes you feel any better, I am a psychologist and am honored to meet you, Anthony Amir. I'm in the cottage right up that path. I don't know how long I'll be here, but I'd love to continue this conversation. Drop by anytime. Between my hurt pride and your loony tunes, we should be able to have a few laughs and solve all the world's problems. What do you say?"

"Thank you, Dr. Wyman. I just may do that and . . . I just have to say it," Anthony paused, sweat dripping from his well-chiseled face, "Nice running into you."

Anthony turned to continue his run. I watched as he disappeared along the trail and up into the woods. I heard the sound of a twig break behind me and turned to see an elderly man coming out of the park-like forest and onto the path. I watched as he approached. He had a slight smile on his well-worn face.

Chapter 3

Life is meant to be lived, and curiosity must be kept alive. One must never, for whatever reason, turn their back on Life.
-Eleanor Roosevelt-

"Good evening. You must be Michael. My name is Favor." His smile widened as he extended his hand. "I'm staying in the cottage next to yours. Did you have a good rest?"

His handshake was firm and strong. I felt an unusual energy from him. His hand moved from the traditional handshake to the more intimate handclasp, one that draws the arms closer toward an embrace. It was a gesture of brotherhood and greater caring. I'd learned it years ago in college.

Our eyes met in this reconfigured handclasp. The moment expanded and grew. Somehow, I knew this older man whom I'd never met. A message beyond words was communicated. Again, I relaxed, remembering to surrender.

"Yes, Favor, I did have a good rest, and my name is Michael. How did you know?"

"I'm an eccentric old man. I call everyone I meet Michael. He or she, depending on the day, is my favorite angel. I see everyone as a messenger, how about you?"

"I'm just getting my bearings. I'm not quite sure where I am or maybe even who I am. It's kind of you to greet me. Have you been here long and where is here?"

Our hands released as he turned toward the lake. The sun was dropping lower in the sky. The horizon was beginning to show streaks of color on the low hanging clouds. He took three deep breaths, which I thought would last forever, and finally spoke while looking out across the lake.

"I've been here quite a long time. I love it here. It's so amazingly beautiful. Each season has its own special wonders. The sights, sounds, smells, tastes, and touches of this place are very healing and empowering. The movement beyond the five senses is filled with mystery."

Favor turned to glance at me, chuckled, and continued. "You simply have to experience it. These great north woods are so close to the Great Lakes. Most people don't feel the connection with the energy vortex here. It's amazing to me that so few feel it when they travel through. Maybe that's it. We're mostly just traveling through, not taking the time, or making the effort to arrive anywhere. It really takes a prolonged time of stillness to understand what this life has to offer. It's in staying that we can leave. It's in receiving that we can give. It's in retreat that we get to advance. It's in silence that we learn to listen. It's in solitude that we learn how to be together. It's in dying that we learn to live. I could go on forever, Michael, and I know this is just craziness to most folks, but after a lifetime as a priest and a monk, I've finally become a holy fool and wild angel. It's quite liberating."

After a long pause, he turned and looked at me with a great smile. "Have you had anything to eat since you've been up and about?"

It was then that I remembered yesterday melting into today: the long drive, getting lost, the lack of sleep, arriving at the café, the exchange with the mystery woman, the cottage, the Arabian knight, and now this holy fool, priest, monk, eccentric wild angel. Have I crossed over into a parallel universe to find a new kind of reality?

"Food? Uh, no, I haven't eaten. I think I ate something yesterday before I got lost in the darkness. I just woke up a little while ago."

"Would you like to have some breakfast or dinner or supper?" he asked.

"I could go for a cup of coffee and a glass of water. Then maybe consider eating something."

"If it's okay with you, I'll walk you back to your cottage, and then over to the café."

"Sounds good," I responded.

We turned and headed up the slight grade through the trees to the cottage. I still needed some answers, so I asked a few more questions.

"Really, Favor, how did you know my name was Michael?" He shrugged and kept walking. "Okay, and then who was the woman who waited on me last night in the café? I never told her my name or asked of hers, and where's my car? I think I left my luggage, wallet, briefcase, and computer in it."

The more I questioned the more fear and anger seemed to arise within me. As the calmness and serenity disappeared, I began to feel like my old self. The back pain I hadn't felt since waking up started throbbing again. The sky was turning dark, and Favor's wry smile never left his face, which made me even more edgy.

"All of your questions will be answered in due time," Favor responded. "Your car is off the street in a safe and secure place not far from here. Would you like to walk over and get your bags now? I'll take you there if you'd like. Do you have another set of keys? You left the ones you drove with in your car last night."

In that moment, it occurred to me that I hadn't really given any thought to staying or leaving. I knew nothing about this place except what Anthony told me, which wasn't much. I was still lost and didn't know specifically where I was. I also began to feel like I didn't know who I was anymore. I'd met three people who treated me with kindness and care. I'd been given a place to rest and stay. What was all this fear and anger? What was I afraid of losing when I had nothing to lose? Why all the fuss about my stuff? What was the problem? Was it me? I looked up to see Favor looking at me with that curious smile.

"The keys. Do you have an extra set? Or do we need to pick up the original set? They're in the office."

"The keys, yeah, the extra set is in a magnetic box on the frame of the car. Let's get the set in the office. Where's the office?"

"It's part of the café. Do you want to get your stuff before or after we eat?"

"How close is the café from the parking lot? How far is it from here?"

"I'll show you," Favor responded, as he stepped off the deck and headed north. I followed with apprehension.

The path up the slight hill from the cabin led to a much larger one circumambulating the lake above the cottages. It led to the main buildings of the compound. Anthony Amir had returned to his cottage, showered, and was hurrying to meet someone for evening prayer and dinner.

Favor and I walked up the cottage path, connected with the larger one, and slowly made our way toward the café. Anthony, on the path behind us, recognized Favor's slow, deliberate, lighthearted stride, and nervously frowned. He slowed his pace and clenched his jaw disconcerted by something. The front of his shoe hit a large rock on the path. He cursed as he caught himself from falling. Favor and I turned in surprise. Favor's face broke into a smile as he stretched out his arms. "Anthony Amir! How good to see you!"

"It is you, Favor. I was about to call out to you. Good evening, and Dr. Wyman, it's you again. I wondered who was walking with Favor. What a surprise. It looks like we're on the same schedule. I'm on my way to meet Clare for evening prayer and dinner. Are you on your way there too?"

Favor clasped his hands joyfully. "Yes, we are, unless Michael wants a tour of our many playgrounds and work areas. Come, let's walk together."

Anthony fell in step beside us. "What brings you here, Dr. Wyman?"

"Truthfully, I don't really know, and well, what brings us anywhere?"

Anthony accepted the response as a signal to be quiet. He checked his watch, anxiously excused himself, and hurried toward the Sunnyview café.

Despite having the weight of the world on his shoulders, Anthony felt giddy to see Clare. When he was in her presence, the feelings within him were powerful and disturbing. They added to and took the edge off his extreme levels of stress. It was confusing and comforting at the same time.

When Anthony entered the café, several heads turned to acknowledge and greet him. He walked past the patrons, politely nodded, and stopped at the booth where Clare was waiting for him. She stood and hugged him.

"I'm so glad to see you, Anthony."

He returned the embrace and inhaled her fragrance. He instantly felt better about life. He pulled back a bit and looked into her eyes. "How are you holding up?"

She was silent for a few seconds. "Mmm . . . good, considering. You're a welcome break from all the family matters and having to play the professional." She smiled and sat down.

"I've been thinking, Clare. It's none of my business and we've only known each other a couple days, but did your dad say anything out of the ordinary the last time you saw him before he . . . left?"

Puzzled, Clare looked at Anthony. "Why do you ask that?"

"I know this event has consumed you ever since you heard the news, and I just thought maybe I could help bring some clarity to the situation." Anthony paused, closed his eyes, placed his elbow on the table, bowed his head, and rested his forehead in his palm.

He didn't want to push on, but it was his assignment, so he forged ahead. He looked up and confronted his fear. "Did he say anything to you about a mission he was on or any concerns he had about an important project he was engaged in with his colleagues?"

Finally, he'd asked what he needed to. There was no way to dance around it anymore. He needed to find out what she knew or didn't know. Clare's facial expression made him regret the question instantly.

"I'm sorry, I don't really understand what you're asking me, or why," said Clare. "I haven't been able to think clearly since yesterday. I don't feel like I can accurately remember my last conversation with Dad. I'm sorry to be so blunt, but why do you have this sudden urgency to know what he was working on? This seems out of character for you."

Anthony couldn't believe what he was seeing on Clare's face and in her eyes. There was no anger, no degradation, and no judgment. All he felt from her was an empathetic concern for him. His body heaved with a sigh.

"I'm sorry, Clare. I guess I'm a little out of sorts too." Anthony hated how he went soft around Clare, but he couldn't help it. He'd have to find his information elsewhere.

"The entire community hasn't felt the same since we received the news yesterday. We'll get past this, it will just take time." Clare continued talking while Anthony pretended to listen. He was now thinking about retrieving confidential information from sources other than Clare. His colleague, Ihsann, was waiting for his report containing useful information from Dr. William Clarence Fischer's family and closest associates, but Anthony was finding it impossible to retrieve. Would he have to fabricate some stories to avoid a failed mission or could he simply tell him the truth?

"Thanks for listening, Anthony. It's time for evening prayer. Let's get ourselves realigned and centered in the kiva. We'll do dinner and continue the conversation after that."

Anthony Amir smiled and followed Clare into the kiva, wondering about love, loss, and quantum entanglement.

Chapter 4

Artistic growth is, more than anything else, a refining of the sense of truthfulness. The ignorant belief that to be truthful is easy; only the artist, the great artist, knows how difficult it is.
-Willa Cather-

Favor and I continued our slow walk toward the café. The sun was low in the sky and casted shadows through the trees in the well-manicured forest. The outer silence and order were in contrast to my inner noise and disorder. My rational mind tried to categorize and evaluate the situation and it dominated my attention. "Favor, would you mind if we talked while we walked?"

"Not at all, what's on your mind?"

"I remember Gandhi saying you must be the change you wish to see in the world, and Socrates saying the beginning of wisdom is wonder, knowing you don't know. What about this change and not knowing? If everything is open to question, change, and new possibilities, is anything possible?"

"What do you say?" he asked.

I looked down at the ground and kicked a small rock off the path. "As I observe my perceptions, attitudes, and behaviors, I see myself wanting change and then complaining when it comes, because it doesn't meet my expectations. I complain when I am stuck in an unappealing cycle and do little or nothing to create a new way of doing and being within it. In the short time I've been here at Sunnyview, I'm beginning to see how my perceptions and beliefs create my reality. Is it possible that the outer world really does reflect the projections of our inner world?"

Favor was looking up at the trees and the changing environment as the earth rotated away from the sun casting longer shadows and coloring the clouds. The glow from his face reflected the light. "What have you experienced during the past twenty-four hours, Michael?"

"When I arrived at the Sunnyview café last night, my world was dark and depressed. I was lost in the dark wood of my own creation and didn't even realize it. It was about my job, family, career, and students, everything outside of me. Having received some distance from my complaining selves by being in a very different environment, I'm coming to see how lost I was. I stumbled upon a flower, Sunnyview, and stopped long enough to truly see what was here, inside me!"

"If the destination is the journey," Favor continued, "then it only makes sense to wake up to the journey and learn to appreciate it, to take what you have and help make it grow. It is advantageous to check out your perceptions and beliefs while awakening to what is. Opening to this 'not knowing' may be one of the greatest tasks you will ever accomplish."

I stopped walking to look at the changing sky and the diffused light sifting through the forest. My mind stopped processing for a moment. I realized I hadn't seen anything but my thoughts since we stepped on this path. I took a deep breath, looked at Favor, smiled, and continued our slow walk.

Trying to stay conscious of my environment, I put my hands together and brought them to my lips. I could now speak with a greater awareness. "I remember when I was young. Everything was new, everything was filled with awe and wonder, everything was worthy of exploration and discovery. Reconnecting with this creative naïveté, this childlikeness *is* the journey. The wonder of life shows up in the people, places, situations, and things that are right in front of me. It's all happening for me, not to me. This is part of what I need to learn at this time; to embody it so I can effectively help others do the same. Wow, what an awakening! Every journey takes place one-step at a time, just like this walk. It begins by seeing through the eyes of a child and ends with joy and reverence."

A new energy surged through my body, an exuberance that wasn't there before. I sensed my heart smiling and felt it reflecting on my face. Favor took my arm, stopped, pointed ahead, and posed a new question.

"What do you see?"

We had come out of the woods and were standing at the edge of a clearing where the backside of the village was located. I was stunned. Thirty yards away stood a seven-story glass and aluminum pyramid. Attached and running east was a long, three-story rectangular building that ended in a large domed kiva. The shift from the rustic, woodsy cottages to this twenty-first century architecture was mind blowing.

I stood unmoving in my tracks. Favor stood silently behind and off to my side. I was looking at something from out of the future having just walked away from something out of the past. The moment held them together in the present. It was compelling.

I moved forward into the clearing just south of the buildings, all the while looking, listening, and leaning into the feeling of what was inside and around me. The clearing was bordered to the north by the pyramid, café, and kiva, all connected. The south, east, and western sides were bordered by the forest that led to the lake and whatever else was out there. I noticed a fire pit in the center of the outdoor area. I also saw a volleyball court, a couple of horseshoe pits, and what looked like an observatory. There was a ropes course in the southeast section and an archery range near that. An impressive twenty-foot wide deck ran along the rectangular portion of the building extending around the kiva to its north side. It ended at the road. *I must have come in on this road*, I mused. We walked east one block. I noticed greenhouses and a series of gardens, solar panel plots, and some small wind generators.

Favor had been following me around this self-guided tour of the compound without a word. He stopped when I stopped, moved when I moved. When we returned to where we started, having walked around this oblong circle, I turned to him and smiled. All I could say was, "Wow!"

"Want to have supper?" Favor extended his arm and pointed to the café. I nodded and followed his lead. I completely forgot about the car and my stuff.

We walked to the front door of the café. I noticed a variety of vehicles parked along the sidewalk: pickup trucks new and old, a Cadillac, a classic Porsche, a couple of Hondas, a VW van, and an assortment of others. I was surprised to see what looked like three Amish buggies with horses tied to a hitching post. I hesitated in front of the café door. I was here in this exact spot some fifteen hours earlier and I didn't recognize a thing. I opened the door and heard the small bell above the entry jingle. We took a few steps into the café, closed the door, and the bell jingled again. *Was this another wake-up call for me?*

Chapter 5

Living is the dialog between fixity and change.
-Julia Cameron-

The only thing I recognized inside the café was the row of booths to the left that lined the windows along the north wall and the wooden model of a sailing vessel next to the host's stand. The room was brightly lit and full of people. Strangely, the conversations were rather quiet and reserved giving an air of peacefulness to the café that I'd never before experienced in a crowded eatery.

A young man greeted us with two menus and led us to the very booth I sat in the night before. Favor excused himself and disappeared down a hall I presumed led to the restrooms. A server immediately adorned our table with two glasses of water, a cup of coffee for me, and a cup of green tea for Favor. I started to wonder aloud why he'd brought me coffee without first asking, but the server returned to the kitchen before I had the chance to ask him.

I looked down at the same blank front page of the menu I'd seen last night and opened it. Nothing on the left page. On the right side in block print it read, SALAD BAR—ALL-INCLUSIVE. TONIGHT'S SPECIAL: EGGPLANT PARMESAN (WITH OR WITHOUT FRESH, FIRE-GRILLED WALLEYE). My stomach growled.

I turned the menu to look on the back cover. In the lower right-hand corner it read, "Why are you here?" I smiled and almost burst out laughing. Why am I here? Where? In this café? In this emotional state? In the Upper Peninsula of Michigan? On this planet? In this body? Why am I here? What a great question!

As I drilled down into what I considered one of the great cosmic jokes of all time, Favor slipped back into the booth, took a sip of tea, and knit his eyebrows together at my smile and shaking head.

"What's the joke?" he asked.

"The question on the back of the menu. It's great. If I didn't know better, I'd say it was directed at me."

"It is," he said.

"I suppose you wrote it," I chortled.

"Right again. Why are you here?" he asked, wearing a smile of a Cheshire cat.

My face turned sober. Wanting to deflect the implications of this examination, I flippantly fired off an answer. "I have no idea, not a clue."

"And if you were to slow way down and sit with the question, letting it drop from the top of your head to the very bottom of your heart, what would arise?"

Anxiety clenched my chest and throat. Emotional distancing was one of my specialties, and I was on the hot seat with this wise old man. I had the sense that to continue was to open the gate of the same dam that flooded me last night. I didn't want to enter that hall of mirrors again, and I didn't want to reveal any more of my well-guarded repressions and denials. I wanted to get up and run.

"Isn't that what you've been doing most of your life?" Favor continued.

"What? Trying to figure out why I'm here?"

"Yes, and more especially, running?"

Somehow, he pressed the emotional button of my deepest fears. *Had he just read my mind?* My feet wouldn't move. My body seemed glued to the bench as I tried to excuse myself for an escape.

Just as I was beginning to lose it, I heard a soft melodic chant coming from somewhere I couldn't identify. The sound grew louder and I slowly relaxed. When my breathing found a slower modulated depth, I realized I had closed my eyes. I opened them to look at Favor. He was staring at me with the same eyes of compassion I'd witnessed last night. I noticed the café was nearly empty. Where had the people gone and how had I missed such a significant change in my environment?

"They're all in the kiva for evening prayer, healing, and realignment. It happens every evening at six o'clock. The chant and music you hear is coming from there. We have an amazing variety of very creative people here at Sunnyview. It's helpful, yes?"

My throat was still relaxing from the tension. I picked up the cup of warm coffee, took a soothing sip, and gave myself a couple extra moments to regain my composure.

"I really don't know what to say," I responded. "There are so many questions bouncing around in my head. Shouldn't you be in there with them? Aren't you a part of this place?"

"I'm exactly where I need to be at this moment and so are you." Favor's words were matter of fact and indisputable for him, but I wondered if they were true for me. How could I be exactly where I needed to be at this moment when it felt so disjointed? How could he be so sure of his statement?

Favor interrupted my thoughts. "Did you decide on what you wanted for supper? The salad bar is great. The eggplant Parmesan is marvelous, and the fire-grilled walleye was caught yesterday, so it's about as fresh as it gets."

I wasn't used to this kind of acceptance and patience. My usual experience was to follow the appropriate policies, procedures, and protocols to gain approval. There were usually no exceptions, and those who pressed for them were summarily dismissed and chastised as examples so others wouldn't transgress. To be here eating supper with Favor while everyone else was participating in an important community practice seemed exceptional.

"Are you sure this is okay?"

"Is the OPEN sign in the window on?"

I turned to look. "Yes, it is."

"Then it's *Ola Kala*."

"Pardon?"

"It's Greek for it's all beautiful, just fine. Over time, the expression was shortened to *OK* and was even given a hand signal." He put his index finger to his thumb and held up his hand with the other three fingers extended. "It's an acceptance and an appropriate handling of what is, despite the conditions. Is everything okay?"

"Somehow, being here with you makes it okay," I said, holding up my hand with this well-known gesture. "Let's start with the salad bar. Do we have to wait for the server?"

"No, he's good with whatever we decide, and he'll show up when we need him."

I stood and surveyed the layout of food, which consisted of an amazing variety of fruit, vegetables, mixed salads, two kinds of soup, pickled herring, shellfish, multi-grain breads, and cheese. I took small helpings of my favorites, which filled a dinner plate and a soup bowl. We returned to the booth and ate without talking, listening to the chant in the adjacent room. I'd never before been comfortable with silence at a table with another person unless it was mandated. There was no mandate here, just a relaxed sense of well being that floated through the closed doors of the kiva. As we sat in that relaxed state, I couldn't help but wonder how this was all happening, and why was I here.

Chapter 6

*The contradiction so puzzling to the ordinary way of thinking comes
from the fact that we have to use language to communicate our
inner experience, which in its very nature transcends linguistics.*
-D. T. Suzuki-

The server walked to the table as we both finished our supper. He
cleared the plates then returned with a pot of steaming green tea and
a new cup for me. He poured the tea, placed the ceramic teapot on
the table, smiled a cordial salutation, and returned to the kitchen.

"How did he know I wanted a cup of tea instead of coffee, and
how was it that he appeared at the exact moment we finished?"

Favor stirred his tea, looked up with that wry smile, and
simply said, "You already know the answer."

I took a sip and wondered if I would ever get a straight
answer from him. After reminding myself to be affable, I replied,
"I don't know what you know, Favor. If I knew the answer to the
question, I wouldn't ask it. I don't even know where I am or what
I'm doing here. I came into this café last night lost and confused
and woke up an hour ago feeling even more so. I've seen things
today I've never seen before and experienced things I've never
experienced, and you say I already know the answer to another
phenomenon that is out of the ordinary? Okay, Favor, you want
to know what I think. I think you're a Jedi master connected to
Yoda, or maybe you are Yoda. How about that?"

I stared at Favor willing him to give me answers, or at least react to my somewhat facetious accusation. He continued to stir his tea and didn't offer a word. Defeated, I slumped back in the booth and tried to regroup when I heard the doors to the kiva open.

People walked quietly into the café from a connecting hallway. A few sat in the chairs and booths and others walked through the dining room to another set of doors or out of the café. Some stopped at our booth and said a few words to Favor. Some introduced themselves to me and then moved on. I heard automobile engines start and vehicles move out into the evening. A couple of children noticed Favor and came running over to him. They gave him hugs and kisses, shared a few words, and smiled at me before galloping away. Anthony waved as he passed by on the other side of the café and headed down the hallway. In these few minutes, the café was again humming a familiar tune of common unity and cordiality.

A smile began to form in my heart. As it did, I saw her coming through the open doors walking toward our booth, the mystery woman who wore the robes. She was as beautiful as I remembered, and with every step she took toward us, I became more nervous. Favor slid toward the wall when she arrived to sit across from me.

"You've already met, but let me formally introduce you. Angelina, this is Michael. Michael, this is Angelina."

She held out her hand and I responded. Her touch was magical. The smell of wild roses with a hint of mint seemed to overwhelm me. I saw my mother, wife, daughter, sisters, past lovers, grandmothers, women I didn't recognize, and the reflection of myself all in an instant. Then I saw the images of my father, son, brothers, grandfathers, compadres, enemies, friends, and the whole creation of male beings. It was like seeing a moving picture of life with all its craziness and wonder in an instant. The women were inviting, alluring, assuring, and coaxing me toward them. The men were curious, stern, inquiring, and challenging me to prove myself. Then it all vanished, as if the electricity had turned off. Angelina let go of my hand. I was in awe. What had just happened? What strange and wonderful places did this mystery woman have access to?

"Love is the energy of the cosmos, the energy of life," I heard her say, bringing me back to the present moment with a focused intent to listen to her every word. "It's magnetic, attracting, and repelling. It holds all things together, pulls all things apart. You can go with it or against it. You can be in harmony or discord with it. You can fight or surrender to it. The choice is always yours. You have been drawn here because you have come to a crossroad in your life. You have a choice to make, and it will determine your life trajectory. You know exactly what you need to do, and you are looking for the affirmation and strength to see you through into the next phase of your awakening." She paused.

"That's why you are here. That's why we are here, Michael. We're a birthing room, midwifery, a place called home deep inside you, a place where you don't have to be someone else. The invitation and challenge is here. You will find solace and strength as well as pardon and renewal. It will take as long as it takes, and it will be difficult and easy. You are not alone, never have been, never will be. Favor and I, along with everything else that is here, will guide you, challenge you, and encourage you to wake up to who you are. The time is now. The place is here. Allow the energy of love to inspire and guide you. Your heart and mind is opening. Do not be afraid of that."

A smile that seemed to embrace the entire room spread across her face. She got up from the table, took two steps toward me, leaned down, and kissed my forehead. Looking into my soul about six inches from my face, she said, "You're supposed to be here. Be safe, enjoy, and remember who you are." Standing up, she glided across the floor and disappeared through the double doors at the other end of the room.

"I'll walk you back to the cottage," I heard Favor say.

I'd forgotten he was here. I got up without thinking and walked out into the twilight. The bell at the top of the door casing woke me up, as did the cool autumn air. I stood looking at the sky, Favor beside me. We turned, walked along the sidewalk past the pyramid, and entered the forest. We made our way toward the cottage and the lake. Had it not been for Favor, I wouldn't have found the cottage. He stepped up onto the deck, walked to one of the two chairs, and sat down. I followed. We listened to the silence together and basked in the cool night air.

"I knew your spiritual father, Benedict. He and I went to seminary together a thousand years ago. When was the last time you saw him?" Favor turned toward me waiting for my answer with a gleam in his eyes.

"Father Benedict, Abbot of St. Mary's Monastery in Forest Lake, Wisconsin? Wow, what a flash from the past. I saw him in California a few years ago. He's retired as abbot, and now lives as a hermit in the desert. That was a strange interchange. I met him at his in-town apartment, and what a mess. There were stacks of folders, papers, and books all over the place. He took me to his hermitage in the mountains that looked out across the entire valley, and he talked about UFO's, the military industrial complex, and the coming unfolding and convergence of time. I left there thinking he'd lost his mind."

"That's the beauty of it, Michael, he did lose his mind. That's why he sees as clearly as he does. What he shared with you was a pure awareness that you translated into rational linear thought. You see, Michael, in the quantum field you have to lose your rational mind to understand fully what's being communicated. You have to move to a transrational, multisensory mind to begin to understand the messages coming to you from a higher altitude. What kind of rational sense does the last twenty-four hours make to you? If you were to tell your colleagues at the university the simple story of this past night and day what would they think of you?"

"They would think I'd lost my mind."

"Have you?"

"If I haven't, I'm in the process of it. Nothing is making sense like it did before I landed here."

"So, from a perspective beyond the five senses, what do you think Benedict, one of your spiritual fathers, was trying to communicate to you?"

I looked up into the sky with its million pinpricks of light. The rhythmic beat of my heart lulled me into a restful posture. My back, neck, and jaw muscles relaxed. After several minutes, I looked up at Favor.

"There are benevolent and malevolent forces at play here. I think I see but I don't, because I identify only with the rational programmed data of my five senses. I cut myself off from the multidimensional parts of my being. What I think is real is often illusion and what I think is illusion is often real. I need to wake up from this closed system and open myself to the expanding mind. For those who refuse, the sun is setting and the day is ending. For those who wake up, the sun is rising and a new day is dawning. A convergence needs to take place: the coming together of all apparent opposites, a reconciliation that ends all wars raging in the hearts, hands, and minds of every seventy-trillion celled human being. The old is passing away while the new is birthing."

There was a deep silence when I stopped talking. I hadn't reflected on my visit with Father Benedict since driving out of the desert those many years ago. I was surprised at my own interpretation. This discovery of how to live a new life deserved further, more expanded inquiry.

"Ameyn!" I heard Favor exclaim. "Ameyn! It ends and begins right here. *Gratia*, good job, excellent! It's the end of my day and the beginning of yours. Thank you. A great way to end . . . and to begin. Ponder that reflection, Michael. It has great merit and importance. It's now time for me to be on my way. I'm on a day schedule, and it looks like you're into the night. Feel free to roam around as you choose. This is a safe harbor, most of the doors don't lock, and there's always someone around looking out for you. Here, in this place, you're never alone, never separate, and remember," he said with his wry humor, "the Force is with you!"

Favor stood, stretched, made a salute to the sun, moon, and stars, bowed to me, and ambled off into the night. Filled with gratitude and wonder, I opened the sliding glass door to the cottage, crossed the threshold, and entered in.

Chapter 7

*Always the wish that you may find patience enough in yourself to
endure, and simplicity enough to believe; that you may acquire
more and more confidence in that which is difficult, and in your
solitude among others.*
-Rainer Maria Rilke-

When I walked into my cottage, I was surprised to see the desk
light on and a fire burning in the woodstove. My luggage and
briefcase were next to the desk, on top of which my keys sat on a
folder. These people deserved an award for hospitality. Satisfied
and comfortable, I sat at the desk and looked at the front page
of the folder to see the headline *About Us,* followed by a brief
history and description of Sunnyview Community and Retreat
Center.

The center was located on a thirty-two hundred acre parcel of
land anonymously gifted to a nonprofit educational organization
in 1972. It sat next to the Hiawatha National Forest, midway
between Lake Michigan and Lake Superior in the Upper
Peninsula. It began as an artist community dedicated to the
advancement of human creativity and consciousness. Many of the
cottages and community buildings were from the original family
fishing camp built in the 1920s. A self-sufficient community
of scientists, artists, visitors, religious, and ongoing supporters
held an integral vision of interconnectivity and sustainability for
the global community. A link to their website followed the brief

description. The brevity of the article raised more questions than gave answers, but it was a beginning, so I sat back in the chair and drifted off into my thoughts.

Am I one of the visitors, artists, scientists, or religious who hold an integral, and in my case, somewhat fragmented vision of a new world? Less than a week ago, I was sitting in my comfortable Victorian home near the University of Denver where I enjoy a tenured position as professor. Joanna and I are still adjusting to an empty nest, as our son and daughter are both on their own journeys. I just finished a summer of family vacations and tying up loose ends, so I could take this much-needed sabbatical leave. The three previous sabbaticals were miserable, because the publish-or-perish drama in academic life has always prompted me to prove my worth, competence, and commitment to the cultural norms of my profession. This time is going to be different. I no longer want to prove myself; I want to find myself!

Somewhere along the way, during these past decades, I've lost my essence. I've compromised the vision that set me on my trajectory, and now I need to find my way back home. The seeker and artist that I used to be are still alive and well, albeit much diminished and ignored. The road trip I began a few days ago was a stepping away from the known and into the unknown. I wanted to go places I'd never been, be with new people, and do things I'd never done, and here I am. Am I in a letting go process that will help me melt down my illusions of being in control? Can I discover something different and delightful here, in myself, and beyond?

What was it one of my mentors taught me? "Get out of the classroom and into the field!" he had shouted. "Stop trying to figure things out and just throw yourself into it! You'll learn all you need to know that way. Anything less is bullshit!"

He was a bit of an iconoclast, yet his advice was sound. He taught me to embody what I teach and eventually only teach what I embody. Over the years of learning and teaching, have I come to stand under that directive: turning information into wisdom by living it, embracing it, taking it into my daily life. Have I finally come to know, after a lifetime of academic training, that I don't really know much of anything?

I lived that in my early years, but then I got comfortable. Is the time for my most significant transition always right now? Am I still finding the path by walking it? It seems I've come to a fork in the road. What must I let go of to let come?

This Sunnyview stop was not consciously planned, not in my playbook or even on the map. Maybe it isn't even real. Could I be dreaming in my car at a rest area? Maybe I've fallen into Jung's collective unconscious or into Rumi's field. Maybe the whole last thirty years never even happened. Maybe there really is something more going on in the universe than what I've been thinking—like parallel universes, higher levels of being, angelic messengers, and invisible realities. Perhaps I'm still twenty-four, lost in some psychedelic fairy tale. Whatever's going on, I'm beginning to enjoy it. I'm learning to relax and starting to rediscover the childlike reality of surprise, wonder, and curiosity. Amazingly, I think I'm beginning to remember my Self!

I woke up from this bothersome and enlightening reflection to see the fire still burning in the woodstove. I felt a shiver run through my body reminding me I was here, alive, and well. I heard the wind blowing through the darkness and the trees outside. It was comforting to be next to the calming fire on the inside.

Chapter 8

Everything must be based on a simple idea. Once we have finally discovered it, it will be so compelling, so beautiful, that we will say to one another, yes, how could it have been any different?
-John Wheeler-

A knock on the sliding glass door startled me. I turned to look but couldn't see through the reflection into the darkness. I got up and slid the door open. Standing in front of me was a woman dressed in the same blue and white robes Angelina wore. The white hood pulled over her head created a strange and wonderful kind of halo that framed her young face.

"Dr. Michael Wyman?"

"Yes."

"My name is Clare. I'm the evening guest master. May I come in?"

"Of course," I said, stepping aside, sliding the door closed behind her. I walked over to the floor lamp and switched it on.

She pulled her hood back revealing the same auburn hair and stunning beauty of the only woman I'd met here. She also reminded me of my daughter who was about the same age. A pang of paternal protectionism surfaced in my heart.

"May I sit down?" she asked, already beginning to sit in the wing back chair.

"Please," I said, feeling a bit uncomfortable. The resemblance to Angelina was uncanny. Was she another figment of my imagination?

"Are you Angelina's . . . ?" I hesitated, not wanting to look the fool.

"Daughter. No worries, it happens all the time. We're thirty years apart in age and some people still mistake us for sisters. I'm flattered for my mother and hope for the same when I'm her age. It's genetics and lifestyle." She paused. I sat in the desk chair, and she looked at me. "Has anyone ever commented that you look like a tall version of Robert Redford?"

My eyes fell to the floor and a bashful smile came to my face. I looked up at Clare and said, "No, never." We both laughed. She glanced at the desktop, saw the open folder, and redirected the conversation.

"I see you've been looking at the welcome folder."

"Yes, and honestly what I've read so far raises more questions than answers. I haven't yet opened my computer to surf your website, so I'm in need of some more information."

"That's why I'm here. How long are you planning to stay?"

"I'm not really sure. It feels like I've been here a week and it's been less than a day. Time is a curious thing. As to making a decision about staying on, now that you bring it up, yeah, I guess I have decided to stay for a while, if that's all right."

Clare smiled. "Absolutely. I see someone brought your luggage and briefcase here for you. Is there anything else you need?"

"You folks are way ahead of me in knowing what I need and providing it efficiently and effectively. I'm in awe and it keeps getting more and more curious. You here in this room is just one more example of insightful hospitality that I'm barely familiar with.

"The brief description I read said this community was founded as an artist colony dedicated to creativity and awakening consciousness. I have to say it feels more like some kind of monastic community. Is it?"

"What gives you that impression?"

"The robes some of you wear, the experience this evening in the kiva, the quiet peaceful efficiency, the demeanor of the people I've met and witnessed, the whole feel of the place. I've spent some time in both monastic and artist communities, and there's a strange and wonderful interplay between the two here. Am I on the right track with this?"

"As you know from your training, Dr. Wyman, the English word religion comes from the Latin word *religare*, which means to bind back."

I nodded in agreement.

Clare gathered her hair with both hands and laid it across her shoulder. She folded her hands and rested them on her lap while she continued her explanation. "The question is, to bind back to what? Those who support, visit, and live in this place have the sense that we are binding back to the very essence and source of creativity, connectivity, light, and life. There's an electromagnetic energy in the universe that connects us all. It reconciles all opposites, binds everything together, and awakens us to infinite possibilities and potentialities. In that sense, one could argue that we are extremely religious. We're aware of the many practices used for thousands of years by people throughout the world who have been adept in aligning with this energy and helping Homo sapiens grow and evolve. These are the mystical traditions of the many spiritual masters from which many of today's religions have come. The idea of aligning and connecting with the life source is an amazingly simple and practical one. The mystics of the ages have known these things, and in many cases, been the repositories of this wisdom. Most of them have been very secretive about what they practiced and the connections they made, because people fear what they don't know and understand."

Her knowledge, confidence, and forthrightness took me aback. Even being thirty years her senior, I felt like a student attending her lecture. It was lovely. I leaned back in my chair waiting for more.

"Our primary connection is with the Benedictine communities who trace their lineage back almost four thousand years through the Judeo-Christian lines. They are still quite active in the world today in very open and visible ways. We are also connected to Buddhist communities, the great Hindu masters, the Sufi's, and other Western, Middle Eastern, and Asian communities who embody the mystical spiritual traditions of the world. We work closely with other hermetic, indigenous, and integral groups throughout the world as well as physicists, biologists, psychologists, artists, ecologists, architects, agriculturalists, philanthropists, entrepreneurs, and the like. We're part of a global network of increase and advancement helping birth a new creation. Beyond that, we're also in contact and in communication with the invisible side of life."

"The invisible side?" I questioned.

"Traditional Catholicism has been calling these messengers and guides, angels, archangels, and the Company of heaven for centuries. They are quite real, Michael."

Clare scooted to the edge of her chair becoming more animated with excitement. "A multisensory and meta-rational consciousness is required to connect with them, which can be facilitated through meditation and contemplative training. Since energy has frequency and vibration, it opens to a spaciousness found at various levels of reality. Alignment is crucial in awakening consciousness. So much of what has been misunderstood and misaligned has been corrected over time, because of the advancement of human awareness and awakening presence. We are part of a universal energy system whose mission is to increase and expand human consciousness and end all war that infects the hearts and minds of humanity. This vision is made active here at Sunnyview in all we say, do, and strive to be. You're experiencing this in your visit here, are you not? Dr. Wyman? Dr. Wyman? Did I lose you along the way?"

The cab pulled up to the hotel. I got out, incredulous and elated that I was in New York City. John came out of the revolving doors to greet me. We hugged and moved quickly into the lobby where there were hundreds of people milling around. It was like a holiday for hippies, business people, gurus, college professors, antiwar activists, curiosity seekers, media reporters, and hangers on. John had invited me to come to this antiwar expo to be a part of what he called a Happening.

"You just have to be there with me, man," he had said over the phone. "I'll pay your way, put you up, it'll be so cool. Timothy Leary and Ram Dass will be there. The Chicago Seven, the Maharishi, some political dude, and his wife from Arkansas and Harvard, maybe even Lennon and Harrison. Michael, you just have to make it. I'll send you the ticket. It's in two weeks. You're not missing this event. Everybody who's anybody will be there. It's your destiny. I'll make all the arrangements and get back to you."

It was three days of haze. There were so many people from so many places discussing so many subjects that I barely registered the significance of the event. On the last day during the last group discussion, I met a guy from the Midwest who had recently received a doctorate in quantum physics, environmental science, and art from the University of Michigan. He was the convener of a discussion concerning a future beyond war. He caught my attention at the beginning of the discussion, because he was from my home area, and I was attending U of M at the time. He was bright, articulate, humorous, and had some amazingly futuristic ideas that I thought were visionary, if rather unpractical. I had a private conversation with him after the seminar about Michigan, his research project in the Upper Peninsula, and my interests.

When we parted, he placed his left arm around me, drew me in close, and looked right into my soul. "You'll be there someday for my family to carry on the work. I may be gone by then, but you'll be there. I can see it. It's your destiny. Stay the course and never give up, Michael. It's why we're here. Always remember to remember!"

He smiled and kissed me on the forehead before pushing me away and out the door as if he was giving me a blessing and sending me out to engage a mission of unknown origin and consequence.

"Dr. Wyman? Dr. Wyman?"

I looked at Clare with a blank expression, still lost in thought. Those moments with Will had made the conference for me, even though I had no idea what they meant at the time. It was more than thirty years ago. Why did it arise now? He and I had communicated as I was finishing my degree, and we traded papers after I became a professor. We became colleagues and good friends over the years. I recently heard from him about a major project he was ecstatic about. His name was Will Fischer.

"I'm sorry, Clare. I was lost in thought. What was your question? I—"

Wait a minute. Clare, the Upper Peninsula of Michigan, futurism, ecology, and quantum physics, artistry, mystical theology. William Clarence Fischer. Oh my God! Are you kidding me? Is this? Could it possibly be?

Waking up to the possibilities of the person sitting in front of me, I blurted out, "Clare! Is your father Dr. William Clarence Fischer?"

Chapter 9

I always knew that one day I would take this road. But yesterday
I did not know today would be the day.
-Nagarjuna-

Tears welled in Clare's eyes and flowed down her cheeks. She looked at me with amazement and relief, a look of knowing and friendship even though we'd just met. I felt my heart stir with some unknown emotion, and I sat silently in a compassionate presence waiting for her answer. She seemed lost in thought.

"Angelina Fischer? She's not here now. This is her daughter, Clare. I can take the call for her."

"This is Captain John Garner with the United States Coast Guard, Marquette Station. We had a Mayday call from a William Fischer and his crew of four on Mystic Travelers, a sailing vessel in passage from Copper Harbor to Thunder Bay. Do you know William Fischer?"

"Yes, he's my father. Is he all right?"

"It doesn't look good. We dispatched a helicopter and had a brief sighting but lost them. We've had no further contact, and there's a squall out there with forty-foot waves. I'm sorry but we fear the worst. I'd gather the family if I were you, Miss Fischer. I'm sorry. I'll get back to you when we have more information."

The phone went dead, and Clare stood motionless in her mother's living room. Her dad and his crew were all such competent and careful professionals, yet Lake Superior had a history of swallowing even the best and brightest of them. Clare's body went numb, but somehow she was able to hit the flash button on the phone to call her mom in Marquette and her brother in California, leaving messages to call her cell phone immediately. She then went to her grandmother's suite to relay the news and broke down with all the rage and sorrow of a Lake Superior squall.

I saw Clare pull a handkerchief from her sleeve, wipe her tears, gently blow her nose, fold her hands on her lap, and take a deep breath. She made eye contact and my heart stirred with an unknown emotion, as I sat silently waiting for her answer.

"Yes," she answered, "he died in a storm on Lake Superior with his crew yesterday. You knew him didn't you?"

My excitement was immediately doused by the shock of her answer. Her revelation evoked an immediate and deep emotional response from me. I felt my eyes well with tears and little rivulets streamed down my cheeks.

Clearing my throat and wiping my eyes with the sleeve of my shirt I finally answered, "Yes. I knew him when we were young men back in the seventies. I didn't know of his death, Clare. He was an inspiration to me. His influence led me to places I wouldn't have gone on my own."

She nodded, still visibly troubled. "Many people have said that about him. He and I were so close and shared so much." She quieted as tears welled up again. She reused her handkerchief, regained her composure, and continued. "I know that life and death are integral to each other and that he's moved on to new places, but I just miss him being here with us." Clare leaned back in her chair and stared out into the darkness beyond the cabin. She looked exhausted.

We sat there listening to the silence between us, the sounds of the night, and the logs crackling in the woodstove. I regained my composure as I ran my hand across my forehead and down my face. I leaned forward, folded my hands, and rested both arms on my legs. "The last communiqué I had with your dad was a little over a week ago. Our conversation had me wondering what kind of work he was doing beyond his brief descriptions and inquiries.

He was a scientist and an artist dedicated to the expansion of human consciousness, and he repeatedly pushed the envelope in his work. He told me of some private research that concerned scalar electromagnetic energy, transportation systems, and weather control. He asked a few questions about the social and psychological implications of a world without war, and thinking back on it now, I sense he was asking something more of me than I knew at the time. Unfortunately, I didn't pay much attention, and answered superficially.

"Clare, do you remember the last conversation you had with your dad?"

She sat very still in a meditative position for a few minutes while I waited attentively. Her breathing deepened. She relaxed her eyes, now clear, and she softly focused on the window of the wood burning stove as she recalled the conversation.

"We were walking in the woods out along the south end of the lake. There's a lone cabin over there that Dad used as his hermitage when he wanted solitude and deeper silence. We stopped and sat in silence on the porch for a while. During our walk, we hadn't talked much. He asked about my doctoral thesis, my involvement with the outside world, relationships with Mom, Atom, and Gram, typical stuff." She looked up at me and continued.

"I asked him about his life and work and much to my surprise he was vague. He would usually take off on some tangent he was following, ask me for some advice on a piece of the puzzle, be quite animated and excited about a new discovery he'd made or a possibility he was pursuing; but that day, the day before he left on the trip to Thunder Bay, he was different. He seemed pensive, talking about all we had been able to accomplish here at Sunnyview. He spoke of the great love he had for Mom, Gram, Atom, and me and the global transformation that had to happen in the twenty-first century. He seemed lost in a wonderland of possibilities, and yet there was something else, something he was pondering that he couldn't speak directly to."

She paused and gazed into her reflection on the window of the woodstove. The fire was dancing with popping and snapping sounds. The atmosphere was soaked with remembrance, nostalgia, and hope. I sensed a presence in the moment. This room, this fire, an old friend's daughter, a death, and a new life were all coming together in me. Was I waking up to a destiny that had been far off and yet very near? I listened more attentively.

"He wanted to say something to me." Clare's eyebrows drew together in concentration. "He wanted to tell me something of great significance and importance. Maybe he couldn't, because it would have put me in harm's way, compromised me. That's what I'm picking up. Yes, there it is, he knew something, a message that slipped right past me until now. He conveyed an uncertainty that I rarely saw in him, as if he was entering something unfamiliar, untested, unproven, risky, and dangerous. The conversation ended in a sea of speculation, hopes, and dreams. We walked back to the compound and just as we parted, he turned to me and looked deep into my soul with a profound intention. I can't believe I forgot about it until now. He said, *Clare, remember to remember. The facts are always pointing to facts beyond the facts. An old friend of mine will come to your assistance. You'll know him when he shows up. Remember to remember. Things are not always as they appear. You, your mother, your brother, and Gram are safe. Love is the healing.* He kissed me on the forehead, we smiled, hugged, and I haven't seen him since.

"Michael, you're that friend. You're the one he sent to help! Who are you and what do you know?"

Chapter 10

The Caterpillar and Alice looked at each other for some time in silence: at last, the Caterpillar addressed her. "Who are you?" "I hardly know," replied Alice. "What do you mean by that?" inquired the Caterpillar sternly. "Explain yourself!" "I can't explain myself sir, because I'm not myself." "Not yourself, then who are you?" "I'm Alice." "Are you?" asked the Caterpillar. "I should know who I am!" exclaimed Alice. "Yes, you should," replied the Caterpillar. "Do you?"
-Lewis Carroll-

Was I really sent here to help her and others? I had no conscious awareness of it. I came to this part of the country to reconnect with some family heritage, get away from the encumbrances of my life, and spend some time with the water and the wilderness. Am I part of something that is beyond a simple explanation? Was Will really talking about me? *You'll know him when he shows up. Things are not always as they appear. Remember to remember. The facts are always pointing to the facts beyond the facts.* Why would these be the last words Will spoke to his daughter? What was he alluding to?

I looked at Clare. The emotion had cleared from her face. She was pacing the small cabin now, trading glances with the fire and the floor, and watching me expectantly.

"Why do you think I'm the one he was talking about?" I didn't want to let Clare down, but this seemed a little too supernatural for me. "I had no idea until a few moments ago that Will had disappeared, that you were his daughter, or even that this was his home base. All our communication was through e-mail, phone, or face-to-face in Colorado. I knew he had a place somewhere in the Upper Peninsula, but I've never been here before. How could I be the one?"

She stopped abruptly and focused intensely on me. Her eyes widened then squinted as she clenched her jaw. She raised her hand and pointed accusingly at me. "You said disappeared just now, not died! Why did you say disappeared?"

My arm and hand jerked up quickly as if I'd been slapped in the face. "I didn't mean anything by it. I have no idea why I said disappeared. Should we read something into it, Clare?"

I rubbed my forehead trying to get my bearings. "Can we put this off to the side for a minute? You didn't answer my question. We'll come right back to this, but first you have to answer my question. Why do you think I'm the one Will was talking about, the old friend who would come to your assistance?"

"Because you're here!" Clare nearly shouted. "It doesn't matter that you don't yet know your part in this story, Michael. The fact is you're here and we're having this conversation. *You'll know him when he shows up* is what he said. I now know. You're the one!"

I still wasn't convinced, but then I remembered Will's words when we parted at the conference back in the seventies: *You'll be there for my family; I can see it. It's your destiny.* Is it possible this was what he was referring to?

I refocused on Clare. "*The facts aren't always the facts . . .* What do you think he was talking about in those last sentences? I'm wondering if he was sending you some kind of hidden message. What exactly did he say again?"

Clare reluctantly dropped her energy for a moment. Silence filled the room. She again went into a meditative state, and then recited the words verbatim as she had before.

"I think you should talk to your mom and Favor about this. They can help interpret his message in a way I can't."

Clare nodded, and then held her hand up in defiant protest when I started to get up. "You said *disappeared.* Let's get back to that! The thought that he and his crew might still be alive never occurred to me. When you said disappeared instead of died, a shiver went through me. I've come to trust my body wisdom. It's a compelling thought that Dad and his crew disappeared rather than died. Can you drill down deeper? What were you saying from a transrational level?"

She seemed to forget I was new here, a beginner in their way of life. Favor had recently helped me reinterpret a message that I'd missed from Father Benedict, perhaps I could do this with Clare too. Was it just wishful thinking when I said disappeared, or did a distant revelation come to awaken and unravel the mystery? I stood, gestured Clare toward me, and took her hands. I shifted to a receptive state with a soft focus that I'd learned long ago, dropped into an unknown remembrance with deep breathing, and felt a new mysterious energy enter the system.

Within a few minutes, out of a mist of consciousness, I felt the power of a storm with its massive waves of wind and water. A faint image of a five-pointed star hovered above a sailing vessel as a wave crashed down upon the boat, swallowing it. I heard a helicopter and a faint garbled word that sounded like the wind whispering *energize.* Then I was back in the room with the warmth of the fire, the dim light, and Clare. We let go of each other's hands, and I asked what she'd seen and heard.

"A storm and Dad's boat. I think I heard the word energize. What about you?"

I told her what I saw and heard. "What do you think it means?" I asked.

"I'm not sure, but it gives me enough to begin some further investigation. Something also came to me when we clasped hands that I can't quite grasp. I'll have to sit with it awhile." She paused for a moment. "The report from the Coast Guard was very vague. It gave us nothing to draw from. Your insight adds additional credibility to what others have speculated about."

"What speculation?"

"That Dad and the others planned their deaths." She shook her head fiercely. "I could never imagine my dad taking his own life. Accidental death, sure, we all make miscalculations and life happens, but intentional suicide? No way. A planned disappearance is another story that I can follow up on, and you can continue to help me. That's why you're here. That's what Dad was saying. You're here to assist in solving the mystery of his disappearance, to understand its meaning, and inquire why he didn't bring us in on the plan. I have to share this with Mom, Atom, and Gram."

She picked up her notebook from the chair, gave me a slight hug, and then drew back. She looked at me and sighed deeply.

"From the heart of my heart, thank you for listening and following the bread crumbs that led you to this cottage, to our family, to this compound, and into this mystery. Mother will want to see you. Stop in at the café tonight after midnight. That's her shift. I'll tell her what we've discovered."

Clare turned, slid open the glass door, and walked out into the darkness. I lost sight of her as she pulled the hood over her head. I shut the door, put a few new logs in the firebox, and stretched out on the bed to ponder the facts that pointed beyond themselves.

Chapter 11

It's not what you look at that matters, it's what you see.
-Henry David Thoreau-

The boat rocked gently in the calm waters of the Caribbean Sea. It floated in a protected bay on the leeward side of Roatan, an island off the coast of Honduras. I awoke to a sunny day with a warm friendly breeze blowing across the bow of a large sailing vessel. We were attached to a buoy about a hundred yards off shore. I stood, stretched, took three deep breaths, and did a 360 degree panoramic take on our position. The only noise I heard was the lapping of the water against the sides of the boat and the calls of a few seagulls. I looked for the dinghy but saw none. Walking to the stern, I stepped into the cockpit. Everything looked shipshape. The hatch cover was open, so I climbed down the stairs and entered the salon. The galley was clean, everything in its place. All the gear was stowed except for a few navigation charts that were open on the table. I was onboard alone. The charts were for celestial navigation. They sketched out a path from Thunder Bay, Ontario, to this bay at Port Royal, Roatan. A sticky note on one of the charts had a handwritten message: Bienvenidos Mystic Travelers! Mi casa es su casa. Derick.

The fire was down to radiant hot coals when I opened my eyes. The cottage was warm and glowing. I struggled to identify where I was, and then it came to me. I looked at my watch, twenty-five minutes after midnight. Time to make my way back to the café.

I got up and headed for the shower. While showering, I pondered the dream I just had, the interaction with Clare, and the other events that had occurred since arriving at this north woods port less than twenty-four hours ago. I tried to connect the dream with the events of the day, but my mind drifted to Denver where my wife Joan and . . .

A loud crashing noise came from the porch. It sounded like someone had fallen. I froze, backed up against the shower stall, and listened intently. I turned off the water and grabbed a towel. My whole body tightened. I heard a muffled voice.

"Hello?" I said as I stepped out of the shower. I squinted to see through the darkness and glow of the dying embers. I heard the sliding glass door open.

"Dr. Wyman, it's me, Anthony Amir. Sorry man, I just tripped over a chair. I'll just stay out here while you finish your shower. I couldn't sleep and saw your light. I can come back later."

"Damn, Anthony, you scared the crap out of me!" I relaxed and breathed deeply. "No, no, come in. Just give me a minute." Awkwardly clutching the towel, I grabbed the clothes I'd placed on the seat of the desk chair.

Anthony respectfully turned his back and waited for me to get dressed, and then he casually said, "I saw Clare leave here a while ago. Earlier today, I heard that something happened to her dad. Do you know anything about that?"

I finished dressing, took my jacket off the back of the chair, and noticed a small flashlight on the desk that I hadn't seen before. I picked it up and flicked it on and off. I was again surprised and thankful for the attention to detail and gracious hospitality of this community. I looked up and saw Anthony still standing with his back toward me. He appeared uncomfortable at the door as he looked out into the night.

"I'm presentable now."

Anthony turned. His dark hair and clothes were disheveled and his face was drawn and tight.

"I'm on my way out, believe it or not. I'm meeting Angelina in the café soon. Want to walk and talk? You can help me find my way back to the compound."

Anthony nodded and led me to the path. We walked slowly in the dim moonlight.

"Clare did come by earlier to do her guest master thing and informed me that Will's schooner went down in a storm yesterday. No one has seen the crew or boat since."

"That's what I heard too. What was he doing out on Lake Superior in October?"

"I don't know."

"I wonder how Dr. Fischer's death will affect this place. Do you think they'll keep it running as they have been? It's quite a vast operation from what I've seen and heard. I'd hate to see it change."

I nodded. "I don't think the way the Fischer's manage Sunnyview will change at all. It's perfect, because it runs more like a living organism than a mechanistic organization. There's a natural fluidity here that's rare. Why can't you sleep?"

"Too much on my mind. There's not much for me to do here but think, you know?"

"Yeah, I do. Before you came by I was thinking about my family."

"In Denver, right? Tell me about them. Are you married?"

"Yes, my wife is still trying to save the world from the small-minded people and political bureaucrats." We both laughed and I continued. "She's a top immigration attorney and is always in the midst of splitting hairs between the letter and the spirit of the law. Her dedication to make a significant difference in the lives of immigrants borders on sainthood. When I left home a few days ago, she was embroiled in litigation. I admire that in her, but I'm so tired of the fight. I just want to disappear into the wilderness. The rift between her unending passion and my loss of passion has caused some difficulties in our relationship during the past year. She's still driving hard in a stormy sea while I've lost my rudder and am drifting far from the shore."

"Huh, sorry to hear that. Do you have kids?"

"Our son Jonah finished his doctoral program and is doing fieldwork as a Peace Corps volunteer in Peru. Our daughter Michaela is finishing a graduate program in business administration and culinary arts in Lyon, France. I miss them."

"Wow, sounds like you raised a couple of overachievers. Are they happy?"

"They're doing what they want to do and are making the contribution they feel is important. Yes, they're both happy and excited about life. How about you?"

Okay, I remember what happened earlier today with this psychologist. I'd love to explore my mixed emotions and conflicted loyalties but no, I can't allow it. Some half-truths and a few small lies can help deflect the conversation and get it back to him. "I graduated college and have been working the nonprofit circuit helping with economic and community development. It's my fieldwork leading to a graduate degree."

"Does that bring you happiness and fulfillment?"

"Absolutely."

"Anthony, do you mind being my sounding board for a few minutes? My monkey mind has been working overtime since I arrived here, and I'd like to get some of it out of my head. Your perspective would be helpful."

Maybe this is some of the unknown information I'm looking for about the Fischer family and the secrets they hold. Maybe I'm finally getting a break. "I'm your man, let it flow."

"I sense a great turning, an unfolding, something different emerging in every country around the globe, and I'm recognizing it in me. I can't ignore it any longer and continue with business as usual. A new, more inclusive call is being issued and I need to answer it. I need to do something more than just maintain the system. I used to be a revolutionary thinker, but that turned into a self-centered grab for the good life. I, as well as millions like me, followed the American dream. I traded my beads and long hair for a BMW, an upscale home, and too much debt. I gave up my unconventional ideas for conventional ones and a mechanized stability. My generation has been silent while wars have come and gone, while the military industrial complex has silently and stealthily taken over our country and transformed our values. It seems we have entered the enemy's camp and they are us. This charade has to change. I can't do it anymore. Are you still with me?"

"Right here. I don't know where you're going, but I'm getting what you're saying."

"Being here at Sunnyview has opened my eyes to something that's been emerging for a long time. I've known Will Fischer for more than thirty years and just found out tonight that he's a significant part of this place. I came here not knowing that, not knowing his family, not knowing anything about this part of his life, and now he's gone. I'm still trying to figure out how that's possible."

This guy's sending mixed messages that I'm not getting, but he's known Will Fischer for more than thirty years. He's a valuable informant. He needs to be on our list. Ihsaan will be pleased. "So let me get this right. You're an entrenched member of the establishment who played the game successfully, has seen it from the inside out, and now wants to be an outsider?"

"I'm wondering if one can be both. It seems to me the Fischer's and their community has found the balance; to be in and out at the same time."

"Dr. Wyman, are you playing with my mind? I'm wondering the same thing. My thinking also seems turned upside down in this place. I can totally relate to what you're saying and I think we're both crazy. Have you been drinking the water? It must be the water." They both smiled.

"Have you heard of Arthur Koestler?" I asked.

Anthony shook his head.

"He's the guy who coined the term holon. He's probably another friend of the Fischer's on the forefront of innovation, exploration, and creative change. This conversation reminds me of Koestler's theory of holons. It describes how everything's simultaneously a whole and a part. Could we be autonomous, self-reliant units who possess a degree of independence, while also being subject to some control from a larger whole? Are we part of a holarchy, a hierarchy of self-regulating holons that can function as autonomous wholes as well as interdependent parts? Are we in control and subordinate to controls at higher levels of being, like here in the Sunnyview community? Could we all be part of a vast infinite system that connects everything, like an infinite mind field or a source matrix?"

"I'm not sure I follow, but it sounds like a cool idea. You should write a paper on it."

"I don't think writing a paper is the call, Anthony. I'm more into the deeper personal inquiry. Is it possible that we're all on a journey into the unknown together, and that there's a calling to move beyond where we are individually and collectively into a higher level of being, doing, and understanding?"

Anthony didn't answer immediately. He slowed his walk and scratched his head trying to remember the role he was playing—receiving and deceiving. He then stopped, stared into the darkness, and answered cautiously. "I think that might be true, but there are so many ways of seeing the same things. How is it possible to get everyone on the same page?"

I stopped and turned toward Anthony. I saw him squint as he looked at me. The partial moon was high in the sky casting shadows in the night. I thought I caught a glimpse of anger on his face, so I looked closer. I saw tears. "Are you okay, Anthony?"

"Yeah, fine, I was just thinking about some people I know. Please finish." He swiped his jacketed arm across his eyes and began to walk.

"What were you thinking?" I asked.

"I don't want to get into it. Please continue, it was just a passing thought, nothing really."

He started walking and I followed, letting the silence inform my decision to pursue this line of questioning. I decided to drop it considering Anthony's emotions, for tearful nothings are always something. My healer self wanted to touch his wound, but I resisted. "Would you agree that we all share the same universal energy, the same planet, the same emotions, the same longings, and the same source?"

"That seems obvious," Anthony responded, again drawing his arm across his face.

"Then maybe each of us has to seriously ask ourselves where we're going, who we're going with, and what we really want and need for ourselves, our families, our communities, and our world. Maybe we need to ask ourselves why we're here, why we were born into this place in time, and what our life's mission is for the highest and greatest good. Maybe life is a whole lot bigger than race, creed, color, doctrine, dogma, opinion, ego, personality, status, or politics. Maybe we have to surrender all these things to be free, to find our individual and collective harmony, and overcome our fears. How does that resonate with you and your life Anthony?"

Chapter 12

It is through the fusion of opinions that truth lights up. Con-versation, the process of "together-versing" (flowing together) is the very opposite of contro-versy, the process of "contra-versing" (flowing against). Conversation is the operation of the fusion of opinions; it is a work of synthesis. All true conversation calls upon the transcendent/immanent Centre, the Shmaya, the Chi, the Source of Life, to create a synthesis or fusion of opinions. Life is a fusion of polarities that vivifies and creates. Harmony and cooperation find a home in the heart of the Divine Feminine. This alchemy transforms rigidity into fluidity, facilitating a fusion of all polarities. It brings forth a new awareness of interconnectivity, new ways of being, and infinite creative possibilities. It is the tomb, the womb, the chalice, the eternal receptacle and birthing place of Life.
-Anonymous-

Anthony brought his hands to his head and tried to sort out his thoughts. *I came here to Sunnyview as an informant and spy to gather information against Will Fischer and his family. Instead, I've been turned in a way that is confusing and disconcerting. Every interaction I've had has been accepting, affirming, and disarming. It is so radically different from the paranoid and vengeful environments I've been living in these past years. How can these people be my enemy when I have so much in common with them?* Anthony stopped mid-stride and looked at Michael.

"I think I'm going to head back to my cottage. It's been a great conversation with much to ponder. The cool air has cleared my head, and all those mind-blowing ideas you've shared have confused me enough for some good sleep. Thanks for letting me hang out with you. It's been helpful." The half moon was high enough in the sky to cast a dim light on Anthony's face. His eyes were swollen and half-open. His face looked tired and worn.

"We're all fighting our own battles, Anthony, so be kind to yourself and take your rest. Thanks for your companionship, and thanks for listening to the ramblings of an aging boomer. I reached out, put my arm around his shoulder, and looked at his downturned head. "See you tomorrow Anthony, and take good care of yourself."

He smiled as I let go and pulled a small flashlight from his back pocket. He pointed it down our footpath. "Just keep following this until a larger path comes in from the right. That will take you directly to the backside of the compound. There's a door off the deck. Have a good night, Dr. Wyman, and thank you for your kindness."

I walked on in silence pondering the many paths that are available to us all. I saw the large path, made the right-hand turn toward the compound, and caught a brief reflection of what I thought was the top of the pyramid. I tried to see it again but couldn't. I finally broke free from the cover of the trees and stood at the edge of the compound.

At first, all I saw was a light coming from a window on the ground level of the rectangular section. While my eyes adjusted to the lack of moonlight, now clouded, the small light in the window went out. The seven-story pyramid, the three-story rectangle, and the large domed kiva, all connected, were suddenly in front of me. A moment ago they weren't. As the cloud drifted, the light of the moon became brighter and the structures became more visible. The light in the window reappeared. I walked toward it. A few hours ago, in the daylight, this appeared to be a different place. Past the fire pit and onto the deck I felt a sense of sanctuary. Strange, how in one moment, I could feel a fearful awe and in another moment, from a different perspective, I could feel a nurturing comfort. I opened the door to the room with the light on and entered.

I immediately noticed the faint smell of roses with a hint of mint and knew I was in the right place. The room I entered was a corridor that ran the entire length of the building. In it were hundreds of plants, herbs, and flowers: a greenhouse! I continued forward on the well-marked walkway to the doorway that entered a hallway leading straight, left, and right. I went straight through the opening into the café, walked across the room, sat down in my booth, noticed the familiar blank menu on the table, and opened it to look for another question. "*Who are you?*" I saw written in the lower right-hand corner. I closed my eyes, became aware of my breathing, and listened for the silence behind the silence. I waited for the intuitive answer that might bring insight to this classical Zen koan.

My monkey mind spewed forth hundreds of words that described how I showed up in the material world: son, brother, husband, father, artist, professor, gadfly, psychologist, consultant, advisor, teacher, priest, outdoorsman, sailor, rancher, king, fool, doer, beggar, bore, player, friend, and so on. I don't know how long the list went on, but it finally unwound itself leaving me with a fresh awareness. After all these years, after all the education, all the experiences, I didn't really know who I was!

I sat with that curious thought, and then allowed it to drop into a deeper place. I could feel a shift from a rational linear thought into a vastness that I'd never experienced before. I was fearlessly falling through inner space, knowing all would be well. As I reached the base of this new place, I landed gently in some kind of energy field. It was spacious, infinite, loving: beyond all duality, right and wrong, pain and sorrow. It was a peaceful, serene, ineffable feeling.

"Who are you here?" a still small voice asked.

"Not knowing," I answered. "I simply am."

As I heard my inner voice say this, I began to laugh. The inner laughter burst out into the empty café. It was uncontrollable. I laughed in a way I hadn't in decades, as if I finally got the cosmic joke that made absolutely no sense. Tears of joy were running down my cheeks when I finally regained some control of the moment.

Was this enlightenment? As I explored this new awareness, my whole body smiled, and I awakened to the foolishness of my former perceptions. They all melted in this moment as I began to see how life in the material world was simply a reflection of the essence, a hologram of the source. The illusions of my created thought opened for me to see.

"Can you live with that?" a different voice asked.

"Yes," I replied, "and I'll need some help."

"This place needs a name so you can recall it at any time, like a string on your finger that you can touch to remember, reconnect, and realign with whenever you choose. What name would you like to give this place, this infinite sea of possibilities, to help you remember?"

The question dropped right into the middle of this boundless space. When it hit, it bounced back a name that had me chuckling. Bob? Another joke on the whole world and me. Not something serious, pious, erudite, scholarly, or mystical, just Bob? I couldn't stop laughing. Whenever I'd calm down, the smile would arise and again burst into this place of wonderful hilarity. My friend, the infinite cosmos, the boundless base of being—Bob! What a joyous ride. I don't think I'll ever be the same again. Thanks Bob!

I was finally able to take a couple of breaths, but the smile on my face and the water in my eyes kept shining. I was in a world that had changed and rearranged, and here I was! Where? My god, I was in the Sunnyview café, the dining room of a retreat center in the middle of the night. My eyes opened. I had no idea how much time had passed or who had witnessed this hilarious revelation, and I had absolutely no concern. In these few moments, the cosmic egg had cracked and opened for me. I felt more free and alive in these moments than at any other time in my life. There could be no apologies for this experience; my angst had become my liberation! What a gift!

A cloth napkin touched my hand. I took it to wipe my eyes with glee and refocused my attention back to the booth. My eyes connected with a radiant smile and gleaming eyes. Angelina. Beautiful Angelina who, in that moment, truly looked like an angel from the other side of a stained glass window.

In our last two meetings, I had experienced a kind of adolescent shyness and infatuation with her. Now, a new collegiality and camaraderie was present. All my barriers had melted in these several moments. I now saw into the heart of the matter, into the very soul of what keeps us apart and draws us together.

My smile widened as I said, "Greetings!"

She replied, "Welcome home."

Chapter 13

*There is no wilderness like a life without friends; friendship
multiplies blessings and minimizes misfortunes; it is a unique
remedy against adversity, and soothes the soul.*
-Baltasar Gracian-

Angelina laid her folded hands on the table and looked at me.
"The wars that rage everyday in the hearts, minds, and hands of
humanity are due to the illusion that we are separate from each
another and creation. We see the surface of reality and call it the
whole. Our perceptions create our beliefs, which open and close
us to what we can receive. The conditioned limitations we place
on one another and ourselves are the grand illusion, Michael.
Our lives change when we wake up to the underlying truth that
we are ultimately all one. Walking in the middle of a forest at
midnight looks, feels, and sounds very different from walking in
the same forest at noon."

I nodded and said, "Last night when I walked into this room
and met you, I had absolutely no idea who you were, and how we
were connected. I'm in awe at how my perceptions have changed
in the last twenty-four hours. I'm here to help you and your
family in any way I am directed. I'm only beginning to know
how much I don't know and want to embrace that uncertainty.
Will and I didn't talk much about the intimacies of our families.
I've known about you, Clare, Atom, and your mother Gloria,
but only in the abstract. To meet you in person and under these

circumstances is a bit overwhelming and confusing. These last days must have been difficult for you."

Angelina looked down at her hands a moment, and then looked back up at me. "Will's departure wasn't as sudden as it appeared, and I must tell you that I knew you were on your way. I knew who you were when you walked in the door last night. We live a very different life out here, Michael. It's set apart from many of the day-to-day dramas that distract the rest of the world. The common union with creation and the cosmic order is more apparent here than it is in the order most people have created. There's a different spatial and energy alignment away from the fray. It's our calling to be here doing what we do, just as it is other people's calling to work for the Company out in the world. We all function in our specially appointed ways. Some of us simply have more awareness of whom we are and why we're here than others do. Our need is to provide a more fertile environment in which people can consciously evolve and co-create with intention. We need to more fully awaken to who we already are, wouldn't you agree?"

I nodded in agreement.

"It's simply about remembering to remember." Angelina paused to smile as she said those words I'd heard so many times since I'd arrived.

"As a species, we're beginning to wake up to what's been experienced and taught by the few for thousands of years. We're now at a critical stage in our planetary history for this revolutionary or evolutionary change to speed up and take place for the many. We at Sunnyview are part of the vanguard of that unfolding movement and that's why you are now here."

"So I'm here to help you and you're here to help me?"

"Exactly. When everyone understands this and aligns with the natural order of things, we'll see what has been called heaven on earth. We're here to awaken the consciousness of humanity to what's already here. The energy needed to awaken the collective has to reach a critical mass for the quantum leap to take place into the next altitude of consciousness. You, Will, and I, like many others, have been working on this since before we were born. We are now, more than ever before in the history of humankind, coming together in response to this critical mass of creative energy. It is happening and will continue to happen in our lifetimes and beyond. Our children, their children, and we are bridge generations. That's why we're together here at this time.

"We experienced the outpouring of this energy at the end of World War Two, in the fifties, sixties, and seventies in massive new ways. In the eighties, nineties, and during the past ten years, we internalized it to do the important individual work of deepening. People followed their personal trajectories, did their work, and forgot the collective. The incremental adjustments and course corrections took place, the world changed, and the evolution continued without much attention. The adjustments and corrections were subtle transformations of darkness and light in classrooms, laboratories, churches, mosques, temples, factories, offices, homes, boardrooms, retreat centers, associations, and in millions of hearts and minds around the globe. That effort now needs to be brought into the collective consciousness in new ways for this emergence to take place. We boomers, our children, grandchildren, and great-grandchildren, are the generations positioned to make this quantum leap for humanity." Angelina paused. "Are you still with me, Michael?"

"Yes, please continue, I'm fascinated by what you're saying."

"It's time to consciously connect with the alignment we've felt all along. It's time to bring the dispersed community of humanity back to the garden of conscious creation for the Great Unfolding. That's our assignment. It's time to fully wake up to our interconnectedness, our destiny, our sacred unity with all that is, has been, and will be. Everything that's needed to assist this birthing is in place, except the necessary convergence of energies in the field. That's where you come in. What does the Reverend Dr. Michael Jacob Wyman, PhD, DMin, have to say about this?"

Angelina's enthusiasm was contagious. I was ready to jump up and hold every hand in the world if I could. What she was telling me made so much sense. I could already feel the changes she spoke of happening inside me. I didn't know what I could say to match her inspirational harangue, so I settled on a wide smile and said, "That's what friends are for!" feeling like the Cheshire cat in Alice in Wonderland.

Angelina smiled cautiously, trying to figure out where I was coming from. I stopped laughing and took a deep breath getting in touch with another side of myself.

"Look, Angelina, this great turning or unfolding, as you call it, sounds great, but it's just another movie. This can't be a realistic mission. I'm not trying to be irreverent or condescending, but there are seven billion people on the planet and you think a few thousand or even a few million of us can cause a change that hasn't happened since the beginning of time? I know that some have been working on the fulfillment of this dream for a lifetime and even longer, but it's not getting any better. Do you get the news out here? I'm talking about wars, rising domestic violence, divorce, homelessness, economic disaster, famine, ecological destruction, denial, fear, greed, authoritarianism, rampant narcissism, extraordinary indebtedness, market collapse, educational illiteracy, pandemics, addictions, depression, mistrust, racism, sexism, nihilism, resource depletion, militarism; you name it, these things are in every corner of the globe. Five of the most notable scientists in the world die mysteriously in a rogue storm and this is where I come in? Do you have the white horse and cowboy hat waiting for me so I can ride in and take out all the bad guys, rescue the damsels in distress, and live happily ever after?" I paused a moment before continuing.

"Where is this grand unfolding, this new convergence? What do you know that I don't know that brings you to these conclusions? Listen, I'm a lowly professor in the middle of the country who is just waking up from the seventies. I'm not sure we've come much farther than that. Globally, our institutions are so bogged down with bureaucratic ineptitude; greed, self-indulgence, and outdated thinking that it's a wonder people find their way. I'm sorry, but my hopes seem to have turned into pragmatism and border on pessimism."

I sat back to catch my breath, scratched my head, and reflected on the craziness of the situation.

Angelina now had the smile of the Cheshire cat as I ranted like the Mad Hatter. Unruffled by my brief tirade, she patiently sat in a radiant energy of understanding before she spoke.

Chapter 14

We must always go beyond, always renounce the lesser for the greater, the finite for the Infinite; we must be prepared to proceed from illumination to illumination, from experience to experience, from soul-state to soul-state . . . . The Ineffable refuses to limit itself to any form or expression.
-Sri Aurobindo-

"I appreciate your passion; that's one of the reasons Will admired you and chose you to be one of our partners and senior advisors. Work with us, Michael. We want you to be part of our inner circle. We need your passion, insights, connections, and expertise. We need your pragmatism, honesty, integrity, spirituality, and your openness."

"Do I sound very open to you?"

"Yes, and hopeful. You see, without this kind of dialogue there is no synthesis. The openness and honesty you just demonstrated is extremely important. We need to have as many pieces of the puzzle on the table as possible to discover the picture we need to see. To know what we're up against is a great advantage.

"The limitations you listed can all be transcended and transformed; it's simply up to us to find the appropriate corrections and alignments. The critical mass, a point the creative energies need to reach, takes place with positive and negative energy. We're here to tip the scale toward a greater synthesis and expansion of what has been accomplished during the past millennia. We're at a critical time in the history of humanity, and we must help the creative expression unfold from the lesser to the greater. Every one of the difficulties you mentioned are caused by the ignorance we human beings choose to participate in, and every one of them can be transcended and transformed by expanding our consciousness and realigning with the ineffable. You know this through your research, teaching, and practice. It's simply about creating fertile environments that facilitate this kind of transition. The environments being created by the powers that be are sterile and life threatening, not fertile and life enhancing. They are exploitive, unsustainable, and like everything else, in the process of change."

I held up my hands, near exasperation. "I agree with you, and there are millions of people on the planet who also agree, and yet all we seem to do is slow down the bleeding, bandage the wounds, and do the emergency room work while the war against humanity and creation continues. How do we stop the wars? How do we transform those who continue to want more at the expense of others? How do we enhance and sustain the entire planetary community? How do we help people see the futility of this narrow-minded path we're on and empower them to expand their consciousness and positive influence? I've been working on this for decades and don't seem to have even scratched the surface. That's why part of me has become so skeptical. It all seems so futile. What's your plan, Angelina? What are the actions involved? Surely, it's not just about sitting in a kiva meditating for years on end?"

Angelina replied with a terse smile and further explanation. "We've been working on this very question for more than forty years with a loosely knit group of people from around the world. You're one of them. You were put on the list way back in the seventies after you and Will made your connection at the conference in New York. We've identified hundreds of thousands of people just like you in all fields of endeavor who share the vision of a transformed planetary condition. They are upright citizens of their respective countries and each of them has tens of thousands of their own connections that have influence throughout the world. The time has come to unify the vision and action of these cellular structures into a more focused mental, physical, and spiritual movement. The work each of us has been doing is extraordinary, and as we bring this creative energy together in a collective and focused way, it will generate the kind of quantum energy bundle that will create a natural unfolding. That, combined with major global events, will accomplish the turning and provide the infrastructure to sustain it. Will and his immediate team have been working diligently on the logistics of bringing everything together for this transformation.

"I have to believe that a compelling vision with comprehensive, consistent, and compassionate action by the few can accomplish anything. When two and three and fifty make a billion, we'll see that day come round."

She paused, smiled in a way that filled me with hope and confidence, and then asked, "Would you like a cup of tea? I'll be right back. I have some great mint and rose hip tea simmering on the stove."

Not waiting for my answer, she got up, walked across the dining room, and disappeared through the opening in the hallway.

I turned to look out the window and saw my reflection in the glass. Staring back at me was a man of many seasons. I saw myself as a boy, an adolescent, a hip adventurer in my twenties, a responsible young professional in my thirties, a devoted husband and father in my forties, a mature contributor in my fifties, and finally, an unfulfilled elder in my sixties on his way to who knows where. My already graying hair turned white, thinned, and fell out as I watched this drama unfold before my eyes. The smooth skin wrinkled and folded over as I watched my body age and my mind become younger. I saw myself at a very old age lying on a bed and smiling. The luminous body departed from the aged material form and traveled on to the next level of life. A new energy filled me as I foresaw my life unfold.

New generations were being birthed and humanity was making its transition. The new emergence had occurred and there was a harmony in the sounds of the cosmos that resonated with every cell of my being. The elders had stayed the course while the children and the children's children had embodied the vision and action to carry it forward. The global community was united and on its way to ever-greater awakening and accomplishments. A new peace was manifest and smiling hearts were everywhere in view.

I saw the face of a woman. She was everyone. She was the mother, daughter, sister, spouse, lover, grandmother, life giver, and nurturer of this new humanity. She was the Theotokis, God bearer, Fire carrier, Life giver. She and He, the two had become one. The lion and the lamb were now together. The spirit of wisdom and understanding had converged. The spirit of counsel and might, of awe and wisdom, of compassion and righteousness were all in a sacred unity led by little children. The dream of peace on earth was becoming reality. The Great Turning had taken place.

I heard gentle footsteps. The vision ended and yet lingered in the silence of the dining room. I was staring at my present day face. The youth and elder were together, watching me look at the whole of creation. My eyes shifted and refocused to see the reflection in the window of an angel approaching the table with tea. The fragrance of roses with a hint of mint touched my nose and my heart. The visible and invisible messengers and helpers were everywhere. How real is any of this? Bob?

Chapter 15

*There is an exchange of information, at a very basic level between
all living things . . . which allows even radically different organisms,
as different as a human and a bush, to borrow each other's ideas.*
-Lyall Watson-

*The wolves howled intermittently through the night. It was the dead
of winter and the moon was full, the snow had stopped, the sky had
cleared. I walked out into the cold of the Canadian Rockies from my
one room cabin at eleven thousand feet to feel the night and look at
the magnificent scene that spread out around me. The only sounds I
heard were the sounds of a deep and profound silence. It was as if I
could hear the invisible energy of the universe, the cosmic sound of
white noise. Before arriving here in this place, I had never heard this
kind of silence. I had never experienced the profundity of solitude. I
had never communed with nature in its raw form this far away from
humanity for this long. It was my third month of what turned out
to be a five-month stay in this place of solitude, silence, and glory.
I had fallen into a deep dark hole of despair. I was directed to this
place of solace and strength; much needed rest, contemplative insight,
and renewal.*

*Moon Dog had told me about this place, miles away from any
human habitation, when I'd talked to him about the desire to escape
my life. It was an old mining cabin from the late nineteenth century
and in excellent condition. It had been in his family for more than
a century, and they maintained it for summer use. Because of its*

remoteness and relative inaccessibility, it was rarely used in the winter. Moon Dog and I had a moment of synchronicity in a bar one night in the small town down the valley. We hadn't seen each other in years. I was waiting for the universe to show me a way out of my darkness, hoping the sign would come from the depths of my frosty glass of brew. Moon Dog was in town to have a few drinks and connect with old friends. The next day, I was snowshoeing up a mountain with a backpack and sleeping bag, making my way to this remote cabin, which appeared for this turning point in my life.

Tonight, the moon was full and high in the sky illuminating the small, tree-lined valley that stretched out before me. The night light was fascinating and strange, turning the landscape from a Technicolor picture to black and white. A surreal quality touched places in me that daylight did not. Tonight was exceptionally brilliant. The snow had started falling mid-afternoon in one of those gentle storms that sometimes roll over the Rockies. There was no wind, just the gentle falling of infinitely unique snowflakes that added another six inches of white cover to the landscape. I had stayed in my outdoor sitting chair under the cover of my hooded down parka, gloves, and snow pants watching and listening to nature's display of grandeur until the darkness settled in around me. I had finally stood up, brushed off the snow, walked into the cabin, and lit the oil lamp. After starting the fire in the potbelly stove and downing some soup, I was outside again to experience communing with the essential order of Mother Nature.

The trail I had created snowshoeing in and out from the nearest road ran from the cabin, across the meadow, and into the trees. The track was visible even though there was six inches of new snow upon it. Standing on the small porch overlooking the meadow, I watched at what looked like a dog walk slowly up the trail from the trees and into the clearing about a hundred yards away. Every ten yards or so, it would stop to look, listen, and sniff the air. I was a bit curious and afraid: the trail led right up to the cabin where I was standing. The closer the animal got to the cabin, the more I thought I needed to let it know I was here. I raised my arm and spoke aloud with the first words that came to mind. "Do you know I am here?"

About twenty yards away, through the break in silence of my words, the dog stopped with all its senses and looked directly toward the source of the words. I could feel its attention riveted on me. I took a deep breath, dropped my fear, opened my heart, and sent a welcoming message out to meet its concern. We stood in this place for what seemed like both an eternity and a moment.

The dog was a wolf. She knew I was here. She wanted me to know she and her family was here. They had been monitoring me for the past months. She was the matriarch of the clan and a messenger. They had determined they could trust me.

I don't know how this all happened. I had never communicated with a wolf before. I'd had some wonderful relations with a couple of dogs and horses that connected with me and yes, there was telepathic communication with them, but not like this. The wolf and I were communicating with each other in some kind of holographic thought form: talking through the silence in the invisible reaches of inner space. It broke through my cultural conditioning and imprinted my consciousness in a way I had never before experienced.

The silence was loud, the night was bright, the mystery unknown, but the wolf and man connected. She walked another ten yards toward me with calm vigilance and then stopped. I transmitted another welcoming prayer to her. She slowly walked to the edge of the porch. I sat down on a log bench and leaned back against the cabin wall. She sat down at the edge of the porch. We surrendered our fearful notions about each other. This was a completely new world for me.

Through the holographic communication, she spoke to me of the encroachment of humanity into the natural order, the present and future destruction of habitat, the demise of the four-legged families, the over-population and lack of concern for the imbalance created by humans. I listened, hearing the compassion and concern of a wise matriarch and elder. Connecting with the creative order of life and opening to the spaciousness within the collective heart were her themes.

Her parting message was very personal. "You are here for more reasons than you know. Continue to love and learn the ways of the earth and heavens. Return again and again for solitary stays as you now have, and remember to remember that you are connected to all that is visible and invisible. There will be times when you will be called upon to stand up and confront the powers of forgetfulness, ignorance, and destruction. When they come, stand up, stand firm, and stand for all your relatives. We need one another. We are all part of this glorious web of life, each intricate to life's purpose. Know that you, with us, are stewards of this creation. Hold her gently. Treat her kindly. She is our mother. Hold this moment in your heart and let it grow within you. My name is Shmaya and my mate is Arha. Learn what these words mean in your own language, for they point to universal truths. We will meet again. We are one."

We sat there in a peaceful grace of a cosmic embrace. She got up after several minutes and walked the short distance between us to put her paw on my knee. Looking into those eyes took me back to my primal roots. I placed my ungloved hand on her paw and made a promise I always carry with me, yet sometimes forget. She turned and walked back down the path, stopping just before she entered the trees. I sat for a long time wondering about our untapped possibilities—how we might all be angels, messengers, Mystic Travelers, and soul connecters—united in this infinite sea of hidden potentiality.

Angelina placed three cups with saucers on the table and poured tea into them from the teapot. She turned around to acknowledge someone walking across the floor toward us. I immediately stood up to greet the elder image of Clare and Angelina. Standing in front of me with an outstretched hand and a broad smile was the matriarch of this clan.

"Michael, this is my mother, Gloria. Mom, this is Michael Wyman."

We shook hands holding each other's gaze as we gave a slight bow. Her eyes were aged with wisdom and clear with insight. The lines on her face marked her years. Her white hair crowned her glory. This line of women, Gloria, Angelina, and Clare, were the roots of the tree planted here in Sunnyview. They were the lineage holders of this movement. Will Fischer had come into their line and them into his, to create a new synthesis. They were the lightning rods, the ground beneath the structures, the wind within the sails, the perennial torchbearers. They were the reason I was here.

Chapter 16

*Sit down before your facts like a little child, and be prepared to
give up every preconceived notion, follow humbly wherever and
to whatever abyss Nature leads, or you shall learn nothing.*
-T. H. Huxley-

We slid into the seats of the booth. I was in awe at the revelation
of these two women who looked so much alike. The image
reminded me of the visit earlier in the night by Clare, the daughter
and granddaughter of these two remarkable matriarchs.

"What brings you to this place at the guru hour of three a.m.
today?" I asked.

"I'm here to meet you." Gloria spoke slowly and clearly,
her hands folded in her lap. "I knew this moment would come,
but I didn't know yesterday that today would be the day. I am
pleased that it is. We've heard quite a bit about you over the years
from William and others. You seem to make quite an impression
with everyone you meet. Clare told me earlier of her insightful
visit with you. Favor spoke highly of you this past evening, and
Angelina here has given me some intriguing insights about you.
These personal interviews we've had in the past twenty-four
hours along with the file we've been keeping on you since you
met William in the seventies have created a very comprehensive
picture of who you are, and who you are not. At some further
place in the continuum, we'll have additional talks about this.
What questions do you have for me?"

A file on me since the seventies? Interviews over the past twenty-four hours? Scrutiny and observation during the past thirty-five years? What? Calm and center, calm and center.

"My first questions are," I spoke calmly and deliberately after the few seconds it took to get over my emotional charge, "why have you been monitoring my life for the past thirty-five years, and what kind of organization is this? What, exactly, is going on here?"

Gloria's gaze was deep and penetrating, yet peaceful. Somehow, I was receiving a holographic image in my mind's eye from her; the place I stayed in the Canadian Rockies for those five months. Shmaya was there looking through Gloria's eyes. I immediately recognized that I, like Gloria, was the observer as well as the observed. I was in the fabric of the universe, inseparably woven into everything. A smile emerged on my face, my defenses dropped, and I awakened to Bob's presence.

"*Gratia Om.* Thank you, Gloria," I said. "That was quite an inexplicable explanation. I see I'm exactly where I need to be, even though I don't understand the intricacies of it. Do you do that mind-merge thing with everybody?"

"No, only with those who are open and willing to receive it."

"On another occasion, I'll beg for an explanation on how that's possible, but for now, I have other questions. What really happened to Will and his associates on the boat? A couple hours ago, I had a lucid dream and woke up on a sailing vessel in Port Royal, Honduras. Nobody was on the boat except me, and there was a note from a Derick welcoming the mystic travelers and inviting them to his home. Was the name of Will's schooner *Mystic Traders*? Do you know a Derick, and is there some connection with a Port Royal in Honduras?"

Gloria and Angelina glanced at each other with raised eyebrows. Gloria looked back at me, smiled, and said, "You've done well in the short time you've been here. I'm impressed." She paused and took a long sip of tea. "It is not, however, an appropriate moment for these questions to be answered. What we're looking for will be revealed in the discoveries you must continue to make. The unraveling of the mystery demands more than a few supposed facts. It's your job to help us answer these questions.

"Your knowledge and experience as a transpersonal psychologist, quantum theologian, eco-entrepreneur, and priest after the order of Melchizedek puts you in a very unique position in the holographic hierarchy of things. Your mission, should you agree to accept it, is to unravel this mystery and help us take the next steps into the ever present unfolding of the implicate order. How intimate are you with the work of David Bohm, Karl Pribram, Brian Josephson, Nikola Tesla, Albert Einstein, Stanislav Grof, Ken Wilber, Thomas Keating, Matthew Fox, the Dali Lama, and William C. Fischer?"

Gloria was telling me to find my own answers to the questions I had for her. Strangely, I wasn't perturbed and trusted her decision.

"I've read some of their writings and have a good resonance with what they're pointing to," I replied. "I've used their understandings to help me come to some expanded awareness, and for me, there is much to be experienced, learned, and researched. It seems to be a lifetime journey.

"I've spent time with Will over the years. He and I have had a relatively significant personal and professional relationship, but I don't know much about his work. What you are suggesting is an intriguing and interesting inquiry. I somehow knew this sabbatical year was going to be different. It seems my new project is sitting right in front of me. Of course, I accept it, thank you. I've only been here twenty-four hours and have already uncovered things in myself that I have forgotten and cry out to be remembered. Where do we start?"

Gloria pulled a map of the compound out of her pocket and pointed to different parts of the pyramid as she spoke. "We have an extensive library that you have access to. Here's the research laboratory and computer lab you'll want to experience. You'll have computer access to the world and much of William's work. We have databases that hold all personal files on people of interest with substantial biographical information and confidential commentary. We'll direct you in that research.

"Clare told you her father had a hermitage at the south end of the lake? We locked it down after his disappearance and have it monitored for unfriendly intrusion. The interior hasn't been touched since he left. We'd like you to start there and see, with your rational and intuitive mind, what you discover. We would also like to meet with you on a regular basis. This research circle will be very small. We will bring Clare into the circle soon, but for the time being, it will be Favor and the three of us. I will be directing the project. Angelina is my right arm, Favor is my left arm, and you will be my private investigator and research associate. There has already been much work done in this investigation and we continue to be surprised. Our preconceived notions have led us down some slippery slopes and dead-end roads. We will eventually put all our cards on the table to prevent you from repeating our mistakes. But for now, less is more."

Gloria paused before continuing. "Go to the hermitage today in the daylight. You'll be able to observe more of the layout. Then go there during the night. You might even want to stay there for a time. William spent significant alone time there, so it holds a great deal of his energy. You'll be the first to enter that domain since his departure. Be awake to the subtleties. Here's the key." She turned the map over and he saw a small envelope taped to the back. "I'll see you again when the time is ripe. Favor will meet with you this afternoon. He'll find you and take you to the hermitage. You may visit our library at will, and we'll direct you to the research and computer labs when we feel it's necessary. You have much to receive and much to give. Rest well."

Gloria slid out of the booth and stood up. I followed her lead and stood with her. Angelina remained seated. The elder matriarch leaned forward as I bowed, kissed me on the forehead, smiled, and walked across the room to the hallway. I remained standing for a moment watching her energy trail before taking a deep breath and sitting back down in the booth. Angelina was staring at me. I looked into her eyes.

"Gratitude," she said, "simple gratitude that you heard the call and responded even though you didn't consciously know your behavior was being organized by the whole. That says a lot about your connection to the deeper levels of reality. I have experienced Will's presence, and somehow I know he's alive somewhere in some way, but it's not clear, and there's something going on beyond our knowledge that we're missing. I wasn't surprised when he disappeared. I knew something was different about this voyage, but I couldn't put it together. All the connections and disconnections have been running through my mind—the people, money, foundations, universities, and governments that are part of his circle. He was working on something very big, something he couldn't completely share with me," Angelina paused.

"Clare thought the same thing after her last conversation with her father. What he said to her about our safety keeps coming back to me. I've never had the sense that we've been in any kind of danger. I'm not into conspiracy theories, but my mind keeps wandering into the possibilities. The work with his handpicked colleagues from all the major continents was on the forefront of change, maybe over the edge. I'll earmark their names, biographies, and publications for you in the database. Will stopped publishing a year ago. Maybe there's a thread you can find in his writings leading up to that point, or in his notes or journal entries? Michael, it's crucial that nothing leave the hermitage without our permission. You might have to stay there awhile until you exhaust the possibilities or make some discoveries. Be who you are. Take your time. We're all in this together."

"What's your theory to date? What are the leads you're tracking?" I asked.

"We need to have this discussion after you spend a few days doing your own research. You have enough to get started. It's important we do not skew your investigation with our observations and theories. Your discoveries will lead you down a path. Your independent inquiry will help us infinitely more at this time than anything we could direct. You have been chosen very carefully for this task.

"As far as anyone outside our hermetic research circle is concerned, you are here on a personal retreat for rest and realignment at the start of your sabbatical. This is, of course, true. Unfortunately, we must cloak everything concerning this inquiry in secrecy. Be attentive and awake to everything you experience during the next days. Remember that your knowing may come through the most subtle of impressions and observations. It's time for you to heighten your awareness, attention, and intention. Be sensitive to your intuitions, dreams, telepathic communications, and tremulous whispers in the silence. Odds are you will discover the knowing we're looking for in your not knowing." She winked. "You know what I mean."

Angelina slid across the bench seat of the booth, stood up, and collected our empty teacups. She gave me a slight bow before turning and walking across the room into what I assumed was the kitchen of the café. A fatigue washed over me that demanded I fall asleep in the booth or get up, make my way back to the cottage, and find the comfort of my bed. I chose the latter.

Chapter 17

It isn't that the world of appearances is wrong; it isn't that there aren't objects out there, at one level of reality. It's that if you penetrate through and look at the universe with a holographic system, you arrive at a different view, a different reality. And that other reality can explain things that have hitherto remained inexplicable scientifically: paranormal phenomena, synchronicities, the apparently meaningful coincidence of events.

-Karl Pribram-

Marquette, Michigan, is a beautiful small town built on a hill that runs right down into Lake Superior, the largest and deepest fresh water lake in the world. Marquette is home to the University of Northern Michigan and attracts thousands of tourists in the summer. In the winter, its biting cold and massive snowfalls make it a wonderland that few choose to experience.

I was sitting in one of the local restaurants overlooking the lake on a brisk winter day waiting for a colleague. I was here on university business. Two men in business suits walked to my table, unexpectedly sat down, and began asking me questions about quantum physics, holography, teleportation, time travel, cloaking devices, and weather control. I had no idea what they were talking about. They told me if I came across any information that even hinted at these subjects to call them, as they represented a company that was very interested in helping develop these ideas.

"As an academic and entrepreneur yourself, Dr. Wyman, you can understand our company's interest in these undertakings and the tremendous opportunity available if you would help us develop these discoveries. We're talking impressive sums of money for you and your other interests."

"Sounds great, but I have absolutely no connections with these theories or anyone who does. I don't know where you got your information, but I'm not your guy."

They stood, handed me a card, and told me to call anytime with information I gained or collected. I looked at the card as they walked away. All it had written on it was, "NSA, Inc. ID code: Cathar, UPUSA" and a phone number.

A knock on the cottage door disrupted my dream. The knock came again while I struggled to gain my bearings. My feet hit the floor; I reached for my robe, and slowly made my way to the sliding glass door. There stood Favor. I slid the door open to greet his smiling face.

"Good afternoon, Michael."

"Hey, Favor. What time is it?" I squinted against the sun.

"It's one o'clock in the afternoon and I've brought your brunch. The sun goes down fairly early this time of year, so we must slowly get a move on toward Will's hermitage. Here's your food tray with coffee. I'll be back in a half hour so we can hike to the hermitage."

He handed me the tray, gave a humble bow, and departed. The aroma of coffee, eggs, and oatmeal with maple syrup was welcome. I placed the tray on the desk before dressing, and then sat down to enjoy a hearty breakfast and ponder the dream I'd been in before the interruption.

These lucid dreams were becoming part of my daily life. I wondered if it might be from an over-active imagination or the vibrations of this environment in between two of the largest lakes on the planet. Maybe I was being given messages from the unseen world of who knows what. Maybe, maybe, maybe? There was no need to figure it out with my rational mind. I just needed to write it all down and report it to Gloria. Everything connected to something somehow, including this dream about the NSA, and I was simply an investigative reporter, a research associate assigned to stay awake, take it all in, and be part of the team.

I finished breakfast, put a few things in my daypack, and stepped out onto the porch to test the temperature. The day was overcast. There was a chill in the air with a slight breeze. I turned and entered the cabin, retrieved my jacket and hat, making sure my digital camera was still in my jacket pocket, and returned to the porch. I sat down to wait for Favor and listen to the midday activities of this awakened world.

The background hum of the present universal energy field was subtle yet audible. I marveled at how loud it sounded now, while during other times in my life, when distracted by my own dramas or activities of the moment, I was unconscious of it. Did it come and go from me or did I come and go from it?

The few trees without leaves looked naked and vulnerable amid the lush environment. I observed how they seemed protected by the dominant and ever-greening pines. Even in the preparation for winter, the whole place seemed alive with a subtle energy of receptivity and retreat. There was a gradual cloaking with the inevitability of the seasons, as the whole environment prepared for the cold, dark, snowy months of winter. The movement from autumn danced with a gentle grace of acceptance and a longing for hibernation and rest. Everything was exactly as it needed to be. I watched as squirrels and chipmunks made their preparations for the snowy blanket that would cover everything they had not yet stored. Migratory birds made their way to more hospitable climates, while the natives held vigil and brought forth their best. Crows called to one another, alerting all to their presence, while finches followed their instincts toward more silent delights.

What a gift to observe these many cycles of nature. I wondered at how much I had forgotten by living inside my own restricted world of deadlines, schedules, dramas, and disconnections. I wondered at the ongoing rhythms of life, and I wondered how we humans seem so separate and disinterested. How did I get so far away from my essential nature? How can I get back to the garden, to the verdancy, the fertility, the rhythm of life's natural order? How can I rediscover the essence in me? How can I . . .

I felt a new energy approach. It was Favor, smiling his great smile. He stepped up onto the porch, sat down, and held his silence for a few moments as he simply became present. We sat there in the silent beauty. Although I appreciated the importance of stillness, I felt a sudden urge for activity. It was time to move. My mind became active with thoughts of disconnection, conspiracy, rejection, misunderstanding, despair, alienation, and destruction. My dualistic rational mind was running a marathon of fear.

I shifted in the chair, looked at Favor, and broke the silence. "I was in a lucid dream when you knocked on the door earlier, and I'd like to share it with you. It may have some importance to the investigation."

Favor turned toward me and nodded, encouraging me to speak.

"I was in a restaurant in Marquette. Two men in business suits walked in, sat down at my table, and questioned me about quantum physics, holography, teleportation, cloaking devices, time travel, and weather manipulation. They offered me money for information. I told them I knew nothing of what they were talking about. They left a card and told me to call with any information I discovered concerning these subjects or anyone connected with them. The card was very simple." I described the card to Favor and continued. "A few minutes ago, I fished out my cell phone from my briefcase and called the number. A real person answered the call, identified the National Security Agency information hotline, and told me to speak the ID code so I could be transferred to an agent. I ended the call immediately. I think I had a telepathic dream and am wondering what the National Security Agency has to do with us?"

Favor stood up, looked at me, and said, "Let's walk. We can talk on the way to Will's hermitage."

There were two footpaths circumambulating the lake. The one above the cottages was wider, seemingly for groups. The one below the cottages ran close to the water. It was narrower and meant for much slower walkers or the occasional non-conforming jogger like Anthony Amir. Favor led me down the gentle grade to the lake path where we met yesterday. It looked different today. The docks were stacked on the shore, and the rowboats, kayaks, and canoes were out of the water and turned upside down next to the docks. The scene was pristine, ready for winter. The leaves were mostly off the oak and maple trees, creating the skeletal strength of the land, and the pines clothed the water and landscape with a gentle perception of containment and safety. Favor led the way southward around the lake. I followed beside and sometimes behind him.

"Let's start with the NSA," he said in a low voice. "The National Security Agency was originally the Armed Forces Security Agency in the late forties and early fifties under the command of the joint chiefs of staff. It became the NSA in fifty-two, initiated by a memo from the CIA director to the head of the National Security Council. A survey and proposal was initiated and approved to morph the AFSA into a separate agency, thereby extending its power beyond the armed forces. President Harry Truman wrote a letter that created the agency. For more than a decade, the letter remained classified and unknown to the American public. The newly named NSA then became a separately organized agency within the Department of Defense. It's under the control of the secretary of defense for the performance of highly specialized technical functions for the intelligence activities of our country. The use of the agency was originally designed for foreign intelligence activities. Over the years, it has increasingly been used for surveillance in domestic activities. After September 11, 2001, there have been significant allegations that the NSA poses threats to privacy and the rule of law toward US citizens as guaranteed by the Fourth Amendment to the US Constitution. That's enough for a starter on the subject." He looked at me as we let the implications of his brief description sink in.

"How about the ID code? Cathar, UPUSA?" I asked.

"My guess is that the UPUSA is a location descriptor. Because the NSA is no longer just a foreign surveillance and intelligence agency, they have to direct or route calls to the appropriate departments for efficient handling. The UP is most likely directing attention to the Upper Peninsula where we're located, and the USA is obvious. They may have more than one location they're targeting with the Cathar label."

"That makes sense, but what is the Cathar label?"

"That might be a little more difficult to unpack. If they're targeting us, we have to wonder about their motivation. Do they see us as a threat or as a citizen group being threatened? Cathar is the root word for catharsis and cathartic from the Latin *catharticus* and the Greek *katharsis*, kathairein, which means to cleanse or purge. Its meaning, then, has to do with purification or renewal.

"It was a label given to a significant group of Christians in southern France in medieval times. Do you remember the Lateran Council of 1215 CE from your medieval church history, or the Albigensian Crusade, which was also called the Medieval Inquisition?"

I scrunched my face and tapped my head trying to remember. "There's a vague classroom recollection here. I'm remembering the church as being into serious command and control in those days. I've lumped that period into one big heresy binge by the fear and power-based buggers who were in control."

Favor laughed at my brief commentary, shook his head, and said regretfully, "It was one of its darkest days. The Albigensian Crusade and Papal Inquisition reportedly exterminated somewhere up to half a million Christians in southern France starting in the latter portion of the twelfth and into the first quarter of the thirteenth centuries. The church, along with the French monarch who claimed all the land, destroyed entire villages of men, women, and children. It was an all-out extermination. The Dominicans were reported to have had the mop-up executions after the major population centers were wiped out. Pope Innocent the Third was the pontiff at the time. Ironic name for such a perpetrator."

"What could possibly have prompted violence of that magnitude?"

"The official position of the church was that the Cathars were devil worshippers, participated in love masses that were sex orgies, they didn't hold marriage sacred, practiced witchcraft and sorcery, and thumbed their noses at the papacy. The unofficial view was that all of that was a ruse, that the threat was more about ancient secret documents, and lineage holders that dated back to the beginning founders of the Way. When people and institutions are threatened, they will invariably demonize those they wish to silence, so that it appears they are simply protecting the faithful rather than suppressing truth and protecting themselves. It's always about fear, power, and control."

"So back to the code, Cathar. What does that have to do with Sunnyview, Will, and his colleagues?"

"It might point to us being viewed as innocent victims and/ or heretical perpetrators. With an ID code name like that, who knows? In either case, there's a threat. Maybe that's what Will had wind of before he departed. He and his colleagues might have been working on something that came to the attention of some very powerful people. That's what we're here to discover. What an informative vision, Michael. Do you think we should invite the fox into the chicken coop?"

"Excuse me?"

"We might just want to track that phone number all the way to its source. It's amazing to me that you had the vision, called the number, and connected with NSA. What are the odds of that? The next move might be to talk to an agent and get him out here for our own interrogation. I'll brief Gloria and Angelina before our next meeting."

"I still don't get how this Cathar thing relates to Sunnyview. What kind of threat could this small community and retreat center possibly be to anyone?"

"Your perception and the perception of those who go looking for trouble are quite different. As you well know, there have been persecutions and destructions of small, quote unquote, secret groups over the centuries. Those who don't conform and fit into neat little boxes that the dominant powers want are often rooted out and destroyed. The monastic movements have always been targets, and while the church had power to protect, it also had power to destroy.

"The same is true of governments and their rich, powerful, and insecure corporate supporters. Will was working on some innovative and experimental technology that many governments and corporate interest groups would kill for if they knew its extent. That's probably one of the reasons he had to be a brilliant entrepreneur and judge of character. In the work he was doing, he had to know whom he could trust and whom he could not. He had to have many rich and powerful friends to keep the wheels in place on his pet projects, insider information, and technological breakthroughs. He had many different waters to navigate to keep all of his supposed supporters happy." Favor paused to refocus as they continued their walk along the lake.

"Power and wealth love power and wealth. To be a true believer in the midst of sharks and barracuda demands tremendous shrewdness and secrecy. Will believed that knowledge, money, and power could be used for the greater good rather than the selfish greed of simply having more while ignoring the basic needs of the planetary community. He believed that war was simply a byproduct of ignorance, profiteering, and self-indulgence. He was a peacemaker. His work revolved around ending war in all forms, starting in the hearts and minds of humanity. He was a Renaissance man who had a mission of transforming the world. To be known as anything but a crazy scientist could have had serious consequences.

"Will walked a fine line in his dealings. He was in bed with a whole lot of conflicting interests. When Sawyer Air Force Base was doing their backdoor research on the site just thirty miles from here, he was right in the middle of the mix. They were working with electromagnetic interference, underwater communications for submarines, quantum computing, teleportation, entanglement, avionics, intrusion detectors, ELF research, and weather control. After the government closed the base in ninety-five, he continued to have access to certain research facilities there as a private contractor. He used those twenty years to come up with some amazing discoveries and connect with a host of inventive and innovative scientists. I'm thinking now that his secrets weren't secret enough."

Chapter 18

Two of the disciples were going to a village named Emmaus, about seven miles from Jerusalem, and talking with each other about all the things that had happened. While they were walking and talking together, Yeshua himself drew near and went with them. They did not recognize him. As they drew near the village to which they were going, he appeared to be going further, but they constrained him, saying, "Stay with us, for it is toward evening and the day is now far spent." So he went in to stay with them. When he was at the table with them, he took the bread, blessed, and broke it, and gave it to them. Their eyes were opened and they recognized him; and he vanished out of their sight.
-The Gospel of Luke-

Favor and I continued our unhurried walk along the path around the lake. A few Canada geese were making their passage south. We heard them call and stopped to look at their V-shaped flight formation overhead. We paused to listen to their conversation, and then watched them fly until they were out of sight. When the moment passed, we picked up our walking conversation.

"Another thing I need to tell you, Favor, is yesterday I woke up on a sailing vessel named *Mystic Traders* in what I think was a multisensory experience. The boat was on a buoy in Port Royal, Honduras. Nobody was there. I saw a note left on the table in the galley from some guy named Derick welcoming the mystic travelers. Did Will know a Derick in Port Royal, Roatan, Honduras?"

Favor's demeanor changed instantly. He stopped walking and quickly turned to me. His face was stern, his body tense, seemingly ready for a fight.

"Where did this information come from?" he asked as if he didn't hear my reference.

"In a lucid dream about thirty-six hours ago, after we first met. I didn't get any response from Angelina and Gloria when I told them about it last night in the café. Your reaction tells me this is troubling news. You look like you've seen a ghost. Why?"

Favor drew his jacket tighter around his frame and began walking again along the footpath. I followed, fearful now about what my vision might have suggested. As we made a long arch from west to south past the last cottage, I struggled to keep my mouth shut. I knew Favor would lay my doubts to rest in his own time, but the suspense in waiting had me on edge. He finally stopped, found a bench just inside the forest, and sat down. He invited me to do the same. Now, at the southern end of the lake he spoke, this time with an unsteady voice.

"Derick is Will's brother. Their grandfather bought an island off the coast of Honduras back in the thirties, and he became quite influential in the politics of the country. He built a compound, secured a portion of a larger island, and became involved with the locals. He, his son Pierre, and eventually his grandsons, Will and Derick, became advisors to influential Honduran families and made a fortune in the import export business. Will shared time between here and there back in the seventies and eighties while they built the two family compounds. You've only seen a fraction of the infrastructure here. The extent of it is expansive. The compound in Honduras is equally efficient and very well disguised. The personal connections Will and Angelina's families have with wealthy and powerful people around the globe are unbelievable. I've never inquired into their lineage, but their families are connected in significant ways with people of various backgrounds in every continent. Did Will ever mention his affiliation with Honduras, Port Royal, or Camp Bay Island to you?"

"No, never. He spoke of research associates he had in South America and alluded to projects in a variety of countries but never specifically talked about Honduras. He was instrumental in getting my son Jonah placed in a specific Peace Corps program in Peru. Hmm, the two of them spent quite a bit of time together researching the program and redesigning it for the corps last year. I might need to contact Jonah about this. Maybe he can lead us to some connections."

"What was, or is, your son's field of studies?"

"His interests are quite similar to what I've experienced here. His doctoral dissertation was on depth psychology, shamanism, and the quantum. He was and still is very interested in the ecology of consciousness and the interaction between the organism and its environment. He's doing ongoing field research under the banner of the Peace Corps. That's where Will came in."

"How many other research projects do you think Will was connected with?"

"That would be hard to say," I replied. "His career seemed to be that of collaborating with as many specialists as he could as an advisor, research associate, funding director, and synergistic agent. He was associated with the most prestigious research organizations in the world. He sat on the board of the Joint Institute for Laboratory Astrophysics, the global center for astrophysics research in Colorado, as well as SRI International in California, and who knows how many others? We always got together when he came to the Front Range meetings in Colorado. He had significant relations with the most notable players in experimental research. As you probably know, he was instrumental in developing the new ultraviolet and X-ray telescopes launched by NASA and very much into Einstein's theory of special relativity, a deep and subtle area of physics based on the properties of light. Every time we had theoretical conversations, I was in awe by the height, depth, and breadth of his knowledge and wisdom. I hardly kept up. What does all this have to do with your reaction to my dream of *Mystic Traders* in Port Royal?"

"I was stunned that you had the information concerning the location, the name of his brother, and visualized *Mystical Traders* in the bay of Port Royal. That is a very well kept secret by the family. What do you remember about the vessel?"

"It was a large cutter with main, jib, and genoa rigging. I think it was a vintage Hylas, but I can't be sure. It was immaculate with teak decks, galley, and berths. Everything was clean and in its place, except for a celestial navigation map on the table in the galley with the note from Derick. There was no dinghy attached to the boat. The hatch was open but no people in sight. It was flying a Honduran flag, and the name on the stern was *Mystic Traders*."

"That sounds like the vessel that went down in the lake, except for the flag and the name. Gloria's husband, David Alexander, bought it new in the seventies, and it's been in the family ever since. It's a great performance cruiser. Will learned everything possible to become skilled at sailing that boat. He became a great skipper just as David did. They spent weeks on Lake Superior and the other Great Lakes during the many summers they shared after Will married into the family and before David died." Favor paused a moment.

"I've had a difficult time reconciling Will getting caught in a storm in his own backyard that would have taken him, his crew, and his ship down. How could it possibly be anchored in Port Royal, and what does the flag and new name point to?"

I shrugged. "Has anyone been in contact with Derick recently? We need to find out if that sighting was just an imaginary scene or something else. How can we get in contact with him to find out what he knows without being monitored by our friends in the NSA, or any other surveillance hackers of our phone or computer systems?"

"We'll have to wait and bring this information to Gloria and Angelina. We have many ways to communicate and a stable of perceptive technicians who know how to keep eyes and ears off us. What kind of communication did you receive that led you here?"

"That's another mystery. I didn't receive a physical call."

"Really? So you just got in your car to take a drive one day and ended up twelve hundred miles from home in the middle of the woods that just happened to be the residential and research center of a longtime associate whose family needed your help on a whim?"

"Now that you put it that way, I'd have to say that the call came through my unconscious mind. A kind of telepathic impression that I was unaware of until after I arrived. Do you know if there was a message sent to me by someone here?"

"Yes, there was. I was part of the calling team along with Gloria and Angelina. We started the call when we found out about Will's disappearance. It was a directive by Will before he left for Copper Harbor and Thunder Bay. We were to get in touch with you that way and bring you here if anything went wrong. That in itself was out of the ordinary. So, nobody knows you're here?"

"Nobody except the NSA, but that was a call to a service operator, and I was on for less than three seconds. They can't trace a call that fast can they?"

"Have you ever heard of caller ID?"

I rolled my eyes at my ignorance.

"Have you sent or received any other calls or e-mails?"

"Nope, I've been quite preoccupied since I arrived less than thirty-six hours ago. I do need, however, to connect with my family. What's the protocol for that?"

"This is a retreat center. We have guests coming and going all the time. To everyone outside the research circle, you're on retreat. In that context, calling your family is fine. For now, let's continue on to Will's hermitage. We're very close to the cabin. Did you remember to bring the key?"

I checked my zippered pocket to find it safely there. We stood up and continued along the path to our next stop, which came about a hundred yards along the path. A rowboat and a kayak turned upside down and two lengths of dock lay just to the left of the path along with a two-person swing that faced the water.

"This is the water access to the hermitage. The path up the hill from here leads to it." Favor pointed. "Do you see the cabin?"

I shook my head.

Favor smiled. "You lead and I'll follow. Signal me when you see the cabin."

We followed a narrow footpath up a slight grade to where Favor had pointed out the hermitage. About thirty feet up the grade, the path suddenly forked left and right, and the two new paths circled back down to the lake. I stopped.

"What is this?" I asked.

"It's a ruse."

"A ruse? I thought you said the path led to the hermitage. There's a fork here and both paths look like they lead back down to the water. What's the ruse?"

Favor smiled. "The ruse is that the path ends, forks off, and goes back to the water. Assume the path doesn't fork left and right but that it continues straight. What will happen?"

"We'll go off into the woods up the hill and depending on how far we go, we may find another path or get lost."

"Follow the invisible path up the hill," said Favor. "Simply perceive and believe that the path continues, and keep your eyes in soft focus looking forward. Move slowly and report to me what you see. I'll be right behind you."

"Okay," I replied. "What am I supposed to be looking for?"

"The path and the hermitage. It is right in front of you. Go ahead."

I looked up the hill and saw nothing but standing trees and leaves on the ground. Everything looked perfectly safe and in place. In no more than three steps, the scene began to change, and almost before I could stop, the hermitage came into view not more than ten yards in front of me. I turned to look back down the hill, and there was the straight path with the two forks leading back to the lake in full view. I turned back to look at the hermitage and it was still there. I walked the ten yards, stepped up onto the porch, and sat down on one of the two chairs, surprised and bewildered.

"What just happened?" I asked after a few moments of confused silence.

"We just walked through a holographic cloaking device. It surrounds the hermitage, and as you discovered, it's easily penetrated. The illusion of nothing being here is part of the security screen we have. The rest of the surveillance is composed of audio-video monitors hidden in the cabin and trees. It's all wireless micro technology, and we monitor it in house at Sunnyview. We have a staff of very sophisticated technicians and research associates.

"Will has been building this research facility and ecological experimental station for thirty-eight years with Gloria, David, and Angelina as primary investors and founding partners. It's called an artist colony and retreat center, because that's really what it is. The art is science and the science is art. All who have come here to live, research, or take retreats have come as artists seeking a new way to live and create a sustainable future for the planet and the entire created order. The whole place is a research center for the Art of Living. That's why I ended up here and it's why you showed up. There's much to learn here, Michael."

Chapter 19

*The discovery of truth is prevented more effectively, not by
the false appearance of things present and which mislead into
error, not directly by weakness of the reasoning powers, but by
preconceived opinion, by prejudice.*
-Arthur Schopenhauer-

Messages poured in from all across the globe concerning Will's
untimely death. Colleagues and supporters registered shock,
curiosity, and concern. Clare was in Gloria's living quarters, both
of them going through the paper and electronic mail together. It
had been less than two days since the incident. The global wire
services and social media networks had picked up the story and
because of the notoriety of Will and his colleagues, the incident
had gone viral. Two laptop computers and paper covered the
large dining room table. Clare looked up from her computer,
stared off into space, and finally spoke. "Do you think Dad set
this whole thing up?"

Gloria looked up from her computer and stared at her
granddaughter. "Why do you ask that, Clare?"

Clare lifted her hands off her keyboard, sat up straight, and
addressed her grandmother. "Last night while talking to Dr.
Wyman, a whole new thought came to me, because he used
the word disappeared instead of died. The difference in those
two words started a new series of thought projections. When
the Coast Guard Captain spoke to me about the storm and the

boat capsizing, I immediately jumped to the conclusion of death. They never found any part of the boat, the bodies, or anything. Isn't that odd? Dad was such a great sailor, almost as good as Grandpa was. Every time I sailed with him, he knew exactly what he was doing and how to make a safe passage, no matter what the conditions. This is all starting to seem a bit odd to me, and you've been unusually quiet these past couple days. What are you seeing?"

Gloria smiled, folded her hands, and raised them to her chin, "Clare, there's sixty years between us. You're twenty-nine, and I've lived through most of the twentieth century and now a decade into the twenty-first. It's been like living a half dozen lifetimes, at least. The changes I've witnessed and experienced have been extraordinary. I remember my grandparents' time when electricity and indoor plumbing were luxuries only a few could afford or have access to. Just heating the house and drawing water were time-consuming projects. Their regular mode of transportation was on horseback or on foot, communication was in person, and letters took weeks or sometimes months to reach their destinations. We now live with instant communications, global travel, central heat, indoor plumbing, and just about anything at the flip of a switch, press of a button, or touch of a glass screen.

"Back in the days when people disappeared for whatever reason, they were just considered dead, because there was no other acceptable explanation. Out of sight, out of mind, out of life. That's all we thought we could know, so our opinions, prejudices, hopes, and dreams were all we had. Today, it's difficult to know what is real and what is not. Your dad was a scientist who loved exploring the unknown to make it known. With what I've seen and experienced in my lifetime, I'd have to say that we live in a unified field of infinite potential and anything is possible. I wouldn't be surprised if your father walked in here right now and told us stories that would be both believable and unbelievable. There's a whole lot more of what we don't know than what we do. The open secret is to know you don't know and stay open to the possibilities, potentialities, and probabilities. Then you can begin to see. You've been taught that all your life, Clare. Stay curious and be open to the discoveries.

"More especially, what I am seeing is a beautiful granddaughter who I'm so in love with I can hardly stand it in a life that's filled with mystery and purpose. I'm seeing a universe that's magnificently generous with ongoing transition and change with everything coming and going, ebbing and flowing. I'm seeing that we live in a state of flux, and it's all tolerable and can even be magnificent." Gloria paused to evaluate her granddaughter's reaction.

Clare was breathing deeply with rapt attention.

"Honey, your mom and I are now working with Favor and Dr. Wyman to solve the mystery of your dad's death or disappearance. We'd like you to be part of this inner circle and investigation. How would that work for you?"

Clare snapped out of her reverie and tears welled up in her eyes. A childlike smile spread across her face as she got up, walked to the other side of the table, and knelt down beside Gloria. She wrapped her arms around her grandmother and leaned into her, feeling the power of love that connected innocence with maturity. She then looked into the eyes of this venerable sage and said, "It works wonderfully well for me. Thank you so very much."

The door opened and Angelina walked in to see her mother and daughter in the grace of their embrace. With a smiling heart, she walked across the room to kiss each of them before sitting down in an adjacent chair.

"To what do we owe this empowering scene?"

"Clare and I were just discussing the implications of Will's disappearance, and she's decided to become an integral member of our small investigative team and hermetic circle."

Clare patted Gloria's knee, wiped her eyes with the back of her hand, and stood up. "I was telling Gram about Dr. Wyman's intriguing use of the word disappearance regarding Dad's most recent experience."

Angelina widened her eyes and nodded her head in agreement. "I'm glad he said that to you; it opens up a whole series of new possibilities. Speaking of Michael, he and Favor are presently sitting on the porch of the hermitage. They just experienced the holograph. We'll see what discoveries they find today. Meanwhile, we must attend to some of the other details that have come to us in the past couple days and Clare, I'm really glad you and your grandmother talked. It's very important for the three of us to be together in this new adventure. Your father and I have been aware of these possibilities and potentialities for quite a while. It's now time for your tutorial, to let you in on what we already know, what we speculate, and our approach to all of this. The public is now involved, which creates more simplicity and complication. Having Dr. Wyman here is also changing our perspective. I like him, trust him, and sense his great gift of discernment. We'll all be speaking with him later today."

Chapter 20

A quantum is a quantity of something, a specific amount.
Mechanics is the study of motion. Therefore, quantum mechanics
is the study of the motion of quantities. Quantum theory says
that nature comes in bits and pieces (quanta), and quantum
mechanics is the study of this phenomenon. We are forced to
develop a more inclusive view, a more comprehensive view to
explain all that we can observe.
-Gary Zukav-

I put the hermitage key in the lock and opened the door. Transitioning inside, I felt a strange sensation that heightened my attention and awareness. A curious energy permeated the room, a presence, an energy field I couldn't identify. I opened myself to the possibility of an expanding consciousness, and let my fears drain to the floor.

"Favor, come in here and stand beside me."

Favor passed through the open door.

"What are you sensing?" I asked, hoping he would validate my sensations.

"Relax, Michael. Eyes in soft focus. Give attention to your breath. Stand grounded with intention. Open yourself. Nurture receptivity."

We stood there side by side experiencing the moment.

A sense of radiant energy filled the room. It came from everywhere and nowhere. Wanting to contain the feeling of this phenomenon, I stepped back to shut the door. In soft focus, my eyes seemed to witness a swirl of colorful cosmic movement. Favor and I stood in the swirl of energy for an eternal moment. It was as if the cosmos had been waiting here to greet us, to welcome and reveal to us the magnificence of life. The energy streams were passing in, around, and through us as we stood together in the radiant glory of the moment. I could feel my heart dancing in time to a rhythm that wasn't exclusively my own. It was as if the whirling dervishes were present, as well as the indigenous peoples of the planet, dancing around their fires. I can't say how long this went on. I lost all awareness of time. Eventually, the cosmic dance slowed, the energy dissipated, and some resemblance to normalcy returned. We stood silently wrapped in awe and expanding consciousness.

I closed my eyes and my mind sailed off to *Mystic Travelers* in the great storm. I watched as the five-crew members each became the point of a vaporous star that hovered over the boat and disappeared like that of a scene from *Star Trek*. I felt the crash of a massive wave and then the calm of a ship at rest in a tropical bay. I sensed a lively expectation and congenial comradeship with everything I was experiencing. My eyes opened to see an expansive smile on Favor's face, his eyes closed.

As I closed my eyes again, I was transported to my North Country experiences above the fiftieth parallel where I'd first seen the aurora borealis, a luminous phenomenon consisting of streamers, bands, and arches of light in the night sky, electrical in origin. It was as if these phenomena were flowing in, out, around, and through all ninety-nine percent of the empty space in my physical body. I then imaged being an eleventh century indigenous native from the East Coast of the Americas standing in Times Square, New York City on the New Year's Eve celebration at the turn of the twenty-first century with all the people, flashing lights, electronic billboards and sounds, fireworks, helicopters, and more.

In my mind's eye, I could see through matter into space where invisible waves and particles of energy seemed to change at will. I saw myself as part of the whole, connected to all things, physical and non-physical. I could feel the interconnectivity in these fields of energy and the illusions of separation. I entered the dreamtime of the ancestors to see the manifestations of the invisible transform into the visible. At the subatomic level of reality, I saw the impossible as already becoming possible. I felt my body breathing, but somehow I was removed from it.

As I continued to open my heart, mind, and awareness to the subtleties of these sights, sounds, sensations, feelings, intuitions, inner knowing, and unknowing; I was brought to the awareness that these fluctuations of the cosmos were happening in every breath, heartbeat, and nanosecond of being, whether we knew it or not. I awakened to the importance of being in alignment with this present flow, as it is the eternal flow of life itself. There were no labels, no judgments, and no fears, just a simple, awesome, and all-embracing presence.

As I began coming back to the normal physical reality in my body and in the room, I felt a reverence for myself and every other sentient and non-sentient being that had ever been, is, and ever shall be. The amazing magnificence of this all-inclusive creation was overwhelming and powerful. I remembered my breathing and felt my embodiment in a new way. In this place, right here, always here, I recognized how much more everything is than it appears to be. Breathing in and breathing out, with conscious awareness, my limited and unlimited selves were brought back into my normal contracted physical reality.

I opened my eyes and felt the energy of the room from a new perspective. I turned and looked at my soul brother, Favor. He smiled and bowed. I did the same. When the time was ripe, we turned and walked out onto the porch. I locked the door. In communion with each other and the whole of the universe, we walked silently back to our cottages.

Chapter 21

The solution to our crisis would be to reinvent ourselves, at a species level, in a way that enables us to live with mutually enhancing relationships. Mutually enhancing relationships, not just with humans but with all beings, so that our activities enhance the world.
-Brian Swimme-

I heard my cell phone ring as I walked into the cottage. I picked it up off the desk after the last ring and put it in my pocket as I went into the restroom to wash my hands and face.

I had just returned from the hermitage with Favor. We discussed schedules before parting. We agreed to gather in the café for a meeting in Gloria's apartment at 5:00 p.m., which gave me an hour to myself. We would then go to evening meditation in the kiva at 6:00 p.m., followed by supper in the café. I gazed into the mirror above the sink still processing my experience in the celestial realm and basking in the afterglow of the experience when my voice mail notification prompted me. As slight as the sound was, I felt jerked out of my reverie by this alien sound. I walked the short distance to the desk, unlocking my phone on the way. I sat down and found four messages.

The first one was from a colleague and friend, the head of the physics department at the University of Denver. He was calling about Will and his associates. He'd seen the post on one of his social networks and wanted to talk since he knew Will and I were friends. The next two calls were from Jonah and Michaela, my children. They wanted me to call them, and both reported all was well. The fourth was from my wife, Joanna, who wanted to know how my trip was going, where I was, and to tell me about the messages she'd received from our son and daughter. I decided to drop the department head an e-mail later and called Joanna back first.

Before touching the contact name on my phone, I noticed a headline and a picture on my small screen that read: WORLD RENOWNED SCIENTISTS LOST AT SEA! I touched the icon and followed the link to the story. In it were the names of the five members on the expedition, the strange circumstances of the rogue storm, and a short description of the known details. I found it surprising to see the story, as scientists rarely attract headline attention in the news media. It also struck me that this significant event happened less than two days ago while I was driving northeast from Denver, unaware of where I was really going. I sighed, touched the magic pad, and listened to the electronics reach out to my wife over a thousand miles away.

"Hello, Joanna Wyman, go ahead."

"Joanna, hi. It's me."

"Michael! Great to hear from you, just a minute." I heard her tell her administrator to hold her calls.

"Sounds like you're busy," I said, leaning back in the chair and smiling into the phone.

"You know how it is, always somebody with something. Where are you?"

"Michigan. I'm southeast of Marquette at a retreat center. I got in late about thirty-six hours ago. It turns out that Will Fischer's family owns the place."

"Will Fischer? I was shocked to see a news story this morning about his death. Is that real, and how did you end up there?"

"It's real as far as anyone knows and it's a mystery. I was driving very late into the night, looking for a place to stay and ended up here. It's been a magical mystery tour. I've met his family . . . well . . . Benedict . . . Abbot who helps . . . place.

Really great . . . and . . . awesome center. I'll . . . I . . . umm . . ."
I paused to reorient myself, because I found myself completely
discombobulated, phasing in and out like I wasn't really here.

"Michael, are you there? I think you're breaking up. Can you
hear me? Hello?"

My mind felt like a blinking light. I thought I was going to
pass out, so I put my hand on the desk to stabilize myself, took a
deep breath, and was finally able to speak again. "I'm here, and I'm
not. I just got back from a walk and had a very strange and hard
to explain experience. I don't think I'm fully present yet. Sorry,
honey, I . . . Will's disappearance, untimely, not knowing . . .
mystery, I'm still dealing with it." I paused. "What did you want
to tell me about Jonah and Michaela?"

"Are you sure you're okay? The reception, the cell phone . . .
spotty. Are you—"

"Yeah, just talk slowly," I interrupted. "I'm in another world,
and I'll, uh, change my position."

I walked to the wing back chair, sat down, and rested my head
on the back. "Go ahead. I'm in a new place. Is this any better?
Can you hear me now?" I still did not know if I could carry on a
cogent conversation. *Was the phone breaking up or was it me?*

"Yes, that's better, thanks. Where were we?" Joanna asked.

I didn't know, so I silently waited.

"Oh, yeah, I was really busy yesterday with clients, briefs,
and court appearances, so I didn't answer my phone. When I got
home last night and checked my messages, I found that both kids
had called. That's a strange coincidence. They just said hi and
that everything was going well for them. They wanted to know
how I was, where you were, and wanted you to get in touch with
them. Did they call you?"

Reorienting to the present, I was able to follow the conversation
and find the appropriate context before responding. "Yes, each
of them left a voice mail saying the same things. This is weird
timing. They both seem to want to tell or ask me something. Do
you have any idea what they want?"

"Yeah, they just want to talk with you. Great, isn't it? We're in four parts of the globe and able to talk, listen, and leave voice messages with a few touches of an instrument. Our grandparents wouldn't have believed it."

I grinned. "Yeah, it's an amazing time, and I'm hoping they're still where I can reach them. I'll call you back, will you be available?"

"I'll make myself available, this is my family. Even though it doesn't seem like it anymore, because we're all off to the four winds, you and the kids are still first in my heart."

"You too, Love. I'll try to call them when I hang up, and I'll get back to you either tonight or tomorrow depending on how everything goes."

"Perfect. Thanks for getting back to me so quickly, and I'm sorry about Will. I don't know what's cooking, but whatever it is, we need to be together in it. With all the people I see coming and going, I'm increasingly realizing how important we are to each other. Love you, and please, take good care of yourself, we need you!"

"Will do, thank you, and all that right back at yah, Love. Bye."

I laid the phone down on my lap, closed my eyes, and wondered at the distance between us all. How could I convey to Joanna or anyone else what I was experiencing? How could I bridge the gap between our realities? How could I bring words to something that is beyond words, and how concerned do I need to be about this fragmentation of my reality?

After a few minutes of reflection and focused clarity on the present moment, I opened my phone contact list again, scrolled down, and touched the name Jonah Wyman. The phone magically sent an impulse to a satellite that beamed it back to a tower somewhere in Peru, South America. The voice of my son came to me through thousands of miles of space.

"Hey Dad, that was a quick response time. Thanks for getting back."

"Great to hear from you, Jonah! How is everything in Peru? I don't expect you to catch me up on everything, but after a month of briefing and living in a radically different culture I imagine you're over the culture shock and beginning to settle into a new rhythm. Give me the highlights, *por favor*."

Jonah was sitting in a café in Cusco writing, going over his upcoming assignments, and having a great cup of coffee. "That's why I called. You keep coming to mind and my adventure has been amazing. I flew into Lima for the first week of orientation; too much traffic, and scads of people. I toured some historical sites, walked the streets, and spent hours on end in a conference room with a dozen newbie's like me, being briefed on the general history and customs of the country. I was glad when that first week was over. I then traveled by minibus to Cusco, the capital of the Inca Empire. In the native language, Quechua, Cusco means center of the world, like the Latin *axis mundi*. The Incas considered this area the center of the universe. Ha, just like most of us feel about our communities, right? The architecture and history of this area are fascinating, but you know all that stuff. I keep seeing myself walking in your footsteps when you were doing similar work a few decades ago. It's a place out of time, so I doubt much has changed since then."

"Probably not, but there are definitely more people. What else?"

"I have a solo assignment as the liaison between the government officials, the local native groups, the scientists, and the eco-tourist contractors in Manu National Park, a four and a half million acre wildlife preserve in the most beautiful, least disturbed, and least developed area in Peru. It sounds like an impossible task, but I'm handling it; it's not as huge a job as it could be. I'm stationed in Puerto Maldonado and Manu, which are a few hours apart by river. Manu is a dream placement. Out there, I'm totally cut off from the modern day world. I've been coming into Cusco on a weekly basis to meet with my field manager, but eventually that will change to once a month or even once a quarter."

"Have you had much time to engage your research yet?"

"That brings me to my point. I'm so glad you and Will helped me get here. It's amazing. I want to get your thoughts on something." Jonah looked up to make sure there were no people within hearing distance of his conversation. He brought the microphone of the phone closer to his mouth and turned his head toward a wall.

"I met the shaman I was guided to, the one I will be doing my initial research with," he began. "On my very first soul journey three days ago, I traveled to a place I'd never been before in dreamtime. It was like being in a movie that would speed up, slow down, and then run in regular time, whatever that is.

"It started with you standing on the edge of a lake. I came to stand by you and a friendly she wolf. The three of us simply stood there in silence looking out across a huge expanse of water. Then there was a fast-forward to a submarine, a giant cargo ship, an enormous storm, and Will's voice in the background repeatedly chanting, Alaha Elohim Shmaya Yod Arha. The scene fast-forwarded to a jungle where a beautiful goddess with auburn hair tended a garden, and who looked up at me when I appeared. Our eyes met, and it was as if a bolt of lightning struck my heart. I fell backward into a tree and slid down the trunk to the ground. I was stunned. She smiled, reached out her hand, and then disappeared. The wolf appeared where the goddess had been, and then transformed into a puma who bared her teeth, hissed at me, and melted into the ground.

"Another fast-forward, a slow motion, and then you appeared. You were in a priest's robe walking toward me and followed by three women of different ages, all looking like the goddess. Mom and Michaela were standing with me. The sky opened, and I saw an energy beaming down through the clouds from the sun with a thousand images playing in the light. Will's chant was still swirling through me, Alaha Elohim Shmaya Yod Arha. I thought I woke up, but I was still in an altered state floating down the river in a dugout canoe traveling from Puerto Maldonado to Manu. My guide was sitting in the canoe with me smiling suspiciously. Another fast-forward flash and I'm on a secluded beach on an island in the Caribbean with the goddess. We're drinking coconut milk and watching two little children playing and laughing. Will's mantra continued. Movie over. I woke up in the shaman's hut in euphoric confusion. You're the doctor of psychology. What do you think this means for me?"

"What did your shaman say?"

"He just looked at me and told me to be patient and continue to awaken."

"I agree with him. These revelations take time to process within you. Simply relax and let the process be the process. Will's chant in the background might be a clue."

"Do you know what the words mean? Are they names or something else?"

I paused to reflect, raised my head, and leaned forward transferring the phone to my left hand. I then stood up, walked to the sliding glass door, and looked out over the beauty of this heaven on earth. "Some might think them to be names, but they're really not. You know the problem with labels Jonah, they have a tendency to limit and diminish deeper meaning.

"This is a great chant about presence, ongoing contemplative action, and awakening. The words are alignment tools. Alaha, Shmaya, and Arha go back more than two thousand years into the ancient spoken language of Aramaic. Alaha refers to the sacred unity and infinite source of everything. Shmaya and Arha refer to what we call heaven and earth, the radiant vibrating energy of life in the invisible and visible realms coming together as a process of creativity and compassion. Elohim and Yod come from the ancient Hebrew language meaning the most high, an all-inclusive oneness and energy of the universal I Am, the active principle of life's non-dual vibrant and circulating energy in everything. These words were used in ancient times to point to the ever present essence and source of all that is; to the wave and particle interactions and co-creative potential of everything, the non-dual, both/and nature of the universe. Many people, in dualistic either-or thinking, would translate them to the smallest meaning of the word God, thus attaching an artificial anthropomorphic, subject/object meaning to them. They're beyond that; vast, infinite, ineffable terms that point to that which cannot be defined and categorized. Life is All. All is Life."

I stopped to breathe into what I had just said and to breathe into what I had just experienced. An aha moment just happened as I mouthed these words, a subtle and causal moment of awakening. I started to drift as the mantra rolled through my system.

"Dad? Are you still here? Hello?"

"Jonah, chanting these words can take you into the infinite within the finite. All the stuff you studied in quantum physics shows up here in five small ancient and mystical words. They all point to the visible and invisible radiant renewing energy of the cosmos. I sense you were given this mantra for a very special reason. To begin, it will help inform you as to the meaning of your inner and outer journeys. You will want to practice it, breathe it, embody it, feel the vibration and frequency of the sounds, and consciously make it part of you as you are part of it!"

I paused again, turned, and looked at the picture hanging above the bed. "How does this inform you?"

"Your words somehow took me back into the experience in an emotional way. I felt the compassion, the common union, the certainty of presence. It was awesome and you're amazing. I knew I could count on you. Thanks, Dad."

I turned, walked to the bed, sat down, and looked at the cold woodstove. "I have some different kind of news that might be difficult to receive," I said, trying to soften the blow. "I want you to put it in the context of the mantra that was given to you for further enlightenment."

Jonah was now looking out the window of the café in Cusco sensing something stirring in his stomach. He frowned as he watched a little boy with his father walk along the sidewalk. "Go ahead, Dad, what is it?"

"Our friend Will Fischer, his ship, and his crew disappeared in a rogue storm two days ago in Lake Superior. They're presumed dead. His family runs the retreat center I'm staying at in the Upper Peninsula of Michigan. I arrived the night after his disappearance. I want you to give attention to anything he might have said or done with you the last time you were with him that might hold a clue to his disappearance. Look at it from a transpersonal perspective."

There was a long pause at the other end of the phone where Jonah now stood as the explanation of his first shamanic journey and the news of Will's disappearance dropped into his field of everyday reality. I stood up, as if to stand with him, and allowed the silence between us to do its work. We held the silence together breathing in what was unable to be spoken. After a couple of minutes, I felt the necessity to put on my good father hat and began speaking again.

"There's an enormous amount to process here, my son. We're not alone in this world. We're not just living our own lives anymore. We're connected to the whole, and Will's departure has set in motion a new series of movements that we're a significant part of. It will all come into greater focus as we continue to cultivate our contemplative vision and action. Everything is what it needs to be, and we must continue to be vigilant: to listen and follow the subtle and causal energy of what is manifesting. Are you getting what I am saying?"

"I don't quite know why, Dad, but my emotions seem to be running away with me. I need to be quiet. Something of my last conversation with Will is showing up. We need to continue this conversation later. I'll be back in Cusco a week from today and will call you then. If you're not available, I'll leave a message. It's spring in the southern hemisphere, so it's raining a lot and sometimes the roads are impassable. If I don't call in a week, it's because I can't get to the city. Let me give you my field supervisor's name and number in case you or Mom needs to reach me. My new laptop with a satellite connection should be here by then, so our communications will be a lot easier."

He gave me the name and number of his supervisor and rang off with appreciation, love, and a request to convey his care and concern to his mother, sister, and the Fischer family. I watched the screen on the phone change as the electronics took me to my home page. I closed my eyes, feeling the presence of Will's hermitage and mantra in my heart and the heart of the universe: Alaha Elohim Shmaya Yod Arha.

Chapter 22

When the soul wishes to experience something, she throws an image
of the experience out before her and enters into her own image.
-Meister Eckhart-

I sat down in the wing back chair with the energy of my son and all that had transpired to let the experience settle and align with what I was feeling. I sensed a reconfiguring taking place within me as my system worked at processing the past few hours. Finding my center, I prompted the phone to signal my daughter in Lyon, France, where she was doing graduate work in hotel restaurant management and the culinary arts. My little girl was now twenty-five years old, living on a different continent, speaking fluent French, and learning how to serve others using her artistry. After the third ring, I heard her voice.

"Papa, is that you?" I heard her ask with enthusiasm.

"Yes, my darling, it is. I got your call and was extremely happy to hear from you. How are you enjoying your work and the ambiance of central and southern France?"

"Oh, Dad, it's absolutely marvelous! It's radically different from the US. The people here at the institute are fabulous at hospitality. I'm meeting people from every part of the world. The education is comprehensive and international. The environment of the city and the surrounding country is, well, you'd love it. When are you and Mom coming over to visit?"

"We'll have to look into that. It would be a great gift to see you in your new environs."

"Yes, please do, I'd love you guys to come here. You and Mom could have my bedroom and I'd sleep on the couch. It would be cozy and I'd love it. It would give me an opportunity to introduce you to some of my favorite new people and do some of my favorite new French things. An incredible amount of history lives in the architecture, the streets, and the whole environment. It's like being in a multiplicity of worlds at the same time, as if the past and present somehow converge and create something new. Raised in Denver, I never had the sense of place that I'm experiencing here. Every weekend I go out exploring and am always discovering something new and challenging. This past weekend, some friends and I traveled south to Carcassonne, the largest fortified city in medieval Europe. My friend Stephanie, who's from England, took me to meet her cousin. Her family has a small chateau in the country around Limoux. I met her extended family who I may be related to through Mom. When they found out that Mom's maiden name was Stewart and that Grandma was a Sinclair, they nearly fell over. You'd have thought I was their long lost daughter or something. I was shocked at the reception. Have you ever heard Mom talk about her English and French relatives?"

"Can't say that I have."

"They also knew of both your Wyman and Martin family names from the past. I don't know what it is about these folks, but ancestry is a really big deal to them. Have you ever heard of the Cathars?"

"The Cathars? Is that another family name?" I asked, playing dumb and a bit taken aback at the synchronicity of having just discussed the Cathar code with Favor.

"Not a family name, but a historical one given to a group of people who settled in this area way back in the first century, supposedly family and friends of the historical Jesus. That's what I wanted to ask you. I thought you might have some information and insight into this. I'd never heard of the Cathars, but Stephanie's family laid out a whole lot of history for me, from their perspective, after they discovered my four family surnames. Could you do some research for me and send it over?"

I found myself pausing again, lost in thought and wonderment. *What was happening here? In the past two days, I seemed to have crossed over into a new reality. There were too many puzzle pieces fitting together for this to be a random series of happenings. What could this all mean? I came back to my dear daughter Em's question about doing some research on the Cathars for her. I stroked my chin, got up, and walked to the sliding glass door again.* "I could, but you'd probably be able to do so with greater success in that you're in the backyard of where it all happened, right? It's my understanding that southeastern France is where most of the Cathar settlements were and most of the inquisition and persecution took place."

"See, you already know more about it than I do."

"Not so much. I'm in the middle of my own research project and some of it touches on what you're asking. If I find something that relates, I'll let you know. In the meantime, you can do some computer research, on the ground investigation, and follow your own leads. Together we may be able to bridge the past and present to discover something new. How does that sound?"

"It sounds just fine. What are you researching?"

"A friend of mine disappeared in a boating incident in Lake Superior with some of his colleagues. There's no sign of the boat or the bodies, so I'm with the family helping them sort out the details here in Michigan. It's a very intriguing situation."

"Wow, my condolences to your friend's family. Did he have kids?"

"Yes, a daughter named Clare, who's the same age as Jonah, and a son named Atom who's your age. They remind me of you two. Clare is finishing her dissertation in residence here, and Atom is finishing his graduate work at Stanford."

Michaela sighed and ran a hand across her forehead. "I can't imagine losing my father at this stage of the game. It must be awful for them."

I heard some conversation in the background that interrupted her focus. "Friends just came in, so I better sign off. Thanks for calling back, Dad, and I'm really glad we were able to talk some. Drop me a line with your research and/or advice. Let's try to keep in touch more regularly. I like having these ongoing dialogues with you, and well, just hearing about Atom and Clare's loss saddens my heart, even if I don't know them. Your call has helped refocus my priorities again and allowed me to slow down for a moment. I'm seeing how extraordinarily blessed I am to have you and Mom and Jonah as family. I really do miss being with you guys. Let me know how your investigation plays out, will you?"

"Yes, and Jonah will be getting a satellite connection and a new laptop within the next week or so. I'll have him send you his link. You two are living in radically different worlds. It will be very interesting and intriguing for our family to compare notes over the next year. Give our best to the Cathars and everyone else from all us peacemakers, lovers, and contemplative servants in the world. Love you, Em!"

"You too Dad, and thanks for everything! It's such a gift to be here."

Chapter 23

There is a vitality a life force, an energy, a quickening, that is
translated through you into action, and because there is only one
of you in all time, this experience is unique. And if you block it,
it will never exist through any other medium and will be lost.
-Martha Graham-

I sat in the small cottage after connecting with the three most precious people in my world, reveling in the new warmth in my heart and brightened, yet confused outlook. I got up to retrieve a glass of water before leaving for the compound, and suddenly I felt a wave of sadness for the Fischer family. Will could no longer simply pick up a phone and talk to his loved ones as I could. He couldn't participate in their lives or stand with them in place. Loss and gain took on a new face.

I looked into the mirror while filling my water glass and saw a man I thought I knew but didn't. What was happening to me, and what had Will discovered that took him over the edge? Was his disappearance part of a plan or did the plan go awry? Knowing Will, there was always a plan, a very detailed, well-thought-out plan with many contingencies. Where was the sailing vessel? Where were the physical forms of those five people? How did Derick and Honduras fit into this? What did the Fischer's know that they hadn't told me? Who were all the high-powered friends and associates Will had worked with over the years? Who would work against him and his team, given the chance? What did the military industrial complex have to do with this? What are the meanings of my dreams, clairvoyant images, insights, and reconfigurations? Why me and not another? How much of what is happening right here do I even know? A hundred questions and a few answers. Was I a fly in a vast spiderweb?

My mind swirled with confusion as I left the cottage and walked the wooded path to my meeting with Favor and the research team. The time was four fifty-five in the afternoon when I stepped through the back door of the café. I placed my jacket on a rack, walked through the hallway, and saw Favor. He led me to the elevator, the door opened, we walked in, and he pressed A5, which took us to Gloria's apartment on the fifth floor of the pyramid.

I had learned from Favor that Angelina, Gloria, and he shared the executive leadership roles of Sunnyview twenty-four hours a day, seven days a week. They each had three associates who also had three associates and so on, out into a large network that managed and operated every facet of this contemplative artist colony of science, spirituality, and transformation. They each headed an eight-hour shift that ran around the clock. Angelina had oversight of the first shift from midnight to eight, Favor the second, and Gloria the third. They met every day at four o'clock to check in and discuss whatever had come up during the day. There were occasional exceptions to the meeting time and who attended. Today was one of those exceptions.

Favor and I were in the elevator that ran through the very center of the pyramid from B6, six floors beneath the ground, to A6, six floors above. The seventh floors, both above and below, were accessed from a stairway from A6 and B6, respectively. There were private inner and outer observation decks reaching from and to the heights and depths of the structure.

The elevator came to a slow stop. The door opened to a small circular room that surrounded the elevator shaft. There were four doors, one at each cardinal point—north, south, east, and west. We walked around to the east door. It opened from the inside where Clare greeted us with a smile and a hug and then ushered us into the living area where Gloria and Angelina waited. The apartment was spacious with a nine-foot ceiling. The outer glass wall had a commanding view of the park in front of the compound and the road leading in and out. Beyond the park were solar panels, greenhouses, and wind generators. The view looked out over and through the trees and rolling hills. The sight was spectacular.

The main room was a combination living and dining with a couch, three wing back chairs, and appropriately placed end tables and lamps. The large dining room table with eight chairs stood close to the kitchen hidden from view. A bedroom and bath were also hidden. Clare brought us to the table where Gloria and Angelina sat. The walls were painted in pastel colors with an eclectic array of modern and classical paintings perfectly placed on the walls. I sat down in a chair next to Favor, across the table from Clare. Gloria sat across from Favor and Angelina sat at the head of the table.

Angelina made a few opening comments concerning the intention of the meeting to evaluate and assess my position in the circle, and then she struck a small temple bell three times. We all sat in silence. I was thankful to be able to sit in that stilling place. I straightened my back, took a deep breath, and relaxed. My mind became still, and the events of the day rested in some sacred place inside of me. Time ceased to exist. Again, the bell rang three times, and I gently opened my eyes, shifted in my chair, and waited for the next movement.

Favor began, turning to look directly at me. "The experience I had with you this afternoon, on our walk, and at the hermitage, was revelatory. The insights you brought were compelling and stunning. The information that came through your lucid dreaming about the NSA and Camp Bay Island were, well, surprising. Your simple, open presence in the hermitage gave me confidence and helped me be present. I have absolutely no doubt that you are the man Will sent to us, and I am pleased to be your associate." We nodded in mutual understanding.

Gloria continued the evaluation. "Each of us has had at least one significant encounter with you, Michael. You've come to us through a long relationship with Will and Spirit. You seem to be part of the family, even though you've only been here physically for a day and a half. I'm impressed with your openness, vulnerability, honesty, and energy alignment. I want to hear more about the insights you shared with Favor this afternoon, and I am looking forward to sharing much more space with you." She looked right into my soul. I could feel her acceptance and appreciation. I felt honored to be in her presence.

Clare raised both hands high up in the air as if she were offering complete attention and total surrender to the process. Everyone's eyes went to her. She slowly lowered her arms, placed her hands flat on the table, leaned forward, and stared deeply into my blue eyes. "When I visited you last evening, I thought you were just another guest. It was a routine visit. When I left, I had the sense that I'd known you all my life. I was surprised at how you put things together so quickly. You touched my heart in a way that is rare. You were so insightful and caring. That's not something that can be faked. I see why Dad chose you to work with us at this time. I trust you. In some ways, you're just like Dad. You have to help us!" She waited for a reply. I nodded at her assessment and silently gave my affirmation.

Angelina always seemed to have the last word, as each of the others recognized the authority bestowed upon her by her deceased father, David Alexander, each of those present, her husband Will, and the Sunnyview community. Gloria had once held this authority as had Favor in their own time and place. Clare would one day have it passed to her. Angelina embraced her role with grace, dignity, competence, and unwavering commitment.

"When Will told me of the plan to make this move, I was extremely hesitant and resistant. To believe in the wisdom of uncertainty is one thing, to step into that uncertainty is another. We knew the potential risks and benefits. They are still to be experienced and evaluated in their fullness. Michael Wyman, you were the wild card Will decided to play. He knew how difficult it would be for anyone to fill the void of his absence for an interim time, and it would be utterly impossible unless everything aligned in the proper way. Of all the associates and colleagues Will has had these past thirty-five years, the one who stood out above the rest was you. I knew you only through Will and the significant research I conducted concerning you and your family. On paper and through interviews with associates, you came to the top of the list just as Will predicted. Now that I've personally engaged you, I find you more sensitive and open than I expected and you're more insightful and reflective. You have a lot to bring to the table, and I honor you for your response to our call. Welcome to the family!"

Angelina sat up straight and leaned forward to make her well-chosen points to the group. "We must be vigilant as we continue to be tested in this fire. We must continue to test one another, and who or whatever comes to us, so we can discover the best outcome with grace, compassion, and forthrightness. Our discernment is critical. I am *all in* with everything that has been said, and I continue to be open for further enlightenment. I am eager to hear the latest revelations that continue to come through all of you."

It was my turn to speak. I was in awe and a little uncomfortable with the comments. I looked at each of the members and kept a straight face. "I appreciate all that's been said concerning my part in this amazing drama, and I am humbled by your assessments. I'm still learning about you, your community, and Will's many personal dealings with the world. I've spoken with my family, and I am committed to seeing this through. I will do all I can to be helpful to you, to Will, and to the highest good. It's been an amazing couple of days, and I know that I hardly know anything except that we're being assisted in our investigation from the transpersonal dimensions of reality. I'm learning to trust and discern the many clues, and I am reserving my judgments. I'll share my revelations and insights as requested. I'm definitely here and in. Where else could I possibly be?" I placed my elbows on the table, folded my hands, looked down for a moment, and then up to Angelina. "Everything is all right."

Angelina held my gaze and then looked at the others. "Thank you, Michael, and thank you Favor, Gloria, and Clare. We will reconvene in the café after evening prayer. Clare, you're leading the chant this evening, are you ready?"

"Yes, and it's five-thirty, so I have to go meet with my team. I'll see you all there, and thanks for letting me sit in this circle. It's important for me to be here."

She got up, walked around the table, and laid her hand on my shoulder as she passed and made her way to the door.

Angelina, Gloria, Favor, and I concluded our conversation with talk of the hermitage experience. We then sat in silence for a few moments preparing ourselves to join Clare and the rest of the community for evening prayer. Smiling at one another, we realized the significant step we had just taken into the mystery of compassion, appreciation, and transition.

Chapter 24

Hope is a light-force which radiates objectively and which directs creative evolution for the world's future. It is the celestial and spiritual counterpart of terrestrial and natural instincts of biological reproduction. Hope is what moves and directs spiritual evolution in the world.
-Valentin Tomberg-

I was surprised to see more than a hundred people already sitting in silence around a vast circular space that had been carved out of the earth and reached into the sky. The kiva was built with native logs that went up from beneath the ground to the roofline. Additional logs reached across the wall beams of the structure to the center that formed the ceiling. Wood planks ran between the logs and created a warm, earthy feel. Natural light entered from the circular space between the wall and roof that was wrapped with windows.

In the center of the concrete floor was a circular oriental rug. On the rug was a round mirror with a single red, long-stemmed rose in a vase surrounded by four burning candles in the cardinal positions. Around this center, people were quietly sitting on meditation cushions, zafus, and zabutons. From this inner floor, three six-foot wide circular concrete tiers rose up, creating more seating space. Community members and guests were scattered all around the tiers and sitting on blankets, cushions, and pillows. It dawned on me that the cushion in my cottage was also to be here. Just as that thought came to me, a young man approached with a zafu, handed it to me, smiled, bowed, and walked back to where he came from.

Clare was sitting at the east edge of the carpet in the center of the kiva. I noticed Favor, Gloria, and Angelina sitting in the other cardinal positions with three people sitting in between each of them, forming a sixteen-person circle around the rug. Others had gathered around them extending to the first tier.

I found a space on the second tier that gave me a comprehensive view of the whole room. People continued to arrive until the two double doors closed. The man sitting next to Clare rang a large temple bell similar to the ones Tibetans use. Those gathered made their final seating adjustments and came to their sitting posture with straight backs, folded legs, and either closed or half-open eyes with a soft focus. The bell rang again; three sets of three and then nine continuous rings. It reminded me of the Catholic Angelus. By the time the bells stopped ringing, a new vibration was palpable in the room. The acoustics were magnificent. We sat in the vibrating silence for about ten minutes. The bell rang again and kept ringing at intervals to match the chanting of a psalm from a voice resonating throughout the chamber with clarity and humble access. A young woman's voice sounded like something from another world. After a few verses, I realized it was Clare.

Bell. "Show me your ways, Oh, Love." *Bell.* "Lead me into Truth and Life."

Bell. "For through you, I know Wholeness." *Bell.* "I shall reflect on the darkness and light both day and night."

Bell. "I know of Mercy and Steadfast Presence." *Bell.* "You are Presence, from beginning to end and beginning again."

Bell. "Forgive the many times I have walked away." *Bell.* "From You, Oh Love."

Bell. "Choosing to separate myself." *Bell.* "Afraid and Forgetful."

Bell. "Now with every breath I take." *Bell.* "I awaken to Companioning along the Way."

Bell. "For you are Serenity and Peace." *Bell.* "Oh Breath of Life, Infinite Presence."

Bell. "All who are Open, enjoy an ever present teaching." *Bell.* "For you are Ineffable Life, Radiant Energy permeating the Cosmos."

Bell. "Your paths are Loving and Sure." *Bell.* "Oh Sacred Unity, Infinite Source."

Bell. "For those who give witness to Love." *Bell.* "Breathe and embody Life."

Bell . . . bell . . . bell . . . .

The whole room was a single breath of life. The resonance of the one voice, the deep sound of the temple bell, the vibration of the atoms, electrons, and molecules, the silent pulse of every heart, the cadence of the words, the harmony of intention, all came together in the simplicity of this contemplative moment.

The silence lasted for an eternity, the sounds behind the sounds resonated in the present mystic revelation of the cosmos. This is what the mystics knew and have known since the dawn of creation. This moment. This alignment. This vibration. This expansion.

I couldn't tell if it had been ten minutes or ten hours when the deep resonance of the kiva bell rang again. This time, the clarity of a male voice, resonant and pure, followed the bell. The words came out in a rhythmic chant of such beauty that I felt my heart well up within my chest. After the fourth time, he sang the mantra and the community joined him. Within another few lines, the chant became a resounding orchestral arrangement of harmony vibrating throughout the room within, around, and through every fiber of every being.

"Alaha. Elohim. Shmaya. Yod. Arha . . . Alaha. Elohim. Shmaya. Yod. Arha."

"Alaha. Elohim. Shmaya. Yod. Arha . . . Alaha. Elohim. Shmaya. Yod. Arha."

I briefly registered the words as the same that Jonah had reported hearing in his experience. I then lost track of time again as the sounds and vibrations continued to travel throughout the circular height, depth, and breadth of the kiva. Slowly and gently, the chant began to wind down. Eventually, it ended as it had begun, in celestial silence. A spoken voice eventually penetrated the silence with, "Namaste. Ameyn." The response by the assembly was a quiet, unified voice of two hundred responding with the same two words, a shorthand understanding that the divine within me recognizes and honors the divine within you. All is sacred and united in the moment, always ending, always beginning; always here, always now; always healing, making whole.

The community stood up together and everybody folded their hands and placed them in front of their hearts. With their eyes faced forward, they bowed slightly and smiled when they heard two blocks of wood clapped together. The double doors opened, and the participants filed quietly out into the corridor to put on their shoes and continue with their journeys.

I stood there a few moments watching and breathing in everything I had just experienced. I noticed Angelina, Favor, and Gloria as they walked out, each acknowledging my presence with a slight nod and a smile. I nodded and smiled in response. I also noticed Anthony, who was frowning. He appeared to be waiting for something, stared at me, and with a concerned look, turned, and made his exit. Clare and her liturgical team were clearing the area and putting everything back in its proper place. When all was cleared, they walked up the ramp to the open doors. Clare stopped at the second tier and turned to look at me. I knowingly responded to her message and walked over to her. With the affection of a proud and loving father, I embraced her and kissed her on the forehead. In that moment, I felt Will standing beside me somehow awakening my heart. I had another daughter.

Clare and I walked silently to where our shoes were placed, and we stopped to look at each other. Something had changed since we walked into the kiva just a short time ago, something profound and unspoken. We were both breathing a new bond, a new spirit.

I heard three words come out of my mouth, which sounded like something I'd heard Will say so many times to me. "It's all ripe!"

Clare looked at me and smiled, and then she reached up to pull me forward and kiss my forehead. "Yes, Father Michael, it is all ripe!"

We walked through the corridor into the light of the café. Angelina, Favor, and Gloria were sitting at a round table at the end of the room with another woman. We went over, sat down, and entered into a family conversation.

Chapter 25

In the middle of winter
I discovered in myself an invincible summer.
-Albert Camus-

Atom Ion Fischer was finishing his doctoral dissertation in electrical engineering at Stanford University. He was studying something his father Will had helped him formulate concerning scalar electromagnetic energy, string theory, quantum entanglement, and the potential effects of these phenomena on the environment. He had run into roadblock after roadblock in his research that made the project more difficult than he'd expected. A breakthrough came when Will helped his son rework a mathematical formula that changed the direction of his project. Atom was busily reworking his dissertation in hopes of finishing by May. His discovery could potentially eliminate the global energy crisis and expand human consciousness in transformational ways. He was completely absorbed in his work. He was at his desk, lost in his numbers and formulas when he was unceremoniously interrupted.

"I just saw a report on your dad and his colleagues on my *Science Today* app. I can't believe you never said a word to me about it. I mean to lose your dad, that's big! I'm really sorry, I didn't know."

Matt was Atom's research associate and closest friend at Stanford. They'd met in a theoretical physics class as undergraduates and had become close over the years of study, examination, late night beer discussions, and a mutual interest in wireless electricity and experimental research. They presently shared a modest, off-campus house the Fischer's owned near Stanford University in Palo Alto, California.

Atom turned in surprise to see Matt's animated gestures and frowning face. "I'm sorry I didn't mention it Matt, but quite frankly, it hasn't hit me yet. We weren't your typical American family while I was growing up, or even now. We lived and worked in a community for as long as I've been alive. I was raised with my family and a host of other artists, scientists, and spiritual seekers. I never wanted for companions. I always experienced life as an individual in community. Everyone I ever knew before coming to Stanford was part of a broadly based extended family that either came to our home in Michigan or we visited somewhere in the world. My life was a continual adventure. Being here in Palo Alto has been more confining than what I experienced in Sunnyview." He paused a moment.

"It's difficult for me to relate to the thought that Dad is no longer with us. It doesn't seem to fit my mindset. I don't sense that he's really gone, just transitioned into a different space that he'll make known to us. Does that sound weird?"

"Yes, it does." Matt went to the only other chair in Atom's study and sat down. "The report I read said that your dad and his four colleagues went down in a freak storm in Lake Superior and nobody was found, not even the boat. Lake Superior is huge and reaches depths of more than a thousand feet. It's ice cold at this time of year, too. I hate to sound crass, but *went down* and *never found* sounds significantly final to me. That was two days ago, and the report said the search has been called off with no leads."

"Yeah, I know, but you don't know my dad. He's a magician. I remember so many incidents about the so-called miracles he's been a part of. I've come to think anything is possible for him. It's like he's tuned into a multidimensional world, while the rest of us ignorantly slog through a three-dimensional one."

Matt gave Atom a look that clearly registered his skepticism.

"All right, look," Atom continued. "I remember a time when we were exploring a mining cave in the Rockies. Somewhere behind me in the dark, Dad yelled, STOP! I did. He caught up with me, lit a match, and dropped it into a giant break in the floor that dropped a couple hundred feet straight down. Another step and I would have fallen into that abyss. He'd never been in that place before and yet he knew. How? Another time was my motorcycle accident."

Matt cocked his head to one side and raised his hand, indicating he didn't remember the incident.

"Remember when I wrecked my bike outside Green Bay? Dad was in India at the time. I was in critical condition, not expected to live. That night in the hospital, he showed up out of nowhere, gently laid his hands on my body for a few minutes, breathed with me, chanted an undecipherable message, kissed me on the forehead, and disappeared. The next morning I was fine. The hospital had no record of any visitor that night. When I asked my dad about it later, he just smiled and told me that India wasn't very far from Wisconsin. Should I go on?"

"Atom, I'm not trying to make a case for your dad's demise, I'm just a graduate student in electrical engineering committed to a rational and analytical perspective. Your experience is not mine, so I defer." Matt held up his hands as if to surrender. "I'm somewhat in awe of your perspective but still skeptical. There must be some reasonable explanations to these stories. It seems like you want to defy logic and reason, which I have serious difficulty with."

"It's not that I want to defy logic and reason," Atom responded. "I simply have a lifetime of experiences that have led me to move beyond simple logic and reason into a much larger field. I've learned that truth always seems to point to a truth beyond the apparent truth. This is why I've chosen a career in science, because there doesn't seem to be an end to what can be discovered. Every evolving pattern seems to lead to another and another. We live in a world of infinite possibilities and potentialities. Dad taught me that and is still teaching me. I know he's still here, and we're infinitely connected. The question for me is simple: *Where is here?* There's something going on that's bigger than the events of the disappearance; something that's pointing to a greater truth, a more expansive view."

Atom paused and his face grew stern as if he was concentrating on something. He put a hand to his forehead and squinted. He looked down at the floor and up at Matt. "Wow! I just woke up to something I'd forgotten. What if . . . ?" He held up his hand as if he was holding something in it. "What if . . . ?"

Atom's remembrance propelled him into action. He turned off his computer, gathered all his papers, put them in a file cabinet and then turned and addressed Matt. "The research for this dissertation can wait. I have a new, immediate project. Thanks for the conversation and the inquiry Matt. You've been a great help. I have to get out of here. If anyone inquires, tell them I went north for a few days of hiking and camping in the Sierras. I'll get back with you."

Before Matt could protest, Atom stood up, grabbed his laptop, went to his room, threw a few things in his pack, and headed out the door. Enthusiasm engulfed him as it hadn't since the time his dad, uncle, and he had departed on a three-week trek through the mountains of Nepal a year ago.

He was now a hound on the scent of a compelling mystery that fired his imagination. The possibilities running through his mind were staggering. He blew out the door of his house, down the sidewalk toward a store a block away, bought a disposable phone with thirty minutes of time on it, and took a cab to the private airport where he had access to an aircraft.

The voice on the other end of the phone at Custom Air Travelers, CAT for short, asked for routing and security codes. Atom spoke into the mouthpiece, "Undercroft. Fish. ATMCB Honda. IT. One, four, five, seven, nine, CANE."

The reservation was confirmed. He then sent a text message to his sister who was sitting in the Sunnyview café enjoying a great supper and discussing the news of the investigation and events that had transpired through the day. The text read, "Clare,

Atom, In, MT, engaged DDU.Me, Guru H tnt, Your Tz. *Capa Negra*. Lv."

Message sent, he sat back and tried to relax as the cab snaked its way through the traffic to the airport. His heart was beating quickly in anticipation of this spontaneous adventure.

He had been a mystic traveler from before he was born. The vehicles changed but the intention did not. He was always on his way to a higher purpose for the common good, always standing in the questions until he found the answers, which always seemed to lead to further questions. On the back of his passport, he had written, "Destination: Further."

Chapter 26

An Epiphany enables you to sense creation not as something completed, but as constantly becoming, evolving, ascending. This transports you from a place where there is nothing new to a place where there is nothing old, where everything renews itself, where heaven and earth, converge as at the moment of Creation.
-Kabbalah-

Clare received Atom's text while she was sitting at the table in the Sunnyview café. She contained herself but was inwardly excited that Atom was now engaged. Accompanying her at the table were Sophia, Will's personal administrator, Favor, Angelina, Gloria, and Michael. Clare had introduced Michael to Sophia when they joined the others for supper. The conversation revolved around the massive number of inquiries received about Will's disappearance and presumed death. Most came from family, friends, associates, former colleagues, the media, and some from crackpots hailing the event as an act of God against the evil scientists. The six agreed it was imperative for the message they conveyed to be brief, concise, and unified. They also agreed that Sophia should be the press secretary for the media, Angelina the spokesperson for the family, and Favor for Sunnyview Retreats. The number of inquiries and international attention had forced them to limit the flow of visitors by shutting the gates at the highway entrance and increasing security at critical locations. All of this was news to Michael, who had been out of this inner communications loop until now.

Clare broke in at an appropriate pause to inform the others that Atom had entered the circle and was now a unique part of the investigation.

"He's giving the directive for *Capa Negra*," Clare announced.

"What does that mean?" questioned Michael.

"Black Cape, he's directing us to cloak all communications," explained Angelina. "This is parallel with our decision to be very sparing with our messages to the outside world. There are many ears listening and eyes looking at us through the numerous satellite surveillance systems around the world. Atom has learned well from Will and Derick's teachings regarding the covert ways of the global military industrial complex.

"With the technology of today, it's imperative to keep whatever cards you want to play very close to the vest as distortion, conjecture, and outright fabrications are part of the various information systems of the world. We've been here before, although under less radical circumstances. Anything else from Atom, Clare?"

"He'll be connecting with me later tonight telepathically. He's cloaked himself." She deliberately failed to mention her understanding that his coded message also indicated he was on his way to see Uncle Derick at Camp Bay Island off the Honduran coast.

Gloria's eyes were clear, her back straight, and her head erect as she raised her hand to her forehead and saluted. "That's our boy," she responded, knowing exactly what Clare was thinking.

*   *   *

Atom arrived at the airport and found his way to the office of Custom Air Travelers. He nodded his head in greeting to a trusted friend of the family and member of Fischer Enterprises.

"Hey Tom, still flying the desk I see." Tom stood up and the two men shook hands. "How long will I have to wait to get that charter to Derick's place?"

"We have a Hawker Beechcraft 1000 flying in from Vancouver in an hour and heading out again with two passengers to Belize. That flight leaves in about two hours and you're on it. How's that for service?"

"That's great; I'll be there before midnight. We're flying directly to Camp Bay Island's private air strip as usual?"

"Yup, just like you requested. The pilot's a close friend of your dads. Have you ever flown with Captain Jack Hawkins? He's an ace pilot and a hell of a guy. Your dad and he put on a whole lot of miles together. By the way, I'm sorry about what happened. Jane and I saw the report on the news. Any new developments?"

"A rogue storm, forty-foot waves, a distress call, capsized boat, and the lake swallowed them. That's all I know."

Tom looked at Atom curiously. "And you're heading to Camp Bay instead of Michigan?"

"Thanks for your condolences about Dad, Tom, and I can't offer any more information. As far as you're concerned, I'm not even here. If anyone insists that I was, I came looking for a flight to Tahoe, you couldn't help, and I left."

"Oh, right, yes, that was the CAN code. Sorry, I *did* register that on the reservation, just a little brain fart there talking about your dad. I still can't believe it. So, back to Captain Jack Hawkins, you couldn't have a better pilot. Let him know who you are and what's up and he'll do anything he can to help you. He and your dad are, or, I just can't believe this, *were* really tight. He's part of the family. You can trust him with anything."

"I appreciate your help and sensitivity around the situation. I know what you're saying about not being able to believe it. I'm in the same space, which is why I'm going to see Uncle Derick. He's now the main guy in the family. And again, you know *what* about all of this?"

"I don't know nothin'. Atom Fischer? Yeah, he tried to get a flight to Tahoe, but we didn't have anything so he left. Sorry."

"Thank you, Tom. I knew I could count on you. By the way, how's Lydia, is she walking yet?"

"Oh man, my little girl. I can't believe you remembered! Yes, she started walking a couple weeks ago, and she's really getting it. How did you remember to ask about her?"

"I flew in about six weeks ago from Marquette and your wife and daughter were in here visiting. I'm a real pushover for little kids, and Jane was just so enthralled with Lydia it made an impression on me. You have a beautiful wife and daughter. You're a very wealthy man to have those two traveling with you."

"Thanks, Atom. I'm honored that you recognize what I've been blessed with. In my experience, that's rare to find in guys your age."

"Say hello to Jane for me, and I'm happy to hear that Lydia's taken the next step in her development." Atom chuckled at his pun and started out the door. "I'm going to pick up a few things at the store and my cab should still be waiting, so I'll be back in what, an hour or so?"

"Yeah, an hour and forty-five minutes will be good. The departure is scheduled in exactly a hundred nineteen minutes. Is that small backpack all you're carrying for luggage?"

"This is it. I like to travel light. See you in a few."

Atom got in the waiting cab and rode to the nearest grocery store. He paid the fare, got out, and slowly walked into the store. He needed a few supplies for the trip and wanted some space before the next leg of his journey. After picking up some dried fruit and nuts, a new toothbrush, a bottle of water, and a couple of bananas, he paid the cashier, walked out of the store and stopped at a park before heading back to the airport.

He walked a slow pace and reflected, awakening to the gravity of the situation and his place in it. He checked his inner guidance systems and felt balanced and aligned in the decision to see Derick in person and connect with whatever was waiting for him. He was feeling the strength of his participation in the family business in a new way. Without his dad to lead, Atom knew his position in the system had significantly changed.

He now remembered the last words his dad had spoken to him four days ago on the phone. "No matter what happens, always take care of the family, always stay together, and always seek the connection to the Source in our common unity. In alignment, you'll always know exactly what to do. Connect with Derick and remember to remember!"

All these lofty ideals and practices he'd been raised with seemed to come together in this moment, creating the path of discovery by walking it. At the park between the grocery store and the airport, he sat, reflected, and wrote a few lines in his journal. He entered the date 10/10/10 and wondered at the significance of the number convergence as he began to write.

Waiting to take another trip with CAT. Unlike so many times before, I have a sense of not knowing that invites a calming, a centering, an opening response. I've tried to escape the emotions that have welled up since I found out about Dad's disappearance and possible death. I've poured myself into my work to hide from all of what I haven't wanted to deal with emotionally. I'm now wondering what this emptiness is and why all of a sudden I'm up and moving right into the mouth of a dragon when just a few hours ago I was still in denial. What do I expect to find at Camp Bay Island? Why do I feel like I'm in a play without a script?

Dad, I'm wondering where you are, what you're experiencing, why I've lost contact with you. Ever since I can remember, we've had an unspoken connection, like we've known each other from other times and places. I've looked to you as one who would always be with me and in this moment, I'm no longer sure of that. I'm thinking of Mom and Clare and G.Ma. I'm feeling a river of emotions that are ready to overflow their banks. I'm wondering if I'm ready to receive what Derick and the universe might give me.

At the thought of Derick, Atom stopped writing, took out the disposable cell phone, and keyed in a text message to him. He knew Tom would send a message to the flight controller at the private airstrip at Camp Bay, but he wanted his uncle to hear directly from him. Because of all the family business enterprises, Derick always had his cell phone turned on, so Atom expected an immediate response. The message came back within a minute: "Expecting U. M here. OK. D." Atom continued in his journal.

Just connected with Derick, and somehow his message sent a ray of hope through me. Was I closing myself off? Am I isolated, hidden in the dark woods of my doubt? Probably. Ever since I received the call from Clare, I've cloaked myself. I've retreated into a hiding place within. That was two days ago, and it seems like two years. How is that possible? This time space thing is a mystery. Maybe time is simply a human creation. Maybe all of what we call reality is simply illusion, a mental creation through unknown neural pathways. More questions, more wonderment, more waves and particles interchanging and smiling at my foolishness. It's time for some new solutions. I'm glad to be on my way to Camp Bay. Somehow, I know Derick is in the know and I need to be there. That's what Dad directed me to in that last conversation. It's all right. It's all ripe. I'm on my way.

Chapter 27

Daylight, full of small dancing particles and the one great turning. Our souls are dancing with you, without feet, they dance. Can you see them when I whisper in your ear?
-Jalaluddin Balkhi Rumi-

Michael was taking in all the information shared by Angelina, Gloria, Favor, Clare, and Sophia. The most compelling piece of data was that a United States submarine performing routine maneuvers in Lake Superior today discovered *Mystic Travelers* split in half in a trough at a depth of 630 feet in the area where she was last seen by the Coast Guard helicopter. The sighting was confirmed, so speculation about the deaths of the crew was verified, closing the official investigation.

"It may seem like a dumb question," Michael quietly blurted out, "but what does this mean to us? What do you all think about the report? I was tracking a different story line that had the boat and crew somewhere else, not at the bottom of the lake. Does this come as a surprise to anybody but me?"

Everyone was looking at Michael with rapt attention.

Angelina leaned into the table and broached the subject. She spoke softly and with clarity. "We now know where the schooner is. That mystery is over. As far as the crew is concerned, we're still uncertain and not counting out the many possibilities we're tracking."

"What possibilities are you tracking?" I asked. "I have my own theories, but I haven't heard any of yours. It seems to me our conversation should be a compilation of the theories and speculations we're tracking. I've had some very curious dreams, reflections, and experiences during the past two days and have shared some with you Favor, but I don't know if the rest of you know of them. I also think it's important for me to know what you've been experiencing and talking about. Let's sort it out. You invited me to be an integral part of this investigation for the family and I'm in. On the other hand, I'm sensing that I'm not in. I need some clarification as to my role and how much disclosure I can expect."

Gloria set the napkin she was holding down on her plate and spoke. "This is a perfect place for the transition. Is everyone finished with supper?"

They all nodded and began stacking their plates.

"Then let's reconvene in B2."

Michael looked at Favor in frustration. The old sage smiled and cocked his head as if to say, *What you're asking for is coming soon.* Michael kept his silence and sighed as he stood up and followed the group. They all entered the elevator, and Favor touched the down button. Silently, the group exited the elevator two floors down that opened into in a vast and spacious arena of science and technology. The room was alive with the hum of electricity and at least twenty technicians moved about among computer screens, phones, security systems, satellite feeds, and other technological wizardry.

Angelina addressed Michael directly as she held up her hand to halt the entourage. "This is our command center for all communications and security on the property as well as all communications to and from the outside world. We're connected to a variety of satellites and a series of networks that we collaborate with. About forty percent of our people at Sunnyview work in our communications department, because like most of what we do here, it's a twenty-four-hour operation. We're a major player in the global communications network and under the radar to all but the most sophisticated players. We've been working on this project since we began in the early seventies when computer technology was an infant. We've placed many computer science majors from the Big Ten universities here over the years. Our network is broad and deep." Angelina's tone was matter of fact and without emotion. She continued to address Michael, not looking at anyone else.

"We monitored *Mystic Travelers* from the time she left Copper Harbor until she capsized and went down. Clare was not in on that information until today. Mom, Favor, and our most trusted technicians were the only ones who knew of the surveillance. We have the whole trip on file."

Michael's face contorted and tensed. "This is mind blowing. What's this all about?" he queried, walking a few steps to the nearest computer screen, squinting down at it and then turning to Angelina. "I don't know what to say. The conspiracy skeptic in my head is running around yelling fire not knowing what to think or what to do. He's wondering what he's fallen prey to. The rational professor is curious and waiting for an explanation, and the inner adventurer wants to dive in and have some fun. Would you please enlighten me?"

Gloria was still standing near the elevator. She touched the down pad and the door opened immediately. "There's more," she said. "Get in."

The group turned and again entered the elevator. Michael and Angelina were the last ones inside. They all rode one floor down to B3. The elevator stopped, the door opened, and they stepped out into a long wide hallway with doors on both sides. They followed Gloria to Room 11 at the end of the hall.

Favor walked in first and flipped on a light switch that illuminated a room the size of a small gymnasium. There were an assortment of odd-looking mechanisms scattered about as well as workstations and a variety of doors along the walls. At each end of the room was a glass box that looked similar to the old-style phone booths that used to populate city streets. These Plexiglas boxes were expandable both horizontally and vertically.

The tops and bottoms were connected to some kind of apparatus that Michael couldn't identify.

A technician came out of one of the doors holding a white rabbit. Two other technicians came out and collapsed the boxes to the size of a rabbit cage. A high-frequency sound entered the room as if someone had turned on an energy device. The technician with the rabbit placed it in the box closest to Angelina and her team. The three technicians then led the group to a viewing room behind thick glass walls.

"Watch carefully, Michael," Angelina directed. "The rabbit will be transported from the place it now rests to the other side of the room into the other box."

Michael's brow wrinkled and his eyes squinted as he concentrated and then moved closer to the glass.

Gloria gave a signal to someone out of sight. In an instant, the rabbit transported from one side of the room to the other, from one glass box to the other without any visible movement whatsoever. For once, Michael was speechless.

Chapter 28

Mystery and manifestations arise from the same source. This source is called darkness . . . . Darkness within darkness, the gateway to all understanding.
-Lao Tzu-

Atom finished writing. He was waiting for the next stream of thought when a young woman walked past him pushing a stroller with a toddler in it. They were both smiling. He watched as they moved to a bench in the park where the mom took her child out of the stroller and placed him on the grass. The toddler immediately started walking around exploring his surroundings. He would stop walking from time to time and reach down to pick something up, look at it, and either carry it or drop it to continue his exploration. The mom shadowed him, ever vigilant and protective as he wandered the area. Occasionally, the toddler would sit down on the grass and be so engrossed in what he was doing that he would lose track of where he was. When he became aware of this lapse, he would immediately scan the surroundings for his mother. Connecting with her, he would go back to what he was doing or move toward her.

Atom put his pen to the paper.

Is this how it is with us humans? From the time we gain mobility and some small independence, we begin to explore our environment to discover where we are and what it's about. Our built-in curiosity pulls us out of our known world into the unknown, from safety and security

141

into danger and opportunity. At some point in our lives, we turn and no one is there. We find ourselves alone with what we think we know. We long for the connection the caring mother or father gave us. For some, this disconnection comes early. For others, it happens later in life. This connection and disconnection from safety and security, from affirmation and affection, from the power and control of others, comes and goes as our external reality changes and rearranges. How do we ever find the inner connections for ourselves, in ourselves? As people, places, and situations change, can we find the longing for connection within, rather than always having to look outside to find it? The answer has to be yes and yet, looking out upon the world of humanity it seems that most do not find it. Is this because we don't know "It" to be here within? Have we not been taught this most primary lesson? Is this where I am at this point in my life? Is this another lesson from the universe? Is this another lesson from Dad?

A disheveled man approached Atom and interrupted his train of thought.

"Hey man, can you spare money for some food? I haven't eaten in a couple days, and I've swallowed my pride long enough to know it doesn't satisfy the hungry stomach. You look like the kind of guy who would help a stranger."

Atom looked up at the man who looked to be in his early to mid-forties and calmly assessed the situation before he responded. The man carried a small backpack and looked like he hadn't seen a shower in quite a while. He wore tattered jeans and a wrinkled T-shirt. His face was worn, his eyes tired.

"Yeah, I have some money for food, but you'll have to earn it."

"Earn it how?"

"You'll have to answer a few questions."

"What kind of questions?"

"Who are you? Where have you come from? Where are you going, and why are you here?" Atom checked his watch for the time. He was well within the window to catch his flight.

"My name is Frank. I'm from Clear Spring, a small town in southern Indiana. I don't know where I'm going and I'm not sure I know what you mean in asking why I'm here?"

"I mean, why is a man like you standing in front a man fifteen years his junior asking for money for food? What kind of choices have you made to put you in this position?"

"You writing a book? What the hell difference does that make? I'm just asking for a small handout."

"From my point of view, you're asking for more than that. What happened?"

"Look man, I don't want to get into it. Just get off your high horse long enough to give me some money, and I'll be on my way."

"What way is that, farther down the slide into shirking your responsibility as a human being?"

"You're starting to piss me off man. What's with you?"

"Maybe if you'd really get pissed off you'd push through the wall of fear that took you down. What would it look like if you'd start caring about yourself again, stand up, and use this latest defeat to wake up to the attitudes and ideas that helped take you down?"

"What the hell do you care? I just asked you to help me buy some food, and here you are trying to psychoanalyze me. You don't know shit, forget it."

The man started to walk away, but Atom stood up, stepped in from of him, and continued. "You're right, I don't know shit, and I care, because I see a man who has great potential and a magnificent life to live. I see a man throwing it all away, because he's forgotten who he really is. My gift to you is a different kind of food. It's to help you wake up, stand up, and find the Who that is You. I'm a mirror reflecting back to you, because I see you through all the pain, suffering, defeat, and depression. I care about you, because I care about me, and we're together in this world, not as strangers but as fellow travelers. What I know is that you appear to be down and out. I'm willing to buy the down, and I'm trying to help you up and out. Mostly, you have to do that for yourself. You're so much more than you appear to be, and when you see that, you'll be able to see some light in the midst of your darkness and find a gateway to a deeper understanding that will change your life. The darkness and difficulty you've experienced is a gift happening for you to wake up and live into your magnificence, your potential, your greatness."

Atom stood tall into his six-foot-three-inch frame and looked deep into the man's eyes. "I see two women and children. I see a bright career dimmed to darkness. I see tears and anger, desire and disconnection. I see extreme loss, defeat, and numbing out. That's all past. Moving forward, I see angst turning into liberation. I see a man standing tall with his son and daughter laughing again. I see a white lab coat on that man standing in another man's office being congratulated. I see a sad and angry woman's mistrust and sorrow turning into hope and happiness. It's time to make your way back to that place called home deep inside yourself, Frank. It's time to find that place beyond right and wrong where all is forgiven, all is loved, and all is reconciled. It's time to be the man you've been created to be."

Frank's angry face softened. Atom saw tears in the man's eyes and watched as his jaw muscles flexed every couple of seconds withholding emotion. Atom pulled out four fifty dollar bills and handed them one by one to Frank.

"The first one's for you. Get some good food and savor it. The second one is for your wife. Get a room, clean up, sober up, and resolve to step up. The third one is for your son. Be the father you never had. Make him proud of you. The final bill is for your daughter. Show her what forgiveness and reconciliation look like. Show her real love and teach her how broken hearts can be mended. Let this gift be a symbol for your new beginning. It may take awhile, challenge your beliefs, and be difficult, but through grace, persistence, and determination, it will be worth it. You are not alone."

Dumbfounded, Frank took the money and said an almost inaudible thank you. Atom offered his hand and Frank sheepishly took it. They connected, released, and Atom turned, took a few steps and turned around again and said, "Frank, remember to remember who you really are at the very depths of your soul. Remember that love is the healing."

Frank nodded as Atom turned and walked slowly away.

Chapter 29

Our whole business in this life is to restore to health the eye of the heart whereby the Light may be seen.
-Saint Augustine-

Walking back toward the airport, Atom was surprised and thankful for his experiences of the mother with child and the lost man. For the first time since he'd heard about his dad's disappearance, Atom felt his dad's presence. It was as if he was allowing Will's energy to direct him in his musings and interactions. Maybe he was waking up to how much of an impression Will had made on his life. Maybe there really was a bond between them that could never be broken. Maybe this adventure was more about finding himself than finding his dad. Whatever it was, his resolve to step into it rather than hide and run away from it left him pleased, even though he'd have to find an ATM before he got back to the airport.

Atom arrived at Custom Air Travelers with time to spare. He checked in with Tom and sat down to wait the brief ten minutes. There had been a last minute change with the other travelers; there were now three passengers instead of two. The Hawker Beechcraft 1000 was built to transport twelve passengers comfortably, so it was not a problem. Just as Atom settled on a couch in the waiting area, a man in a pilot's uniform approached him.

"Hi, you must be Atom Fischer. I'm Captain Jack Hawkins."

Atom stood up to shake hands with him. "Pleased to meet you." The handclasp was strong and powerful and both men looked directly into each other's eyes.

"Tommy told me about your dad. I'm finding it hard to believe, and my condolences. We became really good friends over the years and . . ." Captain Jack looked down at the floor, pulled a handkerchief from his pocket, wiped his eyes, blew his nose, and replaced the handkerchief in his pocket. "I'm sorry, allergies." Captain Jack cleared his throat and regained his composure. "It's great to have you aboard. I understand we're dropping you off at Camp Bay. I've been there many times. It'll be good to see Derick again. I've arranged to lay over a few hours before heading on to Panama," he paused.

"Well, I have to do the preflight now. Just wanted to introduce myself. When we get to altitude and everything's clear would you be willing to share the cockpit with me so we can get to know each other a bit? It would mean a lot to me."

Atom smiled at Captain Jack's demeanor and attitude. "It would be a pleasure."

They shook hands again. Captain Jack walked down the corridor and out to the CAT jet that was waiting twenty yards away. Atom sat back down and watched this aging jet jockey walk outside to his aircraft and prepare for yet another flight. Atom thought it curious that in all the flights he'd taken with CAT, he'd never met Captain Jack Hawkins. He texted an inquiry to Uncle Derick: "CAT pilot J Hawk, info, fam, Y/N?"

While he waited for a response, he noticed three people talking to Tom, or Tommy, as Captain Jack had referred to him. When they finished their conversation, Atom noticed Tommy point to him and the doorway Jack had walked through. The threesome walked to the waiting area where Atom sat. He was looking at his phone when he heard the man in the group introduce himself.

"Greetings. My name is Robert Jameson. This is my wife Aisha and our daughter Inana. We'll be flying with you as far as Belize."

Atom stood, gave a slight smile, and shook hands with each of them. "Pleased to meet you," he responded. "I'm Atom Fischer."

The man and woman were in their early to mid-fifties. Robert was six feet tall with blond hair, light skin, and a youthful California look. He was dressed in a blue blazer, light brown slacks, a white shirt, and tie. Aisha was a very attractive woman with dark hair, dark skin, and the look of royalty. Inana was also beautiful, in her mid-twenties with dark hair like her mother, olive skin, an angular face, and penetrating brown eyes. She was dressed in designer jeans, a white blouse not tucked in, and a tailored sport jacket. Atom thought they were a strikingly handsome family.

"So what takes you to Belize?" Atom questioned.

"We're mixing some pleasure with business. Inana's between things so we thought it would be a good getaway, a way to slow down and reconnect. It's been hectic these past months," Robert answered.

Atom looked at Aisha and Inana and said, "Inana, that's a very interesting name, not one I've heard before. It's Arabic, right? And translates into English as I Am? And Aisha, that's Arabic for *life* isn't it?"

The family members looked at one another with surprise as if some barrier had melted. They all smiled at Atom and Inana spoke. "Atom, you're the first Anglo man your age I've ever met who identified our names with spot-on accuracy. I'm impressed. How do know Arabic?"

Atom blushed slightly. "I know a small amount through my family. They're into the mystical traditions of the Middle East and that's part of our ancestry."

"Your name is Adam. Is that not the English derivation from Adama meaning human being in Arabic?" Aisha asked.

"Everyone thinks so," Atom said smiling, "but my name is spelled A-T-O-M, which comes from the Greek *atomos* meaning indivisible. My dad's a scientist. He thought it would be fun to name his son after a source of vast potential energy. I've grown to appreciate it."

The conversation stopped as Jackie, the CAT copilot, approached the group. She introduced herself and then ushered the four passengers to the flight-ready Hawker Beechcraft 1000 just outside the waiting area.

The Jameson family sat in the seats at the front of the plane. There were six sets of two seats facing one another on each side of the aisle. Atom went to the rear of the plane to sit in the back seat that faced forward. After adjusting his seat belt and stowing his backpack under the seat, he looked up and saw Inana looking at him. He smiled, nodded, and checked his cell phone for the message from Derick. It was there: "J Hawk, fam, Y, Bro. Stay CAN Extreme Joy, C U!"

So Captain Jack is part of the family circle, and I'm to keep everything close to the vest. Just convey information about what the public reports are relaying, which means I know nothing. I agree with that. I really don't know much of anything, and I'm hoping the mystery reveals itself at Camp Bay Island. Ola Kala, it's all beautiful. And speaking of beautiful, this young woman Inana . . . wow! What a beauty, and she's my age. Her mom and dad are a curious couple and . . . that's not why you're here, Atom. Sit back, relax, and enjoy the ride. Get a little sleep, because it could be a very long night. Maybe even have a revealing dream or two. Ola Kala.

The Beechcraft took off in a steady climb and headed south toward the Caribbean where warmth, palm trees, clear blue water, and an unknown adventure awaited. Atom was asleep before the plane leveled off.

A half-hour into the flight, the jet hit some significant turbulence that bounced Atom awake. He grabbed hold of the arms of the leather recliner, sat up, opened his eyes, and blinked rapidly, trying to determine where he was. He calmed himself and noticed someone sitting in the seat across the aisle from him. A smell of musk was in the air. He turned to see Inana sitting with her seat belt on and smiling at him. He smiled back.

"What?" he asked.

"I've been sitting here wondering who you are," she responded. "You're not like the other guys I've met. You seem much older and wiser and much more grounded. Who are you?"

Atom turned away and stared at the empty seat in front of him. *I'm not going to get into it. This is not why I'm here. This can't go anywhere, and I don't know anything and don't want to know anything. I have to be cordial. I can give a brief answer that might satisfy and turn the conversation back on her. People like to talk about themselves, right?*

He turned to look at Inana. Her stare was gentle and innocent. She didn't seem to be playing a game. She was too serious for that and yet, he saw playfulness in the lines around her eyes and mouth, and sensed an aura of curiosity and authenticity about her. *Maybe she is someone to know. She sure is beautiful. Who knows why certain people cross paths?*

"I'm not at all sure how to answer that question, Inana. I could give you a thousand descriptors, but that wouldn't tell you who I am. Even if I gave you my ancestral background, where and how I was raised or what my interests are, it still wouldn't answer your question. At the very source of it all, maybe the only thing I can say is I Am. Just like you, Inana, I Am."

"That's what I'm talking about. You talk differently. You look like any other person sitting on the beach, but when it's time to get in the water, you dive in and go deep. In my experience with guys from their teens, even into old age, that's not the case. You are unique and I'm intrigued by you."

Atom didn't say anything. He just sat quietly in his own curiosity looking at her.

Inana continued. "My father is a wealthy American entrepreneur and my mother is a wealthy Arabian heiress. They met in college in the late seventies at Stanford. Dad was an athlete and Mom was on a student visa from Saudi Arabia. She was studying business and English, because she wanted to get out of her father's house. Her father wanted her to help him with American business. Dad was also studying business for his father. Opposites attract and the rest is history.

"I'm the product of a cultural merger. I rarely meet people who have much depth or knowledge of who they are, where they're going, or why they're here. You look like a hundred people

I've met, well, maybe more attractive, but that's not it. It's as if you possess some kind of ancient wisdom, some kind of shmaya arha. Do you know what that means?"

Atom smiled. "In English, it's heaven and earth, and in the Middle Eastern translation, it's so much more. It's the energy of the universe manifest. It's the waves and particles at the subatomic level interacting in the dance of the universe that create radiant, vibrant, life-giving energy. It's the interaction of all apparent opposites coming together in joy and celebration, sometimes with great subtlety, other times with great vociferousness, and other times in every place in between. Shmaya arha is an experience, a consciousness, a state and stage of being and doing. Shmaya arha is shmaya arha! It's a powerful communion!"

A very long pause and open silence transpired between Atom and Inana. There was electricity in the air. They both felt it with their own interpretations. Neither wanted to speak. Atom turned to look at the empty leather seat in front of him, breathed consciously, and slowed his racing heart. He felt as if some strange passion had overtaken him, as if he'd been caught in the very energy he was explaining. He felt like he may have overwhelmed Inana and wanted to apologize, but then he sensed a warm and a deep understanding emanating from her.

Inana broke the stillness by reaching forward and placing her hand gently on his hand. He felt a power surge through his whole body. She felt it too and sat back, almost jerking her hand away.

"What was that?" she asked.

"Not knowing," he responded.

"Me too."

They both sat back and rested in the causal energy of the moment. Inana eventually reached into her purse and took out a pen and two personal cards. She gave them to Atom. "You keep one and put your contact information on the other one and give it back to me."

Atom wrote his name on the back of the card along with his personal website, e-mail address, and cell phone number. "This should do it." He handed the card back to her and put the other in his shirt pocket. "I'll be unavailable for an undetermined amount of time, but I do have a place in Palo Alto. Where will you be?"

"The Bay Area after Belize. We'll connect. I'll make sure of it," she responded.

The energy between them wasn't so much sensual as it was soulful. It was as if they'd known each other from another time and place. Something mysterious that neither of them had ever experienced in this lifetime happened in those few seconds that somehow seemed to change everything. It was beyond words and yet, they both knew that many words would be spoken at another time in another place. Without knowing each other, they knew each other. It was beyond personality, beyond culture, beyond heritage, beyond gender. It was the momentary realization that separation is an illusion.

Inana unbuckled her seat belt, stood up, bent over, and kissed Atom on the forehead. She glanced at him over her shoulder as she made the short walk back to her seat. He smiled at her, closed his eyes, and drifted away.

Chapter 30

The artist is extremely fortunate who is presented with the worst possible ordeal which will not actually kill him. At that point, he is in business.
-John Barrymore-

Jackie, the copilot of the flight, woke Atom about forty-five minutes after he had fallen asleep for the second time. She informed him that Captain Jack was ready to talk with him. Atom asked for a few moments to wake up.

What to say to Captain Jack? It should be simple. He'll probably want to do most of the talking. He'll want to ask some questions, but what he'll really want is to tell me about himself. Just give a little and listen a lot. Maybe you can learn something you don't know. Remember to remember who you are and not forget why you're here. Find out about him. Be kind. Be present.

Jackie sat across the aisle from Atom. She watched him expectantly until he got up and walked toward the cockpit. Inana looked at him as he passed by. They smiled at each other and gave a slight bow of acknowledgment. He opened the door to the cockpit, stepped in, and took the copilot seat.

"Greetings, my new young friend. How's the flight been so far?" inquired Captain Jack.

"Mostly smooth and . . . interesting passengers. What do you know about the Jameson's?"

"It's a curious thing, Atom. I fly people, some famous and all rich, all over the world, and unless I see them a lot, I hardly know anything about them. I'm the captain of the ship and therefore, simply a servant, one who makes sure passengers and crew get safely to their destinations. It's lonely and isolated behind closed doors. Why do you ask?"

"I'm always curious about people. As you said, catering to the rich and famous is a servant business, and I think that holds true for any business. We're all here to serve in one way, shape, or form, and I'm not sure people at the so-called top really get that, and I'm interested in those who do."

"Your interest couldn't possibly have anything to do with the beautiful daughter, who's about your age sitting just outside this closed door, could it?"

"Isn't it quite rare for wealthy Arabian gentry to marry outside their culture?"

"Yes."

"That's my curiosity. The beautiful daughter? I hadn't noticed."

They both laughed.

"So tell me, Captain Jack Hawkins, how is it that you've come to work for Custom Air Travelers, a subsidiary company of Fischer Enterprises?"

"How much time do you have?"

"All the time in the world and not a moment to lose. Give me the high points."

"Vietnam, late sixties, I met a medic named Michael Wyman from Michigan. He graduated college, got drafted, was a conscientious objector, and became a medic. I flew medivac at the time, and we were stationed at the same MASH unit. He was assigned to my chopper, and we flew more than a hundred missions together. I saved his life once. He saved my life twice, once in Nam and another time in the states. That created a bond between us that will never be broken. He went on to become a priest, psychologist, college professor, and entrepreneur. He married, had a couple of kids, and became successful.

"I became a commercial pilot, womanizer, drunk, and a lost soul. We communicated on and off for years, but our lives took radically different turns. I called him one night when I had hit bottom for the nth time. I was in a hotel in Denver on a layover. He came to see me, put me into rehab, and stayed with me for three years. He turned my life around. He helped me work through my post traumatic stress, my addictions, my negative self-image, my attitudes about life, and most importantly, he helped me see how all the darkness always pointed to the light of what he called the shmya. He helped me see the play of opposites that can cloud our vision when we only see one dimension. He helped open my mind to the infinite possibilities of what he called the human-divine condition of forgetfulness and remembrance. He stood by me when I couldn't," he paused.

"When your dad and uncle started CAT, Michael hooked me up with them. Will and he met in the early seventies after Michael's hitch in Nam. They became friends and associates. I was the first pilot CAT hired, and I've been with the family ever since. Strange how life comes to meet us when we least expect it and when we need it most."

"Where's Michael Wyman now?"

"He still lives in Denver. We get together from time to time. I was just there a couple weeks ago having dinner with he and his wife Joanna. Quite a family. I feel fortunate being connected to them. I'm inspired every time I think about how they live their lives. Not to say they don't have their bumps in the road like the rest of us, but they always seem to find a way to end up, rather than down, at the end of the day. That in itself is an amazing quality that I haven't come across in most people. Your family seems similar. How about you? Tell me about this boating incident with your dad and his associates. It's a hard one to digest and get my arms around. I've known your dad a long time and this smells fishy."

"Fishy? What do you mean?"

"Your dad is a planner. He has a unique ability to conceptualize, analyze, and execute very complicated plans that most folks would never imagine, let alone be able to figure out. Speaking of executing plans, what were your principle studies in college?"

"Physics, math, engineering, philosophy, and art."

"That's quite a combination. Chip off the old block. Did you ever get into an area that was just so complicated you had to ask for outside help?"

"It just happened a few weeks ago. I was running some formulas that refused to work out. I worked them over and over with a variety of permutations but couldn't get them to bring forth the results I knew were there."

"When you reached the end of your rope, what did you do?"

"I put the work aside and walked away from it for a while and then went back, worked it through again, and still came up empty. I did that for a couple of months until finally, when Dad was out visiting, I asked him to help me. We spent two whole days walking through every step of the problem. At the end of the process, he sat back, reflected, made a few additional computations, rearranged the formula, and asked me to check it out. I ran through the reconfigured program and bingo, it landed me right where I knew I should be."

"That's what I'm talking about. Your dad is a master planner and a facilitator of the material world. I sometimes think he's connected to something the rest of us can only dream about. So, fishy, it smells like something's not quite right or ripe, or that it's overripe and there's something missing or there's too much of something. When you've been around the block as many times and with as many people as I have, you have a scent for things. What do you know that you're not telling me?"

"I don't know anything. Really. I live in Palo Alto and my family is in Michigan and Honduras. I'm out of the loop."

"Is that why you're heading to the island to see Derick?"

"Captain Jack, I've checked you out, and I know you're in the family and can be trusted. I also know that I share your skepticism and concern for what's going down, or up, or wherever it's going, and I can't talk about what I don't know. Like you, anything I say would be pure speculation and right now, I don't want to go there. What are you thinking, what insights are you having?"

"It's all new to me, but as I've been sitting here for the past hour, I've been wondering what implications this could have at a global level. Your dad is connected to so many influential people and of all those people, I would say he's more influential than any of them are, because he doesn't have a stake in any one of them. His interest is in the whole as well as the parts. He sees the picture from the vantage point of the individual and the collective, the macro and the micro. His vision is larger than anyone I've ever met except for Michael Wyman, which is probably why they stayed connected over the years. Your dad sees how all things work together for better and for worse. I'm wondering if this whole thing might be an illusion to deflect attention, disarm the resistance, find the weakness and strength of the apparent opposites, and use it to transform the global situation."

"I'm intrigued," Atom replied. "Please go on."

"I've shuttled your dad all over the world. Because of our connection through Michael, we came to have a unique relationship. Whenever he wanted me to pilot him, wherever in the world and for whatever reason, the whole CAT system would reconfigure to accommodate his wish. My sense is that CAT exists because your dad needed a way to connect globally. Rather than fly commercial, with all its hassles or owning a private jet with all its expenses, he and your uncle Derick put together Custom Air Travelers to fund Will's network and generate a profit, as well as provide a service for his many colleagues. It was a stroke of entrepreneurial genius.

"There's always more to the situation than meets the eye. The facts always point beyond themselves to something smaller and larger. Your dad's entrepreneurship took on a global vision somewhere way back. He came to the planet to do some very special things. To die in a freak storm was not one of them. The specifics of the plan elude me, but the general scope of what I'm sensing spells significant change at a variety of levels.

"Back in the sixties, millions of people were committed to positive change, but the system was already too thick and had too much force. Most of us either went off the deep end or just quit and joined the chosen frozen. We got married, pursued the so-called American dream, and went back to sleep while the military industrial complex continued to grow, and now we're part of their status quo army. Your dad was one of the few who never went to sleep. Your Sunnyview colony is a testimony to his innovative and creative thought. That experiment is an amazing success, and you're a product of it. What's your take on Sunnyview?"

"I've been living outside that cloistered environment for seven years now, and at the depth of my soul, I dearly miss it. The world outside is so amazingly fragmented. Everyone goes every which way with no real direction, except toward more separation, consumerism, ecological destruction, control, and fear. The pervasive energy of the planetary condition is dense, thick, and difficult to transcend. We're in a real mess, and very few people in power seem to have any viable solutions to the many problems we face as a global community. It's definitely time for evolution and new solutions. So you think my dad and his associates are part of a plan to execute this evolution?"

"Just look at his life. What has he been about for the past forty-plus years? He's been a creative force in the world. Michael Wyman told me where and how he met your dad in the early seventies. Will was already on the scene attending global conferences as a presenter. He was giving speeches, networking, writing papers, doing research, connecting with people in politics, government, military, industry, academia, religion, business, media, communications, science, arts, sports, philanthropy, and about every other field of endeavor. He had the skills to listen to every viewpoint, the charisma to find common ground, and he brought people together who could help one another create a new world. He created an interconnected global community that is vibrating with every fluctuation of events. It's really very exciting.

"Maybe he saw the time as being ripe for a major turning that he and his colleagues could help facilitate through a radically different approach. I don't know Atom, I'm just an aging flight jockey who has seen way more of the dark side than I could have imagined, and still have hope that the Source is a transformational consciousness in every present reality. With people like Will and Michael and a million more I know, we'll see that day come around," Captain Jack stopped and turned to Atom before continuing.

"Then here you are, traveling to see your uncle, your dad's brother, and closest colleague at this time; this is no vacation or casual business trip. Look Atom, I'm just the bus driver, the pickup and delivery guy, which means that none of this is my business. It is, though, because I'm part of the whole, like every other particle on the planet. I'm pleased and proud to be a small part of whatever positive change is in the air and to have had this opportunity to sit with you. Whatever comes of this, I want you to know that I am your servant, as I have been for your father and your whole family. You can count on me, not matter what!"

Atom felt the atmosphere in the cockpit change from when the conversation started. He sat in silence while he pondered the words of this aging warrior. His heart was touched as he reflected on all that was said. He felt the pain and suffering of Jack's life that could have been lost a thousand times. He thought of all the souls in the world who manifest physically and lose the memory of their essence to rediscover it through their angst. He also felt the liberation of one who had been cradled back to life through the compassion of fellow travelers.

The magnitude of this meeting registered significance. Atom stroked his chin and drifted off into reflective thought. *Does anything happen by chance, or is it all part of the vast network of being and doing? The awakening I had a few hours ago in Palo Alto seemed to have come out of nowhere and created a completely new series of potentially life-changing events, bringing me to this moment. What an incredible field of mysterious energy we live in and which lives in us.*

"Captain Jack Hawkins, you're another man wearing a coat of many colors, and I thank you for your insight, your honesty, and your loyalty. You've been very helpful in giving me your perspective. This is the first time I've had a real conversation about Dad's disappearance. You've given me hope and a lot to reflect upon."

They shook hands, pleased with their connection, and knew the journey they were on together was just beginning.

Chapter 31

We have it in our power to begin the world all over again. A situation similar to the present hath not appeared since the days of Noah until now. The birthday of a new world is at hand.
-Thomas Paine-

Atom turned, partially stood, and opened the door of the cockpit. He hunched his back and ducked his head as he made his way through the cramped space and into the main part of the cabin. Being three inches taller than the six-foot ceiling made it impossible for him to stand straight. As he began to make his way past the Jameson family, he noticed Robert holding up his hand and signaling a halt.

"Would you be willing to sit down here for a few minutes? I'd like to talk with you."

Atom looked, nodded, backed up, and sat down in the seat facing Robert Jameson. Two feet away, across the aisle, sat Inana and Aisha.

"We've been talking about you. It seems you've made a very positive impression upon our family, and we'd like to know more about you. How do you happen to be here? What's your story?"

Here we go again, another inquiry. Our daughter is interested in you, so we're interested in you to see if you are worthy. Give it a rest for God's sake; we just met. Yes, there was a significant connection, but to put me on the grill this early in the game is ridiculous. My dad just disappeared or died or who knows what and all you can think of is . . . hey, what's with all this criticism and condemnation? The man simply wants to get to know you and feel good about what his daughter has told him. He's curious. Loving-kindness, remember? What's the problem here? Get over yourself.

Atom took a breath and the high road. "Mr. Jameson, I'm flattered that you want to know more about me and that I've made a favorable impression. I was taught, however, to question the questioner before answering to find out what is really being asked. Do you mind answering the same two questions before I do? How do you happen to be here? What's your story?"

Robert Jameson was used to getting his way without question, and here a man half his age was rebuffing him. *Who the hell does he think he is turning the questions back on me? Okay, settle down, it's all for the good of the family, and he does have a valid point. If he is whom I think he is, it would make sense for him to answer exactly the way he did. I'll trust the process and answer my own questions. This should be interesting.*

"Fair enough," Robert began. "As I said earlier, we're on a pleasure trip, and I'll be doing some small amount of business while in Belize. We have a few interests there that need attention. Because of our busy and varied schedules, the three of us haven't been able to spend much time together during the past few months so we decided, at the last moment, that it would be a good time to catch up. Sometimes it seems that everything, except the most important things, are attended to. Family has been, and continues to be, extremely important to us, even though our son has . . ." he paused.

A slight grimace appeared on Robert's face. He looked at his wife and daughter, did an emotional and conversational reset, and continued. "We've had our difficulties, and through them, we've become stronger, individually and as a family, with some exceptions." He paused again, rubbed his hand across his face, replaced his hand on the armrest, looked back at Atom with a slight smile, and continued.

"My story is typical for the affluent Californian. Born and raised in the Silicon Valley, Dad was a successful executive in the new world of computer technology. I was raised with a silver spoon in my mouth, went to the best schools, and played soccer well enough to keep playing into my college years. I attended Stanford, studied soccer, girls, and business, in that order. I fell in love with Aisha, married against both our parents' wishes, had a beautiful son and daughter, worked hard, became a successful entrepreneur in a variety of business ventures, and wonder occasionally what I'm going to do with my life when I grow up. It's been an amazing ride and yet, something seems to be missing. How can you have it all and still think there's something missing? That's a rhetorical question. You don't have to answer it. So, that's me. It's a beginning."

Atom nodded thoughtfully and wondered at the two references Robert made concerning his son and why he had made a decision not to pursue it.

"Thank you," Atom began. "That makes it much easier to answer your questions. My story is anything but typical. I was raised in a small village in the Upper Peninsula of Michigan with my nuclear and extended family. It is a self-sustaining spiritual community of artists, scientists, and progressive thinkers. We have farms, studios, research labs, retreat facilities, educational resources for all ages, and a full complement of diversity at every level of life. The facilities sit on more than three thousand acres of forests, lakes, and fields held by a nonprofit corporation. I sit on that board and the boards of two other family businesses. We have interests and holdings globally. This airline is one of our subsidiary companies."

Robert raised his eyebrows in response.

"I'm on my way to one of our interests in Honduras. I'm finishing a PhD at Stanford in electrical engineering and plan to continue my research and participate in the oversight of our family interests."

"Is your father Dr. William C. Fischer?"

"Yes, do you know him?"

"Only by reputation. He's one of the top scientists in the world, as I understand it, and is a strong advocate for eco-stewardship.

His accomplishments and influences are vast. I think my dad had some dealings with him about an oil pipeline years ago. They were on opposite sides of the proposal and your dad won."

"Does that mean your family holds a grudge against mine?" Atom asked rhetorically with a wry smile.

"No, not at all. I view business like a sporting event, Atom. Everyone on the field is trying to win and when the game is over, we shake hands, congratulate one another, and move on to the next event. Each game can be a learning experience that takes coaches and players to a higher level of play. I think my dad learned something from yours in that encounter. I'm actually on the eco-stewardship side of things too. What's he up to these days?"

My inner skeptic and protector are wondering if this is a set-up. Has he read the accounts of the accident, the supposed deaths, and disappearance of Mystic Travelers? Is he leading me into an interrogation trap? I don't know anything about this guy, except the connection I made with his daughter and what he's told me. If his father is connected with the oil and gas industry, he probably is too, and there's the Saudi Arabian connection with Aisha's family. Dad knows many top Saudi engineers and wealthy oil families. Be careful. This may be a slippery slope. So far, we've given him nothing but public information. The public information on Dad is that he and his crew are presumed dead, and I don't know if the investigation is over yet or not. Throw the ball back into his court. Be attentive to his body language as well as his answers. He had that glitch about his son, but he's been very relaxed and confident since then. Walk softly and stay vigilant.

"Have you seen the accounts in the media?"

Robert shook his head.

"Two days ago, Dad and his crew of four went down in a rogue storm in Lake Superior. They're all missing and presumed dead. I don't know if the investigation is over or not, and I don't know anything beyond that."

Aisha and Inana had courteously been acting as if they were reading their magazine and book, but were instead listening to every word of the men's conversation. Hearing this news, they both looked up at each other and then to Robert and Atom. Robert remained contained, but Aisha and Inana responded almost simultaneously with shock and apprehension. Aisha gasped and said, "Oh my god, Atom. I didn't know."

"I'm so sorry," said Inana.

Robert continued after a long pause. "On the way here in the cab, I read a brief article on my phone about the incident. It said the sailing vessel had been found by a submarine on a routine mission six hundred feet below the surface of the lake in two pieces. The investigation was called off and the crew was presumed lost. I only put the story and you together a few seconds ago. I'm really sorry. I feel awful for bringing this up here."

Atom read concern from the entire family and felt confident their feelings were genuine and sincere. He also felt the sting to find out that *Mystic Travelers* was found in two pieces six hundred feet below the surface of the lake.

"Thanks for your concern. You probably know very well how difficult it is being from a family with high-profile people, no matter how under the radar you try to stay." Atom paused and looked down at his hands. "I hadn't heard about the submarine identification of our schooner. Probably a recent update." He paused again, feeling the subtle energy of loss. "It's quite the mystery, and if you don't mind, I have to excuse myself now. I look forward to continuing this conversation under different circumstances. I'd love to hear more about your ideas and activities concerning eco-stewardship and entrepreneurship. It's a passion of mine as well."

Atom stood, shook hands with Robert, Aisha, and Inana, and walked the short distance to his seat. Jackie stood as he approached. With a tired smile, he held out his hand. "Jackie, I want to formally introduce myself and apologize for not doing so sooner. My name is Atom Fischer, and I'm pleased to meet you and am glad you're flying with Captain Jack. Thank you for your courtesy and care. I take it you've met my father, Will?"

Jackie returned the handshake. "Yes, a really great man. He always made me feel special and part of the family. That's always meant a lot to me."

"Do you know of his disappearance?"

"Yes, Captain Jack briefed me when we got on board. I'm terribly sorry for your loss."

"A loss yes and I'm also looking for the gain. It's so easy to get lost in the end and forget there's also a beginning, don't you think?"

Jackie looked quizzically and nodded slightly.

"I thank you for your concern and ask that you keep your heart and mind open for the silver linings that show up in the strangest places when least expected. Tell Captain Jack that we just found out *Mystic Travelers* was identified six hundred feet below the surface in two pieces. Also, tell him we'll talk again after the Jameson family departs. I see you've left tonic water with a twist of lemon for me. *Muy bien y gracias.*"

Jackie returned to the cockpit. Atom went back to dreamtime. The Jameson family went into silent containment.

Chapter 32

It is only with the heart that one can see rightly; what is essential is invisible to the eye.
-Antoine de Saint-Exupéry-

"Did you speak with Atom before coming in?" Captain Jack asked Jackie while she was fastening her seat belt.

"We had a very brief chat just now. He spent time sitting with the Jameson family. I tried not to hear the conversation, but some of it came through. Robert and Atom were exchanging brief autobiographies and the subject of Dr. Fischer came up. I had a sense that whatever they said concerning that part of the conversation was not good news, because it ended shortly after that. Atom returned to his seat and wanted me to tell you that *Mystic Travelers* was identified six hundred feet below the surface of Lake Superior in two pieces and that the two of you should talk again after Belize. That's the extent of it, Boss."

Jack laughed at her formality. "You did good. The new information fits perfectly into my speculations concerning Will and the others. There's a reason this airline is named CAT: cats have at least nine lives. I've been with Will Fischer for eleven years, and he still has a few lives left. This is getting more interesting as we go along.

"I'm also wondering why, in these eleven years, I never met Atom. I flew Clare, Angelina, and Gloria, but never Atom. Will talked a whole lot about him, so I'm asking myself why now is the time and here is the place? Like my favorite character Alice, in Alice in Wonderland, what I'm sensing is getting curiouser and curiouser. Don't you just love it?"

Jackie smiled and went back to checking the controls to discern their exact location and the condition of the weather. She knew very little of what Jack was talking about concerning the Fischer family, and she counted it as not being her business.

The balance of the flight was uneventful. The cabin lights brightened as the plane began its final descent into the Belize airport at San Pedro on Ambergris Caye. The aircraft touched down and the passengers prepared to depart. Jackie opened the door, exited, and waited for the travelers at the bottom of the five steps while the ground crew unloaded the few bags the Jameson's had stowed. Atom and Captain Jack were the last to exit. The Jameson's monitored their bags as they came out and cordially said their thanks and good-byes to Captain Jack and Jackie. Atom was standing by himself basking in the warm humid night air of the Caribbean.

Robert Jameson walked over to Atom, shook his hand, and again apologized for his seeming impropriety. He handed Atom his business card and said, "If you ever need a friend, you have one in me. I lost my dad awhile back. We were close. It was a great loss for me, and I still don't think I'm over it. You and I share some common ground, and I'd deem it an honor to be able to cover it with you. I'd also like to pursue our mutual interest in eco-stewardship from an entrepreneurial point of view. We could be helpful to each other. Please call when the time is ripe."

Atom was surprised at Robert's demeanor, his desire to reconnect, and his use of the word ripe. It was all quite unusual. "I honor your candor and kindness. I'll call when the mist clears. Thank you."

As Robert walked away, Aisha approached Atom with a smile and a gracious handshake. "We just met and I haven't said a word to you, my son, but my daughter's correct. There's something very different about you, and I want you to know that you are welcome in my home. Please come and visit us." She bowed and joined her husband standing beside their luggage. Atom returned the bow.

Inana stood silently waiting her turn to say good-bye. She stepped forward, took his hands in hers, and looked deeply into his dark blue eyes. "This is the strangest and most wonderful flight I've ever experienced, and I don't completely know what happened in that plane, but I do know that something turned in me. Something rearranged itself because of you. You have inside you something I've been looking for all my life. If I could, I'd walk right back into that plane with you and take on whatever we'd find together. I know that's not possible now, and it may never be, so this is a good-bye and a hello. Know that you are anointed and blessed for the journey you are on. We are together and will be together *inshallah*." Inana kissed him on both cheeks, smiled, and bowed slightly before joining her parents who were walking toward the customs officials waiting at their limousine.

Captain Jack and Jackie walked to the office of the private aircraft section of the airport, a much more casual place than the public areas. Here, there was an understanding of the clientele's effect on the politics and economies of the country. No one flying private faced the rigors involved with international flights. The paperwork was extensive, but the passengers never saw it. They simply paid, answered a few questions, had their passports stamped, and went their way.

Atom stood silently watching the dramas unfold, not knowing how, or why it was all happening. He felt a deep emotion that had somehow come to him through this strange and intriguing trip. He watched the Jameson's walk toward their ride, the ground crew move toward their next jobs, and Captain Jack and Jackie disappear through the door of the customs office. He used this opportunity to stretch and enjoy the warm autumn night breeze rustle the palm trees and blow through his sandy blond hair. Despite the disturbing news regarding *Mystic Travelers*, he felt invigorated by the conversations he'd had with Inana, Robert and Aisha Jameson, Jackie, and Captain Jack. He couldn't help but feel flattered by Inana's forthright admission of her attraction to him. He allowed himself the flattery and then shook it off, refocusing on the deeper movements of the day.

He wondered at the further enlightenment he would discover flying into Camp Bay Island and meeting with his uncle Derick. Atom was excited for the meeting and the drama of this unfolding adventure. What would he find? What did Derick know that the rest of his family did not? What strings was he pulling in what parts of the world to do whatever Will had directed? So many questions. Jackie and Captain Jack returned before he could sort them out.

Captain Jack greeted Atom as he approached the plane. "All clear and all aboard! A hop, skip, and a jump, and we'll be on family ground at Camp Bay Island." He put his arm around Atom's shoulder for a moment, let go, and followed him up the five steps into the Hawker 1000.

When they got inside the aircraft, Jack stopped Atom, pointed to a seat and said, "This time you sit where Mr. Jameson sat. It's the best seat in the house, and I'll come out and talk with you here after we get to altitude." Jack turned and entered the cockpit to start the engines while Atom buckled his seat belt. Jackie pulled up the door, locked it down, and moved from flight attendant to copilot. Within a few minutes, they were taxiing down the runway, lifting off, and climbing fast toward the Bay Islands of Roatan off the coast of Honduras. Atom looked out the window onto the water that reflected the moon in the sky. *What a night to be flying.*

Within ten minutes, they had reached altitude and leveled off. The cockpit door opened and Captain Jack came out to park himself where Inana had sat, diagonal to Atom. He pulled a lever beneath the arm of the seat to slide it a bit into the aisle, as did Atom. The corners of the large leather seats were almost touching. This gave them both more head and legroom. Captain Jack began the conversation.

"We don't have much time as we're already cleared to land at Camp Bay and it's less than an hour away. Jackie said you wanted to speak with me?"

Atom leaned forward, rested his left elbow on the arm of his leather chair, and looked directly at Jack. Captain Jack relaxed as he observed and listened. "You gave me some significant insights into Dad that I already had but at the same time, didn't have. They confirmed the impressions and speculations I didn't really want to deal with. This whole series of events over the past two days caught me way off guard, Jack. Maybe it was because I thought my dad was invincible or that I've been so wrapped up in my own research. I'm probably in denial. Despite all that, I woke up this afternoon and remembered the last thing Dad said to me after talking about commitment to the family, the vision of our ancestors, and all the rest. The last thing he said was 'no matter what happens, go see Derick.' That message just popped into my consciousness this afternoon. It was like a direct message from him in that very moment. So I shut down my research, threw a few things in a bag, and here I am. It's led to an amazing array of events I couldn't have predicted, each significant in their own right."

Atom paused to breathe in that thought, shifted his position and continued. "The conversation I had with Robert Jameson was strange. At first I was put off, I thought he was just another arrogant rich guy setting me up to put me down. We actually found some common ground through our fathers and eco-stewardship, of all things. He ended up giving me his business card and invited me to connect as a friend whenever the time was ripe. That was an interesting phrase, too. In all the flights I've taken with CAT, my connections have never been so intimate, impressionistic, or mysterious. What do you make of it?"

"What do you make of it, Master Atom?" responded Captain Jack.

"Master Atom? Why did you just call me that? No one has ever called me that except Dad."

"Really? It just came out that way. I guess I said it out of respect for who you are. I never heard it before either. Maybe your dad's in this plane with us directing what we're experiencing. I'm ruling nothing out when it comes to him and all the synchronistic events that are happening here."

"Dad in this aircraft, on a different astral plane, participating with us in some unknown and yet known way? Hmm, that's a bit of a stretch. Then there's the whole conspiracy thing. Why create an event that figuratively and literally takes him out of the picture so he can more fully be in the picture?" Atom paused to let his intuitive imagination work.

Captain Jack broke the silence after Atom's eyes shifted from the floor to him. "It begs a further question. Why are we together at this particular time, in this particular place, with these particular events? Why, in all these years of travel, have we not met? Do you suppose your dad planned our meeting like this for some special reason?"

"Let's assume that's the case," Atom responded. "What might some of the reasons be? What kind of relationship do you have with Dad? Besides being his personal pilot and captain of the fleet, what roles have you been playing for him? Confidante, intermediary, collaborator, messenger, cover agent, front man, side man, investigator, what?"

Captain Jack sat back in his seat a little farther, leaned his head back on the headrest, closed his eyes, and breathed a deep sigh. He was struggling with how and what to say in response to Atom's very direct question. How much to reveal? What would Will want from him in this moment for his son? What was the appropriate answer? There were so many roles, so many jobs, and so many crosscurrents. Jack leaned forward to address the question.

"To put it very simply, I am your dad's friend, confidante, and driver. I'm a pilot, a transport expert. I know how to deal with people, places, situations, and things. I know how to get people in and out of places effectively and silently, if need be. Your dad and I have been in plenty of tight spots in our globetrotting together, and I'm the guy who knows how to get him in and out. If he is really gone or somewhere between here and there that I can't go, then maybe he set this up so I could stand in with you in the same way."

"Stand in with me? What does that mean?" asked Atom, somewhat surprised.

"On the last trip we took together, he said something kind of weird to me that I've just now remembered. We were talking about the family interests and the Great Turning that the world seems to be going through. Your name came up as it did so many times in our more personal conversations, but in a way that it hadn't before. It was something like, *When the time comes, your charge will shift to Atom. You'll be for him what you have been for me all these years. You'll know when it happens.* I haven't thought of that until right now. This must be the happening! We're together because your dad put us together. You have a new mission, and it looks like we'll find out what it is together." Jack's voice was excited and enthusiastic. "Wow! That puts a completely new spin on this flight. We may be in a whole new chapter of the book!"

"What are you so upbeat about? I'm not sure I like what's being set up here."

"What were the words you got so excited about that put you on this plane?"

"Go see Derick."

"So, in going to see Derick on this particular day, who is here to help you but good old Captain Jack. Your dad is a genius. The joke's on both of us. Here we think it's just another day that we're controlling, but we're part of something much bigger. And then there's the Jameson family. I wonder how they fit into this puzzle?" Jack paused and looked at Atom with the question, then continued. "This is magnificent, Atom. I can hardly wait to see what happens next. I have a sneaking suspicion the answers lie at Camp Bay Island. What do you think?"

Atom's demeanor changed with the enthusiasm Captain Jack brought to the situation. He took a deep breath, and with a great sigh and a large smile he began laughing.

"What a very strange day it's been. It sure is great to meet you, Captain Jack Hawkins. Looks like we're on this ride together, and if only half of what we've speculated is true then we're just beginning, and this ride could last a lifetime."

"Well, Master Atom, what else do you have to do that's more important right now?"

"Not a thing, Captain, not a blessed thing. It's great to be aboard."

They slid their seats back toward the wall, unbuckled their seat belts, stood up, and gave each other an embrace that spanned the centuries. After all this time, here they were on an adventure into the darkness, into the mystery. They had finally met and bonded, brought together by a simple and complicated set of circumstances and unseen forces. They were flying between the earth and the heavens, through the darkness and the light. They were strangers and friends, mystic travelers on a journey into the unknown. What would it bring?

Chapter 33

*Maturity, and perhaps enlightenment, consists in seeing reality as it
is, even when it is at variance with our dearest hopes and most firmly
held convictions. In the Way of Science, one learns to adapt one's
schemes to the world, instead of trying to make the world conform to
one's own schemes. Every Way is an invitation to unlearn.*
-Piero Ferrucci-

The Beechcraft Hawker 1000 made its approach and descent to
Camp Bay Island. The landing lights were on, the runway was
clear, the touchdown was perfect. Jackie, Atom, and Captain Jack
walked down the steps of the aircraft to set foot on an island that
had been inhabited over the centuries by Paya Indians, slaves,
pirates, buccaneers, fishermen, merchants, traders, Puritans,
European explorers, and during the past seven decades, the Fischer
family. Atom's great grandfather was the youngest son born into an
entrepreneurial family from Strasbourg, France, in 1885. Having
three older brothers in the family business, he realized he would
never rise above them, so at the age of twenty, he headed out on
his own to the New World of the United States of America.

He had relatives in New Orleans, Louisiana, so eventually
settled there, got involved in the shipping industry, and
discovered the Honduras of Central America. Over time, he
bought undeveloped property on the mainland and on the island
of Roatan. Camp Bay Island was a purchase he made in the 1930s
as a base camp off the island of Roatan for his personal and family

privacy, security, and serenity. He passed it on to his only son Pierre, Atom's grandfather, who further developed it into a family compound and an agricultural enterprise planting coconut palm trees on every available acre of the private sanctuary.

In the seventies, Will began developing part of the island as his secondary research base where he and his family could spend significant time and escape the severe winters at Sunnyview and the pace of the United States.

Derick took over the operation of the island and the family's South, Central, and North American import, export, and travel enterprises after Pierre died at the age of eighty-three. Derick had his primary residence on Camp Bay Island at the edge of Port Royal Harbor, a half-mile out from the main island where the original family house was still standing and functioned as an office and guesthouse. Camp Bay Island was the passageway into Port Royal Harbor since the shallow reef that created the harbor was only open next to the island, creating a gateway. It had always been a perfect place for smaller, shallower draft ships to anchor, which is why so many used it during the centuries as an anchorage. For the present day Fischer family, it was still a safe harbor.

Derick, and his two right-hand men, Estefan and Pablo, were waiting for Atom when he deplaned. Atom adjusted his eyes to the night as he moved down the steps onto the holy ground of Camp Bay Island. The memories he'd collected during his twenty-six years, along with the stories that were told of the island's history and the Fischer family's place in it, had always fascinated him. Within the marrow of his bones, he sensed this as the one place on earth he could call home. Sunnyview was the home where he'd been taught how to do. Camp Bay Island was the home where he'd learned how to be. This place, this time, this set of circumstances, was touching places within him he rarely accessed consciously.

When Atom looked up to see his dad's brother, tears welled up in his heart and trickled down his cheeks. His uncle stepped forward to meet him. They drew each other close and merged into a family portrait that had been painted centuries earlier and would forever be etched in their hearts and minds. This family, who had endured and celebrated thousands of years of movement was still intact, still viable, still on a mission, still together in the continuum of history.

In that moment, their relationship changed. They were no longer separate entities on the journey of life; rather, they were now consciously united in a bond that had always been there, yet not acknowledged. Derick had stepped into his brother's place. Atom had stepped into his uncle's place. A new cosmic bond had been forged. Without saying a word, they knew their lives would never be the same.

The moment was not lost on Captain Jack. Because of his intimate relationships with Will and Derick and now Atom, he sensed the passage and new relationship. He knew in the depth of his soul that his close friend, William Clarence Fischer, had given attention to every detail within his control in facilitating this transition. He stood in humble awe of the position he was given as guardian and pilot of Atom, who was now stepping up into a very different place in the structure of the family as every son and daughter had before him.

"Atom Ion Fischer," Derick said as he embraced his nephew. "It's so wonderful to have you here with us! I was so happy when I got your message a few hours ago, and now here you are. This whole experience is so surreal it's hard to believe. *Bienvenidos!* Welcome!"

In that moment, all Atom could do was smile and allow the tears to run down his cheeks. He didn't seem to have any words to communicate the feelings and thoughts coursing through him, although some appeared.

"I'm here for the whole family," he heard himself say, reconnecting with the moment and the directive given him by his dad. "What do we need to do?"

"We'll see," replied Derick.

The warmth of their embrace lingered as Atom moved to greet Estefan and Pablo, who had been with the family most of their lives, and as Derick joyfully greeted Jackie and Captain Jack. As the initial greetings concluded, Estefan escorted Jackie to her place of lodging for the night while Pablo tended the Hawker. Atom, Derick, and Captain Jack rode together in an electric cart to the main lodge.

The light of the partial moon reflected off the water as they pulled onto the grounds of the lodge, parked the cart, and walked the short distance to the beach. Derick threw a few small logs on the fire that had burned down to red glowing coals. The wood caught and flamed in the fire pit. They sat down on the three beach chairs, removed their shoes, and enjoyed the feel of warm sand between their toes. The gentle rhythm of the sea lapping the beach was dancing with the slight breeze blowing through the palm trees and the new fire. Derick broke the silence.

"As you both now know, the events of the past few days have been filled with mystery and wonder. I suspect Will and the Company have been working on this plan from before he was born.

"Will and his team are here physically, showing up on schedule. Otherwise, however, they're not here." The words lingered in the night. Atom leaned forward frowning with concern.

Derick held up his hand as if in defense. "When Will brought me in on this end of the plan, he warned me that the whole experiment had a margin of error and uncertainty in it that he and his team were willing to take. What was at risk was the teleportation within the vortex of the storm, the water, and the boat. Timing was critical. He laid out the possible scenarios we could expect, and we got one of them. The team all showed up physically intact but in a state of suspended animation."

"They're all here, on this island, as we speak?" asked Atom.

Derick nodded slowly with raised eyebrows and wide-open eyes.

"Exactly what does suspended animation mean?" Captain Jack asked.

"It's like being in a coma but not. If Will hadn't briefed me on this possibility, we would have thought they were dead and disposed of their bodies. Their pulse and breathing was mostly imperceptible. The glow of their assemblage points was extremely dim, yet stable, which is a sign of life and consciousness. Nobody here had ever seen anything like it. Through our network, we consulted an old shaman from the mountains on the mainland. He told us they were traveling in other dimensions and had left their bodies so they could return if called to do so. That's all we know. Will directed me that if this happened, to simply maintain the physical forms at a constant temperature of seventy-two degrees, keep them lightly covered with cotton sheets, and wait. Tomorrow will be the fourth day, and there's been no change in their physical status thus far." Derick waited patiently for the shock to dissipate while he put another small log on the fire, sat back, and watched it burn.

Captain Jack leaned forward to address Derick. "I knew absolutely nothing about any of this until Atom showed up at the airport today." He ran his hand through his hair and across his face then smiled broadly. "I'm honored to be here with you. Just let me know what I can do."

"They're coming back," Atom interjected, standing up to pace in front of the two older men. "The very last thing Dad said to me as he was telling me about this, in his own coded way, was to go see Derick. That's what I remembered this afternoon and that's why I'm here tonight. When that message arose from my memory, there was no hesitation, no question of what I needed to do. There seems to be an emerging pattern here. If not, why would the three of us be together in this place at this time? The fact that Dad laid out the contingencies to you, Derick, and brought Jack and me together to be with you on this night is filled with possibilities and potentialities. They're coming back soon. I don't know what that means for them, the planet, or us, but there's something going on here that he conveyed to all of us. It's how he does everything. His acts seem random but there's always a pattern, always an intention. A picture here points to an entanglement between countless people, places, situations, and things. It will be made much clearer when they return. We're all in a process of realignment with Dad and his team and the whole Company of Shmya! Where are the vessels, the bodies? I need to see them and sit with them."

"They're in G4 of the research building. I'll take you there."

"Am I bunking in my usual place?" Captain Jack asked Derick.

"Yes, it's waiting for you."

"Then I'm going to bed. I hate to leave, but I have to get up before dawn to be in Panama City by seven, and the two of you should be alone together now anyway. You know how to get in touch with me. I know we're still cloaked, so everything will be coded concerning this mission. Atom, you need to know that you now have your dad's priority booking code. Here's my card with his code written on it. I figured this might happen after our last conversation. It's now yours. Memorize it then throw it in the fire. It hasn't changed since we set it up more than a decade ago. Your old one will be on file for your son or daughter, whichever comes first." He handed the card to Atom as he got up, gave a slight salute to Derick, and headed for his bed.

Derick and Atom stood, dusted the sand from their pants, and walked to the research building and G4 carrying their shoes. Atom found it hard to concentrate on anything except seeing the bodies of his father and crew, but made the effort to change the subject and redirect the focus. "How's Anna, are you guys still together?"

"Going on five years now, and hey, I have some great news. We're pregnant and expecting within the next couple months."

"What? Wow! Congratulations, that's great! Does that mean that after all these years you've finally sown enough wild oats to settle down, raise a family, and get married again?"

Derick laughed. "Anna's a very special person. She loves me, cares for me, seems to understand me, and puts up with me like no other woman ever has. She's kind, compassionate, contained, courageous, really smart, and downright beautiful. I can't imagine finishing this life without her, so yeah, over these years, I guess you could say we've become married to each other. I've never felt this way about a woman. I really care about her. I want to be there for her in every way. We're even talking about making it legal."

"What citizenship will you give the baby?" Atom asked.

"We're still not sure. Now that dual citizenship is part of the equation, it would be much simpler to do the birthing in the states. Citizenship in Honduras after that would be simple. Not so the other way around. So, we're leaning toward a trip to Louisiana."

"It seems you've come a long way since we last saw each other. I look forward to seeing her. I've always liked her a lot and have sensed a depth in her that has nurtured you. Everything's lining up for the newness that is birthing right here in our midst. You're finally going to have an heir, and I'm finally going to have a cousin. I'll have to spend more time with you guys so the little one will get to know me as well as I got to know you when I was a youngster.

"What great news to accompany the other news about Dad and his team. I just knew he was here somewhere, still connected to the earth plane. What an experience he must be having surfing the unknown reaches of multidimensionality. I can hardly wait to reconnect."

They walked into the research building, brushed the sand off their feet, put on their shoes, pressed the down button on the elevator, entered, and descended to G4. The elevator door opened into a hallway. Derick led Atom into a large dimly lit room. Five beds were evenly spaced along the wall. There was another door, with an inset window, at the other side of the room. The bodies of Will and his team were lying on their backs and covered with cotton sheets. What Atom saw was significantly different from what he had visualized. The stark reality before him seemed like a dream.

Atom concentrated on his breath to ground himself and align with what he saw before him. He slowly walked along the foot of every bed, looking at the inert bodies lying as if dead under the sheets. The heads were exposed, eyes closed, peaceful and quiet. At the end of the room lay his father. Atom walked to the side of his bed and stood looking at the face of the man who had helped bring him into this world, nurture, teach, love, and inspire him. A flood of emotions rippled through his body causing him to breathe deeper and more fully ground himself.

"Are they clothed?" he asked Derick, who was standing close behind him.

"Yes, when they arrived here they were soaked with water, so we washed and dried their clothes and put them back on after we also washed and dried their bodies."

Atom pulled the sheet down just below his father's waist and recognized the flannel shirt. "I'm going to touch him," he said to Derick. "I'm going to place my hands over the seven chakras and scan his energy body: the crown of his head, forehead, throat, heart, navel, solar plexus, and pubic bone, and then over his assemblage point. I'd then like to sit with him for a while. I don't know how long this will take. You can stay or leave any time. When I'm done, I'll probably go back out to the fire or take a walk or do whatever I feel directed to do. I promised Clare I would contact her telepathically tonight at the guru hour to let her know what I discovered. I'll have the image when I finish this process with Dad. I won't be able to speak with you until after my communication with Clare. What time is it now?"

"It's almost midnight, central time. Clare's on eastern, so it's one o'clock there. You have two hours if your arrangement with Clare is on her time."

"It is, thanks, that's perfect. When Clare and I do this kind of thing, which we haven't done in quite a while, we never know the timing to get a clear image. I think I want to be on the beach by 2:45 a.m. eastern time, so we're good. When will you be up in the morning?"

"Not sure. I may keep the vigil with you, take a walk, or go rest with Anna. I usually get up before dawn, but with all that's happening I probably won't be able to sleep much." Derick paused and said, "I'm really glad you're here, Atom, this is perfect."

They stood facing each other, put their hands on each other's shoulders, and leaned together touching foreheads. They held the posture until the rhythm of their hearts became one. Their energy merged with vitality and radiance. They slowly parted and Derick quietly left.

Atom touched his father's forehead expecting it to be cold, but it was warm and life was present. He started his scanning ritual and felt the modest maintenance energy still living in Will's body. The diagnosis Derick and his associates made seemed accurate. Atom then went briefly to each of the team members, feeling their energy fields and touching their foreheads. They all registered the same low-level life energy function.

Atom returned to his dad, knelt beside the bed, clasped his left hand with his left hand, and placed his right hand on Will's heart. He held that position for more than an hour feeling the faint, almost imperceptible pulse and breath.

As the time approached to go to the beach and begin his transmission to Clare, the image formed in his mind's eye. Atom placed Will's hands back in the position he found them—left folded over right on his abdomen—and pulled the cotton sheet up just below his chin. He then rested his forehead on the chest of Will's body, over his heart for another minute, kissed his dad's forehead, bowed, and left the building. The warmth of the night air and the gentle breeze soothed his soul as he stopped on the porch of the research building. *They're on their way*, he heard a still, small voice say within the depths of his being. *They're coming back.*

He walked down the porch steps and through the palm trees to the edge of the beach. He stood entranced, embracing the night. The image of the five-team members covered with sheets lying on beds began to form in his mind. Above the beds was a shimmering, teal colored OK sign. His eyes were open in soft focus as he looked north across the Caribbean sea into the Gulf of Mexico, across the continental United States, to a tiny spot in a kiva in the Upper Peninsula of Michigan where his sister Clare was sitting in the silent receptivity of quantum entanglement.

The picture was clear. She saw the beds, the sheets, the faces, and the OK sign shining with shmaya energy, the vibrancy of life and light. Clare smiled as she received the message. She felt a strange and wonderful energy course through her that aligned with Atom. She interpreted it as a body prayer being sent with the image. It was a double message of all rightness and ripeness in form and formlessness. Clare and Atom, sister and brother, connected. The message was clear. The message was truth. The message was life.

Chapter 34

You are the world.
-Krishnamurti-

It was dark in the kiva, save for a single lit candle in the middle of the floor. Clare, seated on a cushion, sat in the silent glow of the moment.

She continued to sit in Atom's presence. Her mind relived the many experiences her brother and she had shared in their quarter century of life together. She saw them playing hide-and-seek in the woods surrounding the compound, experimenting with mental telepathy, tutored by their grandmother. An image appeared of them sailing with their parents aboard *Mystic Travelers* across the calm waters of Lake Michigan. She watched as their younger selves worked together in the fields and gardens of Sunnyview, created meals and washed dishes in the café kitchen, chanted and danced together in the kiva, and walked hand in hand as big sister and little brother along the paths of the lake.

As these memories flooded her, she reflected on the gifts she had received in this incarnation with her fellow travelers. She then saw the distance between past and future coming together in the present moment and wondered at the illusion of time and space.

Where does reality exist? What is reality? Does it change with the seasons of one's life or with the electricity of one's mind? How many realities are there, and can I say anything, or even know anything with absolute certainty? Why are there moments of great lucidity as well as moments of great confusion? How is it that the more I know, the more I come to know I don't know? Questions and answers leading to more questions. It is Ola Kala, O so beautiful, awesome, and wonderful.

Clare gently completed her meditation and blew out the candle. She made the short walk up the steps and through the hall into the Sunnyview café where Gloria and Angelina silently waited for her return. Her walk was brisk as she became more excited to share Atom's vision with them. The two older women sensed her approach. She walked into the light of the room with a radiance that enveloped them. Their demeanor changed in that moment as they connected with her energy. Clare smiled and quickly slid into the booth next to her mother. The three held hands with closed eyes and shared the image Atom had sent, all awakening to the silence and the vision. The joy of the revelation reverberated through their circle as Clare slowly let the image fade. They all came together in understanding and opened their eyes.

Angelina was first to speak. "I'm grateful to know Will still has a connection to form. His absence at all levels has been difficult for me, and I'm so glad Atom is there with him, it eases my concern. It seems we simply need to stay the course and wait for further guidance. We're on the edge of something new that requires heightened awareness, patience, and attentiveness."

"What are you sensing, Clare?" Gloria asked.

Clare's eyes became wide as she shook her head slightly, trying to sort out her impressions. "There's something about this that feels like we are crossing over into another dimension, just as Dad did. Although this new twist is definitely surprising, isn't it what we've been doing all our lives? Isn't this what the convergence of science, spirituality, and the arts is intended to do, to take us into a new expanded consciousness? Evolution seems to move along slowly, and then at certain times, a shift propels everything into a new pattern. I sense this could be what's happening.

"The whole science of teleportation is unknown to all but a handful of people on the planet, and this new twist of suspended animation, near death experience for days, is beyond today's science. It's not like a coma. It's like death but with the option of coming back into the same form. Maybe even changing the form. I'm excited and willing to learn all that's happening here. It's awesome that there's still a lot that hasn't been revealed, and we're on the leading edge of that revelation. I'm sure that when Dad chooses to return, or is sent back to us, we will gain greater access to what's really going on and be able to participate. I sense that all of this is happening *for* us, not *to* us, for very good reasons, and we must appreciate all of it in every conceivable way. That's what I'm getting. What about you, Gram?"

Gloria was always nurturing her granddaughter into expanding awareness. She had inherited the gifts of clairvoyance, clairaudience, and multisensory thought through her lineage. They had become precious to her, as she had been able to perceive them as gifts to be used for the highest good. In recognizing this, she had helped to cultivate the skills in her own daughter and two grandchildren. To watch them grow and use these powers in ways they were intended, always helped to reinforce her continuing role and influence. As sole surviving elder of her clan, she was aware of every possible opportunity to create forward movement for their family mission throughout the ages. She sometimes chose the opportunities with great vigor and other times with reluctance. Today she was both reluctant and enthusiastic as she sought resonance and balance in this new movement.

"I've completed close to nine decades here on this earth. The changes I've experienced have been no less than miraculous. The science fiction of even fifty years ago is the reality of today. Your father is not only a visionary, but also an innovator, inventor, and co-creator. He created social networks with tens of thousands of people before the Internet was invented, and he did it face-to-face, person-to-person. He brought people together from all over the world to work on projects that helped expand human consciousness and serve the greater good. He is a natural born innovator and bridge builder. This recent series of events seems to be some kind of ending and beginning for him, his intimate team of associates, our family, and the world. Maybe what is ending is a business as usual attitude. Maybe the ending is a consciousness of duality that sees everything in either-or terms, thus creating competitive enemies everywhere. Maybe the ending is a recognition that we, as a species, can't keep doing what we've done with reckless abandon and lack of concern for life in all its various forms, creating short-term gains and long-term losses. Maybe the beginning is an awakening to the fragility and shortness of material life and the strength and length of life in spiritual or non-material forms."

Gloria paused to regain focus. She looked at her daughter and granddaughter and then picked up her glass to sip some water. She slowly replaced the glass to the table, folded her hands, and continued.

"There are so many endings and beginnings that need to happen, so many obstacles and limitations that need to be rolled away. Thank goodness, every ending comes with a new beginning. These endings and beginnings happen every day, everywhere. Fear and greed have reached epidemic proportions. They continue to be nurtured by everyone who wants to take selfish advantage. The blind continue to lead the blind. The dead continue to lead the dead. The lies continue to lead the truth, and so few of the world's people are being fed what they really need. Systems are crumbling while those in power try to bolster them, simply by reverting to more of the same, which cannot be sustained." Gloria shifted position, took another sip of water, and went on.

"We're in an opportune time for something great to happen. With the ripeness of all the necessary energies converging, there can be a great harvest of beneficence. The season seems to be upon us, my loves."

She reached out and squeezed the hands of the two younger women. "We as a species discovered fire about six hundred thousand years ago. That simple discovery changed everything.

Maybe we've come to another time where a new kind of fire will be kindled that will again change everything. Maybe with this new fire, those of us who are still here with mother earth and all of creation will be the ones to lead the way."

"What do you think the new fire is?' Clare questioned, leaning forward in anticipation.

"That's what we are being aligned with, Clare. We must continue to listen and give witness from our depths. It probably has to do with compassion, interconnectivity, and non-duality. Teilhard said it would be harnessing the energies of love. I think he's on the right track. We'll see."

Chapter 35

The day will come when after we have mastered the winds,
the waves, the tides, and gravity; we shall harness the energies
of Love. Then, for the second time in the history of the world,
humankind will have discovered fire.
-Pierre Teilhard de Chardin-

Atom had moved beyond time and space while connecting with the modest life force within the bodies of his father and his associates. Time, in a sense, stood still. There was no awareness of passing through anything, just a simple presence with what he was attending to.

He now found himself back at the fire pit where the flames had seemingly gone out. He picked up a stick, stirred the ashes, and noticed a few small glowing coals. He took a machete lying next to a stack of logs and shaved off a few thin pieces of dry wood. He placed the thinnest shavings over the small glowing coals and gently breathed on them. With little effort, the shavings caught fire. He continued to work with the machete, shaving off larger pieces of wood and within moments, the fire blazed. He took a seat in the chair he'd been in a few hours earlier and looked at his watch: four ten a.m. eastern time. More than three hours had passed since he was here with Derick and Captain Jack.

It was the guru hour here and a brand new day. He smiled, aware of his breath—calm, centered, and balanced. He looked into the fire to see what kind of message might be sent to him through this medium. Lost in the meditation of earth, air, fire, and water, he noticed a whole group of men in the fire scrutinizing him with stern expressions. They were evaluating and challenging him to see if he was worthy of their assistance and companionship. They were all ages and races; some bearded with long hair and others clean-shaven with bald heads. All were curious and inquiring. The scene changed as a log shifted, reconfiguring the stack of wood. Suddenly a whole group of women appeared, also scrutinizing him. The looks upon their faces, however, were smiling and inviting. They, too, were testing his valor and character. There were old hags and crones as well as beautiful young maidens and everything in between. All were inviting and challenging Atom, the young warrior. He saw both groups as Ancients of Days.

Are you who you need to be to travel with us? Are you mature enough, strong enough, gentle enough, and aware enough? Are you humble enough, tested, and tempered enough? How teachable are you? Do you have the courage it takes to be a true servant? The questions were from another realm. Another log dropped, having burned to pieces. The images disappeared. The questions, the faces, the generations of these archetypal masculine and feminine images and energies stayed with him as he sat and pondered their appearance at this time in his life.

Why are they showing up now? What assistance can they offer? Are they real or a figment of my imagination? Both? How teachable am I, really? It seems my whole life has been one long series of teachings from the Alexander family to the Fischer family. What beckons from the other side of the veil where Dad is journeying? Patience, persistence, presence. Ola Kala.

Atom put another log on the fire and relaxed in his chair. The day's events were catching up with him, fatigue settled in his muscles and bones. He closed his eyes and saw the glow of the fire through his eyelids as a bright ball of light diminished to a tiny pinhole of light. He drifted effortlessly into sleep. Not knowing how long he'd been sleeping, he awakened upon hearing a voice.

"Wonderful isn't it, the magnificence of creation?"

Atom slowly opened his eyes, trying to break through the fog of sleep. He gently turned his head to see whom the voice belonged. His first thought was Derick. Seeing deeper into the image, he felt a subtle then vital energy charge that sat him upright, upset his balance, and tipped him over onto the sand. He scrambled to his hands and knees reaching out to connect.

"Dad! You're back!" He crawled in the sand seeking an embrace. With awkward agility, they both managed to find the wonder of physical touch. They held each other for a timeless moment, plumbing the depths of this infinite, loving companion presence.

Atom loosened his grip and rolled over in the sand, feeling the warmth of his dad's presence and the strength of his pulse, and with animated enthusiasm, he spoke.

"It's all different now, isn't it?" Atom asked as he gained a new composure and climbed back onto his low-slung beach chair.

"Yes, Atom, it's all very different." Will paused, returning to his chair to bask in the gaze of his son. The glow of firelight cast a halo around the two men and marked the magic of the moment. "These last few days in earth time have been centuries in cosmic time. What we experienced touched infinity and was beyond anything we can ever fully explain. It's ineffable and yet, it's imperative we find ways to share and transmit it. It will take a lifetime to scratch the surface of what's been revealed. That's why we returned to this plane of existence. Our mission has expanded and intensified. There will be no more business as usual. Strangely, though, everything we are being called to do is quite ordinary and fits into the everyday scheme of things. The difference has to do with focused intention and purposeful action." Will paused while they allowed the words to settle and the fire to burn.

"Each millennium, each century, each generation, each decade, has its dangers and opportunities, its challenges and successes, its potentialities and possibilities. Some are radical while others are modest. We are in a period of decline and ascent, of radical endings and beginnings. We've been given a directive to take a quantum leap in our evolutionary trajectory. We have come back to help create an environment in which this change can take place. We are new yeast in the bread of life." Atom listened and wondered what this meant for him and millions of others like him.

"The five of us, each from different continents and cultures, will be working with everyone we know to engage this mission of rapidly elevating and expanding the states and stages of human consciousness. The twenty-first century is a pivot point in the great experiment of planet earth, Gaia, and her inhabitants. Greater assistance is being given from sister realms for us to make this significant inner and outer course correction in our evolving trajectory. Those who are not in alignment with the Divine Source will no longer find the energy to sustain themselves. Their energy will dissipate and be lost, their lives diminished and sent back for review and realignment. Ascending energy will overtake descending energy as we all move beyond our small, constricted egoic minds into the large Meta Mind. Contraction and expansion is giving birth to a new creation and we are *all* a part of it.

"This clarion call is to a Sacred Stewardship of all the resources we have at our disposal, including our own creativity and interconnectivity. We are the New Creation.

"Practically speaking, we're being directed to participate in radically new ways in the highest calling of creation: the Art of Life. It's what we've been doing at Sunnyview and here at Camp Bay most our lives. For us then, it's just bringing what we've been doing and being to a few hundred million more people. The tipping point will be reached and the garden will flourish, because the energy will all be ascending. Any questions?"

"Only a couple thousand and all but two can wait. What's my part and how will it be directed?"

"No questions about what we experienced, who we met, what the other realms were like, the storm, our new powers, the future of Fischer Enterprises, what we learned, timelines, analysis, deployment, et cetera."

"I figure all that will come as needed. This is a lifetime of work, and you were all sent back here to help orchestrate this transition. I'm assuming you'll be around for a good long while. Have all the personal changes necessary for you to engage this expanded mission already been made so they are fully operational?" Atom asked, putting on his engineering hat.

"Yes, and we'll continue to grow in insight and power as the flower unfolds. There are infinite variables, so we must remain vigilant and flexible. I'll be greeting Derick in a few minutes, connect with Captain Jack, convene with my associates, and transport to Sunnyview to make the rounds with our family and friends. Your part is linked to our close nuclear extended family, your energy project, and to me.

"I have a whole new set of formulas for you to complete your dissertation and experimental research. Through your discoveries, we're going to revolutionize the global energy systems, which will significantly turn the tables in the marketplace and seats of power. The walls of greed and control will come tumbling down while the humble and pure of heart will be blessed and empowered with unlimited free energy. It's going to be quite a movie. You'll stay here with Derick and Anna until I reconnect with you."

"Same as always, Dad. You're the man with the plan. It's no wonder you were chosen for this assignment. Who else? I'm proud to be under your authority. The Ancients of Days showed up just before you did. I think they still have some doubts about me, as they should. I still have some doubts about me." Atom chuckled as he stood up feeling the enthusiasm of a child. "I'll follow your lead and do whatever I'm directed to do be do be do be do, Mr. Sinatra! How do I connect with you if I have a need?"

Will stood to join his son, connecting heart to heart. "Remember CAT, it's about Compassion, Appreciation, and Transmission. When you enter deeply into these three awakenings, you'll always connect with the essence and there I am, or as a song from the sixties goes: winter, spring, summer, or fall, all you gotta do is call, and I'll be there!"

193

Atom and Will smiled and nodded a core understanding and appreciation. They held the pose with great compassion and care and felt the alignment and deep connection. Atom closed his eyes for a moment to create an inner picture of his dad standing in the glow of the firelight. When he opened them, Will was gone.

Chapter 36

Magnanimity is the expansion of the soul to great things. Magnanimous people put themselves in all kinds of danger for great things, for instance, the common welfare, justice, divine service, and so forth.
-Thomas Aquinas-

After the tour and teleportation demonstration under the pyramid, Michael needed to get some air. He walked out the back door of the café, and Favor followed at a distance. The long deck stretched out across the length of the building. Michael walked to the edge, stepped off, and sat on the ground, his back leaning against the side of the deck. Favor did the same. They sat quietly appreciating the twilight while breathing in what had just taken place.

"I don't know what to say, Favor." Michael spoke quietly, keeping his eyes forward as if talking to himself. "It's one thing to hold something in your imagination but quite another to physically witness it. The B2 center for communications was beyond my expectation, and the B3 teleportation demonstration was way out of this world. I've held out for the possibility of something like this ever since I heard the resurrection story and later saw the first episodes of *Star Trek*, but to see it with my own eyes and know that a friend and colleague has found a way to make it so is stunning. Our technology is farther advanced than I care to believe, and in the hands of malevolent people, it could be devastating. What was Will thinking when he developed that technology?" Michael looked to Favor, deep concern lining his forehead, eyes, and mouth.

Favor pondered the question, sitting with it in silence before answering. He was about to reveal things he rarely shared. He pulled his legs to his chest and wrapped his arms around them before he addressed Michael.

"Will has lived in a different plane of reality from before I met him. I believe he was born to do all of what he's done. It's as if he came here with more conscious memory than the rest of us. I've always felt he's had one foot on this earth plane and the other somewhere else. He always seemed to have access to the plan for where things were going and how to participate in helping move them along.

"When I first became aware of his work behind closed doors, I was cautious, just as you are. The longer I stayed in the field of his energy; however, the more I came to understand that his motives were all connected to the essence of life and in alignment with what I would call the Divine Source. He's always been committed to the expansion of consciousness and the enlightened evolution of creation." Favor paused to reflect.

"Michael, do you remember the Introit in the Eucharistic Prayer of the church? 'Therefore we praise you, joining with angels, archangels, and all the company of heaven.'"

Favor held up a finger and raised his eyebrows when he said company. "Around here, we joke about being connected to all of what is expressed there, and how we all work for *the Company*. If you remember ancient Hebrew or have studied anything about the Aramaic language from a couple millennia ago, you'll remember *shm*, which expands to shem and shmaya. It is the original root word for heaven and divine name. It has to do with the radiant energy and atmosphere of transcendent life, and can be experienced in the frequencies and vibrations of this realm. To connect with shmaya energy is to tune into a universal frequency that transcends ordinary consciousness. This shining includes every center of activity, the potential abilities of everything, the vibration by which we can recognize the Oneness in all processes of creation, both visible and invisible.

"I bring this up because the marriage of shmaya energy with the recent discoveries of the scientific communities in the fields of psychology and the social sciences, quantum physics, cellular biology, electrical engineering, chemistry, business, and the arts, could be extraordinary. He's been working on those pairings to co-create a new synthesis in the planetary field.

"I know this all sounds really strange, but it appears to be time to break free of our old limiting beliefs and link the twenty-first century with the highest, deepest, and broadest wisdom of the past and future, wouldn't you agree?"

Michael was trying to keep up with Favor's stream of thought. All he could muster was a weak, "yeah," as he pushed his back closer to the edge of the deck in an attempt to straighten his posture and become more receptive.

Favor had already started talking again. "From my point of view, the Yeshua, or Jesus story needs to be reinterpreted and understood in its original cosmic way. In that unique story, we have the historical Yeshua converging with the Cosmic Christ, creating a new being, both human and divine. I sense the ripeness for this old/new Gospel, good news, of an all-inclusive cosmic blessing. I'm beginning to believe Will and his colleagues are helping write it. Their narrative includes the human species and all of creation; a kind of deep ecumenism that brings everything home.

"Then there's the word God, which is a Western translation for the Great Mystery, the I Amness, transcendence, and immanence of being in one divine word. I'm finding it difficult, however, to use that word anymore, because of all the baggage that's been loaded upon it. It's become a subject/object dualistic reference to something that's always inclusive, non-dual.

"A professor and dean of a cathedral visiting the monastery years back, said God was a code word, pointing to the ultimate meaning and mystery of life, which has its center everywhere and its circumference nowhere. I also resonate with an expression from the great mystic Meister Eckhart who prayed to God to help rid him of God. He was inviting the elimination of all constricted human concepts of God, so the essence of it could be experienced. I don't know, Michael, sometimes I just need to speak these things."

Favor paused, drew lines in the sand with his finger, and then rubbed them out with his hand. He spoke again as if he was still trying to convince himself of these new and ancient awakenings.

"We're so anthropomorphic and limiting in our ideas, beliefs, and certainties. It's like we use words as hitching posts rather than guideposts to fight rather than cooperate, to contract rather than expand, to feed our addiction to our own patterns of unhelpful binary either-or and superiority thinking. The mystics awakened to transrational thought and multisensory experiences, and the new physics is discovering the same realities in the quantum realms. Expanding our consciousness is imperative before our technological advancements overwhelm us. Imagine children sitting in a tinderbox playing with matches. Eventually, there will be destruction. Maybe that's just the way it has to be. If, however, we can somehow educate the children through compassionate instructive experiences, there might be greater hope for progress without catastrophic consequences."

Favor stopped talking rather abruptly and squinted. He turned to look at Michael and tried to gauge his receptivity to these newly formulated philosophies.

Michael continued staring at the sky, letting Favor's longwinded response settle into his heart and mind. He lifted himself off the ground, repositioned himself to sit on the deck, and then turned to address Favor.

"I'm surprised and pleased to hear you speak this way, Favor. Here you are, a man who has represented the church as a priest, monk, and abbot for more than sixty years, embracing the very heart of the faith, and shaking its foundations all at the same time. I'm also surprised at how much I agreed with you and how I too, have kept these thoughts hidden. Maybe this is part of what Will and his colleagues have been trying to do, to allow people to put forward their innermost intuitions and concerns. Unless we share our innermost awakenings and wonderments, the walls of oppression and fear will never come down. Greater clarity of understanding and action will not surface unless we are willing to speak openly, honestly, and transparently.

"I want to add something to this discussion that I've been pondering for a long time, and it also comes from the liturgy of the church. It has opened up the mystery and changed the way I see others and myself. It comes after the Words of Institution in the Mass. 'Therefore, we proclaim the mystery of faith: Christ has died. Christ has risen. Christ will come again.'

"From the cosmic perspective, we can speak of Christ as a title and as the original blessing and anointing we all receive at birth. It can be seen as another word pointing to an ever-present reality, to the divine energy of the universe. I see this blessing as dying and rising with our awareness, and our lack of it. It waxes and wanes as we fall asleep and wake up to who we are at the core of our being. What I've come to know is that this Cosmic Christ dies, arises, and comes again and again and again as we remember to remember who we really are, where we've come from, where we're going, and why we're here. My sense is that we are that! It makes me want to shout, WAKE UP to what is here and now in every breath and heartbeat! For me, it's not about a belief; it's about who we've forgotten we already are, and remembering who we've always been! It's about practicing this presence!"

Favor's eyes widened as he nodded an affirmation.

What's the next step? Michael wondered. He felt a sudden urge to research all the people Will and his colleagues were connected with to find a link in the chain that could solve the mystery of these entangled events. His body shuddered slightly with fear as the implications of these deeply held, open secrets became conscious and transparent.

"I'm remembering the experience we had in Will's cabin," Michael finally said. "Was that yesterday, today, or a month ago? I'm losing track of time. I just realized I must go back there and maybe spend the night. I can't tell you why, it's just a feeling I'm having. Something is beckoning me back there right now. I still have the key in my pocket; I'll pick up a flashlight in my cottage on the way. Didn't Gloria mention that I might need to spend a night there?"

Michael didn't wait for Favor's response. Standing, he began moving slowly away from the deck, still addressing the old sage. "I can find my way, so I'll see you tomorrow, and thank you for your musings, honesty, and openness. It's a bit frightening to hear these rather unorthodox words spoken, yet there seems to be a significant call to you and me, and a many other establishment people to heed this call to contemplation and action at this time." Michael stopped suddenly, and Favor saw a strange expression on his face.

"In Will's own methodical scientific and spiritual way, it may be that he and *the Company* have been laying the groundwork for this new awakening of cosmic proportions for a very long time. Hmm. I'm sensing that the time really is now, and the place is always here. I have to go. Thank you, Father Favor."

Michael bowed to Favor and turned toward the path leading to his destiny. For the first time in a very long time, he was full of the energy of passion and purpose. He was on a mission. He was awakened and alive again.

He had no difficulty finding his cottage. He walked in, picked up his daypack, and placed it on the bed. He took a handful of matches from the container next to the fireplace and put them in his pants pocket. He then placed his journal and pen, reading glasses, sweater, and a bottle of water in his pack, which he slung over his shoulder. He took the small flashlight from the desk, put it in his jacket pocket, and was out the door. The light was dimming as he found the path leading around the lake.

As he made the turn south at the lake, he noticed someone sitting on the ground close to the shore. The person looked up. It was Anthony Amir.

"Anthony, what are you doing out here? You look like you've lost your best friend."

Anthony looked up with sad eyes but didn't move. "Dr. Wyman. I . . . well . . . I'm leaving shortly. There's been a family emergency, and I'm really conflicted. I can't go into it now and . . ." he paused, holding back his emotions. "I'm glad to have met you and hope we meet again."

Michael walked up to Anthony and put his hand out to him. "I have a distinct sense that we will meet again and it will be under very different circumstances."

Anthony shook Michael's hand without standing up. "Thanks, Dr. Wyman. I hope that's true," he said as he dropped farther into his darkness.

Michael let go of Anthony's hand and moved on, thinking about how many Anthony Amir's there were in the world sitting in anxiety and conflict. He sent a blessing to them all, refocused, and returned to the presence of the lake and the forest.

He made his way with ease and finally climbed the gentle slope coming to the apparent end of the trail that curved left and right back down to the lake. The cloaking device was still on. He reached out to touch it, but there was no sensation or disturbance. As before, he walked right through the unseen barrier and within three steps Will's cabin became visible. The light of day was almost gone when Michael stepped up onto the porch. He sat in one of the two chairs that looked out across the lake and caught his breath. He collected himself, wanting to feel the place again before opening the door and walking inside. He knew anything could happen and wanted to be prepared.

He took the key out of his pocket and turned it over in his hand. He stood up, placed it in the lock, grasped the handle, and turned them together to open the door. The scent of mint caressed his senses. He crossed the threshold following the flashlight's small path and looked for a light switch. There was none. He noticed an oil lamp on a desk. He removed the chimney, turned up the wick, took a match from his pocket, and struck it. The lamp gave a gentle warm glow to the whole room. The smell of kerosene and the scent of mint mingled in an indefinable combination. The merging of apparent opposites brought a smile to Michael's face as he caught the metaphor of the marriage.

Michael sat down in Will's swivel desk chair and scanned the room. He observed two walls of books, a file cabinet, stacks of papers, wall maps, and a wood burning cookstove. He noticed a cot folded up in a corner, with a pillow, blanket, and comforter lying on the seat of a wing back chair. There were two windows. One directly above the desk that looked out over the porch to the woods and the lake, and the other on the opposite wall that looked out into the woods. He pulled open the drawers of the desk to find more papers, trade magazines, and two composition books. One notebook was filled with drawings, mathematical equations, and notes and the other with journal entries. Michael was drawn to the journal entries. He checked the dates. They ran from July 23, 2010 to October 4, 2010, three days before Will's disappearance. With some quick scanning, Michael was able to discern the entries as mostly self-reflective and pertaining to his relationships with family, colleagues, and self.

An entry on the Wednesday before Labor Day, September 1, 2010, drew Michael's attention. Will was musing over a message he had received from someone he called Bill Black. From the questions Will was asking himself, Michael couldn't tell if Bill Black was a real person, a code name for a project, or both. Will seemed agitated in his writings as he recalled a couple of vague references to the United States, Middle East, Russia, the global community, climate change, and the weather. None of it made any sense to Michael, but something about it waved an orange flag of concern.

> *It disturbs me that a discovery I made and passed on in good faith is being considered as an economic weapon against innocent people. I'm wondering now who I've been associating with these many years. Breaking trust is a major violation and doesn't sit well. Deceit is not a behavior I take kindly to and even thinking this way is a breach of trust with my colleagues, the global community, and me. This thinking and possible action deceives and undermines the decency of our humanity. The real*

economy is simply good management of the household. More short-term gains with long-term losses are not the sacred stewardship required for the management of the household that is our local and global home. No! Know! What's happened to compassion, appreciation, and the sacred trust? What's happened to conscience? What's happened to the highest good? Not sure what to do. Must act if possible to get this off the table. Must sit in remembrance, offering, and discernment to proceed.

Michael checked the rest of the entries for a possible stream of thought concerning this thread and found none except at the very end of the last entry on October 4.

Found a way to remove the card. Very risky at all levels. Colleagues on board. Plan in place. Launch set. Company's in. Danger and Opportunity. Major transition. Capa Negra. Open Secret. Little stream, Big River. Ola Kala, no matter what. Will be fine.

Michael sat in the stillness of the hermitage, focusing on the oil lamp's glow and steady presence. The light radiating quietly off the wick reminded him of those days in the Canadian Rockies where he spent the winter in a cabin much like this one. He was also reminded of the visitation by the she wolf Shmaya and her message concerning the new consciousness that needed to protect and sustain the many endangered species of the planet, including Homo sapiens. Was this entry in Will's journal the thread he was looking for? Who or what was Bill Black? What did weather and climate change have to do with anything that could be manipulated for economic advantage regionally or globally?

Michael walked to the corner of the room, picked up the cot, and unfolded it. He went to the wood box beside the cookstove to put some kindling in the stove's firebox. He lit and fed it until the fire sustained itself. He placed the blanket, comforter, and pillow on the cot, lay down, and stared at the fire dance on the ceiling and walls. He closed his eyes, his head buzzing with conspiracy theories, scenes from movies and books, and the experiences he'd had at Sunnyview. He released the pressure of responsibility tensing his back muscles. He calmed himself with slow breathing to find the stilling place where he could hear the silence, the crackling of the fire, and the hoot of an owl in the distance. Serenity overtook him as his mind slowed and quieted its chatter.

He was home again with himself and the cosmos. His body wisdom was becoming conscious and reminding him of his place in the great mystery. *The answers will come.* It was time to empty, surrender to the Divine Source, and receive any formless gifts that would be given at this time, in this place. In himself, he sensed a flowing river and a rooting tree reconciling all the apparent opposites within and without as he gave thanks and drifted off. *Here, there are no problems, no solutions, only presence within breath, fire, darkness, and life. No wonder Will spent so much time here.*

Chapter 37

In times of change, the learners will inherit the earth while the learned will find themselves beautifully equipped to deal with a world that no longer exists.
-Eric Hoffer-

Atom stood on the beach in a state of reverence and wonder. The juxtaposition of his interactions with the form and formlessness of his dad left him speechless and transformed. He urged himself to move, walked over to the woodpile, and put another log on the fire. The night surrounded him like a warm cape while the fire created a glow that for the moment, carved out his place in the universe. He sat down to experience the fire, the water lapping upon the shore, the wind rustling the palm fronds, and the heart beating in his chest.

Let go to let come, he heard in the stillness. *Shlama, peace is within and all around you. Breathe it in. Surrender. Trust. Open. Presence.* He listened attentively to the earth, air, fire, and water. *All is well and all will be well. Compassion. Appreciation. Transition. Embrace the wonder. It's all happening for you and the whole of creation. Trust the reception and continue to be grateful.*

He couldn't tell how long he sat in that contemplative place. He couldn't tell in what reality he had traveled to or awakened from. He felt weightless, like a scuba diver with a buoyancy control device hovering motionless over the bottom of the sea, feeling the rhythm of the current, at one with the ocean of life.

As he returned to the beach from the outer reaches of inner space, his eyes and ears opened to see the dim light of a new day filling the sky. The songs of a few birds welcomed another new beginning.

He stood and stretched every muscle, reaching to the sky in a salute to the sun, moon, and stars as well as to the earth and all its wonder. He brushed the sand from his clothes and looked out across the water of the bay trying to make sense of the last twelve hours. He felt the pull of the tides, the flow of the ages, the dying that leads to life, and the ongoing reconciliation of all apparent opposites. He also felt hungry for a hearty Caribbean breakfast and the companionship of Derick and Anna.

He walked toward the lodge where he hoped breakfast and the closeness of family awaited him, even though the morning was just dawning. He quietly climbed the front steps and made his way through the screened porch. As he crossed the threshold into the house, he heard Anna singing in the kitchen. The tune was familiar and took him back to his childhood.

"This little light of mine, I'm gonna let it shine. This little light of mine, I'm gonna let it shine. This little light of mine, I'm gonna let it shine. Let it shine all the time, let it shine!"

Atom slipped off his shoes and silently walked across the room toward the kitchen. When he came to the doorway, he stopped and leaned against the doorjamb admiring the beauty of Anna's voice. She had her back to him, preparing something on the countertop. A few seconds passed before she felt his presence. She whirled around, recognized him, and with a great smile, left what she was doing and ran with glee to greet Atom with a gracious hug and twirl, as if dancing to the music that was still singing in her heart.

"Atom, Atom, Atom! How wonderful to see you and hug you and be with you! The day just keeps getting better, and Will, he's back with his whole crew and amazingly transformed. He's risen right up from that apparent death sleep and walks and talks and even eats like a new man. I can't believe it and yet, here we are. I'm so happy, and the new baby in my womb is moving around this morning like he knows what's going on too. Derick will be back soon. He and Will went for a walk."

Atom couldn't stop smiling at Anna, who was acting like a child in reverie, instead of the thirty-eight-year-old pregnant woman she was. He needed this kind of welcome.

"Have you had breakfast? I made an egg casserole with black beans, vegetables, and white fish, not knowing who would be here this morning. Are Captain Jack and Jackie still here?"

"I'd love some breakfast, thank you," Atom responded, following Anna to the other side of the kitchen. "I heard Jack say they had to be in Panama City by seven this morning, so we may see them. What's this I hear about a baby? That is definitely a cause for congratulations! How did you snag my uncle, the uncatchable fish? I had hopes for you two, but wow, what a wonderful surprise; a marriage and a baby."

Anna pulled out a chair and motioned Atom to sit. She joined him at the kitchen table. "It was rough at first. Derick definitely wasn't an easy catch, but then again, neither was I. It was just meant to be, because through all the difficulties, we kept growing stronger together as a couple and as individuals, and now with Will's new thing and all of what that means, which, by the way, I don't understand, everything seems to be falling into place."

"Speaking of Dad, did you see his colleagues? Are they still here?"

"No, I don't know where they are. We got a call from Carla, the medical technician who was monitoring their vital signs this morning. She told Derick he needed to get over there pronto! She said the whole room was radiating a blinding white light. Poor thing, she was really freaked out. Derick was up and over there in minutes, but by the time he got there, everyone had disappeared. Derick came back here after questioning Carla, who reported that after the light dimmed, their vital signs spiked and returned to normal. She watched through a window in the door to see them all come back to life together, shed their sheets as they stood up, and disappear into thin air. She was extremely shaken up."

Anna smiled compassionately while she stood, went to the stove, and returned with two cups of tea that she placed on the table. She sat back down again. "Estefan is still with her at their house. I'm sure she's fine, and I'll go see her when Derick returns." She took a sip of tea and then continued. "Not long after Derick returned, while we were talking at the table in the great room, your dad just appeared out of nowhere! We were both shocked and overwhelmed. The baby leaped in my womb, and I about fell out of my chair. When the surprise and excitement subsided, the three of us talked awhile before Derick and Will excused themselves, and now here you are. I understand your dad saw you on the beach before he saw us."

"Yes, and what a wonderful revelation. I'm still in awe by the sequence of events and the realization that he's here and not here."

Anna leaned back in her chair, placing her hands instinctively over her expanding stomach. "What do you mean?"

"Well, he's here, but there's a separation between what he was, a brilliant human being, and what he is now, a brilliant, super-conscious human and divine being who has traveled across the great divide and back. Have you read anything about NDE's, Near Death Experiences?"

Anna shook her head.

"There's been significant research into the phenomena of near death experiences. Thousands of people who were presumed dead returned to life and then interviewed for the research. The difference between them and Dad is that the NDE's were only gone or presumed dead for minutes, not days. They all returned with reports of white light, crossing a divide, being greeted by other beings, some of whom they knew, experiencing a holographic life review, remembrance of their life mission, telepathy, profound peace, great beauty, wanting to stay, and being sent or called back into their former lives and bodies with a new awareness. Those few minutes of so-called death seemed like days to them. Dad told me that the three days, now into the fourth here on earth, were like centuries on the other side. It's also been reported that time can be reversed; minutes can seem like months, and months can seem like minutes. Time changes beyond our frame of reference, and the discipline of new physics verifies that. Dad's scientific team verifies that. They were transfigured and transformed."

Atom paused to see if Anna was following the explanation. She was listening raptly, soothing her in utero child with gentle strokes of her hand.

"Maybe it's a combination of Dad's change and the change in me. I couldn't ask him about it at the time, but I really want to find out as much as I can about what he and his colleagues experienced, even if I can't understand it now. If what we call death is not really death but simply another transition and a new beginning, imagine what that could mean for us. If we all have a life mission that we often forget, and earth is like a school where we have to repeat lessons until we get them, then attention, remembrance, and ongoing learning would be a priority. Attachment to fear and carnal desire would no longer rule our lives. If we could see death in this new way, we could transcend fear. Transcending fear and forgetfulness would radically change the games we play here on earth.

"Imagine a world where there is no fear and no death as we've come to know it, and no amnesia of our life mission. Imagine life without a localized hell or heaven except the ones we create in this reality. Imagine ongoing transition into greater awareness by simple spiritual practice and participation. Is it possible that we all come from and return to those formless places reported in the NDE's and that there are more than three dimensions, maybe five, ten, or a thousand dimensions?

"Having experienced all that, Dad's different. How could it be otherwise? So am I, and so are you, and so is the world. Wow, I just got goose bumps. What a shift, what a change in perspective when what we accept as real becomes unreal and what we have believed to be unreal becomes real. I feel like I just woke up after twenty-six years of sleep. I think I've lost my mind and found a new one!"

Anna's smile broadened and radiated an inner knowing she couldn't articulate. They both sat there pondering the implications of these revelations and the expansive effect they could have on the global community. Something had changed. Putting their experience into a cosmic perspective had expanded their consciousness. The newly forming being within Anna's womb also seemed to join in the wonder of the moment, as Anna felt a strange sensation and communication move within her. She invited Atom to put his hands on her abdomen.

"Do you feel it? He's receiving our vibration, our new frequency, and making contact. I think the newest space cadet of the family is letting us know he's with us. This is too weird and I love it!" She broke out in laughter. "This whole thing is amazingly hilarious."

Atom also got the joke and broke out of his containment into a liberating laughter.

Derick felt the exuberant vibration as he walked into the kitchen and smiled. When the wondrous energy of the moment subsided, he poured himself some tea and dished up the breakfast casserole for Anna, Atom, and himself.

While they ate, he briefed Anna and Atom about his meeting with Will and the other four. He reported that he and Will had met with Captain Jack, Jackie, Estefan, Carla, and Pablo. "All is well and back to normal, or paranormal, depending on how you look at it," he joked. "All five of the team members have departed to their designated assignments and will be moving in and out of Camp Bay Island during the next few months. Anna, I've directed each of them to check in with me upon their arrival so I can introduce them to you. Is that satisfactory?"

Anna nodded yes, as she chewed her breakfast casserole.

They spent the next couple of hours discussing the various plans Will had shared with Derick concerning Fischer Enterprises, the global village, geopolitical entanglements, strategic operations, short and long term transition initiatives, possible outcomes, Atom's trip back to Sunnyview, and the upcoming birth of Baby Fischer with family in New Orleans.

Atom's fatigue was catching up with him, so he asked a summary and follow-up question to conclude the conversation. "So we're all to simply build on the lifetime work we've already accomplished?"

"That's the plan to date," responded Derick. "The major difference is that the individual, collective, and global transition will be focused on forward movement in a unified field for the welfare and benefit of all beings. Out of compassion for all, there will be more emphasis on collaboration across the many divides that have been created. The greater good for the whole of creation becomes the highest value in all endeavors. The conscious awareness and honoring of our interconnectivity and collective evolution is the platform for our sustainability!"

"I wonder how many people on the planet are consciously aware of this transition and if those presently being birthed around the globe are coming in with a more awakened consciousness to this new balance, harmony, and interconnectivity?" Atom questioned.

"I can't speak for the rest of the planet," responded Anna, "but I've been aware of it most of my life and our developing baby seems to be aware of everything we're aware of through osmosis. My sense is we all have a longing for this transition. I think it's inherent in the hearts and minds of everyone, whether we consciously know it or not. We have to move forward with this hope, intention, and illumination. I'm inspired to reach out farther than I have in the past. How about you?"

Derick and Atom looked quizzically at each other and then back at Anna, both nodding in appreciative agreement of her earthy wisdom.

Chapter 38

The human venture depends absolutely on the quality of awe
and reverence and joy in the Earth and all that lives and grows
upon the Earth. In the end, the universe can only be explained
in celebration. It is all an exuberant expression of existence itself.
We must feel we are supported by that same power that brought
the Earth into being, that power that spun the galaxies into
space, that tilt the sun and brought the moon into its orbit.
-Thomas Berry-

Angelina was by herself in the kitchen of the café as the sun
peeked out over the horizon on the fourth day of Will's absence.
She hummed a tune she used to sing to her children and recalled
the wonder of those early days as a family. She glanced up to
see a man standing in the doorway between the kitchen and the
hallway and looking at her in a way she thought curious.

"May I help you?" she asked.

"Angelina!" he replied.

"Will! How can this be?" She dropped what she was doing
and ran into his arms with childlike abandon. They hugged and
kissed as he lifted her off the ground and enfolded her in his arms.
Coming to a stop, Angelina stepped back holding his hands to
look closer at what she felt might be a mirage.

"I knew you'd come back, I knew you'd find a way and yet, it's
hard to believe you're standing right here in front of me." They
drew close again in a silent embrace, wrapping their arms around

212

each other, leaning into the warmth of this new communion, and feeling the pulse of life coursing through their bodies and souls. Angelina relaxed and stepped back again. Still holding her husband's hands, she looked deeply into his eyes and asked, "What happened?"

Will released one of his hands and softly ran the back of it across Angelina's cheeks and lips. He gently caressed her hair and led her to a chair where she sat down and he knelt down beside her.

"The risks we talked about were real," he began. "We came close to losing our connection with visible form. Our physical bodies made it to Camp Bay, but our ethereal bodies were taken on a journey reserved for the few. We were transported to the other side, educated in the ways of angels, bodhisattvas, and saints, and then returned as new beings with supernatural powers. It's an extraordinary phenomenon to have happened and quite unexpected.

"You were right about *the Company*, Angelina. The crew and I were chosen to help the inhabitants of planet earth with the unfolding and expanding of consciousness to fulfill our human destiny and that of Gaia. We still have much to do as a species. The transformational process we have just gone through is a precursor to what the whole of humanity is called to do. It's the wisdom and compassion of the One to the many, and the awakening and receptivity of the many to the One!"

Will moved closer to Angelina. He wrapped his left arm around her and leaned his head against her chest while she held his right hand on her lap. Angelina cradled and caressed him. They stayed in this contemplative embrace realigning with the present heavenly and earthly energies of the cosmos. The smile in their hearts radiated out through every cell of their beings as the frequencies vibrated a hymn of the universe. Angelina felt the ascending and descending energy as never before. Life lovingly embraced them as they merged with each other. Silent music played in the background.

Parting, they both knew the next move of the dance without words. Will walked to the hermitage in silent form. Angelina returned to her duties, wiping tears of joy from her eyes.

*   *   *

Favor had awakened earlier than usual to check on Michael at the hermitage. His walk along the lake was opening him to the wonder of the new day as he took in the briskness of the October air, the songs of the autumn birds, and the sheer stillness of the transition between darkness and light. He made his way slowly to the bench swing that marked the transition point just before the path to the hermitage. He sat in the stillness observing the mystery of the moment.

He saw another man coming along the trail. It was impossible to identify him due to his hooded sweatshirt and the darkness of the early morning. Maybe Michael had taken an early morning walk too. The man approached and without a sound sat down on the swing next to Favor. The movement of the swing cradled them both. Favor sat comfortably, sensing the stranger's presence as peaceful and full of repose.

"You've been a faithful and loving companion and friend. We are infinitely grateful," Will said, breaking the silence.

The words burned in Favor's heart. He turned to look at the man but no one was there. He turned back, looking across the lake as the sun began to increase the available light. What had just happened? The urge to move came but he could not.

Favor relaxed, breathed in the cool morning air, and went to the familiar contemplative place of not knowing. He stayed there until he again felt the energy of a joyful peacefulness come from within. He stood, stretched, gave thanks, and walked to the porch of the hermitage. He sat down in one of the two chairs on the porch and heard the voices of Will and Michael inside the cabin. He knew it was important to be here.

The questions Favor wanted to ask Will were legion. The past four days had created so many opportunities for his imagination to engage that he felt exhausted and elated at the same time. The disappearance and reappearance of Will was just the beginning of the mystery and the adventure that was unfolding. He knew the time would come to ask his questions. He also knew that many questions would remain unanswered. His many years of disciplined life had taught him this difficult and liberating lesson.

He sat patiently, waiting his turn in this revolving cycle of engagement and disengagement. He listened quietly to the ebb and flow of the conversation inside the hermitage, not knowing what was being said. He felt the closing of one door while experiencing the opening of another, the strings of binding and unbinding, and the new vibration of an ancient universal song.

The door of the hermitage opened, and Michael walked out with an inner smile on his face, his body glowing with a golden aura. He shared a silent space with Favor for an infinite moment, and then stepped off the porch and disappeared on the path along the lake. Favor waited. A bell sent out its vibration, resonating with the call for awareness and attention.

Favor stood and walked into the hermitage. He closed the door and sat on the zafu in front of Will who was sitting on the floor. The two men bowed reverently and then gazed into each other's souls.

Favor felt the penetrating compassion and joy Will was radiating. Will felt the loving companion presence of this venerable elder who had dedicated his life to the universal sanctification and unification of humanity through his priestly mission he had come to embody.

The scene was as ancient as it was modern. Words became unnecessary, as the two became one. They understood the common union. They were both under orders from the same Divine Source. They each knew their place and understood how the Company worked. In this most extraordinary meeting, the necessary transmission was given and received. Favor had nothing to say. Before they parted, Will said one thing, knowing the change it would create. It was the next step, and Favor would understand and make it so.

"Invite the fox into the chicken coop."

Chapter 39

The face of the wise is not somber or austere, contracted by anxiety and sorrow, but precisely the opposite; radiant and serene, and filled with vast delight, which often makes them the most playful of all, acting with a sense of humor that blends with their essence. The goal of wisdom is laughter and play, to become laughter itself.
-Philo-

There was a festive atmosphere in Gloria's living room on the sixth floor of the pyramid as the light of a new day filled the sky and the hearts of those gathered. Angelina, Favor, Michael, and Sophia, the most recent member of this hermetic circle, had joined Gloria, Clare, and Will. They all shared their experiences of the past four days with rapt attention, providing every detail and drama. The laughter at their own inner uncertainties helped each of them to know and understand the situation from a variety of perspectives, expanding their perception and awareness of the human and divine conditions playing within them.

Will's presence had galvanized them into a sacred unity that had been growing but not consummated. The radiant shmaya energy swirled in, around, and through each of them, transforming what could have been danger into opportunity. The crisis was no longer. There was opportunity for growth and change in ways that none knew in fullness, yet knew in faith. Each had a unique part to play in the grand scheme of things and each would be empowered, inspired, and illuminated through the ongoing revelations in this unfolding story.

Will had laid the groundwork so there would be no personality cults, no divisions, no them and us. Each person and situation would be treated as sacred, significant, and successfully leaning toward the turning points, the flowering moments, and the emerging patterns that were now taking place for the benefit of all. Even apparent setbacks were to be viewed with appreciation, retreat leading to advancement. There would be no significant attachments to any expectations. Trusting the process, the Company, and their free interconnected presence would rule, along with ongoing alignment and realignment, giving significant attention to course corrections for the most effective set of outcomes. The reality of all things, working together for the highest good, was being held with resonance and confidence.

Will waited for the appropriate moment to make an announcement. "I've directed Favor to invite the fox into the chicken coop. You all know that we've been under the scrutiny of the National Security Agency for a very long time. My experiments and research have been monitored and investigated ever since we joined and expanded the research team at Sawyer Air Force Base in Marquette back in the late eighties. When they closed the facility in ninety-five, I kept a significant staff in place to continue our own research by subcontracting some of the research facilities. We knew we were being monitored. I scrutinized all my staff and research associates over time and discovered some leaks in our security. NSA paid significant sums of money for some of our associates to pass on reviews and updates on our research in various areas under the banner of national security. After September 11, two thousand one, everything changed. We had ongoing difficulties with the Department of Defense, which culminated in them shutting us down and confiscating significant data.

"Fortunately, we saw it coming, changed the files to render them unimportant, closed ranks, and neutralized all potential possibilities of having our discoveries deciphered and compromised. That's when we moved everything we needed to Sunnyview and Camp Bay. Over time, there seemed to be more covert operations into our intellectual property, which is why the five principles decided to take a calculated risk. That is, disappear and reverse the pursuit. It's turned out better than we hoped. The Company stepped in, gave us the help we needed, plus new knowledge, wisdom, and powers we couldn't even imagine before our journey to the other side. We will be revealing what we can, but most of it will have to be experienced.

"Since our return today, we have destroyed all evidence of that data in the files at Camp Bay and here at Sunnyview so it no longer exists, except in the holographic memory banks of our five-member team and possibly with those we are yet to know. Since we have connected with a consciousness beyond the limits of present day beings, and crossed over into what we call the sacred, we five cannot be compromised in any way. We are invincible and immortal in ways that are impossible to describe. It's a quantum leap in human evolution and it's been happening incrementally over millennia. It will continue to happen until we all transcend the lower levels of human consciousness. It appears to be an impossible task and yet, we are all here with this new inner-evolutionary technology. Each of our team has taken the bodhisattva vow: we are connected to the earth plane until we have all transcended the barriers of dualistic thought and five sensory physical experiences." Will paused.

"Our mission is to become conscious instruments of transformation. All of creation is crying out for this intervention and it is here and now. All of us are part of it, and we will be assisting in more active and transformational ways. Soon we will be privately contacting all of our associates around the globe and work to diffuse every threat to the livelihood and sustainability of all sentient and non-sentient beings on the planet.

"When Michael's call was received by the NSA hotline yesterday, the number was immediately recorded and sent to a field agent for investigation. I have given Michael and Favor the name and direct phone link to Randy Dirk, the NSA regional director whom I know. He and his two closest field agents will be joining us today for lunch. We will exchange information and find the underlying cause of this apparent mystery of the Cathar label given to us. We need to know what that means to them and determine if we are in danger. I will take an invisible position until it is necessary to reveal myself. It may not be necessary at this time, we'll see."

Clare shook her head. "I'm sorry; Dad, but I don't get it. They may be coming here to steal the eggs and maybe even eat the chickens. What makes you think we can convince them that we're the good guys when they may be thinking we're the bad guys?"

"That's the beauty of it, Clare," Will responded. "The fox always believes it is smarter, more savvy, and in greater control than the chickens. We have powers the fox doesn't know about. So the tables are turned, and we can potentially transform the fox. The new powers I've been given can, to some degree, be transmitted to others. It's not about belief, argument, or force. It's about the energetic power of the universe, which is creative and connected to everything. We are now able to transmit the necessary energy frequencies to facilitate a transmission of illumination in just a few moments when the time is ripe and the subjects are receptive. Sometimes all it takes is a look, a handshake, or a power surge from one being to another. Other times, the subject simply goes unconscious and wakes without the memory of the event or what preceded it.

"We're all made of the same waves and particles and all connected to the same source. Movement of energy is fundamental, and we now know how to move energy in ways we never did before. We're not in control; rather, we're conscious transceivers receiving and transmitting energy messages. When the energy is resonant with the vibrations of the universe, change can happen instantly. Some small examples of this are eureka events, the aha's, the epiphanies that show up occasionally. We now have the power to direct this energy. The enhancement of these powers is something we will all learn. We, as a species, have been working on this project since we began to stand upright and play with fire. It's beyond the either-or thinking of most humans toward an inclusive both-and consciousness. Everybody wins. Everyone is in when we awaken to it."

"Last night, when I heard Michael say disappeared instead of died my whole perspective shifted," Clare responded.

"When I met you, Angelina, you shook my hand and I felt a surge of energy that shocked and transformed me," Michael said.

"And this morning, Will," Favor added, "when you spoke to me on the swing, and Michael, when we looked at each other on the porch of the hermitage, something unfolded in me."

"All of this and more," Will continued. "You've all had some experience in this alignment, this at-one-ment. The power of concentrated focused energy can melt the resistance of anyone and move through the defenses to the receptors in the many brain centers of the body. It is a power of healing and wholeness, a gift that can be given and received. When a person receives it from another, it realigns the assemblage points of the body, mind, and spirit connections. Until now, it was something we experienced at times of coincidence, or not at all. We are now in a historic period of coincidence. We're the ones to lead the way and help others develop this illuminating power of surrender, receptivity, and transmission."

"It's brilliant, Will," stated Gloria. "In all the years I've been around to imagine conflict being overcome by compassion, I never thought I'd see the day where it could be accomplished like this. What you're talking about and beginning right here today in our presence is a dream come true. Many family lineage holders have been envisioning and working within this possibility and potentiality for millennia, and here we are in the midst of experiencing it! I can feel it in these old bones of mine and in this infinite soul. The time is ripe and I'm ready to pick some fruit."

Angelina concluded. "Remember the air of lightness, creativity, and joy? It can happen anytime. It's about being in a state of resonance, receptivity, and alignment with the source. Joy and peace brings forth the illumination. It's quite a dance. See you all at eleven-thirty this morning in the kiva. The final preparations will be made then. Enjoy the balance of your morning."

They all stood up, bowed in reverence to one another, and went their various ways. Will stayed with Gloria in the silence of the pyramid's apex. The energy was subtle and sweet.

"What are you sensing?" Will asked the matriarch.

"There's a very positive and powerful vibration here at Sunnyview and yet, I sense danger at a distance. It's not here or even close to us in proximity, but it's present. I don't sense that your friend Randy Dirk and his associates are part of the danger; it's too scattered for the denseness of the NSA. The danger is both large and small. It will come like a thief in the night. That's all I'm picking up. What about you?"

"I'm still getting used to the height, depth, and breadth of my new powers. It's as if I'm learning to ride a bicycle and still have the training wheels on. I can ride and find my balance most of the time, but at those other times, not so much. I'm finding a resonance with what you're sensing and yet, I can't find the channel to tune into the danger and its opportunity. I'm sure, however, that when the time is ripe, the tuning and refinement will occur. The intensity of the new powers increases with use. I seem to have an unlimited power supply connected to the source. It's a wonderful gift. I'll check in with you from time to time and if you want me just remember CAT. You'll always find me in Compassion, Appreciation, and Transmission. That's where I live now." He smiled and vanished. A faint scent of coconut and mint lingered in the air.

Chapter 40

Any path is only a path, and there is no affront, to oneself or to others, in dropping it if that is what your heart tells you. Look at every path closely and deliberately. Try it as many times as you think necessary. Then ask yourself, and yourself alone, one question. Does this path have a heart? If it does, the path is good; if it doesn't, it is of no use.
-Carlos Castaneda-

Michael and Favor met Director Randy Dirk and his two associates as they walked through the door of the Sunnyview café. They fit the stereotype of government agents: dark suits, sunglasses, of medium muscular build. It was fifteen minutes until twelve when the small bell rang over the door announcing their arrival. Introductions were cordial and formal. Michael and Favor briefed Director Dirk on the protocol. The three men removed their sunglasses and were led through the café to the kiva. They would sit with the community for noonday meditation before the lunch meeting.

"What's your connection with Sunnyview?" Dirk asked Michael as they stood waiting in the hallway just outside the kiva.

"I'm a friend of the family and am here on retreat. Why do you ask?"

"We traced your first phone call to Denver. It was very low priority. We had no idea you were connected with Dr. Fischer and Sunnyview. The call today was surprising and obviously got our attention, especially considering the recent events with Dr. Fischer and his colleagues. What prompted the calls?"

"A dream," he answered. "I'll expand on that over lunch. Right now, it's time to do a little inner work and connect with something more expansive. The community here at Sunnyview offers prayer and meditation to the public three times a day. The noonday prayer lasts twenty minutes and is usually very simple. We'll all sit together in silence with whatever community gathers, and then have lunch with the other members of our circle. You'll get to meet Dr. Fischer's wife, daughter, mother-in-law, and his personal administrator. We hope to clear up all the necessary details of our investigations so we can more fully collaborate in our mutual interests. Is that satisfactory?"

"It's a bit odd, but it's your call. What religion is this organization connected with?"

Favor spoke. "It's connected to all deep contemplative traditions in that we experience one river with many wells. We're here to reconnect to the essence of life for greater participation and creative collaboration. We're a nonprofit educational institution that connects science, spirituality, and the arts. We're self-sufficient and inclusive. Our security starts within and radiates out. It's a different approach than most. We come from a great variety of backgrounds and are committed to eco-stewardship, inquiry, and awakening consciousness. I'm sure you have all this in your files. It's different, however, when you personally experience what you read from impersonal documents. That's why we wanted you to come today. We want you to know who we are experientially, and we want to know you. We sense we can be beneficial to one another."

"We'll see," responded Dirk. He nodded at his two associates to follow Michael and Favor through the doors of the kiva. After removing their shoes, the five men found a place to sit together. The three agents were exchanging doubtful looks while following Michael and Favor's lead.

The temple bell rang promptly at noon. Clare opened with a brief meditation from the Upanishads.

> *Bell.* "Truly it is Life that shines forth in all things . . . ."
>
> *Bell.* "Vast, heavenly, of unthinkable form it shines forth . . . ."
>
> *Bell.* "It is farther than far, yet near at hand . . . ."
>
> *Bell.* "Set down in the secret places of the heart . . . ."
>
> *Bell.* "Not by sight is it grasped, not even by speech . . . ."
>
> *Bell.* "But by the peace of Wisdom, one's nature purified . . . ."
>
> *Bell.* "In that way, by meditating, one does behold that which is without form . . . ."

When she finished the reading, the temple bell rang three times. The silent meditation began and lasted for twenty minutes. At the conclusion of the time, the reading was again given, and the bell rang at the end of each line. Everyone stood, bowed, and moved from the kiva.

Michael led the group to the private dining room just off the main part of the café with Favor following. In the middle of the room was a round table set for nine people. Gloria, Angelina, Clare, and Sophia entered the room, made their introductions, and sat in their designated places around the table. Favor offered a brief blessing and Michael introduced the check-in etiquette. One by one, each individual introduced themselves by name, relationship to the organization, why they were present, and what they wanted from the meeting.

Michael started. "My name is Michael Wyman. I'm a friend of the Fischer family. I live in Denver, Colorado, and work as a psychology professor. I'm here because of a dream I had and a phone call I made. I'm also here because the family asked me to be here. What I want is to clarify the relationship between Sunnyview and the NSA. With that I'm in."

The check-in continued around the table until everyone had spoken. The atmosphere changed. The three suits from the NSA were good sports, despite their nervous glances and chuckles among themselves. The doors opened and three servers appeared with salad plates and a pitcher of water.

Michael spoke up. "A couple days ago, I woke up with a dream. Two men visited me in a Marquette restaurant asking about quantum physics, holography, teleportation, radio waves, and weather manipulation. They left a card from the NSA with a phone number and an ID code. The ID code was Cathar, UPUSA. After I woke up, I called the phone number out of curiosity. I reached the NSA hotline, which asked me to speak the ID code so I could be transferred to the appropriate department. I was stunned at the coincidence and clarity of the dream. I talked to Favor about it, and we tried to decipher the code. The word Cathar brought up some concern about how Sunnyview was viewed. Does the National Security Agency perceive Sunnyview, Dr. Will Fischer, and his colleagues as threats to the security of the United States or are we being perceived as victims of a hostile threat?"

Everyone was now looking at Director Randy Dirk. He put his fork down, took a drink of water, wiped his mouth with his napkin, and took a deep breath.

"Dr. Fischer and I developed a collegial relationship twenty years ago at Sawyer Air Force Base in Marquette. At the time, I was working for the Department of Defense as Security Advisor at Sawyer. My job was to make sure there were no security breaches in the system. The research we were doing was top secret, and I was to make sure it stayed that way. It was necessary to have informants inside the research facilities to make sure everything was secure. We paid researchers for information. I became very close to Dr. William Fischer, who was the senior researcher and director of operations. He knew what we were doing and he cooperated with us. We found his operation almost flawless, and his integrity and those closely associated with him impeccable. However, we discovered a glitch that eventually led to closing the whole research operation.

"The Cathar designation comes from an ancient group in Europe who were persecuted and mostly destroyed by what were supposed to be friendly allies. NSA has seen you as those who were being threatened, *not* those who were a threat."

He paused to take another drink of water. "We have had, and continue to have, the highest regard for Dr. Fischer, his colleagues, and their research. He's been connected to the highest reaches of our national enterprise and has been of utmost importance to us. The latest incident in Lake Superior has significantly affected the president, the secretary of state, defense, and all other department heads and associates who have known Dr. Fischer. We bear the message of condolence from the president and his associates. That is why we are here. We also hope you may be able to provide some information to us concerning these events.

"We have suspicions about some highly technical terrorist cells operating deeply undercover in the Americas who may have intercepted some valuable data generated in the Sawyer research that Dr. Fischer was engaged in. Our research and investigations span decades. We received a message from Dr. Fischer recently that was very disturbing and informative."

"Did it have to do with Bill Black?" Michael asked.

"How do you know about that?" Dirk asked with an edge in his voice.

"I was in Will's hermitage last night and came across his name in a journal entry he made on September first, just a month and a half ago."

Dirk relaxed a little. "That's the code name he used for a significant security breach he discovered, and he passed it along to us concerning some research his team had done at Sawyer. It was abandoned because of its dangerous implications. He found out that some interests close to him had stolen the research and developed it during the past ten years for destructive economic reasons that cut at the very fabric of national and global security. It involved weather manipulation and scalar energy. He was extremely concerned about the discovery and its implications in the hands of the wrong people. We think those people had something to do with the demise of Dr. Fischer and his colleagues," he paused. "What else do you know?" Dirk asked, directing his question to everyone at the table.

A heavy silence followed. The group waited for discernment from the Fischer family and everyone's attention turned to Angelina. She breathed deeply; making sure the time was ripe to reveal a truth.

"We know that Will and his colleagues did not die. This morning we discovered they are alive and well."

Dirk and his associates stared in disbelief at Angelina and then at the rest of the group.

Before another word could be spoken, the doors of the dining room opened. Three servers came in to clear the salad plates and serve the chicken Marsala. As one of the servers cleared plates, the other two served the main course and refilled the water glasses. Everyone remained silent and waited for the servers to finish before they resumed the conversation.

When Dirk's plate was placed in front of him, the server touched his hand, looked into his eyes, and whispered, "Randy."

Dirk was stunned. He wanted to speak and stand up but could not. He paled when he recognized Will Fischer. A silent message was transmitted from Will to Randy. The director received it, managed himself back to calm, and silently watched everything continue as if nothing out of the ordinary had happened. The servers finished their work, left the room, and closed the doors behind them. The meeting was suspended while the meal was eaten.

Randy Dirk picked at his food, having lost his appetite. His heart was pounding hard and his head was spinning with thoughts he couldn't seem to control or make much sense of. When he found the appropriate moment, he excused himself to go to the restroom. He signaled his associates to stay at the table.

Favor escorted him to a private office next to the library where Will was waiting.

Chapter 41

If the only prayer you say in your whole life is "Thank You," that would suffice.
-Meister Eckhart-

"Dr. Fischer, what the hell? How in the world?"

Will shook Director Randy Dirk's hand and smiled, gesturing for him to take a seat in the plush wing back chair that faced Will's desk. Favor stood at the door in a relaxed posture, hands folded in front of him.

After sitting down himself, Will began. "Randy, thank you for being here. I need you today for my community. Not only Sunnyview, but for America and the world. Everything's changed and you need to know about it directly from me. The information I sent you and the plan we devised last month has proven to be more enlightening than we imagined. The fish took the bait. As you know, the storm that could have killed us was created, and we've tracked where it was engineered. We now know at least one perpetrator whom I'm confident will lead to others. This technology cannot be in the hands of the unenlightened. It will heap great destruction and disaster upon many innocent people and will collapse the economies of the Western World.

"We lost the schooner and almost our lives. Our physical bodies were teleported to a safe place. We then traveled astrally in realms beyond this earth plane for three and a half days of earth time. We returned early this morning with powers that can only be transmitted and received willingly, without malice of intent. This transition is of epic proportions and over time, we will communicate it to everyone. The whole team is communicating globally right now with those in trust who need to know. We are urgent in our communication and abilities to stem the tide of violent destruction taking place by humanity. We're here to awaken and liberate the consciousness of humanity in a new expanded way. The senseless destruction and violence in the world must stop."

Dirk wanted to interrupt but decided against it. He repositioned himself in the chair and prepared himself to listen and ask questions at the end of Will's explanation.

"As you well know, there are many threats by many people who are unable to see the power of their actions or simply don't care. The time for new solutions is at hand and we're leading the way. The unfolding we experienced in the invisible realms of formlessness is now being transmitted with a higher frequency and urgency to make this global transition while it can still be made. We're on the threshold of great danger and an even greater opportunity.

"Your report to the president and the secretaries of state, defense, and Homeland Security will be followed by a personal conversation with me within the next few days. Tell them not to be surprised when I show up. It will be private and informative. Much of what my colleagues and I will do, you will not know. What you need to know, however, is that we are all working for the highest and greatest good and are connected to the Company beyond all companies, beyond time and space. This is bigger than our country alone; we're talking the entire cosmos. The lower levels of consciousness must be rapidly raised to keep up with our technology or it will destroy us because of our ignorance and lack of wisdom. Humanity must awaken to the interconnectivity of all realms of being. There can be no more business as usual. Time is no longer on our side. We are in a crisis of consciousness."

Uncharacteristically, Director Randy Dirk was speechless. This debrief from Will Fischer was unlike anything he'd ever experienced. He wanted to ask a hundred questions, but he couldn't find the words. He sat staring at Will in disbelief and seemed a bit discombobulated by all the information conveyed.

Favor walked forward, tapped Dirk on the shoulder and said, "It's time to go."

He turned and reluctantly nodded his acknowledgment to Favor. Dirk turned back to Will to say good-bye. His eyes widened when he saw Will had already gone.

Dirk used the office restroom that Favor had directed him to. He stared at himself in the mirror and wondered where this would all lead and what the implications would be for him, his agency, and his family. He checked his digital recorder, pleased to see it had recorded everything. Thankfully, that would make reporting this interaction much easier and more believable.

He splashed water on his face, dried himself with a towel, and again looked at his face in the mirror. "Crisis of consciousness? Danger and opportunity? No shit!"

Favor led Dirk back to the dining room. All attention was focused on Dirk as he took his seat. He felt surprisingly confident and contained.

"I've just had an informative conversation with Dr. William C. Fischer, who is very much alive, as you said. I appreciate your candor and hospitality. I'll have my associates communicate with yours concerning the origin of the storm that came in over Lake Superior the other day and of the tracking that took place. You can give them the name and code for that contact information, and we'll coordinate our findings with yours for verification. This is a very curious time and set of circumstances unlike anything we've experienced. I hope to return soon to continue this conversation, but now we must go. Thank you for everything."

Randy Dirk and his two associates stood up to leave. Gloria, still sitting, spoke. "Remember, Randy, there can be no more business as usual. Hold onto that directive and observe its meaning as each day unfolds. Let it be your guide."

Dirk looked at this wise woman forty years his senior with respect. "I'll remember that ma'am, thank you. I'm not sure what it means at this juncture, but it's the second time I've heard it in five minutes, so I'll look into it."

Favor and Michael saw Dirk and the other two men to the door, gave their salutations, and returned to the dining room.

"What's your assessment?" Michael asked the group as he and Favor returned to their seats.

"It seems the fox wasn't really the fox after all, unless I missed something," Clare responded.

Angelina laughed. "I think the fox came into what he thought was a chicken coop to find the lead chicken was himself a fox. It's a unique experience to see what you thought was a dead chicken turn into a divine human being. I don't suspect Director Dirk has met many resurrected, shape-shifting chickens."

"That's a good one," said Sophia. "Did any of you notice Will when he came in as a server? Did you see the expression on Randy's face when Will whispered to him? I was watching the director very closely when you told him Will and his colleagues were alive and well. That was a jolt in itself. Then the doors opened and the servers walked in. He was still disoriented when Will made his presence known and never seemed the same after that. I sense the transmission Director Dirk received was more than what Will spoke to him about in the office. There was a noticeable shift in his consciousness from the time he sat down for lunch to when he walked out a few moments ago."

"The real clincher came in the office when he turned from looking at Will to me and then back to Will. In those two seconds, Will had disappeared." Favor smiled broadly, closed his eyes, and shook his head with glee.

"So, for the moment, mission accomplished. Now what?" asked Michael.

"No more business as usual," responded Will, who was leaning against the closed door. Smiles erupted throughout the room at his appearance.

"You just experienced the new expanded collective mind in action," began Will. "It was not just Randy Dirk who was changed. His two associates, all of us, everyone changed by this participatory interaction. To truly experience compassion, appreciation, and the transmission of high-frequency ascension energy, is to be transformed in ways we are just beginning to know. It is a collective consciousness brought forward through the participatory experience.

"Have you noticed how your energy has shifted from the time we began the planning earlier this morning? There are differences in your focus, the ways you experienced the meditation, and the lack of anxiety in meeting with the regional director. Did you notice the subtle shifts within you, and in those who you interacted with this morning? How awake were you to the softening that took place in our three guests from the time they arrived until the time they left? This is all a part of the way we will help transform the consciousness of humanity."

Will walked slowly around the room and rested his hands on his colleague and family's shoulders as he passed by them. "Much of the power used by humans for change has been forced. It has been about power *over* rather than power *with*. We have forced change without due consideration to whom or what we were changing. Too often, we humans have deigned our power over one another through manipulation, thus creating more disconnection and less love. Everyone is fighting a battle. What we need, in every interaction, is the power of loving-kindness and compassion. I sensed all of you experiencing that this morning. This is exactly what we've been about at Sunnyview, and it is what wants to increase within the whole fabric of humanity. Others and we who are awakening to this energy are the seeds of a new creation. What we've known and not known ends and begins right here."

Will took a deep breath. "Alert the community that tonight's contemplative gathering at six o'clock is a Code White. Put all systems in place. I will be addressing everyone who is here, and Sophia, notify our AV team to record it for those who will not be here and the media who are waiting for a story. Put all protocols in place, and thank you so very much for being the magnificently beautiful human-divine beings you are. We must continue to remember the interconnected common union that includes everybody and everything. Remember to remember, no more business as usual. There's urgency in our mission."

Chapter 42

As we acquire more knowledge and wisdom, things do not become more comprehensible, but more mysterious.
-Albert Schweitzer-

Atom opened the door of his second floor room in the main lodge at Camp Bay Island. The view of the bay was beautiful. The windows on both walls were open, allowing a gentle breeze to waft through the room. He heard a rustling of palms outside and reveled in the smells of a place he'd known from boyhood. The memories of a lifetime greeted and embraced him, welcoming him home. He sat down on his bed and then laid back to reflect on the adventure of the last twenty hours and wondered where it might lead.

Was it just yesterday afternoon I had the remembrance that brought me here? Had I just met Captain Jack? Did the interaction with Inana really happen? Had I physically touched and talked with Dad who was presumed dead only a few hours ago? As these and a thousand other thoughts and images crossed the movie screen of his mind, he relaxed on his bed, closed his eyes, and drifted off from beta to alpha and into the dreamland of theta consciousness. His sleep took him across the waters of time into another place.

"What the hell do you want with me? I have absolutely nothing to do with anything you're talking about! You have the wrong guy! What are you up to anyway? What's your motivation for doing violence to me or anyone else?" Atom turned his face and shielded it with his arms as he shouted at his captors.

Three masked men were interrogating him in a small dingy room. One of them held back his arms while the other one backhanded him across the face before spitting on him.

"You arrogant bastard. We're asking the questions! We don't have to answer to your kind anymore. We're in charge here, and if you want to get out of here alive, you'll cooperate. Your value is your information. Without that, you're just another roach that needs to be exterminated. Now answer the fucking questions!"

"How can I answer your fucking questions if I don't have the fucking answers?" *Atom struggled against the man holding him back until he was forced to his knees and held in that position.*

The interrogator backhanded him again on the other side of his face. The pain was startling.

"There you go again with your questions. We ask them. You answer them. Get it? Now let's try this again. Is your name Atom Ion Fischer?

"Yes."

"Is your father Dr. William Clarence Fischer?"

"Yes."

"Are you a graduate student in the Engineering Department at Stanford University?"

"Yes."

"Are you writing a dissertation on scalar electromagnetic energy?"

"Yes."

"See how easy this is? We ask the questions. You give the answers. Is your father alive or dead?"

"Yes."

"Another smart-ass college boy answer. He's either alive or dead. Which is it?"

"Both."

The man backhanded Atom again and snarled. "Nobody can be both alive and dead. WHICH IS IT?" *he shouted.*

Atom's vision was beginning to cloud over with darkness. He struggled getting his words out. "He was in a drowning accident, *dead but not, a state of suspended animation. He came back different. Something died and something new came to life, so he's both."*

One of the men gave a nod.

"Do you know how, or does your father know how to alter the weather?"

"No."

"Do you know how to trap and transduce the longitudinal scalar EM waves of the time domain into ordinary transverse EM energy in our three-dimensional spatial world?"

"No."

"You lying son of a bitch. We know you know."

Atom felt a massive electrical shock and jolted awake. Soaked with sweat, he felt some pain in his face and didn't know at first where he was. Looking around quickly, he remembered the familiar sights of his room at Camp Bay Island and laid his head back down, relieved. He took a couple deep breaths and wiped the sweat from his face. The dream felt uncommonly real. He sat up and looking out the window, squinted through the palm trees at the tranquil blue-green water of Camp Bay.

The vividness and realism of the dream troubled him. What did it point to? What part of him or of the collective unconscious did the characters and their behavior illustrate?

Unable to rest anymore, Atom walked to the restroom, splashed water on his face to clear his head, and went downstairs. He was relieved to find Derick in his office and walked through the open door with intention.

"Hey, Atom. I thought you'd be taking a rest. It's been a long night and day for you. What's up? You look different."

Atom sat down beside the desk. "I just had a very violent and disturbing dream. Can I share it with you?"

"Sure, but I'm no expert at dream interpretation and don't have the clairvoyant insight that the other side of your family does."

"I just need to express it. Maybe we can figure out what it's pointing to together."

"Fine, let's have it."

Atom told Derick the dream, leaving nothing out. The clarity of the scene, the feelings, and the verbatim dialogue was compelling.

"What do you think?" Atom asked.

Derick sat quiet for a long time. He got up, closed the door, moved to one of the windows, and looked out across the bay, his back to Atom. "It's the dance between darkness and light, between duality and non-duality, between what's traditionally been called good and evil." He turned, walked back to the door, opened it, and said, "Let's take a walk."

Atom nodded, stood, and joined Derick. Their silent bond ushered them to the porch, down the stairs, and out into the coconut grove.

Derick picked up a rock and smoothed the surface with his thumb as they walked through the maze of the small plantation. "This island has seen your dream and all of what it costs in human misery. This has been a place of piracy, slavery, exploitation, violence, poverty, pain, suffering . . . and all their opposites as well. It's been a microcosm of the human condition. It's no different today. The energy of all apparent opposites exists everywhere in everything. It's the electromagnetic energy field of the universe.

"Your dad and his colleagues are now highly evolved beings; prototypes who have access to immense power others want but cannot have. The present technology your dad has spent lifetimes developing and gaining access to is the stuff of prophesy, mythology, speculative fiction, and dreams. He, nor his associates, can any longer be compromised. We, on the other hand, and the rest of the immediate families can, because we're still attached to our form, flesh, and limited consciousness. We feel pain. We fear the loss of this body and that of those whom we love. We're still identified with this reality, because we don't clearly remember the other ones. We are susceptible to those who would do us and our loved ones harm."

A lone sailboat was tacking across the bay, painting a moving metaphor with each change of course.

Derick continued. "Nobody's safe in this world and yet, we're all safe. We all live in some kind of crisis from time to time. The Chinese word for crisis is composed of two words: danger and opportunity. At every turn in our lives, we face danger and opportunity. The danger in any given situation is that we'll take the low road of scorn, revenge, destruction, enslavement, and fear. The opportunity is in taking the high road of courage, trust, hope, forgiveness, wisdom, love, peace, and enlightenment. Too many people spend too much time on the low road without knowing they also have within them the high road. It's built into the system. It's part of the entelechy of our nature, like the oak tree in the seed of the acorn.

"Our choice-full-ness is what makes us human. Our awareness is what makes us divine. It's taken me a very long time to know this and be able to live it with some consistency. Your dream might be a wake-up call to this dark and light in you and in the world. There are people all around the globe who will create massive and violent destruction to have any useful technology to gain power and control. It's our job to raise our consciousness to receive and give from the opportunities of the high road and encourage others to do the same in constructive ways. Did you notice in your dream how quickly the victim mirrored the perpetrator? There's a significant lesson in that."

Atom weighed his thoughts and feelings, not ready to speak. They stopped walking at the end of the grove to enjoy the calm, gentle waves lapping the beach.

Sighing, Atom finally spoke. "Self-mirroring is a significant lesson. I was off in a place of pain, suffering, not knowing, and fear wondering what I'd do if that situation were really happening. It's not a thought I want to ponder too long. Why would someone come after me?"

"Why would someone come after Anna, your mother, your sister, me, or any of the close family members of the Mystic Travelers crew? Because we are something they could use. We might have access to information that could be compromised, especially you, because of your work with your dad on experimental projects. Isn't your dissertation dealing with the infinite energy permeating space and time and the ability to tap into that energy with a very simple dipole device that could be made inexpensively and available to everybody on the planet? Look at what that would do to the vast global energy industries. Free energy? There are major interests that would do anything to keep that technology off the market so they could exploit it for their own advantage. What about weather alteration? Imagine what special interests could do with that. If weather could be altered anywhere at any time, imagine the implications. Your dad was involved in that research at Sawyer. It's one of the reasons the facility was shut down. Will was very concerned about that information getting into the wrong hands. It now looks like it did and competing interests want it."

"I've been naive about Dad's work, as well as my own," Atom said. "All the codes we have as a family, here, and at Sunnyview have a real purpose beyond shorthand communication. I'm now realizing that the outside and inside threats are very real. All of what you've said, and the feeling I have in my gut, brings me to a place I don't want to embrace. The low road fed by fear has a huge energy vortex that can suck the life right out of me. Maybe that's part of the CAT code Dad gave me when I asked how I could contact him. The Compassion is maybe to step into the pain and suffering of others to understand where they're coming from, what drives them, and how it can be redirected. The Appreciation may be taking what is and growing it in such a way that something new is birthed. The transmission then, coming from a field of higher energy, is always possible. We can consciously live in that transition from one pole to the other, choosing the appropriate alternating energy for the task. That's what electromagnetic energy is. That's what Dad meant every time he and I parted when he said, 'Remember to remember.' It's amazing how things can be radically different with an altered perspective."

"So what does your dream mean?"

"It's a very clear message about awareness."

"Awareness of what?"

"Everything! It's telling me that I need to look beneath the surface for what's hidden. That's what scientific research and mystical inquiry is really about. It's looking at life with an inquiring mind, with vigilance and focus, to imagine and analyze the structures, and the relationships that are seen and unseen, known and unknown. I've learned how to do that in my academic and spiritual life, but I have lapses every day where I just trust that everything's going to be all right, because it usually is. Do I have to be attentive all the time . . . with everything?"

"What do you say?"

"No. Like right now, here with you and with Anna and the significant others, there's no need to guard every word and protect myself with hypervigilance. The shields can be down. In other, more unknown situations, it can be a very good policy to be vigilant, especially now with all that's happened."

Atom paused and turned to Derick suddenly. "This is a eureka moment! I just had the thought that I've never seen myself as a target before. I've never seen myself as someone special, a standout in a crowd, either positively or negatively, a man of privilege. Now, for the first time, I'm seeing the other side of it; how others have never had the privilege not to feel oppressed, free. Wow, what a revelation! I'm the rich kid so many love to hate. I'm the symbol of oppression for those who have and continue to be oppressed. Holy shit, I've never seen that before. I am and am not that man. Derick, do you get what I'm saying here?"

Derick nodded and smiled regretfully. "I've spent my whole life living with that paradox. I learned it early on when your grandfather came here to Central America way back when. We were the only white family in the area. We made more money in a day than most people here made in a year. It took me a very long time to find my way into this culture as an equal and now that you bring your perspective to it, I've never been an equal. I feel that I am, but the peoples' perception is different. They don't own an island, fly jets, have boats, and travel around the world. They don't go to the United States to birth their children, converse and dine with corporate presidents. No matter what we think, we're the privileged ones. No matter how many tattoos I have, or how well I speak the language, how funky I dress, or how much I get down with the folks, I'm still not one of them. I do see what you're saying. It's humbling."

"I can't believe I've never seen this before. What does it mean?" Atom asked.

"Be alert. Have compassion. Appreciate everybody and everything. Transition into life's process of creative energy. It all requires patience, insight, and attention."

"I like that. I can live with that formula. Now what?"

Derick looked out across Camp Bay. The schooner *Mystic Traders* was floating on a buoy a few hundred yards off shore.

"How would you like to take *Mystic Traders* for a sail with me?"

Atom's expression immediately changed into the same radiance he saw reflected on the water. "Perfect."

"I'll call Estefan and have him meet us at the dock. We'll stop at the lodge and check in with Anna. Maybe she'll want to come along . . . and Atom?" Derick paused. "Thanks for giving me the honor of standing in for your dad while he's not here for you. I can't tell you how much you mean to me. I'm here for you no matter what."

Atom smiled and gave his uncle a bear hug. "Right back at'cha, Bro. Forever and a day. Let's go sailing."

Chapter 43

Modern physics has confirmed one of the basic ideas of Eastern mysticism; that all the concepts we use to describe nature are limited, creations of the mind; parts of the map, not the territory. Whenever we expand the realm of our experience, the limitations of our rational mind become apparent and we have to modify, or even abandon, some of our concepts.
-Fritjof Capra-

"I don't know why we have to follow up on all this shit. If they're dead, they're dead. If they're not, they're not. We moved the command station to Nicaragua. Even if they were tracking our transmission location, we're no longer there, so what's the big deal?" In frustration, Marc threw the folder he was holding across the table.

Comrade Dmitri picked up the discarded folder and leafed through it. "The big deal is that we don't know what they know. If they're dead then fine, but who in their intimate circles know about what we want to know? Who, in their closed communities, have access to their data that could hinder us or help us expand our research and development? Fischer has a son at Stanford doing graduate work in electrical engineering. That would be a good place to start."

Colonel Chekov furrowed his brow, narrowed his eyes, and raised his voice. "We already have a couple comrades out there trying to find him! We also have another checking into a room at the Fischer compound in Michigan right now. She'll be there for a few days to find out who is in the know and what they know. We had to pull our other operative out for a new mission. He didn't uncover much. We're also working on a Honduran connection. One of our South American cells is tracking Dr. Miguel Santana's connections in Argentina while an Asian cell is looking into Dr. Aya Sakura's people in Japan. The European connections are locating Dr. Sonja Braun's family in Germany and Russia, and our Middle Eastern cells are investigating Dr. Shareef Amari's associations in Egypt and India.

"Will Fischer and his colleagues were all well connected with intimate associations. We may be small, but we're thorough, informed, and well connected through our many networks. This project is too big to leave any stone unturned. We must find all those who have any significant information on us, milk them for what they know, and destroy them."

Colonel Chekov crossed his arms over his puffed-out chest and glanced at Nicholi, hoping his superior was as pleased with him as he was of himself. Chekov, a former army officer and top KGB agent during the Cold War had befriended Doctor Nicholi Billsnev when he was looking for the lifestyle he'd lost when the Soviet Union collapsed. He found his soul mate of darkness in Billsnev, who stood silently listening to his executive team plan their revised strategy.

*   *   *

"Dr. Nicholi Billsnev was a former Russian scientist and politico," reported Director Randy Dirk in a briefing at the NSA headquarters in Minneapolis. "He appears to be the brain trust of the operation. He was a former associate of Will Fischer's from the research institute at Sawyer back in the nineties. It seems he managed to smuggle classified data off the compound to continue his own work on the unfinished government and privately funded experiments that were most sensitive. For more than a decade, he's continued to work with a small group of associates to create a new technology in motionless electromagnetic generation. He's also focused on scalar interferometry involving weather alteration, and it appears he's recently made a significant breakthrough that allows him to manipulate the weather." Dirk looked up from his briefing report, stroked his chin, and reflected briefly. "I was the chief security officer at Sawyer and remember this guy. I always had my suspicions about him but could never prove anything. He's a dangerous genius. We're now receiving reports that he's using that technology to blackmail governments and private industry globally. His goal is world domination. He's moved from fifteen years of obscurity to the top of our most wanted list.

"Dr. Fischer's discovery of Billsnev's plans triggered his wrath and revenge on Will and his colleagues, thus creating the rogue storm that sank their ship and nearly killed them. Will anticipated the possibility and turned the tables. The hunt for Black-ops is now happening on both sides of the divide. Billsnev is a powerful and unseen force we must deal with. I'm taking this to Washington today, so get on it. We have this as our top priority."

*　　*　　*

"Chekov has it right concerning the Fischer group; we're on a search and destroy mission. Whoever knows something that is vital to us will have it extracted. After extraction, extinction. We'll let the ants lead us to the food so we can have it and then destroy them. There are millions of ants." Nicholi Billsnev walked around the conference table, hands clasped behind his back, and scrutinized his team. "We're so close to what I've dreamed of all my life. We no longer have any governments over us to tell us what to do or how to do it. I have no one to interfere with my plans. Finally, *I am* becoming the master. *I am* finding the power of God."

He stopped and released his folded hands. He became animated as he pointed to the globe and then to the maps of the world hanging on the walls. "*I am* in control of the weather as

I choose: earthquakes, floods, droughts, tornadoes, hurricanes, blizzards, ice storms. *I can* control it all. Warm the air over here, cool it down over there, put a curl in the jet stream, create clouds, dissipate clouds, and all from any remote location I choose. *I am* the GENIUS, and the great Dr. William Clarence Fischer's time is up. He led me down this path, right to his own destruction. *I am* the MASTER. *I am* my own GOD and whatever I do is RIGHT!" Billsnev's face turned red as he pounded his fist on the table to make his point clear. The three other men in the room flinched.

Billsnev's eyes drilled into his second in command. "Chekov, you head this project concerning Fischer's colleagues and their closest family and associates. Stay on it until it's complete, and do whatever it takes for as long it takes. When you're done with them, we'll move on to the others. Nobody alive will know anything about us that we don't want them to know. Get on it and stay on it. The rest of you, do whatever he directs you to do."

Chekov and the rest nodded, saluted, and left the room, perhaps too eagerly, but Billsnev didn't notice. He stood alone looking at the map of the world. "It's all mine," he said, laughing at how easy his goal had become. "All mine!"

Chapter 44

*By and large, Western civilization is a celebration of the illusion
that good may exist without evil, light without darkness, and
pleasure without pain. In reality, life is paradox and mystery.*
-Alan Watts-

Matt heard a knock at his door. Irritated at the interruption, he
took his time getting up from his computer to walk across the
living room floor. Two men in dark suits and sunglasses stared at
him through the screen door.

"What can I do for you?" Matt stopped near the door but
didn't attempt to open it.

"We're looking for Atom Fischer. Is he home?"

"Who are you?"

"We're agents Montgomery and Smith from the IRS. We'd
like to speak to Mister Fischer."

"He's not here, and I don't know when he'll be back."

"Where is he?"

"Not that it's any of your business, but he left yesterday for a
hiking trip in the mountains. Can I have one of your cards, and
he can get in touch with you when he returns."

"No, we'll come back another day. Did he drive? Fly? Is he
alone?"

"Look guys," replied Matt. "I don't know anything about it.
I'm not my roommate's keeper; we don't check in and out with
each other."

"Thanks. We don't need to leave a card, we'll find him."

Matt stood and watched as the men walked off the porch and across the street to a black SUV.

There's something strange about those two, Matt thought. He pulled out his smart phone and took pictures of the men before they got into their vehicle and again as they drove away. He went back to his desk, and feeling worried for his friend, downloaded the pictures into his computer. He sent them to Atom and then stared at nothing for several minutes, unable to refocus on his work.

The same two supposed IRS agents also visited Tommy at the CAT office in Palo Alto.

"Yeah, I know Atom Fischer. He was here yesterday inquiring about a flight to Lake Tahoe. We didn't have anything so he left. I haven't seen him since."

"Who was he planning to stay with in Tahoe?" Agent Montgomery asked.

"I don't know. He passes through from time to time, so if you want to leave a business card, I'll be happy to give it to him."

"No, that won't be necessary," he replied. "Thanks for the info."

"No problem." Tommy watched them leave the office and visually followed them. *IRS, my ass*, he thought. *I had better send Captain Jack a message. I don't like the feel of this.*

Back at Camp Bay Island, Atom and Derick had gone out for a sail. Anna had denied their request to join them. Atom hadn't been on *Mystic Traders* in more than a year. Setting the rigging, feeling the wind on his face, and gliding across the calm waters on the leeward side of the Island of Roatan was a holiday in itself.

As a teenager, he'd sailed with his Alexander family on the Great Lakes as well as with his Fischer family on the Caribbean. He now realized those experiences were ones of privilege, even though he'd never considered it that way until today. He wished everyone could experience the freedom, the quiet, and the communion with nature it allowed him to feel.

They were on the west end of Roatan Island heading east, back to Camp Bay a mile off shore, when Atom and Derick noticed a large powerboat coming toward them from the shoreline. They gave little attention, as boats came and went frequently at this end of the island. A few minutes later, however, they both commented on the speed of the powerboat; it seemed headed straight toward them. They maintained their course with an eye to the approaching boat. It was barreling toward them and getting dangerously close. Derick ordered Atom to blow the air horn and prepare to reverse course. Atom blew one long blast and then three short blasts. The powerboat did not adjust direction or slow down. It was on a crash course.

"Prepare to jibe!" yelled Derick.

"Ready!" Atom called back, bringing the boom to center position and prepared to release the jib sail.

"Jibe ho!"

Derick turned the rudder sharply off the tack they were on, bringing the stern across the wind heading the schooner back west. Atom pulled the line of the jib sheet tight to set the sail and let out the boom to catch more wind. The jibe was complete. They were heading away from what could have been an ugly crash.

The powerboat slowed, changed course, and caught up with *Mystic Traders*. There were two men on the bridge and two men with rifles standing on the bow and stern, respectively. They were all dressed in uniform. One of the men on the bridge held a megaphone to his mouth. "Come about and drop your sails!" he commanded. "This is the Honduran Coast Guard!"

Derick was skeptical. He'd lived here most of his life and had never seen a Honduran Coast Guard vessel that looked like this. *Mystic Traders* had sailed these waters for two decades and the Coast Guard knew his boat. *This is not what it appears to be*, he thought.

"Go below and call the Coast Guard on channel fourteen," cried Derick. "Tell them what's happening, and ask them to identify the problem. If they don't know what you're talking about, call Mayday. I think we're under attack. Do it now! I'll hold the course."

Atom went below. "*Mystic Traders* calling Honduran Coast Guard, come in. *Mystic Traders* calling Coast Guard, come in."

"Honduran Coast Guard to *Mystic Traders* . . . go ahead . . . over."

"This is Derick and Atom Fischer from Camp Bay Island. We're two miles due south of West Bay in a Hylas sloop hailed by a vessel claiming to be one of yours. Please verify. The men are armed and preparing to board . . . over."

"One moment please, over . . . ."

To Atom, the seconds seemed like minutes. The response finally came. "We have no vessels in that vicinity . . . over."

"Then we have a Mayday, SOS, and request immediate assistance. Send a helicopter or the fastest boat you have. We're being hijacked . . . over."

"Roger that *Mystic Traders*. We're on our way. We'll get there ASAP. Stall them as long as you can . . . over."

"We'll try to maintain our course to West Bay . . . over."

"Roger, *Mystic Traders*. Stay calm and move slowly, we'll keep the line open."

Atom kept the radio on transmit and returned to the cockpit where Derick was trying to stall the four men in the powerboat.

"The Coast Guard's on its way. These guys are impostors." Atom bent down to pick up a rope while he addressed his uncle so the men couldn't read his lips or catch wind of his words.

"Roll up the jib very slowly," Derick said, talking with his back to the men. "We need to buy some time. We need to act as if we're following their orders. When you finish securing the jib, start lowering the main. At the first reef point, hook it, and make it look like you got jammed. We can only hope the Coast Guard arrives before these guys catch onto our stall. Stay with trying to fix the jam until I give the order to drop the sheet. Follow the order, unhook it, and slowly lower it. Wrap the sail and join me at the helm. We'll figure out where we are from there."

The man on the bullhorn again barked the command. "Come about and drop your sails!" They wanted Derick to head the boat directly into the wind, thereby stalling any forward motion and bringing the boat to rest.

Derick moved the rudder slightly in that direction, keeping his eyes on the sails and the men with the guns. Atom had the jib rolled and was making his way toward the mast to begin lowering the mainsail. They both came to attention at the sudden machine gunfire, hearing bullets split the air close to them.

"One final time!" the man on the bullhorn warned. "Come about and drop your sail!"

Derick brought the schooner about.

"Drop the sheet, Atom," Derick ordered.

He did so, dropping the mainsail and securing it. He then joined his uncle at the helm. They were now like a cork in the water. The powerboat came alongside *Mystic Traders* to secure the bow and stern lines. The two men with rifles boarded *Mystic Traders*. The helmsman controlled the boat while the other traded his bullhorn for a rifle and kept a bead on Atom and Derick.

"You're coming with us," one of the men said.

"Don't fight or you're dead," the other added.

Derick and Atom were forcefully escorted onto the powerboat. The lines connecting the boats were released, and they powered off full speed for the open water heading southwest toward Nicaragua. *Mystic Traders* was adrift by herself. Clouds appeared overhead. A storm was brewing.

Chapter 45

The universe is not only stranger than we imagined, but stranger than we can imagine.
-Sir Arthur Eddington-

The Honduran Coast Guard Cutter in transit from West Bay was able to make visual contact with the abductors a mile out as the boat powered across the water with Derick and Atom. They radioed ahead to their La Ceiba station on the Honduran mainland to report the last heading. The Coast Guard lost them in a storm that seemed to come in from nowhere creating a squall and thick fog. The Coast Guard was forced to turn around. They retrieved *Mystic Traders* and towed her to Camp Bay Island.

Estefan received a radio message to meet the Coast Guard Cutter and *Mystic Traders* at the buoy and hear the detailed report of the abduction. He immediately contacted Captain Jack, who was now on his way to Camp Bay Island from Miami.

Estefan then contacted Angelina at Sunnyview. "Mrs. Fischer, this is Estefan from Camp Bay. I have some news that you need to hear and relay to Dr. Fischer immediately, if you can."

"What is it Estefan?"

"Atom and Derick were sailing *Mystic Traders* this afternoon. They were hijacked two miles out from West Bay. They were taken from the schooner in a powerboat. The Coast Guard lost contact with the pirates in a squall and thick fog. They are still in pursuit, but they have not located them yet. Captain Jack is flying to the island right now from Miami. I'm sorry, it happened about a half hour ago."

There was a long pause on the other end of the line. "How is Anna?" Angelina asked.

"I haven't told her yet. I'll speak with her after we hang up."

"Tell her we're with her and all will be well. I will contact Dr. Fischer, and we'll have them back very soon. Thank you so very much for contacting me, Estefan. We'll be in touch."

Estefan jogged from the CAT hanger to the main lodge. Anna was working in the garden and she looked up as he approached.

"Good afternoon, Estefan!" Her face lit up when she saw him. "How are you this fine day? I haven't seen you since all the mornings' activity. Have you noticed the weather change off the mainland coast?"

His face had concern written all over it. Her demeanor changed. "What's wrong? You don't look well."

"Derick and Atom have been kidnapped. They were abducted from *Mystic Traders*. The Coast Guard is towing her back right now. I'm meeting them at the buoy. The captain said he would brief us and take our statements then. Captain Jack is on his way from Miami, and I've talked to Angelina. She said to tell you they are with you, all will be well, and that Dr. Fischer would be contacted. Would you like to go out in the runabout with me to meet with the Coast Guard or should I have them come to the house?" Estefan felt the heaviness of his message and barely took a breath during his report.

Anna took a deep breath and held up her hand. "Just give me a moment." Kneeling in the garden, she dropped her digging tools and placed both hands on her abdomen where her baby was still growing. She closed her eyes to breath in a peaceful and secure presence. She felt the anxiety of abandonment that was so destructive to children wash over her, then subside, and transform to a fluid, loving companion presence. Slowly, gently, she began to hum a lullaby, the simple act that always calmed the waters and connected mother and child with the peaceful presence of life. The rhythm of the song connected with her body. She slowly rocked as she cradled herself and her child. The realignment with the calm center of the universe was reestablished and all was well. Estefan watched in silent amazement and was touched. With the help of Estefan, Anna slowly stood up and smiled.

"Everything's okay now. We'll find out as much as we can from the Coast Guard, give them what information will be helpful, and be the family who brings our men back home alive. We're good, Estefan. Let's play our part. Let's do this thing!"

They walked slowly to the dock, arm in arm. Estefan lowered the shallow draft twenty-foot runabout into the water and steadied it while Anna stepped in. They motored to the buoy. They could see the Coast Guard Cutter towing *Mystic Traders* in an approach to the rendezvous point.

After *Mystic Traders* was secured to the buoy, Estefan and Anna joined the captain and his first officer on the cutter anchored a short distance away.

Following introductions, Anna and Estefan listened to the recording of Atom and the radio operator. They heard the man on the megaphone, the machine gunfire, the orders not to resist, and the roar of the engines as the boat sped away. There were no clues pointing to why or by whom the abduction took place.

"Who do you know who might want to kidnap your husband and nephew?" Captain Garcia asked Anna.

"I really don't know."

"Estefan?"

"Atom just arrived, he was here visiting. I think he was just an extra fish in the net. As for Derick, he's been very successful in business, but I can't imagine any of his associates doing something like this."

"What about Will Fischer?"

"What about him?" Anna questioned.

"He was a famous scientist who died in a storm a few days ago, and is obviously closely related to Derick and Atom. Do you think there might be any connection between his death and this abduction?"

Anna remained calm but firm. "Captain Garcia, we're still unclear about what happened to Will. A connection is certainly possible and there are still people looking into that, but our present concern is how you're tracking the boat that took our family. What kind of assistance do you have locating it, and what are the odds of finding it?"

"Of course, ma'am. We have the whole fleet on alert, but the storm that came out of nowhere has the entire southern end of the coast socked in with zero visibility. They could be anywhere. We'll stay on it, but our options are limited until the storm lifts. We have to consider that, and by then, it might be too late to track them."

Chapter 46

*I am the flower, part of joy and a part of sorrow. I look up high
to see only the light, and never look down to see my shadow. This
is wisdom which humanity must learn.*
-Khalil Gibran-

Derick and Atom found themselves on the floor of a tiny room
below deck in the powerboat. They were gagged and blindfolded,
their hands and feet bound. Circumstances forced them to
communicate in a multisensory and transrational way.

Each remembered the words Will had spoken to them about
this possibility and their response to it: *It's a RAW wind that
blows in your face as you lean into it with Radical Acceptance and
Willingness. Patiently persevere with faith, optimism, and reverence.
The CAT has nine lives, because she is awake to all possibilities.
Feel the confusion and pain of the other. Find the Compassion to
discover the vulnerability of the opposing force. Appreciate it. Grow
the potentialities for the Transition that is taking place in the
moment. You will always know what to do and help will all ways
be present and on its way. Ask for the help you need and give thanks
immediately as it's already there. Anything is possible, be awake to
that. Vigilance in repose brings patient awareness for the ripeness of
the moment. Remember to remember.*

Derick began humming the song Anna sang when she needed
to remember the light in the darkness and realign herself with it.
Atom recognized it from his childhood and earlier that morning

with Anna. The words formed in their brain-mind bodies. *This little light of mine, I'm gonna let it shine. This little light of mine, I'm gonna let it shine. This little light of mine, I'm gonna let it shine. Let is shine, let it shine, let it shine.*

As they hummed together, a new energy entered the dark cramped space. A familiar mindfulness reawakened, and their hearts sang together the song of faith, optimism, and renewal.

CAT was with them; purring, bringing solace and strength, pardon and renewal. Their dark night dawned into a new day and a new way of being. They began transmitting and receiving messages to and from each other and a plan began to emerge. Help from the depths of their beings was making itself known. They both saw and heard Will tell them to stay the course, because he was with them and help was present. A light was shining in the darkness. They had awakened as if from a bad dream. Humming their childlike song had become their hymn of the universe.

*   *   *

Activities at Sunnyview had increased as everyone received the Code White directive to be fulfilled at the six o'clock evening gathering of the community. The call concerning the abduction of Atom and Derick had added to the activity, initiating a review and scrutiny of the satellite images routinely received from Camp Bay Island and the surrounding vicinity. The recorded images of Estefan delivering Derick and Atom to *Mystic Traders* were retrieved as well as their sail to West Bay and the hijacking. The powerboat's departure point and identification markers were noted and the identity of the abductors was being analyzed.

The senior technical supervisor of Sunnyview's satellite tracking station addressed the hermetic circle at Gloria's dining room table in her apartment. "The trajectory of the boat looks to be Trujillo on the Honduran mainland. The line runs from *Mystic Traders* at the abduction point to where we lost them in the cloud cover. They could have changed direction after that, but if they stayed on course from that point of departure, they would be headed directly to Trujillo. There's a busy port at the east end of the bay and a private airstrip down the beach from the Christopher Columbus Hotel. It's a large green architectural curiosity that would make a good landmark. They may be headed there to make a transfer by air. From there, who knows? With all the preparation for Code White, we got busy and missed the event in real time. I take full responsibility for the oversight."

"It's okay, Phillip, I understand. I appreciate the briefing, thanks. Do any of the rest of you have any questions for Phillip?" Angelina asked the others.

"Make sure this information gets to Estefan and Captain Jack. We need to keep them informed. They are vital links to this operation," Sophia responded.

"Done." Phillip, the technical supervisor nodded.

"Anything else?" Angelina asked again. When the group collectively shook their heads, Angelina put her hand on Phillip's arm. "Thanks again, you've been very informative. You can get back to work now and keep us informed as events unfold."

He nodded his consent, bowed slightly, and left the room. Gloria, Clare, Sophia, Favor, and Michael all looked to Angelina expectantly.

"We will continue with the plans for this evening's events. Code White is in effect until we complete the process or Will calls it off. NBC, CNN, and the BBC are already here being briefed and setting up. We have a public announcement to make for the greater good. Have any of you had any contact with Will?"

"I have a deep sense that Will already knows about this latest series of events and is on it," said Gloria. "This must be what I was sensing this morning about danger at a great distance. Will said he felt it too but couldn't identify or locate it. Now that his brother and son have been abducted, I'm confident Will is there with them and that Atom and Derick know it. All is well and all shall be well."

"Anything else for the good of the order?" Angelina asked.

"It was brought to my attention that a woman has arrived here from Montreal for a three-day retreat. Her name is reportedly

Barbara Brown," Favor reported. "Our intuitive at the check-in desk picked up some very disturbing frequencies in her energy field, so we ran a check on her. Her reported information is invalid. She's highly suspect. We placed monitoring companions close to her, and we will track all her communications and response frequencies. She feels like someone who might be connected with Bill Black."

"*Ola Kala* then," Angelina concluded. "Be awake to the energies. They seem to be showing up in all kinds of ways, and Clare, I need to see you for a minute. The rest of you can get back to what you were doing. Thank you so very much for all you do and all you are."

The room cleared except for Clare, Angelina, and Gloria. They drew to one another like magnets. Mothers and daughters embraced for a very long time exchanging the breadth of their emotions without words. The divine matrix of primary cause that mothers and daughters embody reverenced itself and reached out to Will, Atom, Derick, Anna, and all with whom they shared this reality, even those lost in the sea of destruction, enslavement, and aggression. The sacred unity and intimate compassion that Clare, Angelina, and Gloria experienced in this receptive embrace was filled with healing and wholeness.

"Love is the healing," Angelina said. It radiated in, around, and through them, and outward into the world as a gift of divine presence and new beginnings for all.

Chapter 47

Death is our eternal companion. It is always to our left, at arm's length. It has always been watching you. It always will until the day it takes you. The thing to do when you're anxious, is to turn to your left and ask advice from your death.
-Don Juan-

The steady roar of the engines running at full speed lessened as the boat slowed. The pounding of the hull on the water stopped and the boat slowed and gradually moved gently through the water. Finally, the engine came to an idle and the boat glided toward the beach. The door flew open and two men grabbed Derick and Atom, forcing them upright and out into a larger space. The bindings around their ankles were removed and they were guided up steps leading to the stern of the boat. The fresh moist air greeted their nostrils and bare skin. The sounds of lapping waves and a small aircraft in the distance registered in their ears. They were pushed to the back deck of the boat and shoved into knee-deep water. An additional guard for each man had walked out from the beach and was now at their sides. The boat made its way back out to sea without them.

In the distance, obscured by fog, was a large green architectural anomaly. Atom and Derick were hustled across the beach, past the green structure to the airstrip without notice, each still bound, gagged, and blindfolded. They heard the noise of a two-engine aircraft grow louder as they approached. The door of the six-passenger Cessna opened. Derick was pushed into the backseat and accompanied by one guard, and Atom was thrust into the middle seat behind the pilot accompanied by the other guard. As the door closed, the plane taxied to the runway and powered up into the dense fog. Ten minutes into the flight, the aircraft leveled off reaching its cruising altitude and breaking into the bright clear sky. Atom and Derick both sensed the difference even though duct tape covered their eyes. A sharp poke of a needle into their arms broke the awareness of light and dropped them into a deep darkness as the sedative entered their bloodstreams and shut down their consciousness.

Each guard pulled off the duct tape wrapped around Derick and Atom's heads that covered their eyes, ears, and mouths. They also removed the handcuffs that had drawn blood from their wrists. It was a short flight from Trujillo, Honduras, to Puerto Cabezas, Nicaragua, or Bilwi, as the locals called it. Puerto Cabezas was a small scruffy port town where everybody was doing some kind of business, from lumber merchants and fishermen, to drug runners and political activists. The region was perfect for the current mission, because the people had little money, lots of guns, and minded their own business.

The plane touched down at an airstrip two miles north of town where a Hummer waited to transport the hostages to a remote outpost in one of the most impenetrable and underdeveloped regions of the Americas. No roads connected the area with the rest of the country, and the back roads in and around the area were unmarked, dangerously under maintained, and difficult to navigate, preventing most non-locals from venturing outside the confines of the gritty little town.

The local customs officials had already been paid off, so the transfer from the aircraft to the Hummer went unnoticed and undocumented. After loading the unconscious Derick and Atom into the vehicle, the two guards climbed into the Hummer.

The driver was an expatriate from the United States who worked freelance for the highest bidder, and had been around these parts for decades, washed upon its shores by drug running, defrauding, and a series of bad choices. The guards were also from the United States but had stories that set them apart and kept them together.

"My name is Sam Smith," the driver said as he lit a cigarette and addressed the two guards who had just entered his vehicle. "I've never seen you guys around these parts before. What's your connection with this operation?"

They looked at each other then back to Sam. "What's it to you?" the one in the front seat answered.

"Nothing really, but you guys look like Arabs, and I've never seen any Arabs doing this kind of work on this side of the fence before, and your youth, what are you, late twenties or so?"

"Are you writing a book or what?" questioned the first responder. "We're just a couple of alienated guys who hate racial profiling and discrimination, and you're starting to piss me off."

"Hey, no offense, man. I'm just wondering if you know what you're getting into. The guys who hired us aren't the kind you want to mess with. They kill people without even thinking about it. We're just the hired thugs who do their bidding. We're nothing to them, so if you're already alienated, you'll be more so with this bunch. We're just as expendable as those two unconscious guys riding with us. Names, what do I call you?"

"What's it to you?" the guy in the front seat asked again.

"Look guys, we're going to a very remote outpost and don't know how long we'll be there. You're going to need a compadre. I need a handle, a name for each of you so the others will think you're part of something bigger than you are. It's not for me, it's for you."

"My name is Anthony Amir and his name is Ihsaan Jameson," the one in the backseat answered.

"Whoa, we need a couple of names that sound American, because we're dealing with Russians, so maybe I'll just call you Tony and James, what about it?"

"That'll work," Ihsaan said.

"Who are the guys we're bringing in?" Sam asked.

"We don't know, and it's none of our business. We were just ordered to be here from our superiors, so here we are. We don't know anything," Anthony replied.

"You're quick studies. A perfect answer. Keep playing like this and you'll be fine. Keep your heads down and your mouths shut. Do what you're told without question and you'll get out of this alive and in one piece. Welcome to the world of Sam Smith."

* * *

Atom woke up groggy and disoriented in a hot damp concrete room. Derick was lying on the floor next to him, still unconscious. There were no windows in the room. A single lightbulb was screwed into a socket in the center of a twelve-foot ceiling adding heat and light to the cell. Two cameras hung from the ceiling at opposite corners. Atom had no orientation of time or place. He stood to stretch, rubbed his sore wrists, and approached the steel door that led into the unknown. Just as he reached the door, he heard Derick groan and begin to wake up. He turned to watch Derick lift his arm up to cover his eyes from the bright overhead light. Atom walked back to him and knelt down.

"Don't talk above a whisper. We're being monitored, and we can't let them hear anything we say. Now that we're awake, they could come in any moment for us. What's the plan?"

Derick dropped his arm from his face, looked at Atom, and sat up to lean against him.

"The truth will set us free, and we have to accept that death is still at arm's length. We may not get out of this alive, so it's time to let go of any fear and embrace what is in whatever way we can," Derick whispered.

"Agreed. Maybe we can turn one or more of our captors toward a different light. That would be a good final act for this play," Atom said.

"That's the attitude. It's just a little hitch in the get along. Remember to remember."

"I'm not sure how," responded Atom hurriedly, "but I sense this little journey might be happening for us as well as to us. It's part of a difficult educational opportunity. I'm starting to feel better already. Let's dance our way out of here. We have nothing to lose, so let's have a little fun with it, if we can. Dad's on his way so we have to buy some time and create some diversion. It's an opportunity to go with the flow and see where it leads. I trust the flowing river and rooting tree."

"Attitude adjustment . . . right." Derick rubbed his eyes. "This morning we were dancing with a new song. Let's see if we can keep it moving along. The guys who brought us here definitely need some lightheartedness in their lives. Maybe we can provide it for them. No more business as usual. No more heaviness. Death can be our new dance partner. What an idea, what a way to go, what a plan. I think we've lost our minds!"

The door opened and two young men walked in, grabbed Derick, and removed him from the room. The door slammed shut behind them. Before Atom allowed doubt to set in, he crawled to the wall and sat against it in a meditative posture. After a couple of moments, he sensed he was not alone. A still small voice inside kept reminding him of compassion, appreciation, and transmission. He imagined a smiling face that looked like his dad's face. He felt encouraged.

Derick was taken to another concrete room, this one with a steel table bolted to the floor and accompanied by two chairs. He was placed on one of the chairs while his hands were cuffed to the steel tabletop. The men stepped away to stand beside the door. Two older, well-worn men stepped into the room and shut the door. It was Colonel Chekov and his accomplice, Comrade Dmitri. Chekov pulled out a chair and sat down. He glared at Derick.

"Well, Mr. Fischer, it seems we've been given a twofer. We thought your nephew was still in California and much to our surprise, we find him with you. You've saved us significant time and effort. Thank you."

"You're welcome and who are you and why are we here?"

"You are here because we want you here. We want to find out more about Fischer Enterprises and your role with your brother Will. So sorry to hear about his death, he was such a great asset to us. What do you know about his work with scalar electromagnetic energy systems?"

"I'm not a scientist. I don't know what you're talking about."

"Come now, Mr. Fischer, you can't be ignorant of his greatest discoveries and accomplishments. You've been working together since you were boys. He never once even mentioned scalar energy?"

"I'm in the import export business. I know commodities, materials, shipping, and handling. I don't know theories and experimental research. I'm just the guy on the ground. Even if he mentioned it along the way, I didn't pay any attention. He and I lived in very different worlds and had very different interests. He has postdoctoral degrees and credentials. I didn't even finish college. I was the roustabout, he the scholar. Ask me about fish and coconuts, bamboo and mahogany, ships and trade routes, and I'll give you tons of information. If you can see it, touch it, taste it, smell it, or hear it, I can talk about it. Beyond that, you need to talk with my brother."

"Unfortunately, your brother is dead, and you were one of the closest people to him so we're talking to you."

Remember to remember. The truth will set you free, Derick heard from within him.

"What if I were to tell you that my brother is not dead?"

Chekov's demeanor changed immediately. "That would be very interesting information. If you could prove it, it could mean your life. Where is he?"

Derick knew he had found an opening. *Now, what to do with it? How can I use this truth to our advantage? How can I buy the necessary time for Will and whomever else is on their way to arrive? What can I say that will help set us free?*

"Exactly what do you want?" Derick asked.

"I want to know everything you know about Dr. Fischer's research on scalar energy, and I want to know everything he knows."

"The first one is easy. I don't know anything. The second is between you and Will, and I'm not at all sure where he is. He travels all the time."

"If, however, he knew you were in trouble and your life and the life of his son were in jeopardy, he'd find you and make every effort to save you, would he not?"

"I'd say that would be a sure bet," said Derick.

Chekov stood, spoke to Dmitri in the corner, and walked out the door.

Dmitri directed Anthony and Ihsaan to take Derick to his cell and bring Atom back with them.

The door to Atom's cell opened. Derick was released and Atom was summoned. They exchanged looks with each other and sent a message of hope and resolve. Atom was escorted to the interrogation room and cuffed to the table. The two young guards waited inside the closed door. Atom sat staring at the two Anglo-Arab men whom he imagined were only a few years older than he was. It was curious to him that they would be part of this operation. He seized the opportunity to engage them.

"My name is Atom Fischer. I'm from Michigan and for the past seven years have been living in Palo Alto, California, going to school at Stanford. What are your names and where did you guys go to school?"

The introduction and questions startled the two guards. Anthony appeared especially agitated. He'd never met Atom but he knew him. He was Clare's brother, Angelina's son, and Gloria Alexander's grandson. He was the male heir to the family he so admired and had so much inner conflict with. He could feel sweat running down his back and beading on his forehead.

"We're nobody and nothing. We're Justice. That's it. That's all," responded Ihsaan.

"Come on, guys. It is just us, and we can cut through all the bullshit and all the false pride and really get to our common parts if we choose to. I don't know the others involved in this mission, but I can guess they don't have your best interests at heart. What do you want? What do you hope to gain by being a part of this operation? My uncle and I are not your enemies. We probably have more in common with you than the people you're working for. Why are you here? What's your purpose? Who do you serve?"

Anthony was starting to crack. He remembered the many hours and days he'd spent at Sunnyview with Clare and the community. It had been like being in his mother's arms. There had been so much acceptance and loving companion presence at Sunnyview. His anger and resentment had melted and when he was called back into the darkness, into the hardness that had controlled him for so long, something became lost. Something had died and been reborn at Sunnyview that he'd not been able to access until this moment. *What am I doing here? What is my purpose? Whom do I serve?*

Ihsaan answered. "I might ask you the very same questions. What is your purpose? You, who knows nothing about prejudice and injustice. Whom do you serve besides yourself and those like you? What have you suffered? What have you lost? What have you been denied that cuts at the fabric of your soul?"

"Ihsaan, that's enough. Be quiet," Anthony commanded.

"Ihsaan, what a beautiful name," Atom responded. "Doesn't that mean kindness, active goodness, helpful, beneficence?"

"How do you know that? No Anglo male I've ever met has known that."

"You're the second person in two days who has said that to me," said Atom. "The other one was a beautiful young woman named Inana. We met on a flight from Palo Alto to Belize. She was with her father and mother, beautiful family. To answer your question, my family taught my sister, the other children in our community, and me Arabic, and the earlier language of Aramaic. We think knowing our roots and ancestry is an important part of knowing who we are. Ihsaan, in your kindness, goodness, and helpfulness, what do you want?"

Ihsaan was stunned. He was putting the puzzle together and getting more agitated by the second. He was about to react when the door opened. Colonel Chekov and Comrade Dmitri entered. Chekov walked to the table, sat down in the chair, and looked at Atom with disdain and admiration. He knew this young man was as brilliant as his father was and as gritty as his uncle. He also knew he needed to lay the snare carefully to catch his prey and have his way.

Chapter 48

*Perhaps the ultimate enterprise of the twenty-first century will
be the establishment of a tranquility base, not on the moon, but
within humankind.*
-Kenneth R. Pelletier-

All the preparations for Code White at the six o'clock evening
contemplative gathering had been made. A simple meditation was
planned to precede a brief appearance and talk by Dr. William
Clarence Fischer, who was still presumed dead by the community.
Code White was a designation given for mandatory attendance
by everyone in residence and connected with the community. All
projects including satellite tracking, farming, energy production,
recreation, and study would be suspended or put on autopilot.

The events of the day changed the talk Will wanted to
give. Since connecting with Atom and Derick telepathically in
transit to Trujillo, he had been monitoring the situation through
his ability of remote viewing. He had seen and heard Derick's
interrogation and was waiting to monitor Atom's examination.
He sensed the direction of the evolving plan and was prepared
to intervene at the appropriate moment if necessary. He knew
Captain Jack was preparing to do whatever was needed as well.
Will was pleased that everything was coming together. His talk
would be brief, he would meet with the hermetic circle in private
immediately after the speech, and depart to Camp Bay.

The evening meditation started with a brief announcement by Angelina concerning the circumstances of the gathering. The outside and in-house media had been briefed and were inconspicuously placed in the kiva, ready to record the event. The temple bells rang three sets of three and then a succession of nine. The brief reading was slowly repeated three times with four minutes of silence between each reading. At the end of the third passage, during a period of silence, the door to the kiva opened and the temple bell rang eleven times. Will walked down the steps and into the center of the kiva. When the bells stopped vibrating, the silence was deafening. All eyes were riveted on Will.

Smiling, he looked at the startled faces that showed joy, appreciation, and love. "If I didn't know any better, I'd think you'd all just seen a ghost. I'm back!"

The silence broke as the crowd laughed and applauded, some shouting out acclamations.

When the noise subsided, Will spoke addressing each person in his audience. "I'm here to tell you and the world that my colleagues and I had near death experiences and are back to relate them to you as we continue our recovery. I speak for Doctors Miguel Santana of Argentina, Aya Sakura of Japan, Sonja Braun of Germany and Russia, and Shareef Amari of Egypt and India. We are all alive, well, and recovering from the events of the past four days. We were caught in a storm that came out of nowhere, were battling it one minute, and the next, four days later, woke up in a clinic alive, healthy, and changed. We're still piecing this happening together.

"The message we want you to hear is simple and will be elaborated on over time. Here's the short version. We are living in a benign and benevolent universe. We are interconnected with everything in an ongoing, unfolding process that is part of a greater whole. The invitation is to outgrow our fears and trust life to this infinite unfolding process of beauty and purpose. It's time to realize and embody the profound meaning of these ancient words: perfect love casts out all fear. It's time to find our way back home, and help is here for us all. Learn to be still, give thanks in all things, and remember to remember who you really are. Together we are the change we've been waiting for. There can be no more business as usual. We're all in, all connected, all a part of the whole. I leave you with the gift of a Haiku you might reflect on and carry with you. Listen deeply." He paused, silenced himself, and slowly turned around three hundred sixty degrees, scanning the audience and transmitting a radiant energy of pure consciousness. Waiting for the ripeness of the moment, he continued.

"Loving-kindness yields . . . interconnectivity . . . wonder overflows."

He paused and repeated his slow circular scanning and the Haiku two more times. Returning to his original position, he again waited in silence for the ripeness of the moment, his smile filling the room.

"Thank you and remember to enter into the joy of life. The One I AM is always here, always with you, all ways for you."

He bowed with great reverence and turned to leave. Applause filled the room as everyone stood. Will walked up the steps humbly bowing and smiling at all who were gathered. After walking through the door, he slipped on his shoes and took the elevator to Gloria's apartment. Angelina, Gloria, Clare, Sophia, Favor, and Michael were right behind him.

After everyone had filed into the living room, Will shut the door behind them, and said, "Thank you for making tonight possible. It was important for me to address the community in person, and now I need to be on my way to help retrieve Atom and Derick. It's all coming together and everything's all right. Somebody will be calling, telling you that Atom and Derick's lives depend on me coming to Nicaragua. Tell them I'll be there, but it will take at least ten hours, maybe more depending on the availability of a plane. We have a plan and we'll be in contact with you." Before exiting, he gave Angelina, Clare, and the remaining group hugs, and then walked out the door and disappeared into the night.

After leaving the community gathering, Barbara Brown walked to her room, picked up her bag, and walked by herself to her car in the parking lot. She made a call to her contact on the way. "Tell Chekov I just saw Dr. William Fischer and heard him speak. He's here at Sunnyview, alive and well. He said the others are also alive and recovering. I'm out of here. You know how to reach me."

* * *

Captain Jack and Jackie had arrived at Camp Bay Island from Miami. Anna and Estefan briefed the pilots concerning the events of the day. They connected with Sunnyview and a cautionary and vigilant Code Yellow was issued. Now they were waiting for further instructions.

The two pilots sat with Anna and Estefan on the screened-in front porch at the main lodge. A fragile and hopeful anticipation hung in the night air and surrounded the group. Nobody could sleep so everyone waited together in silence, only a few words spoken from time to time. Captain Jack had contacted people at the airstrips at Trujillo and Puerto Cabezas, Bilwi, and as he suspected, no one knew anything. He was trying to remember the few contacts he still had on the Caribbean coast of Nicaragua when his cellular phone rang. His three friends turned to him, curious at the news that would come.

"Captain Jack here. Go ahead."

"This is Ricardo Alvarez from Bilwi. I understand you're looking for a couple of gringos who are friends of yours."

Jack smiled broadly at the others to let them know it was good news. "Ricardo, you old dog, I was just trying to recall your whereabouts. It's been a very long time. Are you still active?"

"Not much changes except the wear and tear on the body. It's a hard life out here, and the scum gets scummier and the slime gets slimier, but it's where the family is and somebody's got to stand in for the good."

"How'd you know to contact me?"

"One of my brothers works at the airport. He's the one you talked to. You know how it is down here. Nobody knows nothing unless you know somebody or have lots of money. After he got off the phone, he remembered some of the war stories I've been telling for years about Captain Jack, good old Jayhawk as you use to be called. It dawned on him to call me and ask about you. I knew there could only be one Captain Jack, and I owe you, brother. I wouldn't be alive if it wasn't for you. How can I help?"

"Two men were kidnapped this afternoon off the coast of Roatan by pirates posing as the Coast Guard. I think they made their way to Trujillo and caught a plane to Bilwi. They probably took a vehicle into the jungle. I'm guessing on the logistics, but that's what I would have done, so I'm running with it. Right now, speculation is all I have. The two guys are close family and I'm responsible for them, Ricardo. This is a very serious situation."

"When would they have landed in Bilwi?"

"I'm thinking about two or three hours ago."

"I'll do some snooping. I'm not far from the airport and have people down there. It would require a driver familiar with the terrain—a local, and at least two guards with the hostages. I'm thinking a Land Rover, a Hummer, or a large SUV. I'd include an old four-wheel drive beater, but from the sound of the operation, the ops have money. The vehicle and driver should be easy to locate. I'll get right on it and get back to you."

"Thanks, Ricardo. This is personal so whatever you need, you've got it."

"No problem, Jayhawk. I got it covered. Just like the old days, I'm your man."

Jack signed off his phone and relayed the message to Jackie, Anna, and Estefan. "Looks like we caught a break with that call. Ricardo's an old pro," Jack said, feeling some weight lift off his shoulders.

A gentle breeze was coming across the bay. The rhythm of the waves had them all in a calm trance when suddenly they heard voices in the dark near the porch. Captain Jack jumped up, released his sidearm, flipped on the spotlights that lit up the entire area around the lodge, grabbed a flashlight, and dashed off the porch. Estefan was right behind him. Jackie ushered Anna into the house and locked the door.

Jack and Estefan headed directly toward the voices that were just outside the range of the house spotlights. Guns drawn, they turned on their flashlights and pointed them directly toward the voices. No one there. Both of them felt a pinching pressure on their necks. They dropped their guns and flashlights and fell to their knees. They heard laughter.

The flashlights shone in their eyes and then turned off. When their eyes refocused, they saw Will and Miguel Santana, Will's first mate and colleague from Argentina standing in front of them laughing.

"Damn, you guys. This isn't funny! We could have shot you!" Jack yelled.

"You think so, huh?" Miguel said. "You obviously haven't had any experience with shape-shifters and disappearing acts. I doubt that anybody has."

Will and Miguel helped Estefan and Captain Jack to their feet and apologized for the scare. The four of them shook hands, slapped one another's backs, and walked to the porch. Jackie and Anna were summoned, and they came back out again to enjoy the night air and company.

Will began the conversation. "I've communicated with the whole team and invited Miguel to help us with this retrieval. It's important that we do it in the spirit of loving-kindness, as we know those involved are lost in a darkness of their own choices. Violence begets violence and we're here to bring compassion, so Miguel and I will be doing the recon and direct intervention. Estefan, you'll stay here with Anna and the others as our communications liaison. Jackie, you'll stay at the airport with the plane, and Jack, you'll be my double, if necessary.

"I'm monitoring the interrogations, and it looks like Derick and Atom are setting up Chekov to bring me in. One of their people saw and heard me speak a few minutes ago at Sunnyview.

That call will be directed to Chekov so we'll catch them sleeping with their own plan tonight. It should be an easy extraction. I want to see Chekov personally and have him deliver a message to Billsnev. He's the one person who has personal access and can help us get to him. Now that he's shown us his hand, we have to find him and take away his destructive powers. It seems Billsnev has as many connections with darkness as we do with light. It should be quite a dance."

"I'm waiting on a call from my contact on the ground in Puerto Cabezas," said Captain Jack. "He's tracking the vehicle and driver for us. Will, I have some reluctance in saying this, but this whole nonviolent peace-and-love thing doesn't compute for me, especially with guys like Chekov and Billsnev. They're mass murderers, designers of a death star, and you want to treat them with compassion? I don't get it. I'm just not there yet and maybe never will be."

"I know, Jack," said Will. "It's an interesting observation that the emotional activities like forgiveness, love, kindness, and charity are there for us as long as the violation is not directed toward us individually or toward members of our tribe. When that happens, however, those attitudes and dispositions just become words while we are dragged down into the core of our reptilian brain that's all about survival and instinctual fight flight reactivity. That's why Miguel and I will be doing the extraction. We have the advantage of transrational thought and multidimensional action. Invisibility, shape shifting, teleportation, mind merging, and all the rest of the latent powers of our human-divine species give us a great advantage with all the less evolved forces.

"With our new developments and help from the Company, we can't be threatened. We can't be overcome. We can't be compromised. It's the trajectory humankind is on, and it's our job to help us all get there, no matter how long it takes. It can't be accomplished mechanically, only in alignment with the source. For us, no more business as usual means an embodiment of this evolved and gifted awareness and activity. Our choices are both more limited and more expansive.

"Thanks for your honesty, Jack. That's one of the reasons you're here. Shifting back to the operation, how long would it take to fly from Marquette to Puerto Cabezas?"

"I'd say maybe eight-plus hours from takeoff to landing, depending on the conditions," responded Jack.

"Chekov has received the call by now, will be interrogating Atom, and making plans to bring me into his little spiderweb. Can you have the CAT at the Puerto Cabezas airport in under an hour?" Will directed his question to Jackie and Jack.

"Yes," Jack responded. "No problem. We'll leave right away."

"Then we're a go. Thank you all. Anna, you should have Derick in your arms in a few hours, and Jack and Jackie, stay inside the plane with communication channels on until we contact you. We'll direct you once we're on our way in the vehicle. Estefan, stay in contact with Sunnyview and Captain Jack. They will connect with you as needed. Blessings abound. Let's get to it."

Chapter 49

How did the rose ever open its heart and give to this world all its beauty? It felt the encouragement of light against its Being. Otherwise, we all remain too frightened.

-Hafiz-

Atom focused on Colonel Chekov's eyes and inner vibration as he sat down across the table from him. He saw years of darkness, violence, and loneliness that enveloped his soul. Atom spoke with compassion and forthrightness.

"I see pain, suffering, and sorrow in your soul. It must have been very difficult to lose the nurturance of your mother at such an early age."

Atom's observations and directness startled Chekov, but before he could speak, Atom continued. "My name is Atom Ion Fischer. I am not your enemy. I'm your friend. How can I help you?"

Chekov was again astounded by Atom's question. In all the decades of interrogation, no one had ever confronted him like this. He loved and hated it all at the same time. He felt something inside him stir, grabbed it by the tail, and stuffed it back into his subconscious.

"No, Atom Fischer, you're not my friend, and never will be, and you can help me by bringing your father back from the dead so we can thank him for all his help." Chekov glared at Atom.

"Do you have a phone? I'll place a call to him right now so you can talk with him."

"That's a good smart-ass answer. He died in our storm. How are you going to call him?"

"I take it you haven't heard the news. He and his colleagues survived your storm. Dad's probably back at Sunnyview right now. I'll stay here until he comes, and then you can see for yourself. Let's trade Derick for Dad. He'll come if I call."

"What a remarkable idea. You'll trade him for your uncle?"

"Why not? He's much more valuable to you than Derick."

There was a knock on the door. An agitated Chekov turned to Dmitri and nodded impatiently. A slot opened in the door and an envelope fell through. Anthony brought it to Chekov who opened and read the message. *Agent Brown reports contact with Dr. Fischer at Sunnyview, in residence. All colleagues alive.*

Chekov shoved the message into his pocket and turned back to Atom. "You make an interesting proposal that I'll first have to verify and then consider." He stood up, turned to Anthony and Ihsaan, and said, "Take him back to his cell." Dmitri opened the door and followed Chekov out.

Ihsaan unchained Atom while Anthony stood ready to take his arms. They escorted him back to the cell, opened the door, and pushed him inside. Ihsaan sneered at Atom and spat at him.

"You're some piece of work, Fischer," he said as he slammed and locked the door.

"What was that about?" asked Derick.

"Just a little brotherly love," Atom responded with a smile and a shake of his head.

Chekov went to the communications room where his technicians were monitoring the many projects they had operating around the globe.

He went to the chief operations officer. "Connect us with Dr. Fischer's compound in Sunnyview. I want to speak with him."

The chief hid his surprise and went to his station, found the number, and made the call. The phone rang through to Sunnyview.

"Sunnyview Retreats, how may I help you?" a female voice answered.

"Connect me with Dr. William Fischer," Chekov commanded.

"Just a moment, please." A few seconds passed before the receptionist returned. "I'm sorry; he's not available at the moment. May I direct your call to another person?"

"I'd like to speak with his wife, Angelina. It's urgent."

"One moment, please."

The moment passed before another woman's voice responded, "This is Angelina Fischer."

"This is Colonel Chekov. We have your son and your husband's brother. They will be executed in twelve hours unless your husband reports to me at the Puerto Cabezas airport in Nicaragua between now and then. Do you understand?"

"Yes, I understand, but it may take him longer than that to get there."

"That's not my problem. Someone will be waiting at the airport in ten hours. They will contact your husband on the ground and he had better be alone. No heroics. If he doesn't show or we have any trouble, you'll never see Atom and Derick again. Do you understand?"

"I understand. He'll be there." The phone went dead.

Angelina immediately called Camp Bay Island, reported the message to Estefan, which he relayed to Captain Jack and Jackie. She went to Gloria's apartment and reported to the others. The plan was in place.

*   *   *

Will and Miguel had no trouble finding Billsnev's small and efficient compound in the dense jungle three miles west of Bilwi. They were able to follow their inner guidance systems to hone in, track, and pinpoint energy frequencies.

They scanned the outside for security systems, entry-exit points, and transportation options. A Hummer was parked next to a door. Still in an invisible high-frequency vibration, they entered the building, walked through every room, and triple-checked all the occupants. Derick and Atom were still together in their concrete cell. They felt tired and worn out, yet thankfully unharmed. The technical staff worked their magic on the computers while the second shift watched television together in the lounge. Chekov and Dmitri were conversing in what appeared to be a private suite unlike anything else in the Spartan facility.

An argument in another room caught Will and Miguel's attention. Two young Middle Eastern men paced around in a small room furnished only with two single beds and a fan.

"Ihsaan, what the hell is wrong with you? Are you losing your mind? I hope your little outbursts weren't being monitored. If they were, we could be in deep shit!"

"I don't give a rat's ass, Anthony. That arrogant bastard spent time with my sister! No telling what stories he heard or fabricated. He probably just shook his head in pity when she described her demented, misdirected brother who lost his way and disgraced his family. What do they know?"

"I thought you disowned your family and didn't care about them?" responded Anthony. "Your behavior is saying the exact opposite."

"Oh, so now you're a psychologist? I don't want to talk about it. I *am* a loser. What the hell are we doing here with all these goddamn American and Russian white guys? How the hell is this advancing our cause? What the hell is our cause? We keep being sent on these stupid missions where we're the grunts, the dark-skinned gophers. I'm tired of this shit, and I'm tired of wiping all these white assholes!"

"Calm down, Ihsaan. Do you think I like it? Do you think I like being ordered around by people who don't share our cause? Do you think I like denying myself? When I looked at Atom Fischer, all I could see was his sister, my family, and all my deceit. When you spat at him, I felt like you should have spat on me. What the hell has happened to us? We were so sure of ourselves."

"It's been nine years since nine-eleven and what have we accomplished? We've lost our homes, our families, our dignity, our honor and for what? For our own righteous indignation at the prejudice that was heaped upon us? I want out. I want a new life. I want to start over."

"Ihsaan Jameson, how can you say that?"

"Anthony Amir, how can you *not* say it? I've heard you calling out Clare's name in your dreams. I've heard you asking *why* over and over while you sleep. I felt your nervousness when we brought the Fischer's here and when we witnessed the interrogations. I felt your fear at how we were both going to have to make a life decision in this hellhole that would cost us our lives, one way, or the other. Let's stop dancing around the issue. What are we going to do if we're told to kill Atom and Derick, or be a party to it?" Ihsaan moved to the wall and slumped against it with his arms across his chest. He looked at his friend in defeat.

Anthony nervously paced from wall to wall. He walked to Ihsaan and lowered his voice. "I keep thinking about how Atom pointed to Justice; the way he turned it into how it's *just us, an all-inclusive us.* I experienced that at Sunnyview like never before, except when I was a little boy with my family. What should we do?"

"You can come with us," responded Will, who instantly appeared in the room.

Ihsaan and Anthony jumped backward against the wall, full of fear.

Will stood his ground, smiling and radiating a compassionate presence. "There's nothing to fear. All is well and all will be well. I'm Will Fischer, and I'm here to help you get home, if that's where your hearts really want to go. Is that what you want? From what we've been hearing, I'd say you're well on your way. You just need a little help."

Anthony and Ihsaan both looked at each other and then at their pistols lying on the bed.

"Is that what you want?" Will asked. "Go ahead, pick up the guns, and continue this drama or you can relax, remember, surrender, and renew your lives like you're being called to do from a much deeper place within yourselves. Feel the conflict, the pull that wants to take you down, and the one that wants to raise you up. The choice is always yours and the more conscious you get of these energies, the more clarity you can bring to your situations. It sounds like the direction you've been traveling hasn't worked very well for you and the ones you love. Here's an opportunity to change that."

"What do you want from us?" Ihsaan asked.

"What I want from you is what's best for you, and I sense that after all these years of turmoil, you're beginning to figure out what that might be. It's not about what I want or what anyone else wants. Stop, breathe deeply, and drop into your heart of hearts. From this place, what do you want?"

The two young men took a deep breath, released a portion of their anxiety, and dropped into the heart center. "I want out of this mess," said Ihsaan slowly.

Anthony nodded. "I want to go home and make up with my family. I want to rest, rediscover who I am. I want my self-respect and dignity back. I want peace. I'm sick of this constant war that rages inside of me."

Ihsaan reached for the guns, picked them up, and handed them to Will. "I want to surrender all of it and find some pardon and renewal. Can you help with that?"

Will nodded while he took the guns out of the holsters, unloaded them, and threw them back on the bed.

"Let's get to work. Are you with me, against me, or neither?" Will asked.

"We're not sure if we're with you, but we're not against you," Anthony answered.

"That's a good beginning. Unfortunately, you'll have to decide soon though, because we're going to turn this place upside down, and there will be no escape for you if you're not with us. We're the only ones leaving with a safe place to go. The rest will be apprehended."

"We'll take the offer," Anthony said. "We'll be with you and take you at your word to get us out safely. What can we do to help?"

"Stay put for the time being and firm up your commitment to your deepest selves, your families, and each other. I have a partner with me who can do everything I can do, so if you change your minds, we'll know and you'll be left behind. Your word has to be your bond. Do you understand?"

Ihsaan and Anthony nodded.

"My partner, Miguel, will come back for you in a few moments. Do exactly what he says, and you'll be safe. Do you trust that?"

They nodded again and Will vanished from their sight.

Chapter 50

*Evolution is underpinned by a deep unfolding structure,
characterized by design and purpose, necessitating an unceasing
interplay of order and disorder, randomness and creativity.*
-Diarmuid O'Murchu-

Will met Miguel invisibly in a high-frequency vibration outside
the door to Atom and Derick's cell. Miguel had been observing
the technicians in the communications control room to discern
their operations. He and Will mind mapped their advanced
technology and emerging plans. Captain Jack and Jackie would
be landing shortly. Will had listened to Chekov and Dmitri's
conversation concerning the upcoming rendezvous with him in
less than twelve hours. The compound was completely relaxed
with business as usual for the next nine hours.

Miguel appeared to Ihsaan and Anthony and alerted them of the
plan. He checked to see if they were still committed to the escape.
They were. He also checked to see if their guns were still unloaded.
They were. They strapped them on per regulation. Miguel then
invisibly transported to the communications control room to
disconnect the audio-video monitors to Derick and Atom's cell and
begin his work to plant a virus in the computer control system.

Ihsaan and Anthony walked into the control room just as the
video screen monitoring in Atom and Derick's cell went blank.
"Chief, the screens . . . they're down in the prisoners cell!" cried
Anthony.

"Check the leads to the monitors and audio feeds," the chief barked. He looked at Anthony and Ihsaan and said, "Go there now, double time, and report what you find immediately!" They turned and ran out the door.

Will entered Atom and Derick's cell for a moment to brief them on what was happening. Ihsaan and Anthony anxiously followed Will into the cell, locked the door behind them, and then checked in with the communications control room.

"The room is secure, chief. We'll stand guard until further notice," Anthony reported on his transceiver.

"That's exactly what you'll do. Report in immediately if anything, and I mean anything, changes. You got that?"

"Yes, sir. Report in if anything changes. Got it."

As Chekov walked to his desk, Will invisibly entered his suite. Dmitri was sitting on the couch drinking his second vodka on the rocks. As he put the glass down on the end table, Will touched a pressure point on his neck that caused him to pass out silently. Chekov returned from his desk with a document and noticed Dmitri sleeping. Shaking his head in disgust, he sat down in the chair across from the couch, sipped his drink, and began to read.

Will appeared in the chair five feet from Chekov.

"Having a good time Colonel Chekov?" Will asked, now visible.

Chekov choked on his drink and pulled a handkerchief from his pocket to wipe his mouth. "What the hell?"

"I know I'm a little early, but I have a lot to do these days since you and Billsnev tried to put me out of commission. It's strange how you helped change my life for the better. I thought I'd return the favor and change yours some."

"How did you get in here?"

"If I told you, you wouldn't believe me, so let's just deal with the reality as it is. I'm here, you're here, and I have a message for your boss, Dr. Nicholi Billsnev. I see you have a pad and pen, so would you please write it down so there's no confusion?"

Chekov angrily nodded and reluctantly waited for the transcription.

"The greatest benefit to you is to cease and desist, shut down your operations globally and cooperate with people of good will. The world needs your genius to work for the highest good. We are aware of your plans. We have powers you do not. You cannot succeed in your enterprise, only slow down the forward movement of the conscious evolution that is taking place globally. In good faith, we are opening this channel of communication for dialogue and possible collaboration."

Will stopped to let Chekov catch up.

"Did you get all that?"

"Yeah, and it's all bullshit!"

"Just keep writing, are you ready?"

Chekov glared at him.

Will continued. *"I hold no grudges and will work to move forward together. Further destruction of the global community is unnecessary. It cannot serve you and will ultimately result in your death and dissolution. New life will always emerge after us in ways we can't imagine. Why create an interlude of misery? I am offering you this olive branch as a new beginning, an opportunity for you to change."*

Chekov looked up to see if Will was finished. He put his pen down, regained his composure, and took another sip of his vodka before speaking. "You think you can threaten or persuade the most powerful man in the world? You think he will listen to you? We failed to exterminate you and your do-gooder colleagues this time, but it was our first attempt, a practice run. There will be another. We will not rest until you and your colleagues are dead, along with all your families and closest associates. You are no match for us."

Will disappeared into thin air as Chekov finished.

"Where did you go?" Chekov asked. "What the hell?"

"What the hell, indeed," said Will, now sitting in Chekov's chair behind the desk. "What was the hell you experienced all those years in the killing fields of Europe, the Middle East, and

Africa? What did that accomplish and how well have you been able to repress the dark and violent emotions that live in you and haunt your sleep?"

Chekov was beginning to lose his inner gyroscope. His mind started to reel with the memories of darkness, death, and destruction.

"It had to be done," he blurted out. "Our interests were being compromised, and we were ordered to do it."

"Despite all that effort and misery, your empire still fell and left you where? How is it with you and Billsnev? Is he a friend? If you fail in a mission, what will happen to you? What solace and strength do you get when he's ranting about his power, his control, his plans? What is the benefit to you, your daughter, and your grandson?"

"What do you know about my daughter and grandson? Nobody knows about them!"

"I know that they're alive, that they're well, supported by you, and have become your only link to the world of compassion and caring. I also know that the pain of your mother's death when you were very young, along with the abuse of an alcoholic father, has shaped your life. Everything that happened required you to defend yourself. All the parts within you rallied to protect and keep you alive. Those parts have outgrown their usefulness for you and the world you now inhabit. They no longer need to destroy an enemy. The enemy no longer exists except within you."

Will stood and approached Chekov. "Karl, take my hands."

Chekov startled. *How did Will know my first name?*

He stood up with a jerk, knocking over the glass of vodka and spilling his papers on the floor. He took a step back, preparing for attack.

"Karl, I'm not here to hurt you. I'm not your enemy. I want to return you to the innocence and openness of your childhood. Your daughter and grandson need the gentle mother you lost and the kind father you never had. They're in you, Karl. I can see them longing to be and belong. Take my hands; I want to give you a gift."

"I haven't heard that name spoken to me in a lifetime," Chekov said. "I only hear it in my dreams as a faint whisper that sounds like my dear mother's voice." Tears began to form in his eyes. A crack in the armor was forming.

"Take my hands; we're all strangers in paradise. I want to show you something inside of you."

Karl Chekov had never placed his hands in the hands of another man except to drag them into a ditch or away from a scene of violence and death. His hands now seemed to have a life of their own as they opened while his arms rose to meet Will's hands.

Will received Karl's hands, and for the first time in his life, Karl Chekov felt the trust of another man. In an altered psychological state, Karl closed his eyes and began to drop, as if falling through a long dark hollow cylinder in the earth. He felt no fear, only the falling, deeper and deeper into the darkness. As he approached the floor of the cylinder, a cushion of air slowed his fall and landed him gently on his feet. He saw a pathway lit with soft light inviting him to follow. It led to a large, dimly lit cave hollowed out from the rock.

He stopped and observed a glowing light in the center of the room to which he was drawn. As he approached the light, it began to change. By the time he stood before it, images were appearing and disappearing in a contained energy field. The holographic images were revealing his present life story, the roads traveled and not. He saw the whole of his life unfold before him and the varieties of ways it could have changed. He recognized the mission he had agreed to undertake and how, through his own choices, he had misconstrued the signals and sabotaged his higher self. He was brought to the present and shown the potential outcomes for the world and him. He was awakened to the possibilities as he heard the voices of his mother, daughter, and grandson gently speak his name through the created order. *Remember Karl, remember Papa, remember . . . .* He rested there for what seemed an eternity as he saw the many roads traveled and not. He found himself back at the base of the cylinder and slowly began rising upward toward another light.

When he opened his eyes, he saw himself in the reflection of Will Fischer.

He released his hands and sat down in the chair. The moments felt like years.

"Where do we go from here?" he asked.

"Where were you directed to go?"

Karl Chekov took a few moments to answer. "Into the fulfillment of my original mission and strangely, that path goes through you. I can hardly believe what I've just experienced. I suppose I should say thank you, but . . . and . . . I'm just . . . I don't know what to say. I'll need some time to ponder this. It's tapping into something unimaginable. I can't process it quickly. Everything in my life has just been turned upside down; the perspective is completely different and unsettling."

"You don't have to act now, Karl. We are here to extract Atom and Derick and to shut down your facility. A virus has been planted in the memory of your computer and it will destroy all your systems. We'll be leaving now, and I will return and help you along your new path. Tell Billsnev anything you want about what happened here, and make sure you deliver my message to him. I hope to help him see the light too, but I don't sense receptivity to it as I did with you. Protect yourself and those under you. I put Dmitri to sleep so don't be hard on him; he's had a difficult journey too. You can wake him up any time by putting some ice on the back of his neck and forehead."

Miguel had just finished disabling the vehicles and was waiting at the Hummer. Atom, Derick, Ihsaan, and Anthony were already in the Hummer and buckled up. When Will arrived to meet them, the electricity in the compound went out, all the doors of the facility automatically unlocked, the security systems failed, and chaos broke out. The technicians worked furiously to fix the problems and switch on the backup systems. Miguel started the Hummer and drove slowly through the three miles of jungle on the deserted road to the airstrip.

Captain Jack and Jackie had just touched down and were taxiing to the terminal when Will opened the door to the cockpit and said, "They're on their way. Everything went smoothly."

Jack startled. "Damn! Will, that freaks me out. How do I get used to you just popping in and out on me like this?" He paused to calm himself, taking a deep breath and shaking his head. "How did the mission go, any casualties?" he asked as he turned the controls over to Jackie.

"The mission was accomplished with no casualties and we even retrieved two converts. One of them is the son of Robert and Aisha Jameson."

"What was he doing here?"

"Some righteous indignation and misplaced loyalty," said Will.

"Glad you got him out. My friend Ricardo has his end set up. His brother works here at the airport. I have to make a quick drop and we can turn around and head out."

"That's not going to happen, Jack. I'm sorry. I'll make the drop for you after you're out of here. I need to check out the terminal. You don't leave the plane, and we don't go in any closer to the terminal. When the Hummer gets here, transfer the passengers and get them back to Camp Bay, pronto! They should be here any minute. Let Estefan know we have two more in tow and that we'll have breakfast at nine and a debriefing at noon for everyone. I'll take care of the Hummer and everything else here. Give me a mental picture of Ricardo so I can make your delivery. Visualize him so I can pick up the image. I'll contact him. He's probably in the terminal or close to it."

Captain Jack visualized Ricardo. Will captured the image and was gone.

Jackie taxied to a stop and parked the jet leaving the engines running. Will arrived at the outside of the terminal that looked toward the tarmac where CAT's Beechcraft Hawker 1000 was positioned. He saw three men standing in the shadows beside a large black SUV. They were smoking cigarettes, looking at the Hawker, and scanning the horizon.

"That's the Fischer jet out there," one of them said. "Lorenzo gave us a good tip. We'll have to give him a bonus. Any vehicle moving toward that jet we intercept and then take down the plane. No screw-ups on this one. The Russians reward their victories well and punish their losses severely."

In his invisibility, Will was able to walk around the SUV and make out the machine guns and rocket launchers inside. He needed to move fast.

One of the men turned and pointed. "It's the Hummer. Did you see it? It stopped at the edge of the pavement. Look, it's moving again and heading out to the jet. Let's go!"

Will dropped the driver and the man directly behind him without a sound. He then jumped over the car and landed on the third man. He too went down without a fight or a sound. Will disarmed the vehicle and weapons and then moved to where he sensed Ricardo was waiting.

Ricardo was smoking a cigarette and leaning against the side of the terminal watching the Hummer speed toward the Hawker 1000.

"What do you think is going on out there, Ricardo?"

Ricardo jumped and came to attention. "Who the hell are you?"

"I'm a part of Captain Jack's family, and I just stopped by to let you know that whatever you paid Lorenzo, it wasn't enough."

"What do you mean? I didn't pay him anything, he's my brother."

"I just met three men down the way with enough weaponry to take down a village. They said Lorenzo gave them a good tip. They were waiting for Captain Jack and were about to intercept the Hummer and take down the plane. That tip couldn't have been about the CAT jet coming in now instead of later could it?"

"I had to tell him so he could arrange the customs clearance," responded Ricardo defensively.

"I'd be a little more careful who I trusted if I were you, Ricardo. Seems money is the only thing that buys loyalty here in Bilwi. I wouldn't be too hard on Lorenzo, though. He doesn't know what he's doing or whom he's serving. Maybe you can enlighten him. Maybe you can teach him about integrity, family loyalty, and the higher road?"

Ricardo looked closely at Will, relaxed a little, and then looked back at the speeding Hummer, almost to its destination. He took another drag on his cigarette and then turned back to Will but he was gone.

The Hummer stopped. All four doors flew open as the door and stairs to the Hawker descended to the ground. Derick, Atom, Ihsaan, Anthony, and Miguel quickly departed the Hummer and boarded the Hawker. The stairs and door were up with all passengers on board in less than a minute. Captain Jack powered up, hit the runway, and took off into the starlit sky. The passengers breathed deeply, privately reflecting on the events of the day. It was a silent flight of thanksgiving back to Camp Bay Island.

Will shut the doors of the Hummer and drove it back to where he left Ricardo. He got out, walked around the car, and handed him Captain Jack's bag.

"What's this?"

"It's the bag Captain Jack wanted to give you that would have cost him his life if I hadn't intervened."

"What's in it?" Ricardo grabbed the bag.

"That's between you and Jack. I don't know. It's yours now."

Will got back in the Hummer and drove it off the airstrip into town where he left it parked on the street. He found a Dumpster where he disposed of the two pistols and holsters left in the Hummer by Ihsaan and Anthony. This part of the mission was now complete.

He stood alone in the midst of the darkness. The nightlife was beginning to come alive in this grimy port town. The bars, the booze, the broads, and the back-room deals that were all a part of its fabric felt familiar and foreign to him. As he walked to the beach, he pondered how far away from the ideal the human species had strayed. He wondered at the enormity of the job that his colleagues and he had been given, and he wondered what it meant for them, their families, and the rest of the world. He wondered how two and three and fifty would make a billion so everyone could see this new day come round. He gave thanks for the dangers and the opportunities and returned home to Camp Bay Island.

The Beechcraft Hawker 1000 made a safe landing on the private airstrip at Camp Bay. Will, Anna, Estefan, Pablo, and Carla were there to greet the passengers. It was a great reunion. Ihsaan and Anthony were treated as family. Atom and Derick were washed and bandaged. Jackie and Captain Jack were congratulated. Will and Miguel left the celebration briefly to confer.

"Order and disorder, transition and transformation seem to be the specials of our day," Will reflected as they strolled through the palm trees. "This series of events has changed the game. In this chess match, we need to have a powerful defense and a strategic offense. We can't allow our families and closest associates to be taken like this. It's not part of the plan." Will became silent as he pondered the mission looking up at the half moon in the sky.

"I am optimistic about Karl Chekov, however. He could be the wild card in this heroic adventure. His awakening and transformation will be crucial to the mission. I'll be following up with him regularly. He'll need ongoing encouragement and support. Awakening and conscious evolution is the name of the new game. There are all kinds of people who have lost their way, forgotten their higher calling, and are stuck in situations they don't know how to get out of. We have to be involved in creating new environments in which this change, this awakening and reorientation can take place.

"It's not enough to stop Billsnev. There will always be people like Billsnev. We have to continue to take the high road, hold, and transmit from the sacred center. Our mission, in this crisis of consciousness, is to stop the malignant behavior, heal the hearts of the disillusioned, and bring more conscious awareness and compassionate interconnectivity to the people of the world. We must find new, effective ways to feed the body, mind, and spirit. It's a major project, and it begins with every one of us. We have to help one another remember our original spiritual nature and our mission of service for one another and the whole of creation. It's amazing how far from the center we all get when we don't give proper attention to the helpful transmissions in our transitions.

"We also need to have the rest of the team here today for the debriefing. Aya, Sonja, Shareef, you, and I represent the global community in this new journey. It's imperative we act as one in a sacred unity. It's imperative we all know the new dangers and opportunities!"

"They'll all be here along with Angelina, Clare, Gloria, Favor, Sophia, and Michael Wyman," said Miguel. "It's another ending and beginning. How could it be any other way?"

They smiled at each other, having returned to the celebration, while Colonel Karl Chekov and his technicians were still trying to figure out what happened and people around the globe were saying, "Have a nice day."

Epilogue

We end and begin again, dear mystic traveler and friend, as the mystery continues to unfold. What will you take from this adventure? What one thing resonates with you so strongly that you know it is a special message just for you at this time in your life?

Close your eyes, breathe it in, envision it, and put yourself in the picture. Allow it to speak to you. This small awareness with focused attention will stimulate the change you perceive. The more attention you bring to it, the more it will grow and become part of your life. Feel the radiant energy that subtly vibrates in, around, and through you, and be patient with loving-kindness for all, yourself included.

Allow this step to become part of you before you move on and forget again. Remember that you are so much more than you appear to be! Remember to remember! No separation. All One! Mystic Travelers: awakening, belonging, creating, discovering. And our final hello comes from another friend of the family, Padre Rico, who speaks from within:

Out of death comes new life, and out of new life comes verdancy, unfolding, difficulty, wonder, and eventually death and another new life. The cycles of nature speak to us of the nature of being. At the summer solstice, we are at the height of light. In the winter solstice, we are at the height of darkness. We continue to move from light to darkness to light and everything in between. This is the nature of life as we know it in the gross physical and subtle dreamlike states of being. It is a divided self. When we enter the causal and non-dual states, the evaluation ceases, and we simply allow ourselves and everything else to be what it is; illumined, interconnected, witnessing with awe and wonder. Have you allowed yourself the grace to simply sit in and witness the awe and wonder of any moments today? If not, STOP! Drop into this place of non-evaluative witnessing and breathe in the peace, the radiant energy and wisdom of this moment. Awaken to the stillness and serenity, the trust and tranquility, the openness and opportunity, the presence and prosperity. Strive to be a Mystic Traveler: Awakening, Belonging, Creating, Discovering!

About the Author

F. W. Rick Meyers spent the first two and a half decades of his life in the rolling hills and inland water lakes of southern Michigan. He moved to the mountains, high plains, and foothills of Colorado after college to continue his education in psychology and spirituality. He and his wife Rita have a son and daughter, grandson, and son-in-law. They all live on the eastern slope of the Colorado Rockies. He is an educator, psychotherapist, priest, artist, and eco-entrepreneur. His passions are his family, the outdoors, community development, conscious evolution, music, speaking, and writing. He currently works with the Episcopal Church and Oikos International Associates. This is his first novel. Look for his next novel, *Mystic Travelers—Belonging*. He can be reached at www.MysticTravelersBook.com.

CPSIA information can be obtained at www.ICGtesting.com
Printed in the USA
BVOW021145170412

287861BV00002B/4/P